RENNER

In the Company of Snipers

Book 19

Irish Winters

COPYRIGHT

Renner; In the Company of Snipers, Book 19

Cover design: Kelli Ann Morgan, Inspire Creative Services
Cover image: Paul Henry Serres Photography, www.paulhenryserres.com
My gorgeous cover model: Francis Brunet
Interior book design: Bob Houston, eBook Formatting
Editor: Linda Clarkson, Black Opal Editing and Proofreading

ISBN Paperback: 978-1-942895-74-9
ISBN eBook: 978-1-942895-75-6
Library of Congress Control Number: 2019911452

In the Company of Snipers

You can find Irish Winters

On Facebook:
https://www.facebook.com/author.irishwinters

On Twitter: https://twitter.com/irishwinters1

For news on upcoming releases, sign up for Irish Winters' Newsletter at IrishWinters.com.

For more information about all my books, visit IrishWinters.com.

IN THE COMPANY OF SNIPERS

This series revolves around former Marine scout sniper, Alex Stewart, and his covert surveillance company, The TEAM, home-based out of Alexandria, Virginia. An obsessive patriot and workaholic, he created the company to give former military snipers like him, a chance at returning to civilian life with a decent job, security, and a future.

This is not a serial with each book ending at a cliffhanger. *In the Company of Snipers* is a collection of passionate love stories involving strong women and men who are tough enough to take on the world alone. Each is a stand-alone read, complete in itself.

Spoiler alert: Every story contains adult scenes including sexual situations (some explicit), language, and violence. I don't write sweet romance, so be forewarned.

Book 1, *ALEX*, reveals how The TEAM came to be, as well as how Alex met Kelsey, how they fell in love and fought all odds to stay together. Each of the following books is a complete romance in itself, where, in the course of an active TEAM operation, one agent comes face to face with his or her demons. The men and women I write about are all patriots and warriors, dealing with what they've lived through or mistakes they've made.

It's my hope that you will come to realize along with my heroes...

Love changes everything.

Prologue

Alex Stewart loved early mornings, but especially this particular Saturday morning in December. This was the day volunteers from all over the country converged on Arlington National Cemetery to distribute Christmas wreaths provided by *Wreaths Across America*, one to each and every headstone. Forgetting none.

He had too many friends and family sleeping on these hallowed grounds to feel anything but respect for their service and for the kinds of men and women they'd been in life. Today, he and his little girl were part of a throng of like-minded people headed for Section 60, the parcel set aside for heroes who'd served in Afghanistan, Iraq, and other current conflicts.

People said there was a community of dead below the surface of Section 60, as well as a community of the living above the surface. Those losses there were too fresh, the deaths so recent. And the pain in these survivors' hearts was still a living, screaming beast. Families and friends came here to talk with their fallen brothers and sisters, sons and daughters, as if they were still alive. As if they could hear them. Wives, children, fathers, mothers, brothers, sisters, and friend spread blankets and spent hours among the dead but not forgotten. They left gifts and remembrances, ribbons and photos, bottles of Jack or of Johnny Walker Blue. They planted Christmas trees in December, roses in June. They came with teddy bears and framed photos of baby boys and girls those Soldiers, Marines, Airmen, Coasties, and Sailors would never meet.

Passing McClellan Gate at his right, Alex hoisted Lexie onto his shoulder, so she could see. This morning was different. The humble *Wreaths Across America* event had grown since its inception in 1992. But in 2005, WAA exploded onto the national scene. The once trickling crowd of patriots had become a vibrant, raging river of steadfast patriots with WAA's tenets in mind: *Remember. Honor. Teach. But above all, say their names.*

This was Lexie's first time *'hewping Daddy'*. Alex took special care, teaching her to say to each fallen warrior. How to stand the crisp balsam wreath at the headstone with the red ribbon up top. How to salute afterward, then stand straight and proud when she told that fallen warrior *'thank you'*. Hence the sheen in his eyes and the lump in his throat. He'd lost his first daughter in a past life, and this sweet three-year-old would never replace that first sweetheart, his one and only Abby. But watching this tiny girl perform her solemn duty at the first white granite headstone and mimicking him while she did it, had somehow combined both his girls into one heartbreaking, breathtaking moment.

The rising sun cast a gentle rosy glow over Lexie's pudgy cheeks as she saluted Todd Chandler in her adorably gruff, *I'm-gonna-be-just-like-my-Daddy* way. How often had Abby said those same words? Alex could barely keep from crying out loud at the joy and pain culminated in his heart. But that was the bitter sweetness of Arlington where Joy walked hand-in-hand with Pain. Honor. Respect. His solemn vow to never forget the men and women who had died for him, Kelsey, and Lexie.

Todd was the first agent Alex lost after he'd put out his shingle and declared he owned the best covert surveillance team In. The. World. Alex was arrogant back then. Green, stubborn, and out of his mind. So dumb to the ways of business that he'd simply named his half-cocked idea *The TEAM*. Back then, Alex had balls, but no faith that his harebrained idea would fly. He hadn't truly realized the price of that arrogance until Todd fell during a firefight at one of The TEAM's safe houses.

In her selfish zeal to nail a sensational story, an idiot reporter had unwittingly followed his agents and outed their location on the air. She'd stalked Alex's office like a rabid dog, then followed his agents for days. She was the one responsible for Todd's death. She and the punk who'd thought he'd killed Zack Lennox when he'd ended Todd instead. But none of that mattered when it was one of your own bleeding out in your arms.

Zack Lennox and Ember Dennison were there that day. She hadn't been Rory Dennison's wife then. Before Rory, she'd been head over heels in love with Todd Chandler. They were the buzz of the office. But Todd fell during that operation gone bad, and for months after, Ember went dark. If Alex hadn't assigned her and Rory Dennison to a simple protection detail that began here at Arlington, she'd still be one of the ghosts haunting these hallowed grounds. Out of that singular protection detail had come one of the strongest married couples Alex knew, Mr. and Mrs. Rory Dennison.

"An I am neber gonna forget you, Mr. Todd," Lexie pronounced with childish solemnity. Mimicking her father's straight as an arrow profile, she stuck her chin out, her shoulders back, and extended her tiny fingers to her forehead in a damned good salute.

"Respect," Alex whispered as he also saluted the man who'd lain down his life to protect the woman he'd been guarding that day, the woman who was now Zach Lennox's wife. What else could Alex say? He owed Todd more than anyone could know. Respect and a Christmas wreath seemed small reward for a life freely given, for a humble warrior lost. These men and women deserved to be remembered—applauded even—for their acts of valor on and off the battlefield. Yet this was all they got.

"Kin I do a nutter one, Daddy?" Lexie asked, blinking those big beautiful brown eyes up at him.

What else could Alex say but, "You bet, sweetheart." Dutifully, he handed over the other wreath he'd been given to distribute.

It was still early in the event, barely after nine am. The trucks had just opened. Wreaths were still being doled out. The scent of fresh cut evergreens from Maine was everywhere. Alex had done this often enough to know there'd be plenty wreaths leftover in each of the semis parked throughout the grounds should he and Lexie want to distribute more.

Of the more than seventy-thousand volunteers here today, most laid just one wreath. Some didn't want to stand in the long lines. Few volunteers came here to work. But those few were the same who lined up again and again, who stayed until the job was done. Until each warrior had been spoken to, respected, and remembered. It used to take all day, but last year it took less than a couple hours to distribute the more than three hundred thousand wreaths. Imagine that. All these willing patriots come to serve the nation's honored dead.

It seemed a ridiculously small thing—to remember. But Americans were good at moving onto the latest brainless-celebrity scandal, while red-blooded heroes who'd sacrificed all for their country, were easy to forget. George Bernard Shaw had once said that *'the one thing we learn from experience is that we never learn from experience'*. God's honest truth, that.

A bump on his shoulder had Alex turning to apologize, but Junior Agent Renner Graves' cocky smirk came back to him. Alex gave him a chin nod in recognition.

Renner fluttered his fingers at Lexie. "Hey, short stack."

"Hi, Unca Renner!" she squealed, then ran to him and hugged his leg. "I hewpin' Daddy!"

Stooping, he flipped her giggling little girl body upside down before he planted her upside-right on his shoulders. Renner had a way with little kids. He made a good uncle for all The TEAM children.

Dressed in what passed for TEAM casual wear, black jeans, TEAM polo, a leather motorcycle jacket, and black work boots, Renner clutched Lexie's fluffy fur boots at his neck, making sure she wouldn't fall. Leaning into his scruffy, spiked hair, she giggled as she hugged him again and said, "I wub you, Unca Renner!"

Like her mother, Lexie loved everyone.

A USMC veteran, Renner was a wiry, slightly built guy who'd served three deployments in Afghanistan. He'd seen action in South America, the Philippines, and most recently, Saudi Arabia, though that one was largely redacted. No big surprise there. He had that windblown look, and he was out of breath as if he'd been running.

"You seen Jed McCormack today, Boss?" Renner asked as he stepped to Alex's side, his blue eyes hard, but twinkling like he knew something Alex didn't.

Alex looked over his shoulder. "He's here? Where?"

Jed was a good friend who'd bankrolled Alex, back when he'd started out.

"Up the hill, at the Tomb of the Unknown. He's not alone. He's with some woman, think he called her LuAnn." Renner's cocky smile dropped to the dry December grass at his feet. "But it's *her*, Boss. I'm sure." Renner handed over his cell. "It's Montego. I took pictures. Scroll right."

Heart pounding, Alex couldn't believe what Renner had captured on his cell. Jed McCormack's wife had died less than six months ago. He couldn't be out with another woman—especially not *that woman*—already. *God, no.*

But *son of a bitch! Yes.* There Jed stood as elegant as ever in his full-length black cashmere winter overcoat, a gray striped scarf at his neck, *that woman* clutching his arm like she belonged with him. She'd changed her looks. The blonde short bob now long, shining raven black hair. Her cheeks seemed fuller. Her brows and hairline—different. They were outside Arlington Amphitheater facing the Tomb. Diamonds sparkled at the neck Alex wanted to break. Other sparkles glittered on her wrist and fingers. She looked younger in that long, red leather coat. Thinner. But yeah. The bitch was back in town.

Alex could've spit nails he was so angry, but not with Lexie around. "Damnit," he muttered under his breath as he handed Renner's phone back, palmed his out of his jeans pocket, and rang Kelsey. Because of the massive crowds, she'd volunteered to work the counter at Arlington Visitors Center today, but no more. He needed her here. They were leaving. Now.

"Boss," Renner said calmly. "She won't get far."

Instantly pissed that Jed could be so foolish—what the hell was he thinking?—Alex asked, "Why? What'd you do?"

Still clutching Lexie's boots, Renner fingered a Tattle Tale, one of Mother's infamous inventions. Sasha Kennedy, aka Mother, worked for Alex as his personal secretary/technical genius. She'd invented a bug so small and inconspicuous, it could transmit sights and sounds until deactivated by someone who knew the deactivation code. Or until the battery died.

"I brushed by the two of them while they had their heads together. Stuck one of these babies on her red coat. She won't find it."

"No visual? Just audio?"

Renner shrugged. "Better than nothing."

Alex allowed a frosty breath. The woman he detested most on the earth was now stalking one of his best friends. Maybe sleeping with him. Jed McCormack was the famous billionaire who'd anted-up and given Alex the funding to implement his crazy scheme, now known up and down the Eastern Seaboard as simply, The TEAM. The best and most faithful advocate of the common warrior, Jed had more clout on Capitol Hill than most elected officials. He influenced federal budgets in his practical, pragmatic way. Presidents respected him for his talent to compromise. Hell, the man could run for that office and beat any competition, hands down.

Up until six months ago when his wife fell ill with an odd case of food poisoning at one of her chili cookout events. Within twenty-four hours, she'd died. Alex stared over his shoulder at the trees obscuring the Tomb, suspicious now. Had

Lois died of food poisoning—or Catalina? The witch would've done something like that, kill a man's wife to get to him. How could Jed be so stupid?

"You want me to hang onto Lexie for you, Boss?" Renner offered. "Kelsey'll be here soon. Shouldn't take long. That way you can check on Mr. McCormack yourself."

Alex shook the compulsion to run to his friend and tear that black widow spider's fingernails off his arm. But he'd chosen his job over his first wife and daughter before, and that call to duty had cost him their lives. He'd been deployed when Sara and Abby died. Alex wouldn't make that mistake again.

"Follow them," he ordered his newest recruit. "Don't let that woman out of your sight. If she tries anything—"

Renner's head bobbed. "Understood. End her." Ducking, he handed Lexie over his head into her father's arms. "Consider it done."

Rattled, Alex encased Lexie against his chest while he hurried back to the Visitors Center, fighting a steady current of veterans, military members, and family.

"Alex!" Kelsey called. What a sight. Rosy-cheeked with her winter jacket wide open and flapping, it looked like she'd run all the way. Good girl!

"Here," he shouted, truly frightened that he'd put her and Lexie at risk by not ending Montego after she'd nearly killed Beau Villanueva, another TEAM agent. She'd drugged and kidnapped him, then clipped off his finger. The unholy bitch! Yet she'd gotten away from The TEAM, then fled the United States and returned to her natural hunting grounds in Cuba. Talk about a bungled operation.

The woman was nothing less than a psychopathic, cold-blooded murderer, a dominatrix of unholy appetites, who lured willing young servicemen to her web. Worse, she'd been at it for years. While Beau hadn't been her last, he had been the first to locate the devilish prison where she'd kept her victims. He'd been the hero that day. But they hadn't been quick enough to end her. They'd failed and she'd gotten away.

"What's wrong?" Kelsey asked as Lexie stretched forward into her mother's arms.

"Nothing," Alex breathed, not willing to frighten his little girl, his pride and joy, any more than he already had. "We're leaving. Do you have all your… your things?"

Kelsey nodded, her cheeks red and her eyes bright with concern, but trusting him. As always. That was what he loved most about her. She'd loved him long before he'd been smart enough to admit that he loved and needed her, too.

As he had a hundred thousand times before, he took Kelsey protectively under his arm, ready to die for her if required. He'd guard Kelsey and Lexie like a rabid wolf. Let Catalina try—just once—to come after his family, and he'd gut her.

"Stay close," he ordered, glancing behind them as they hurried west to the exit, then north to the visitor parking lot. Only when they were on the road west to their Shenandoah fortress did he confide in his wife. "Montego's back."

Kelsey shot him a look of disbelief, then palmed her cell, tapped in a code and said, "Ladies. The witch is back. You know what to do."

"What was that about?" Alex asked as he steered them toward home and safety.

"Our coordinated home defense plan," Kelsey explained sweetly, her voice as bright as if she were telling Lexie a fairytale. "After everything that woman put us through last time, the wives and I came up with a plan to protect ourselves and the children."

The wives were the gutsy women who'd married into Alex's nearly all male TEAM. Former military, most of them snipers, less than five weren't yet married. As happened with military wives, these women were a close-knit group who looked out for each other when the men traveled. Alex had always considered the wives his secret weapon. They were strong and, like Kelsey, they could be formidable. Alex was as proud of them as he was their husbands.

Kelsey continued, "Instead of waiting for Montego to turn us into her evil little gingerbread cookies, we're covering each other's backs. Those of us who aren't working at the moment, take turns babysitting. Which is why I'm not always home when you finally get away from the office. It's worked like a charm. You should see what Mei's taught those dogs of hers."

Mei Lennox, Zack's wife, had become a skilled dog handler after her oldest daughter was kidnapped, located in France, then returned, years ago. LiLi, that same little girl, had named their two black-and-white Pitbulls, Spot and Moo. The dogs vacillated between being adorable *'can-I-slime-your-knees-hands-and-face?'* pets, and the more formidable *'I'll-eat-your-face-off'* killing machines, should the wrong person breach the Lennox's defenses. Nobody got past those monsters, nobody but TEAM children.

Alex could've kissed his brilliant wife for this delightful storyline, so he played along. "You want me to push her into her wicked oven like Hansel and Gretel did to that other old witch?"

"Actually," Kelsey said breathily, "I wouldn't mind if you did. Montego's evil. She needs to die."

"She needs to die," Lexie repeated excitedly from her booster seat behind Alex. "Witches all needs to die! Kin I hewp?"

Alex glanced at his darling daughter in the rearview mirror. "You like to help, don't you?"

"Yup!" All bright smiles and big brown eyes, she grinned back at him. "Kin we git ice cweam cones now? I want peppamint."

For the first time since he'd seen that picture of Montego back on American soil, Alex's lungs filled. He could breathe. His family was safe. His best agent was on the case.

Peppamint it was.

Chapter One

Three days and Renner had yet to catch up with Jed McCormack or Catalina Montego, aka LuAnn Something-or-Other. Since that first sighting in Arlington, they'd vanished. The Tattle Tale he'd planted in the folds of that red leather nightmare had transmitted a singular location, but no audio. Which indicated either that pricey coat was now hanging in McCormack's dark closet or the Tattle Tale had failed. If it did, that'd be the first time one of those devices died on the job. Which did not bode well for the conservative statesman.

Montego's past MO, her modus operandi, was to lure a younger man, oftentimes a military member, into her sexual snare, then torture him into subservience. While she worked that poor guy over in the most heinous ways, she often forced him to watch her torture or murder other young men to break him, thus ensuring his absolute loyalty to her. It wasn't uncommon for her to snip off a victim's finger, toe, or even a hand to prove she meant business. She'd been known to toss drugged or dying men into her industrial woodchipper as an effective means of crowd control. And now she had Jed seemingly head-over-heels in love—or lust—with her.

No one knew how many male slaves she'd acquired by now, only that six young male servicemen had recently gone missing from installations along the East Coast. Metro Police were watching Veterans' hospitals, clinics, and memorials closely. Renner had to be careful. Which was why he'd parked his TEAM sedan downhill from Roslyn at the USMC Iwo Jima Monument.

He knew Montego had been born into a family of absolute depravity. Among other horrors, she'd not only witnessed, but experienced unparalleled cruelty, pedophilia, and child rape at an early age. Her mother and father were known sadists, which explained how she and her brother Roland became absolute monsters.

Agent Seth McCray had already ended her brother. Took the bastard out on his own turf in Cuba. Not that Renner cared how bad things were for Montego as a kid. He frankly did not. She'd chosen to follow in her family business. He was just a TEAM exterminator, tasked by contract with the Justice Department to end her once and for all.

Renner fingered his flask up from the inner pocket of his leather cut, a leftover from his after-the-Corps rough-rider days, back when he'd been giddy and free and still raced his Harley. Before reality declared *'get a job'*. The lightweight aluminum flask was solid USMC, embossed with the eagle, globe, and anchor that matched the ink on his left bicep. A label and a brand, it screamed an ethos only warriors understood. Drinking was a bad habit he intended to whip one of these days. Just not today.

He'd spent the better part of the last forty-eight hours staking out the McCormack Industries complex in Roslyn, Virginia, hoping McCormack would show. Across the Potomac from the District, its prime location kept Mr. McCormack in steady contact with congressmen and defense contractors alike. But he'd never showed, not once in two days. So, where was he? What was more important than the billion-dollar company he'd spent his life on?

Tipping his head back, Renner let the whiskey pour down his throat and work its magic. Some called it liquid courage. He called it 'friend'. Once it settled low and warm in his gut, he stared up at McCormack's modern, gold-glinted high-rise apartment building and blew out a breath of frosty air. McCormack had to be in there. At home. With Montego.

Built in the heart of Roslyn, the ultra-modern structure soared above all other buildings. Renner's job was to get inside without McCormack or Montego knowing. The man was obviously compromised. He couldn't be trusted.

Pocketing the flask, Renner shifted his focus on the firearms concealed beneath his leather cut. Two Beretta 92FS Inox semiauto pistols, 9 mm; two extra magazines, fifteen rounds each. Beretta hadn't let him down in the military; wouldn't let him down now.

He walked the several blocks into downtown Roslyn, not precisely sure what he'd do once he arrived at the building. Jed's security might challenge him the moment he put in the secret entry code. Then again, they might not. Alex had provided the code. He'd never been challenged. Why would Renner?

Yet things could get ugly. Maybe he should call ahead and talk to McCormack. Maybe the direct approach was the easiest way in. But if Jed were with Catalina…? Jed could already be dead, or like Beau when he woke that fateful day, bound to a table with a digit missing.

Renner cleared the entrance easily. There were no security guards in the lobby, which was odd. Only the standard drop-down ceiling cameras, and Alex had told him where they were and how to avoid them. So far so good.

Sliding his hands into a pair of black nitrile gloves from one of the many pockets in his tactical cargo pants, Renner keyed in the code one more time. Worked like magic. The elevator ascended smoothly. Quickly. Lined with spotless mirrored walls, he glanced up at the ceiling instead of staring at himself. At the last numbered floor, his ride continued smoothly up four more levels. Which made him wonder why McCormack needed all that space.

At last the elevator doors swooshed open, and Renner found himself in an arboretum and under a glass cathedral ceiling of epic proportion, so epic that full-grown palm trees grew lush and tall. A large, as in twenty-foot tall, smiling Buddha sat off to Renner's right in a grove of ferns. Next to that a small, red wooden bridge spanned a large koi pond. Trickling water sounded from somewhere, and perfumed moisture scented the air. McCormack had created a lovely Japanese garden, complete with flowering bushes, orchids, and vines, high above the city. Soft golden light emanated from overhead as well as from several stone pagodas along the walk. Which made sense. Mrs. McCormack had gotten into Eastern meditation after their son passed. Jed had no doubt built this for her.

Renner proceeded cautiously beneath the drape of hanging ferns. It seemed this entire floor was devoted to things Lois loved in life. It was a wedge of paradise in the middle of busy Roslyn, VA. But McCormack wasn't here.

Backtracking to the elevator, once again Renner keyed in the code. One floor down, the doors again swooshed open, this time to a room that looked more like an entryway. Boot rack to the left. Coat rack to the right. Double entry doors with beveled glass inserts straight ahead. A phone sat on the table alongside the elevator. Hmm. Guess visitors were supposed to announce themselves? Not today.

Tugging his B&E kit out of one of his many pockets, Renner worked his pick and the door unlocked like magic. Within ninety seconds he was in, and McCormack's front door closed silently behind him. Lush carpet underfoot softened his steps as he cocked his head and listened to make sure he was alone. No TV. No music. No quiet conversation. Not that those missing noises meant anything. Still, if present, they were indicators that could spell trouble. Renner didn't want to create problems for his boss, and McCormack finding one of Alex's agents inside his private residence would do that.

So, Renner stepped it up and, one by one, cleared the rooms, looking for Catalina Montego. He hadn't expected to find her in the garden, but there was no sign of her here, either. Chagrined at his streak of bad luck, he headed back to the elevator. It was getting late and he owed Alex a sitrep. Tapping the two-way radio inside his jacket, Renner buzzed his boss.

"Nothing here, Boss." The words were barely out of his mouth when he spied a silvery glint from between the leather couch cushion and the heavy armrest in Jed's living room. Yet when he blinked, the glint was gone.

"Then get the hell out of there," Alex replied evenly. "Rory and Ember are tracking Jed. He's on his way across the river now."

"Hold on a sec," Renner said as he returned to McCormack's private space. He'd spied something bright and shiny where it didn't belong.

Back at the couch, he slid one hand cautiously between the cushion and armrest. A disposable plastic syringe slid to the floor, the sharp still intact as if the syringe had been hidden in haste. Renner picked it up and held it against the dim light of the setting sun, tapping it. The few drops left in the vial were green. Bright, vivid green. Not like any medicine Renner had ever seen.

"Ah, Boss. Is Mr. McCormack diabetic or something? Was his wife? Did either of them take injections? Only asking because I just found a syringe in McCormack's couch."

"No. Definitely not. Jed's as strong as I am, and Lois was, too. They didn't believe in drugs. They are, er, were, health nuts. That's what makes her death suspicious."

Renner knew the story. The entire country had been shocked when Lois McCormack became ill while attending one of her famous *Heat the World* chili cook-offs at the local veterans' home. That was her schtick. Through those amicable competitions, she raised funding and awareness for veterans. She and her husband knew full well the high cost of war. Their only son Brady, a Marine, had returned home a quadriplegic and, years later, died of complications from his traumatic injuries.

But what if... Renner's gut dropped at the thought. Could McCormack be behind his wife's death? He had hooked up with Catalina Montego a little too quickly for Renner's tastes after Lois' funeral. Were the two of them in league for some ungodly reason? The thought didn't feel right. Tugging an evidence bag up from his pocket, Renner secured the hypo for further analysis back at TEAM headquarters. But he had to ask, "Boss, remind me. How long's it been since Mrs. McCormack passed? Five months?"

"Six, why? What are you thinking?"

Next question. But this one was harder. Yet Mother, the TEAM's savvy technical genius, was still on leave somewhere in the Pacific. Junior Agent Beau Villanueva, who was every bit as smart a techie as Mother, was on family leave watching his baby girl while his wife started her new job as Alex's TEAM physician. There was no one else to ask. "Is there anyone in the office who can run this evidence and do a background check on McCormack for me without raising any red flags?" *Or biting my head off?*

The TEAM had recently acquired the dubious service of a Division of Fish and Wildlife Services reject. Agent Camilla Brinkman certainly couldn't do this type of research. She was still acclimating to her *'demeaning'* roles as Alex's secretary and technical assistant—her exact words, not Renner's. At the moment, he couldn't stand the sight of her, and he refused to ask the snarky woman for anything. Even Harley Mortimer, one of Alex's senior agents, had stopped teasing, cajoling, or trying to make friends with Brinkman. Renner couldn't see her staying much longer. The woman had no social skills other than looking down her nose at everyone. And if she corrected him one more time with her caustic, *"It's pronounced 'Kah-me-ah,' you moron. No 'L' sound, got it?"* Damn. Just thinking about her snippy attitude made his blood boil.

"Why Jed?"

"Just checking all possibilities. There's a reason this syringe was hidden in his couch cushions. There's a couple drops of something green in it."

"Are you accusing him of murdering Lois? His wife."

Renner looked down at the carpet. "No." *Maybe.* "But we need to rule him out just the same. It's what you'd do with us,

Boss. You'd make sure we were clean if one of our wives died under mysterious circumstances." Which Renner didn't have and didn't want. A wife. He didn't need the drama.

"Son of a bitch. I sent you to find Montego, not build a case against my friend."

Renner could almost see his boss grinding his teeth when he said that. Didn't matter. Alex was under a lot of stress, he got that, but as much as possible, this covert investigation had to be done by the books. "I need an in-depth history on McCormack, Boss. If you can't get that for me, I'll—"

"Ember will run the evidence and the numbers when she gets in, damn it," Alex said, the steam gone out of his voice.

"Thanks. I'm not trying to railroad McCormack. Just need all the pieces to this puzzle we're working."

"You're sure you saw Montego with him at Arlington?"

That again. Alex still couldn't believe how far off-track Jed had gone. "You saw the pictures. You tell me. Was that Catalina Montego hanging on his arm or not? I know you don't like to hear this, but they looked happy together. He didn't look sad. He looked good."

"Shit," Alex hissed. "Jed wouldn't—"

Renner didn't hear the end of that sentence. The elevator doors had just swooshed open. He ran for the kitchen and ducked inside McCormack's expansive pantry to listen and watch.

Catalina had no more than breezed into the living room when Renner heard a distinct thump coming from the hallway. With Montego on one side and a possible third party on the other, the sniper in him growled to life. Every nerve in his body was suddenly strung tight and vibrating.

Muttering in Spanish, Montego unzipped her jacket and tossed it to the couch. Reaching over her shoulder, she tugged her tank top over her head. Jesus. For a short woman, she was stacked. Voluptuous didn't come close. Her caramel colored breasts hung like thick clusters of ripened fruit any guy would want to finger and taste.

Renner hadn't expected a floor show, but her running shorts went next, and every testosterone-filled cell in his all-male body took notice. Not the distraction he needed at the moment, and he certainly was not attracted to this stone-cold killer. But she was there and nude, and he was just a stupid man.

With one fingertip, he pushed the pantry door open wider. With the kitchen dark, he had a clear view of the strip show in Jed's living room. The last time Montego had been on US soil, she'd been blonde. Her hair was long and black now, which he could see was her natural color given her state of undress. She loosened the tie at the back of her head, her hair spilling like an ebony cape over her shoulders, making her look like a diminutive Eve in the Garden of Eden.

But Renner wasn't an idiot. Montego was no innocent, and this wasn't paradise. If anything, she was a viper through and through, nothing more, nothing less. She might look like a typical Cuban diva, olive-skinned, delicate build, and slender, but she was Roland Montego's evil baby sister, a sadist who enjoyed torturing gullible young servicemen who fell for her— breasts.

Thump. Bump. There it was again. That noise had most definitely come from McCormack's bedroom. What—or who—could it be? Now totally nude, Montego strutted through

McCormack's palatial living room toward his bedroom like she owned the place.

Renner's nose wrinkled with disgust. He was no prude, but the thought of Jed bumping uglies under the sheets with this brutal witch went against the laws of nature. Jed was one of America's finest. Montego was nothing but a deviant. Was the man crazy?

That actually made sense. It hadn't been that long ago he'd lost his war hero son. Now his wife. McCormack might just be insane.

Chapter Two

Once Montego sashayed her ugly ass down the hall and disappeared into Jed's suite, Renner followed. Montego hadn't bothered turning on any lights. Maybe she had some dignity after all.

He waited outside the door to make sure the shower came on before he entered McCormack's bedroom. Extracting flex cuffs from yet another pocket, he whispered as he crept into the bedroom, "Sorry Jed, but this is for your own good."

Was this B&E legal? No way in hell, but Renner meant to get Montego under wraps and out of McCormack's penthouse before anyone knew what happened. Which suited Renner fine. He did his best work in the dark.

Prepared to face down this crazy alpha bitch once and for all, he advanced silently, his weapon in one hand, the cuffs in his other. He'd have to be quick. She'd think she was safe in the shower, and the water would provide the perfect white noise. She'd never see him coming. But if she fought back? Renner didn't mind pistol-whipping the witch senseless if it made her compliant. That was the least she deserved.

He glanced over his shoulder, distracted by the sheer curtains fluttering in a breeze that shouldn't have been there. That window hadn't been open when he'd cleared this room. A shadow skulked behind those sheers. How'd Montego get over there? Did she know she'd been followed? Was she waiting to kill him now, too? Pissed at her cunning, conniving mind, he lowered his shoulder and barreled into her. She wasn't getting away this time. "I've got you now, you bitch."

"Let me go," she hissed, elbowing his chest.

"Not on your life, you piece of shit," he growled reaching for her wrist. On went one cuff even as he mashed her against the glass, his knee between her legs and his arm across her throat. Snap. Zip. She was caught now. To make sure she didn't escape, he clipped the other part of the dual cuff to his wrist.

It dawned on him then. He was touching spandex or something just as skintight, not bare skin. But Montego had been nude. Add that little detail to the black knit cap pulled snug over this woman's head and—

Shit. She'd spoken in clear American English, no accent. The shower door slammed in the en suite bathroom behind Renner, sealing the deal. He peered closer at the woman in the dark whom he now knew was not Montego. "Who are you?"

"Not your bitch, you asshole!" she shot back at him. "Who the fuck are you?"

McCormack's toilet flushed, and Renner's heart damn near stopped. It didn't matter who he was. He'd just made the worst rookie move in the book. He'd forgotten all about that out-of-place noise he'd heard before in his eagerness to catch Montego, and he was trapped. The now cracked open bathroom door at his back cast a long stream of light into the bedroom. Running would land him and this unknown woman in Montego's path. At least he'd cuffed his left wrist to this mystery woman's right wrist. Which meant they could run side by side. If they lived.

"How'd you get in here?" he asked even as the sheer curtain billowed around them in the wintry breeze.

She rolled her eyes. "Are you stupid or just plain dumb?"

Ah, both? "You're shitting me? You came in through the w-w-window?"

"What's the matter, tough guy?" She sent an angry puff of frozen vapor into his face. "You're brave enough to rob one of America's richest men, but scared you're going to fall and go boom?"

That did it. Now fastened to quite possibly the most obnoxious woman he'd ever met, Renner pushed the stranger through the open window she said she'd come through. Then quietly, he shut the slider, careful to not trap the sheer curtain in its track. If only it had opened onto a lanai or a deck, anything wider than the narrow concrete ledge he found himself balancing on. Those cars on the streets below looked awfully small and—

"Don't look down," the lady jerking his cuffed wrist snapped. "You look down, you fall. My eyes only." She pointed two fingers at her eyes, jerking his left hand again. "Look at me, asshole. Like it or not, I'm your way out of here."

Jesus, it was cold up here. But solid. There was no ice on the ledge, not that he couldn't still fall off. Sweating bullets now, Renner's eyeballs locked onto the smart aleck lady in the black bodysuit. Black cap. The tiniest black booties he'd ever seen. Nope, those were definitely climbing shoes. Velcro straps instead of laces. Probably some kind of suction-cupped soles, he hoped. Which weren't going to help him, not with his everyday steel-toed anchors on his stiff as cinder block feet.

There was a reason he hadn't signed with the Army's 101st Airborne. Renner hated heights, that and a little thing called hypoxia, the lower-than-normal oxygen saturation in a guy's blood when skydiving, made him pass out. He hated flying commercial, too, never went anywhere he couldn't drive—unless he absolutely had to. Yet he'd never admit it, certainly not to the chick he was now cuffed to.

Once a year, all TEAM members had to qualify for HAHO, high altitude high opening, and HALO, high altitude low opening, parachute jumps. Adam Torrey, the resident SEAL and the only flying squirrel on The TEAM, loved that shit. He'd even organized the Mile-High-Bastards club to which every agent, except Renner—the only smart one on The TEAM—belonged. They'd all go flying together—in a perfectly good plane—then jump out of that plane like a pack of idiots. Not Renner. He only qualified when he had to. Once a year was enough.

"What now?" he asked, his mouth dry and his heart pounding up high his throat at his two very real possibilities. One, standing on this ledge all night until Montego left. That would suck. Two, dying of a heart attack while standing on the same narrow ledge—that was getting narrower with each passing second—until Montego left.

"Now we let go, tough guy," she replied evenly, her gaze still on him.

Renner couldn't *not* look at her by then. He was frozen. Paralyzed. That third possibility of letting go had never entered his mind. He had to give her credit, though, this gal had guts. But the rappelling rope coiled over her neck and one arm, a thin piece of nylon, wouldn't even begin to hold his weight. She had some kind of pack on her back, too, but it wasn't big enough to be a parachute, certainly wasn't two.

Then this was it, how everything ended. He was going to die.

"How long's your rope?" he asked like a dick, as if she could possibly carry one long enough to put him safely on the ground.

Instead of answering, she reached around his head, ran her glove across his neck, then down his back and asked, "Do you trust me?"

"No," he replied quickly. This was not one of those *"Aladdin"* moments when the sultan's daughter got suckered by a street rat asking the same question. Renner was no princess and there was no damned magic carpet in sight. He would've watched what was making that clicking sound behind him, but he'd lost all capacity to think calmly or logically. To think at all. Fear did that to a guy. "I don't know you enough to trust you."

But she'd also gotten in close, and she smelled like flowers and wind. He closed his eyes, savoring the moment, until a sweeping sense of vertigo spoiled everything. He snapped those eyes back open, needing something—anything!—to hold onto. The window behind him would do. Like an idiot, he palmed his free hand to the cold glass behind him that offered no handhold. Not a one.

Maybe Montego wouldn't notice if they sneaked back in. Maybe there was another way, a better way to get out of this mess. Damn it, the ledge was too high, too narrow. His boots were too large. He was going to fall. Like a pig. A frozen pig. By the time he landed, they'd have to scrape him off the pavement and use DNA to identify what was left of him.

"R-R-Renner Graves," he managed to spit out. It seemed important now. Someone should notify his mother and sister, his niece. Not that Alex wouldn't, but this woman was here and...

She cocked her head like she was really seeing him, as if she'd read his mind. If it hadn't been for the altitude, he might've called her cute in a boyish, pixie, kind of way. She was small like Montego, but her facial features were delicate, not coarse. For certain, this cocky Wonder Woman was strong, but she was also kind, not cold and brutal, certainly no sadist. She didn't give off that kind of vibe. He could tell. There was a warm, motherly light in her eyes, and she had breasts that stretched the front of her jacket just right—like they wanted to be let loose.

Shit! He nearly slipped. Renner palmed that slippery glass window again, mad at himself for getting distracted by two very fine breasts.

The slightest smile quirked her pursed lips, lips that were luscious and wet and shining and—

What a time to be thinking about sex. But yeah, no. His last visit home and the bright smiling face of Frankie, his four-year-old niece, overrode those crazy, wonderful, erotic—but totally inappropriate—sensations bubbling through his veins. He was going to miss Frankie's sweet hugs most of all. Not this woman he didn't know. Frankie adored him, and Renner loved that little girl with every beat of his devil dog heart. This gal didn't care if he lived or died.

But those breasts…

"It's very nice to meet you, Mr. Renner Graves," the woman he was now bound to in death whispered beguilingly as if she'd known precisely what he was thinking.

"Yeah, I'd say the same back to you if I hadn't just jacked up both our lives," he murmured, still trying to get a grip on that glass. Still fighting to keep his eyes off her chest. "Sure sorry about this."

For the first time he realized that, because of his brilliant idea to use flex cuffs, this woman's arm was now extended along with his. She was letting him palm the glass even though she knew there was no support there. The only thing keeping him from dropping to his death was her and this tiny ledge his big feet were now precariously balanced on. Damn, he was stupid, but she probably knew that, too.

She shrugged, that sparkle in her gaze drawing him in. "No worries. It's part of the job."

The bedroom light flashed on behind them. Jesus, Montego could see through those sheer panels!

"But we need to go now, Mr. Graves," his lady of the night said calmly. "We fly together. All the way. Are you with me?"

WTF? Fly? "No," he meant to say, but it came out in one long, "Nooooooooooooooooooooo!" Because his diving buddy pushed him! Him! The guy without a parachute or a rope or a—

She'd pushed him! He was airborne and falling and—

"No! Just no!"

But then his body jerked against the drop like he'd been caught. But he wasn't. Renner peered up. There was no chute, but his cuffed hand was now interlocked with Wonder Woman's, her grip tight and dry and sure. Warm. He squeezed her hand tighter before he noticed she'd also managed to capture his other hand, those fingers now interlocked in the same tight grip. They were facing each other, both falling to their deaths. Only slower than he expected. And her legs were spread wide. Some kind of webbing shimmered between them and under her arms and—

His brain kicked back on. She was as crazy as Adam. That outfit of hers was a wingsuit, the kind that adrenaline junkies wore when they jumped off skyscrapers and mile-high cliffs for the thrill of it. That was what she was doing up there. She was a human bat, a wingnut, with strong tensile fabric-wings now stretched taut under her arms and between her legs. He was still dead weight and still falling, just not as fast.

"We're coming in hard," she shouted across the noisy air space between them. "My chute won't slow us down enough. Whatever you do, don't tense up. Bend your knees when you land or you'll break your legs."

She had a chute? Another good thing to know.

"Did you hear me?" she yelled louder that time.

Renner nodded, his heart pounding like a mother, and the ground coming up like a freight train riding rails of sheer black ice. "I'm going to die," he muttered at himself. "Even if I live, I'm still going to die because Alex will kill me when I tell him I almost had Montego, only not really because I cuffed myself to a flying squirrel. Shit, I'm so dumb."

"What'd you say?" she bellowed.

He shook his head. No sense repeating that. No sense talking at all, not unless he could give himself Last Rites.

The cars on the street below grew larger. His throat got drier. At the last moment, she deployed her chute and it seemed to slow them just enough they didn't crash and burn. But then he'd bent both knees, anticipating crashing on the top level of a nearby parking terrace instead of in the middle of the busy street, and praying, *'Please, God. I'll go to Mass with Mom every Sunday if You let me live tonight.'*

At last, touchdown.

In better control of his senses and his bowels by then, Renner rolled into the landing to lessen the impact. As if she'd anticipated his move, his cat burglar friend rolled with him.

Somersaulted really. It wasn't pretty. By the time they came to a full stop, they were a pair of awkward conjoined twins. Renner was face down to the pavement with his left arm twisted behind his back. She'd ended splayed over him like a rag doll, her face in the crook of his sweaty neck, her right arm between them, and her knee stuck between his thighs. Which he was totally okay with because a simple patch of concrete had never felt so good or so immovable. He let the last of the sun's radiant heat stored in it remind his cheek that life really was good, and he was alive. Yup still breathing. A childhood rhyme sprang to mind. *'God is great. God is good. Let us thank him for our food. And for living. Hell, yeah.'*

"Thank you, God," he whispered to the grime and oil and whatever else was ground into the cement under his face. "Not for the ride down so much, but definitely for the landing."

Wonder Woman whispered in his ear, "The police will be here soon, tough guy. Should we stay and get better acquainted? Maybe they won't notice us mugging each other like we are."

"No, ma'am," he growled. "Let's haul ass."

Still feeling like a pretzel, Renner waited until she rolled off before he climbed to his hands and knees. Which was so not his style. He was in reasonably good shape. He was a fit athlete, jarheads had to be, damn it. He was certainly not accustomed to kneeling at a woman's feet. But after dropping from a penthouse in the dark...

Jesus. Never again.

They made it up and on their feet at the same time. "Hold up," he ordered. Digging into his boot sheath, he pulled out his knife and made short work of that stupid damned flex cuff.

Man, her smile was a beacon that would give their position away all by itself.

Renner still held her wrist. Red and blue lights flashed from the street below. The police were there, but he didn't want to let this mystery woman go. "Who are you?"

"What's it to you?" she asked, eyeing his fingers as if she might bite them. "Are you going to arrest me after I saved your life?" She gave him that cocky chin nod again as she dragged her cap off with her free hand. Shimmering, touchable, scarlet red spilled over her shoulders and tumbled down her back like a gleaming river.

A man could get lost in there, and Renner was. Long hair and breasts, his two favorite kryptonites rolled into one sexy package. He shook his head to clear the sudden steam between his ears. "No, but I would like to know who to thank for saving my life." His voice had gone hoarse and low. It was hard to swallow again. This woman was no pixie. Maybe a siren who called men to their deaths? That seemed a better fit.

He couldn't quite decide the color of her eyes, but he guessed blue. Maybe green. Suddenly it seemed a critically important detail, something he should know after the intimacy of nearly dying together.

The roar of tires squealing up the parking ramp killed his need to know. They both looked toward the sound. "Tara," she said when she turned back around to face him. "I'm Tara Tumulty. Now grab the chute and run!"

Like a dumb jarhead recruit with his first badassed drill instructor, Renner grabbed the chute, rolling it into a ball as he ran. He had a feeling then. Even without the cuffs, he'd follow this woman anywhere.

Chapter Three

Tara led him through the door marked STAIRS, down three winding levels, then out onto the quiet, frigid streets of Roslyn, Virginia. Facing east, she began jogging even as she stripped her all-in-one wingsuit off, stopping only to step out of the pants. Down to black running pants and an Under Armour tank, she wrapped the suit into a tight roll as she ran. Renner had already handled the chute into a neat, tight package under his arm. No longer out in the open, she breathed easier despite the cold sharp air.

Now that he had his nerve back, Renner Graves made an excellent running partner. Not too fast. Not too slow. She'd kept watch on her first ever wingnut trainee. He wasn't even breathing hard. Good to know. The man was in shape, something she respected. Not enough people kept themselves in prime condition.

The quiet slap of their soles against the pavement made Tara smile. So had the astonished look on his handsome face when she'd pushed him off the ledge. That was priceless. This big tough guy hadn't expected she'd do it, which had made it the right thing to do. They hadn't time to argue, and she'd learned long ago arguing solved nothing. Action was what brought results. So, she'd acted, and here they were, still alive and headed east, away from her perfect mark. But only for tonight. She'd climb that landmark apartment building again and soon. She had plans for those diamonds.

"We should stop for a drink," she told him. Too much adrenaline made a person thirsty. This guy had to be parched by now.

"Yeah, sure. I know a place," he said, still running and still keeping up. "Turn left, next corner. On the right. You can't miss it."

He was right. The bright green lights were on and Irish music was thumping at Crazy Eights, a local tavern. Mr. Graves' hand coasted to the small of her back when he pushed the door open for her. That was nice and gentlemanly, but nice was as deceiving as was gentlemanly. Neither made a man kind or a gentleman, a noble hero or an intelligent partner. It certainly didn't make him worth wasting her hard-bought freedom. Tara had learned that lesson well. Small gestures only made men—nice. Barely worth breaking a sweat over.

Mr. Graves waved at the bartender, an older, but pretty, dark-haired woman wearing a green Notre Dame ballcap and matching ND apron.

Her eyes lit up when she saw him. "Hey, boyo of mine! The usual?"

Nodding, he pointed to the back of the place, his hand still on Tara's lower back as he steered her to a corner booth of Irish proportions. As eating establishments were in Ireland, all the booths in the place were different and unique. None looked alike. A stout wooden bench lined one side of this table, two matching wooden chairs the other. The table itself was a heavy piece of antique oak, its top inlaid with ceramic tiles in shades of emerald green and shamrocks, what else? The wall enclosed two sides of the booth while a high-back divider of the same heavy oak separated this booth from the next.

Tara selected the bench since it faced the door. She needed to see whoever entered the pub. Mr. Graves took the chair farthest from the aisle, his back to the door and a knowing smile on his face. Well, he could have it. She would let him know if the police—or anyone else—showed.

They'd no more than settled down when the bartender came by with a tray of two tall waters, two large frothy mugs of beer, and a gigantic bowl of pub mix.

"What'll it be, young lady?" she asked Tara, her bright eyes the loveliest shade of sky blue.

"Thanks, but no thanks. Water will be fine. I'm not hungry."

"But surely you'll be wanting something more to drink than just water?" The bartender made that a question.

Tara looked at the two sweaty mugs. What would it hut? Maybe drinking a single beer wouldn't hurt—just this one time.

Mr. Graves snickered as he appropriated both mugs, sliding them to his side of the table. He grinned like a kid with a secret. "Uh uh. These are mine. Get your own."

How rude. Obviously, Renner was a regular here. Well, okay then.

Facing the bartender once, Tara said, "Since I've come with a piggish man, I'll have a root beer, please." She didn't ordinarily drink alcohol anyway, but she needed something after the fiasco the night had become. There was an interesting vibe to this quaint little Irish pub though, one she couldn't yet put her finger on. It wasn't coming from the steady Irish music the band played, either.

"Aye, he's a piggish one, he is. One root beer, coming right up," the bartender said with a smile as big as could be. "Fish and Chips?" she asked Mr. Graves.

"No, ma'am. Rib-eye tonight. I'm hungry."

"Another tough day?" she sympathized.

"Nah, not really," he grunted, his smiling eyes back on Tara. "Just another day in the life of. Right?"

What else could she do but nod in agreement and say, "You might be right." Something was definitely going on here, but Tara was darned if she could tell what it was.

"How about you?"

Tara looked up into the charming woman's face. Those same dark blue eyes. The same straight nose. She looked tired but determined. And familiar. "Are you…? Is he…?"

The bartender nodded. They *were* related. "Yes, my dear, this handsome man is me boyo. Now what'll you be eating? A rib-eye like him or the cod? I breaded it myself, and it's fresh caught this morning." She pronounced morning with a soft 'a', like marning.

Tara spiked a brow and shot Mr. Graves her best evil-eye even as she extended her hand politely to make the acquaintance. "It's so nice to meet you, Mrs. Graves. I'm Tara Tumulty. I, umm, work with your son—occasionally—but he never told me how young you were."

Mrs. Graves took gentle hold of Tara's hand with both of hers. "Well then, we're even. He never told me he had such a beautiful girlfriend, either. But from now on you'll be calling me Brenda, you hear? Now let me get that root beer for you. I'll be back before you can say Nine Fine Irishmen!"

When she was out of earshot, Tara leaned into the table and whispered, "Your mother's delightful. You should've told me she worked here."

He sipped his draft, his cobalt blue eyes intently fixed on her. "She doesn't. She owns Crazy Eights. This is her place."

"Oh, really?" Wow. Tara took a longer, closer look at the fine woodwork in the tavern, all of it polished, every antique-furnished booth clean, the black-and-white checkered floor swept and as lovely a throwback as the rest of the place. The racked liquor bottles on the antique bar gleamed gold and blue, red and white against a sparkling beveled mirror. Green glass lampshades glowed everywhere. Dainty pink roses in Irish crystal vases graced each table.

"Your mother's an amazing woman."

"Aye, that she is," he replied, his half-empty mug raised in a salute. "My dad's been gone for years, and Mom's been a force in my life. You'll like her."

I already do. Brenda reminded Tara of her own mother. Kind to a fault and willing to work herself to death if it helped her family. "You know," she drawled as she reached across the table and interlocked his fingers with hers. "This could be the start of something fun. If we're going to bump into each other like we did tonight, we might as well work together."

His gaze fell to her hand on his, his eyes bright with—something. At last he looked up. "Why were you there?"

She cocked her head at him. "Are you kidding? You know. For the same reason as you."

"And that would be?"

Was he playing dumb? "The payoff. The jewels and what all those diamonds can buy," she answered earnestly.

He pulled his fingers away. "You're a thief?"

She would've scoffed, but the beam in his eyes was now more serious, not so much light as awareness. Until he tugged her hand back across the table and said, "You like ink."

He had to be a cop who could now identify her by the *Grumpy Cat* tattoo on the back of her hand. She'd always loved that internet celebrity. Until now. "Goodbye, Mr. Graves," she said politely even as she pushed to her feet.

If only he'd let go of her hand. "Do you mind?"

He gave her that cocky head nod guys did so well, the one that told her to sit her ass back down and shut up. Tara's spine stiffened at the temerity of this walking bag of testosterone. He had his nerve. She never should've thought he was different. He wasn't! Okay, so she had thought precisely that for all of ten seconds, but that had more to do with his sweet mother than him. Talk about a night to forget.

"Please," he whispered, the sincerity in his eyes warm and alive as if he needed this more than she did.

Tara balked, her nerves still on edge for all she'd lived through and all she'd accomplished in spite of it. *For that.* She'd never make the same mistake twice.

Fool me once, shame on you. Fool me twice, shame on me. Never again.

His lips pinched, but not with anger. It looked more like regret. Maybe pity. Which she didn't need, damn him. But it was better than what she'd expected from a… a man.

His grip loosened as if he'd realized he'd been holding on too tight. "I'm sorry, Tara Tumulty," he said quietly. "For whatever happened to you in the past, I'm sorry."

"You don't know me well enough to be sorry," she declared, her righteous indignation on fire. Damn him for thinking he knew anything about her when he most certainly did not. For assuming an apology from one male could ever make up for the others. Men were jerks. All of them!

Mr. Graves' fingers let go. He nodded as if he'd lost and she'd won. "You're right, but I'm still sorry, especially if I came across as judgmental. I'm not usually quick to jump to conclusions, but you surprised me, and… Hell. Everything about this night surprised me."

He leaned back in the chair and ran his fingers over his head as if frustrated. The sides of his head were shaved close, the top longer. With each stroke, the darker locks up top lifted like burnt wheat under a stiff wind. As dark as his hair appeared under these dim lights, there were traces of red in there, red she wanted to run her fingers through.

"Listen, we just survived one helluva drop, and I'm thirsty and hungry. Stay. Just to talk. That's all I'm asking. Then I'll see you home. My car's parked not too far from here. After that, you'll never have to put up with me again."

"I'll see myself home, thank you." How she wanted to run. She'd had enough of men and their wily traps. Their conniving lies.

His mother arrived with another dripping wet mug and a raft of napkins. "Here you go, my darlings," she said cheerily as she wiped her hands on the bar towel at her waist, then ran her hand over and through that same dark hair. Mr. Graves sat there taking it in like a little boy who adored his mom. Obviously, she adored him, too. She ended the caress with a thump on the top of his head, which he smiled through.

Then she said, "Steaks will be up in a minute, children. Holler if you need anything."

Yet he hadn't taken his eyes off Tara. Not once. "Thanks, Mom," he said quietly, "but I don't think Tara will be joining—"

"I just realized," Tara interrupted as she patted her pocket like she was searching for something. "I forgot my wallet. I'm so sorry, but I'm afraid—"

"Oh, come now, din't my boy tell you?" Mrs. Graves asked, a mischievous glint in her eye. "Renner…" She drew that word out as if it carried an implied threat.

"Umm, tell me what?"

"That there's never no charge for family or friends, that's what. And if my boyo brought you here, then that's what you be. Now sit your pretty caboose down and enjoy that root beer before it goes stale, young lady. I'll have another round brought over soon as you're done with this one. Drink up."

"Thanks, Mom," Mr. Graves said as his mother turned back to her barkeeping.

Swallowing hard, Tara sat, her spine rigid, her palms sweating. If this was a trap, it was a really good one. Almost— almost—made her want to stay. But she couldn't, could she? Better question, should she? What if someone had seen her jogging away from the scene of the crime. What if Renner was in on it. What if *he* were somehow trailing her… watching her…

"I didn't ask for steak, Mr. Graves," was all she could think to say, her voice no more than a whisper.

"For God's sake, woman, we just fell to our deaths and lived to talk about it," he whispered, glancing over her shoulder at the bar where his mother had just welcomed another couple to 'come, have a few'. "Would it hurt you to call me Renner? Maybe pretend you at least know me? That you might like me, just a little?"

"Hmmpf." That would be the day. She'd just met this guy. What was there to like?

His arm stretched across the table again, but this time he merely rested his hand palm up where she could see it. Open. Trusting.

Tara bowed her head to hide the fear rising in the back of her throat, as well as what he might be able to read in her eyes. Man, he was good. Maybe too good.

He did have a nice manly hand, though. Short, clipped nails, but not manicured. Calluses marked each finger and thumb. His knuckles were chapped. Obviously not a mechanic's hand, it was too clean. Which only proved he wasn't afraid to work hard. But Tara had been down this road before, and it was a long one to come back from. Smarter now, she clasped her hands beneath the table, not willing to give herself away. She'd done easy once before. Never again.

"Mom likes you," he said, pulling his arm back, the tender glint still in his eyes.

Tara made the mistake of looking at him then. "Who are you?"

He cocked his head, perhaps realizing there would be no tit-for-tat conversation. He didn't deserve her trust. Not yet. Maybe never. And he seemed to understand that. "I'm no cop if that's what you're thinking. I do work security, though."

"For Mr. McCormack?" she asked, her nose in the air.

He nodded. "He's on my list at the moment, yeah. My boss asked me to make sure he was okay after the way his wife died. That's why I was there."

Tara wasn't buying that. "In his bedroom?"

A half-smile flittered over Mr. Graves, ahem, okay then, over Renner's face. He was good-looking in a boyishly handsome way. Maybe six-foot tall, maybe just under that guesstimate. But strong. Lean and wiry. Definitely a guy who worked out. She'd felt those tight abs, his muscled thighs and shoulders when she'd landed on him. He'd honestly tried to wrap his arms and legs around her when they'd rolled together onto the parking terrace, as if he'd meant to cushion her fall. But when they'd landed and he'd been breathing hard... When she'd found herself lying on his back, her face between his shoulder blades, feeling his heart throbbing through his entire body…

Yeah. The mysterious Mr. Graves was good-looking, and he was also carrying. That pistol he'd threatened her up top with might've disappeared from public view, but she knew it rested under his left arm beneath his leather jacket, another under his right arm. She'd felt another piece of *hardware* when they'd tumbled together, too, and for that single moment, she'd found a strange kind of peace breathing in the musky, sweaty maleness of him, knowing he was all man.

He cocked his head as if debating what to say next. "To be honest, I'm after the woman McCormack's seeing. I just didn't expect to run into her tonight like I did. Sure as hell wasn't expecting you."

"Why do you want her?"

He snapped his mouth closed, his eyes gone hard.

Tara shook her head. "Not that you want her, *want her*, but is she a threat? Doesn't McCormack have other bodyguards?"

"Why were you there?" he asked instead of answering.

She shrugged. He might as well know. "You're right. I am a thief, but it's not what you think."

"Then what is it?"

"You could say I'm a modern-day Robin Hood. I work for a local charity in the District. They're always short-funded.

Too many kids, not enough money to go around. You know how it goes."

He smirked. "You expect me to believe you steal from the rich and give to the poor, is that it?"

She gulped at what she was doing. Telling him a little but not enough. Just enough to sound credible but never everything. "Actually, yes. That's what I do. I pick pockets and I prowl cars. Occasionally, like tonight, I drop in unexpectedly on wealthy people who have everything everybody else wants or needs. While the cats are away, you know. Don't get me wrong, I've never hurt anyone. But that woman..." Tara shivered thinking about the woman Mr. McCormack deigned to associate with. Yes, deigned. He was too good for her. There was something fundamentally wrong with her, something evil.

"She's always dressed to the nines, slathered in diamond rings and necklaces, and McCormack's just another dumb, rich, older guy with a young woman hanging on his arm. That Cuban chick who's got her hooks in him now? She's a gold digger; I can tell. All she wants is his billions, his wife's diamonds, and for him to drop dead. But my kids…"

Tara pinched her lips tight before she revealed too much. She swallowed hard. Lying didn't usually bother her like it did now. She'd gotten good at it back in her former life on the streets. Yes, she'd told her friend Kelsey she'd tell the truth and nothing but the truth from now on. But this felt like one of those times when a white lie might be the wiser choice.

Mr. Graves was still studying her like a bug under a magnifying glass.

And that was enough. She looked away, dismissing and ignoring him. The steaks were here. Maybe she was hungry after all.

Chapter Four

Man, this woman was tense. Renner finished his first beer, then pulled the second handle within reach. After a long swallow, he swiped the back of his hand over his mouth, refreshed and finally feeling the crash of too much adrenaline.

Tara started out picking at her steak, moving asparagus spears from fore to aft on her plate. But after the first sizzling, succulent mouthful of grade A prime, she dug into that rib-eye like a concentration camp survivor. The buttered asparagus went next, and now, courtesy of Renner's mom, a double helping of Irish bread pudding, complete with a dose of Jamison now burning off and creating a crispy, sugary crust, sat between them. Two spoons. The incorrigible matchmaker that she was, Mom had only brought one dessert but two spoons. If she only knew that this was no date, that Renner was fairly sure he'd never see the mystery woman across the table again.

Daintily, Tara sampled the pudding. A tiny bit of caramel glaze dripped to her chin. He planned to lick it off later, so he said nothing. Just smiled when she closed her eyes and moaned at the first mouthful. Low and throaty. Earthy. Enough to drive a thinking man out of his mind.

He controlled his impulse to slide in next to her, gather her sexy body against him, and kiss that mouth. She was a mystery, but he knew body language. It came with the territory. Snipers employed all skillsets when tasked with a kill order. They alone had to live with what they did, and it was clear that Tara knew pain and betrayal. It showed in the way she flinched every time someone came through the door, and in the many times she'd stiffened her body as if waiting for something to go wrong. He was pretty sure she'd suffered at someone else's hand. That was why she hadn't encouraged his touch.

She might never allow him to get any closer, and that was okay. Not all battles were won in a day or a night. Some took years. Some took forever. And some friendships never evolved into anything more. He'd worked with women in the Corps and on The TEAM. He understood the dynamics between men and women. So, Renner kept his place and enjoyed what was left of the night with her. It might be all there was.

"Tell me about your children," he said, still watching her eat. Still loving the way she licked her lips, and still jealous of her spoon. Caramel, huh? Caramel and whipped cream… that actually gave him an idea… But no. Not with Tara and not tonight. Probably never.

"They're not mine," she sputtered as a spoonful of the custard got away from her and tumbled down the front of her tank top. "Oh, darn. Look at me."

It was hard not to look at her, or to reach across the table and dab the creamy mess away. To cop a feel, maybe get in close. Smear the rest of that caramel over her throat and inch his lips down to her—

He cleared his throat to banish the temptation. Nope. Not happening.

Renner cranked his head toward the bar, stayed on his side of the table, and kept his hands to himself. Tara needed her space more than she needed him, and he needed to get away from her before he lost his mind. Man, she was pretty. All that red hair. Those eyes. Her mouth had a way of turning hard and then soft in the blink of an eye, as if she could read him the riot act, then kiss him better after she had.

Yeah. He needed to get her into an Uber and forget this night ever happened.

By the time she'd wiped her shirt and her chin, his pants were too tight and he needed a long breath of fresh air and a cold shower. If he'd been able to walk. But no. Renner wasn't going anywhere soon.

"Anyway…" She drew that word out with a big smile. "Like I was saying, they're not my kids. I work at a halfway house for runaways. I'm kind of like you. I'm in security, too."

Renner rested his chin on his palm and his elbow on the table. "And…" he prompted. "Kids are still kids. They're smelly and noisy. What are yours like?"

"They're terrific," she said with star-bright enthusiasm. Her smile could've honestly lit the entire Eastern Seaboard.

"For instance…" He made a circle with his fingers for her to keep talking.

Tara set the spoon into the plate of half-finished dessert. "Well, my favorite is Jessica. She's the sweetest little African American doll-faced liar you'll ever meet. When I first arrived, she didn't want help getting away from her abusive pimp brother. She'd just come down from Boston, but she made it clear she didn't need anyone. She was all *'Leave me alone! I can do this myself! Back off and stop bugging me, you crackers!'"*

Renner could've watched Tara the rest of his life. He chuckled at the image of a spitfire like little Jessica. What made that little girl so fierce and so determined? Kids weren't born like that; they evolved into it to survive. So, what had Jessica survived? Just her brother? For that matter, little boys weren't born pimps, either. What had her brother survived to turn him into a user?

Tara's words snapped him back to the moment. "She was just eleven, can you imagine that? But something I said must have gotten through to her. Jessica needed my help, and she got it. No questions asked, just 'thank you, ma'am'," Tara said with attitude. "Her brother got schooled in the law of the jungle, that bigger truly is better, and he got schooled hard. He never touched Jessica again. A guy with broken fingers isn't very intimidating."

"You broke his fingers?"

Tara blinked then. She'd only had root beer, not even all of it. But it seemed to have loosened her tongue more than she'd wanted. "Umm, no," she answered, her enthusiasm squelched. "But in my line of work, I, umm, know people and…" She shrugged. "If I can help kids who are homeless and in trouble like Jessica and…" She coughed. "I mean…" Cough, cough, cough.

Another clue. The covert cough. Renner sat there and took it all in. The way Tara's lashes dropped as if she thought she could shut him out by not looking at him. The hitch in her breath when she thought she'd said too much. The side glances, always looking over her shoulder. He'd seen these indicators before. PTSD, plain and simple. At one time in her life, Tara had been in trouble like the kids she now served and obviously loved. Renner let the moment of truth pass. Tara would tell him in her own time and way. That was just the way it was.

"Any other kids you've taken to heart?" he asked to get her back on track.

Her lashes fluttered as her gaze locked onto him. "Yes. Tyson. He's a local runaway from the other side of the river."

She'd lost the fire that had lit her up from the inside out, and Renner wanted it back. "The Anacostia?" It stood to reason. The most troubled neighborhood in the District lay across the Anacostia River.

She nodded. "Yes, most of our kids are black, but Tyson's special. He's just a skinny little thing, but he's courageous and he's fierce. Only he witnessed a gang murder. He was scared and he wouldn't go to the police, so he came to us, said word on the streets is we'll help anyone. The gang threatened to torture his mom and little sister if he ratted on them. They demanded he join up to prove he was one of them. He didn't know where else to go."

"Would that be the Tufts who committed that murder?" Renner asked. The Tufts, so named by a pack of idiot young men who thought they were 'tough' and who also wore short mohawks of—tufts. Yeah, not the brightest bulbs in that box of dimwitted Christmas bulbs. But they were mean and their crimes were escalating.

She nodded, her eyes on what was left of the dessert, her fingers once more fidgeting with the handle of her spoon. "Yes, um, you know who they are?"

Renner leaned back in his chair. "I've had a few run-ins with them."

It had to be hard, not knowing how much to say without admitting anything that would get Tara or her employer into serious legal trouble. He watched her neck muscles tighten. She was definitely on edge.

But this case sounded a lot like one he'd recently handled for Alex. He and Beau had made a trip across the Anacostia

Bridge one dark night. They'd tracked down the leader of that worthless pack of punks, and made a few points with him, points he'd opted not to heed. So, Beau made a few more points a day later—on that gang boss's hard head. By the time the discussion was done, Mr. 'Big-Mouth-Tuft' wasn't so tough anymore. He also knew Beau meant business when he said he'd be back and that he'd be watching.

"You like working with children," Renner said to move the conversation along. Tara needed to talk, and he didn't mind listening.

She met his gaze then. "Why do you do that?"

"Do what?"

She wiggled out of the bench and rounded the table, sliding in next to him. "Do this."

His heartbeat soared at what he hoped she was doing.

"You make me feel like I could tell you anything." She looked at his mouth.

He looked at hers. They were close enough he was going cross-eyed. "Because you can. I owe you. You saved my life, remember? You're my hero."

She cracked a smile. "You'd better be gender specific. I think that's 'heroine'."

"I think you're right." He leaned in closer, breathing heavier.

Sizzle. Crackle. Boom.

She jerked him into her face and planted her warm, wet mouth on his lips and...

Yessssss. This was what he'd wanted since she'd pushed him off that ledge. This sassy mouth. This warm, moist breath. This sensational wet, wild, unexpected kiss of a lifetime.

Renner circled one hand around the back of her slender neck, not willing to frighten the brave, bold woman now breathing hard in his face. Life was all about timing, and sometimes things worked out, but never often enough. Best-laid plans often fell through. Every jarhead knew strategy never survived first contact with the enemy in combat. Which made this surprise one of the best moves ever.

He didn't know what he'd done to deserve this moment, but it was now, and she was here, and... *Jesus.* She tasted sweeter than the bread pudding on her tongue.

Tara moaned and linked her arms around his neck.

His hands shifted down to her hips, his thumbs on her taut abdomen. Everywhere his fingers went, he discovered solid muscle. Slender but washboard hard. She worked out and it showed. But man alive, she was all woman. Trembling. Moaning into his mouth. Angling her head for easier access to his mouth, so more of his tongue could reach inside her. She wanted him, and that was all it took. Her fingers dropped to his belt. Every all-male receptor in his body sprang to life, and Renner was a man on fire.

But not here. "Whoa," he growled before he lost control. The wall around the booth gave them plenty of privacy for talking. Not—*that.* "Slow down a little."

By then she was nearly on his lap. Renner took firm hold of the situation. He could do one-night stands, but he wasn't good at them. Didn't like the way he felt the morning after. Didn't like being a user or a loser, being used or tossed aside. So, he'd sworn off the bar and single scenes. Until now.

Tara dropped her forehead to his chest, panting hard. "I'm... God, I'm sorry."

He pressed his index finger under her chin and tipped her face up. "I'm not," he told her honestly. "You're beautiful and you're smart enough to go after what you want. Just glad it was me."

"I don't know what came over me," she whispered, her lips swollen and wet, so damned delicious.

"I do," he whispered, his voice hoarse with desire. "Adrenaline and bread pudding will do it every time." This time he coughed into his fist as he soldiered through the erotic image of Tara covered in caramel and whipped cream. "Yup, mix those two together and…" *Cough, cough, cough.* "…you get one helluva…" *Hard-on.* "… aphrodisiac."

A sad little smile lit her face, and Renner was smitten. He peered into her soft blue eyes. A woman of worth glowed back at him, but she came with baggage, and he had the feeling Tara didn't know for certain who she was right then. That she was searching, exploring, maybe fighting her own brand of demons. A smart man didn't take advantage of a woman when she wasn't on her A game, and Renner's mother hadn't raised any fools.

Threading his fingers through her rich red hair, he cupped the back of her skull and kissed her forehead instead of those luscious tempting lips. "Mom makes the best Irish coffee this side of the river," he breathed. "You interested?"

He knew he'd said what she'd needed to hear by the way the tension sighed out of her. Which made letting her go more difficult. But the last thing Tara needed was some pushy guy in her bed. She needed more. She needed something solid to hold onto. Someone who wouldn't let her down. She needed a friend.

He'd only known her a couple hours, but he couldn't help it. Renner wanted to be that friend. He would've luxuriated in that deeply sensitive, personal revelation, but his cell vibrated like an angry wasp in his pants pocket. *Oh, shit, Alex.*

"You lost Montego?" his boss spat without introduction. Yup, Alex was smoking-hot pissed at Renner's lack of a timely sitrep, and as usual, Alex assumed the worst.

"No, Boss, I never had her. Someone else was already inside McCormack's penthouse when Montego showed." Renner stared Tara in the eye. She looked like she might bolt, so he'd grabbed her hand to hold her in place. Just in case.

"Who?"

"Not exactly sure yet, Boss. I'm still tracking her."

"Her? You got *sidetracked* by a female?" Not that Alex was misogynistic. Just a trifle old-fashioned.

Well, yeah. Kinda. Sorta. "Why not? Females are as capable as males." Why that commercial for women's rights poured out of his mouth, Renner hadn't a clue. Yet he did. A kid wasn't raised by an independent woman who owned and ran her own business, only to turn into a male chauvinist.

"Tell me you at least got close enough to lock onto Montego's son of a bitchin' cell."

Ouch. Renner winced. Each TEAM cell was not only ruggedized to endure all manner of shit, but it came equipped with a tracking app. An agent had only to come within feet of the person in question to link their cell identification with that app and begin tracking. "Didn't have time, Boss. Sorry. One minute I was inside McCormack's apartment, the next thing I was standing outside on his window ledge about to fall."

"Son of a bitch!" Alex's favorite curse stung Renner's eardrum again.

"But I'm okay," Renner interjected in case Alex forgot McCormack's penthouse was sky high.

"Well, shit, that's something." Alex wielded sarcasm as lethally as cursing.

"And I landed without breaking my neck," Renner deadpanned.

"You fell from Jed's penthouse?"

So far, Renner had sidestepped every direct question, but he had to come clean. This was Alex. He'd find out later, so he might as well know the entire story now. Renner inhaled a deep breath and said, "Yeah. I did something stupid tonight. Thought I had Montego, so I cuffed our wrists together to make sure she didn't get away. Only it wasn't her. I'd locked myself to a woman named Tara. She was inside McCormack's place to steal a few trinkets, and no, I'm not still tracking her. We're, umm, eating dinner at Mom's."

Tara's eyes widened when he revealed their location. She jerked away from him and jumped to her feet, but Renner held on tighter while he talked faster and explained further.

"She saved my life, Boss. If not for Tara's fast thinking, we'd both be dead, or—you know." There was no way he'd tell Tara what Montego would've done had she caught them. Blood, gore, and torture did not a good first date make.

"You jumped?" Alex finally sounded interested, maybe even a little incredulous.

"Had to. There was no other way out of there. Tara's a wingnut, Boss. She came prepared, and she's good. Damned good."

She stopped struggling then.

Renner kept going, watching her and thrilled he might've said something right. "By the time we touched down, the police were already on site, so we ran. Honestly, I should've contacted you right then and there, but—"

"Yes, you should have. Bring her in," Alex ordered.

"No," Renner told his hard-assed, stubborn-as-hell boss. "She's free to go. I already told her that."

"Junior Agent…"

Renner rolled his eyes at that drawn-out threatening growl. Alex was prone to pull rank on his agents to get his way. Not this time. "I said no. She's not part of this mess. She doesn't need to be, either." It dawned on him that it might convince Tara if he actually released his grip. So, Renner did. He let her go.

Oddly, she didn't jump up and walk away. If anything, she looked interested and sat back down beside him.

"By your own admission, you caught a thief in the commission of a crime against one of the most beloved men in our country," Alex said. "This is no small thing. Bring her in."

Tara whispered, "It's okay, I'll go. I'd like to meet your boss."

Renner shook his head. She might be able to hear both sides of the conversation—Alex *was* loud—but there was no way Renner would take her willingly into the lion's den. Alex could be volatile, downright nasty when pushed. There was no knowing what he'd do when it came to his friend McCormack. Alex had nearly lost Beau to the witch. Then he'd discovered that Montego had kidnapped and tortured one of his USMC buddies from years before. So yeah. Introducing this friendly neighborhood cat burglar to his boss was out of the question.

Until she smiled that sultry, come-hither smile and kissed him on the side of his mouth. "Trust me," she whispered, her fingertips walking up his chest to his neck. Into his scalp.

Stimulating him in ways he hadn't known were possible. "It's still early, and you said your car's parked close by. I don't mind walking with you."

Renner licked his lips, wanting more of her mouth and less of Alex. "But he might have you arrested."

"But he might not," she murmured, her voice low and sultry as sin.

At the same time Alex snarled, "Oh, for hell's sake, Graves, I will not have her arrested!"

Renner knew it was already too late. His boss had just called him Graves. Not Renner. Not dumbass. Yup. They were going to TEAM HQ.

Chapter Five

"We're leaving?" Renner asked the moment the elevator opened to reveal his ornery boss. "Already?"

"Home," Alex retorted, his bulging briefcase under one arm and his gut tied in knots. "You must be Tara," he said to the pretty woman in black at Renner's side. They did look good together. An angel and an assassin, her with all that wavy red hair, him with his usual dark and deadpan expression.

She gave him her chin and a cold glare. "Who else would I be?"

Make that smartass instead of angel. "Tara what?"

"Tara Tumulty. You must be Alex Stewart." Obviously, Renner had forewarned her about this meeting. She stuck out her hand. "Do you want my mother and father's names as well? My blood-type?"

I like her. "That won't be necessary. Pleased to meet you, Tara Tumulty," he said politely as he shook her hand. Alex gave her instant credit. She'd been considerate and courteous when he had not. He reined in his temper. "Good Irish name."

"Yes, it is. Thank you."

She had a firm grip. Another point earned. He hated the oatmeal hand clasps of so many weak-kneed men around the world, including Congress. Give him a strong American girl any day.

"You break into many homes lately, or is it an impulse you can't control?" he asked outright.

Again, with the audacious chin nod. The cool, icy, blue-eyed stare. The way her tongue worked the inside of her mouth like she didn't know whether to spit in his face or answer. "If you must know, I only break in when I want something I can't have. But the bloodsucker who has attached herself to Mr. McCormack's left arm? Her I'd rob just for spite."

His nostrils flared at the implied insult to his friend. "You know Catalina Montego, do you?"

"So, that's Catalina Montego. Thought her name was LuAnn? Huh." Ms. Tumulty shook her head, but she'd said that as if she knew something about Montego. Interesting. "No, I don't know her, just what I see on the news. But every time, she's had her hooks in your billionaire friend. How stupid is Mr. McCormack? Can't he see what she's doing? That she's only pretending to like him?"

"You see her a lot?"

Her upper lip twitched, just enough that Alex knew she'd caught the dare behind his rapid-fire question. *Just how good are you?* "I study my marks thoroughly before I relieve them of... ahem, their heart's desire, if that's what you're asking, *sir*."

Alex nodded despite the sarcasm behind that ultra-polite 'sir'. He couldn't deny it, Jed was a stupid shit to trust Montego. Which tweaked the pounding migraine Alex had lived with since she'd escaped his TEAM's grasp more than six months ago. The awful irony was that Jed's wife had died shortly after Montego fled the States. Murdering Lois was the one crime Montego couldn't have committed.

From that moment on, Alex had kept a close eye on his dearest friend. But not close enough. Alex and his TEAM had been too busy then, stretched too thin, covering all bases, at home and on the job, protecting their families and coworkers. Playing it safe. But when Lois died, everything came to a screeching halt.

How could Jed have moved on so easily? He'd adored Lois. Everyone had. Alex still couldn't get over the phone call that had broken the awful news. Some poor nurse at the hospital had to call him because Jed couldn't speak, he'd been that torn up. The nation and The TEAM mourned with him. Hell, TEAM agents were pallbearers at her funeral. How could Jed have forgotten this quickly? Hell, Alex hadn't yet gotten over the loss of his first wife and child, while Jed had seemingly jumped at the chance to hook up with Montego. It didn't make sense.

So, Alex fretted every day and stayed awake nights, working through all imaginable scenarios. How could he have prevented Lois's death? Should he have provided Jed with security instead of letting him secure his own? Should he have been less about business, more about friendship? Should he have seen Lois's death coming?

Alex wished he had. Because now Jed had gone off-track, shacked up with a dark-haired beauty who called herself LuAnn, even being seen in public with her. The society pages were full of photo ops and coverage of every event Jed and LuAnn attended. The press liked her. Hell, they were making the mysterious, beautiful Cuban 'princess'—her word, not theirs—who'd saved America's hero from a life of depression and grief, a star!

But Alex knew better. Montego might look different. She might have a different name, but she was still the same sadistic bitch. He and his TEAM just needed to prove it. But they also needed to proceed with caution. They couldn't just outright accuse her, not since she'd won Jed's affection as well as America's. The TEAM needed rock-solid DNA evidence to link her to her past and current crimes, which, after months of tedious undercover work, they still didn't have.

Not a trace of Montego's DNA evidence existed at any of the crime scenes. Not at the mansion down the road from Alex's stronghold near the Shenandoahs, where she'd tortured Beau Villanueva. Not at the underground complex in Crystal City, where she'd maintained a disgusting pit for her kidnapped army, all of them now poster boys for the worst kind of post-traumatic stress.

Alex shot Renner's feminine buddy a closer look then. He could see clearly what most others could not. Like so many of his agents, Tara wore the shadows stalking her like a trench coat. They all but hung off her shoulders and encased her small, athletic body. She had definitely suffered somewhere along the line, yet she carried that shroud well, her shoulders back and a go-to-hell chin nod at the world. The fire of a survivor shone in her eyes. He liked her. She was a fighter. Like Kelsey.

"Ah, Boss, are we going home, as in your place or mine?" Renner asked as if he'd asked once already. Which he probably had. Damned migraine.

"I'm flying out to mine. We can talk on the drive to Reagan." Reagan National Airport in Crystal City, Virginia, where Ben Mason, Alex's pilot, kept The TEAM helicopter waiting.

"Sure thing."

Alex liked Renner, too. More like Senior Agent Mark Houston than his other agents, he never overreacted. Some men came back from combat hardened, quick to fight. Not Renner. He was a thinker and a doer instead of a talker or complainer. His jokes were always expertly crafted, quietly delivered, and more often than not, they went unheard and unappreciated. Always understated, Renner stood back from the lead dog until he knew the best way forward. Not that he was passive. Renner hadn't a passive bone in his wiry body.

He never argued, just accepted his place on The TEAM, content to follow whoever was 'lead dog' at the time. To listen and obey. He'd been born a natural sniper, his patience an inherent character trait instead of a learned skill. That he'd screwed the pooch tonight only proved he'd been too intent on ending Montego. He'd leaned too far forward into this job, which could get an operator killed.

How well Alex understood. Only tonight his mind was on Kelsey, and why she hadn't been home when he'd called, why Lexie was at Mark and Libby's place again. Not that Lexie wasn't happily bossing Mark's daughters around, or that she wasn't well cared for. She most certainly was. Alex never doubted his second in command, but Kelsey's group of organized wives seemed to be keeping her occupied. Too busy. She'd been—off—lately. And not in a Christmas spirit, shop-until-she-dropped way. He couldn't put his finger on precisely what, but something was wrong at home, and Alex didn't like it. He needed to fix it.

"Out with it. What really happened?" Alex asked as the elevator emptied them into The TEAM's subterranean parking lot. He headed toward the nearest company car, an armor-plated black Cadillac, bullet-proof, zero-dark-thirty window tinting, and reinforced undercarriage. A man didn't own the best security business in the country without making enemies. Another hard lesson learned.

At the car, Alex tossed the key fob over the Caddie's hood to Renner. "You drive," he said as he climbed in behind the passenger seat and dropped his briefcase on the seat beside him. That way they wouldn't need to change seats at Reagan. They'd be good to go. Like him. Alex needed to be gone now.

Miss Tumulty rode shotgun. Renner took point, adjusting the rearview mirror, meeting his gaze. "What happened, Boss, is I screwed up. I cleared McCormack's apartment, but when Montego showed up unexpectedly, then stripped down to nothing in the foyer, I got a little distracted. I was in the kitchen. The only light on was in Jed's living room, but yeah, she walked through the place like she lives there."

"She does," Alex ground out, mentally cursing his friend's asininity for letting a slimy snake like Montego into his home and his life.

"That was your first mistake," Tumulty purred.

Renner shot her a spiked brow. "Okay, so I assumed once the shower came on that I could easily overpower her. And I could have—"

"Until he interrupted me," Miss Tumulty interjected, still speaking to Alex. "That was his second mistake."

Alex caught the tight smile Renner shot the woman at his side. He had a name for it now. Twitterpated. Renner might act pissed, but he liked this gal.

"And?" Alex asked to keep things moving.

"And..." Renner maneuvered through hectic Alexandria road construction. "I was wrong. I saw someone behind Jed's bedroom curtain. Thought it was Montego. I mean, who else could it have been, right? I'd just cleared the place. She and I were the only ones there. Only it wasn't her. But by then, like an ass, I'd cuffed myself to Miss Know-It-All here."

"And that was his third mistake," Tara teased, a pleasant lilt in her voice. "You assumed. Anyone ever tell you what 'assuming' makes you?"

Yup. Twitterpated.

"Hey!" Renner quipped. "Are you keeping score or something, lady?"

"Maybe," she replied, her tone suggestively low. "Someone has to keep track of you."

"And…?" Alex snapped. "Did you get away with it? Did Montego know you were in Jed's apartment or not?"

"Positive she didn't see us, Boss."

"She might have heard you screaming," Tumulty added saucily.

"Like hell I screamed."

"Oh, yes, you did. Like a little girl," she taunted. "All the way down."

"Did not."

"Did too."

"Guys." Alex didn't have time for this flirty back and forth. "I doubt people inside any building Jed built would hear screaming outside their apartment."

Renner's gaze stabbed Alex in the rearview. "I did not scream."

Tumulty scoffed.

He cocked his head at her. "You want to tell the rest of this story?"

"As a matter of fact, yes." She turned and swung an elbow over the back of her seat. "Actually, Renner is a fast learner,

Mr. Stewart. He did as I instructed on the way down, and we landed safely, so all is well. But I do believe you're right. That woman you call Montego is dangerous. What has she done?"

Alex glared at Renner in the mirror. "You haven't told her?"

Renner shook his head. "Need to know, Boss. She doesn't need to be mixed up in this."

"She already is."

"No. No, she isn't. She won't be going back there."

"I won't?" Tara asked, her eyes boring into the side of Renner's head.

Alex recognized that look. She was daring Renner to tell her one more time, just one more time—what she could and could not do. He'd better watch out. The words all men dreaded might come out of her mouth next. *Fine. Nothing. Go ahead. Whatever.* Best of all, *wow.* None of those meant the same thing to a pissed-off woman as they did to a clueless guy.

The light at the intersection blinked red. They were just south of the airport. Renner brought the caddy to a full stop.

Alex stilled, waiting.

Renner turned to Tara, his brows furrowed as he looked her in the eye and told her, "I sure wish you wouldn't go back to Jed's place. Montego's bad news, Tara."

There went that chin again, this time with a flounce of red mane. "I'm not a child, Mr. Graves. I can take care of myself."

"Never said you couldn't," Renner admitted. He seemed to know how to get around his prickly friend. "But that woman's a sadistic, cold-blooded murderer, and she's smart as a viper. We've been tracking her the better part of a year now, still haven't been able to get ahead of her, much less apprehend her. And most of us are former military. We're trained. Ending lowlifes like her is what we do for a living. I'm sure you've read about the missing Marines from LeJeune. Well, she's the witch behind that ugly mess, and I'd hate to see you in the same room with her. Please, Tara, for me, don't go after her."

This guy's good. Steady eye contact. Continued use of her name. Begging...

Her mouth formed a silent, *Oh.*

Renner nodded. "She's tortured more men than you've met in your entire life. Trust me." His hand went to her jaw as he brushed her hair off her shoulder and tucked a loose strand behind her ear. "The sooner we take her down, the better for everyone."

Just the right amount of physical contact.

Tara's neck worked through a noisy gulp. Renner had her complete attention now. "I'm... I'm sorry I ruined your chance to apprehend her tonight. Because of me, more men might be hurt. Or killed. You're right, I shouldn't have been there."

Intelligent explanation. But most of all, respect.

Renner shrugged. "I'm not sorry. Got to meet you, didn't I?"

Okay, and a little bit of schmooze.

Alex bit the inside of his cheek, watching his agent put some pretty smooth moves on his target.

"If you know she's a murderer, why don't you have her arrested?" Tara asked with a hint of *'how dumb are you'* in her tone.

"Because she's changed her looks," Alex snapped, interrupting the verbal foreplay going on in the front seat. "She's had plastic surgery and she changed her MO. She's pandered to the press and suddenly, she's a media darling."

"And we have no solid evidence to take to the DA," Renner added evenly. "No DNA, either. Not yet."

"But you're sure this LuAnn's the same woman? You're sure she's Montego?"

"Never been more positive," Renner said evenly. "I've seen her. Montego can't change the shape of her head or her retinas."

Alex was impressed. He hadn't known Renner had run her profile through Ember's facial rec program. They were at the Reagan terminal by then, turning onto the narrow road and through the gate that led to the runway and his flight home.

At the thought of Catalina Montego and what she'd done to gullible young military men, Alex's right frontal lobe spasmed, sending a firestorm bouncing throughout his skull like a pinball machine, skewering his retinas. He closed his eyes, every headlight on the street ahead a bright stabbing pain that offered no quarter.

Son of a bitch, he was tired of living with migraines. He'd been doing it for too long. The shitstorm with Jed, Montego, now Kelsey's seeming indifference was taking its toll. Maybe it was time to step away from this business and get a handle on these headaches before he stroked out. Take a long vacation. Chill.

Yeah, no. The TEAM was his blessing and his curse. He'd see this nightmare through. He'd always soldiered through before. He could do it again.

"Ah, Boss?"

Alex looked up at the concern shining bright in his junior agent's eyes. "What?" he nearly croaked as another lightning strike took his breath.

Renner nodded toward the windshield. "I, umm, said we're here."

Damn. They were at Reagan, parked at the waiting helicopter that would whisk him away from the District and onto another problem. Kelsey had better be home when he got there. Alex nodded. "Thanks."

"Are you feeling okay?" Renner asked calmly and evenly. Like always. "Maybe it's just these lights, Boss, but you look a little pale."

Alex scooped up his briefcase, shoved the car door open, and jumped to his feet to prove he was fine. Just fine. It'd take a helluva lot more than a monster like Montego to best him.

Tara had her window down, so he leaned over and talked past her to Renner. "Stay on Montego. Bring her down. Understood?"

"Copy that, but are you sure you're up to this? Maybe you should—"

"I said I'm fine. Steady sitreps from now on, got it?"

Renner touched two fingertips to his forehead. "I won't fail you again."

Alex gave him a curt nod, turned and ran for the waiting chopper. He had no doubt about Renner. But as he settled into the copilot's seat and snapped the noise canceling headset on, he wondered. Who was failing who?

Alex had three agents in Cambodia at the moment, all working the sex trade epidemic sweeping the world. Two more were in Afghanistan, on loan to the current regime, monitoring heroin trafficking as well as the never-ending humanitarian crisis unique to that part of the world. People thought the Taliban were dead and gone. Guess again. The media just didn't report the latest war on terror anymore like they should.

It wasn't popular. It didn't earn high enough ratings. They couldn't make money off it. *Bastards. The Taliban was back, people. More cunning. Still ruthless. But definitely back.*

Then there were his two agents inside China, another three in Russia, and…

His migraine surged back to life with a monstrous left hook that sucked his breath away. Alex leaned back in the copilot's seat and closed his eyes before his head exploded. He'd never doubted his place in the universe until now, and that doubt revolved entirely around Kelsey. She was his only anchor and his whole heart. His reason for living. Hell, she was his reason for breathing.

But if she'd grown tired of him…?

God knew she had the right. His long hours away from home were enough to ruin his health, they could certainly destroy his marriage. But if this was her subtle way of moving on with her life… Of leaving him and his bullheaded, arrogant ass behind…

He couldn't blame her for that, either. This was his fault. What woman in her right mind could or would wait forever for her man to come home?

Yet Kelsey had never failed to support him. Every night he came home to a hot homemade meal. She doted on him, and when he had time, he doted on her.

And there it was. Their problem. His problem. *When he had time…*

Was there such a thing as enough time? He knew damned well there was. A smart man managed his hours and minutes, he put important things first. Only Alex hadn't done that, not since Montego set foot in America. Not since she'd decided to exact revenge on The TEAM for her brother's death.

Which meant Alex had failed. He needed to work harder. Faster. Better. For everyone's sake, he needed to end that bitch before she destroyed the people around him!

Unless you destroy them first.

Shit. Yeah. There was that. Alex drew in a long, slow breath to slow the freight train of despair roaring down the tracks at him. That's precisely what he was doing. Running on empty. Always running...

Doubt Kelsey? *Never.* She loved him, and he knew it. She'd never leave. He knew that, too. Where had these awful questions come from? Was he insane? Another deep breath and Alex opened his eyes to the westward winding trail of red taillights on the interstate below. He checked his home security app, the one that pinged whenever a door or window opened at his house. The one that recorded all approaches and relayed those views back to him. The last time it notified him was when Kelsey had driven away late this morning with Lexie.

Alex refused to call her. He refused to lose hope. He'd be home soon, and Kelsey would be there. Then they could talk. Put Lexie to bed early, maybe open a bottle of white wine and relax together for one damned blessed evening. Kelsey liked wine.

More than anything, Alex needed to see the light in her pretty brown eyes when she first saw him waiting for her. Like the sun, that light was always there, even on bad days. Wouldn't she be surprised?

But more than anything, he needed her safe and warm and willing in his arms again, the heady scent of her hair in his nose. It'd been too long since they'd been intimate. He'd be okay then. Because they'd be okay. They had to be.

God, please let her be home.

Chapter Six

Tara glanced at Renner from the corner of her eye. After she gave him her address, he'd grown quiet. Pensive. Wintery clouds hung low over the landscape. They were a block from her apartment in Wakefield, a neighborhood in the Northwest quadrant of the District, but he had yet to say anything.

The home itself was an older Victorian, complete with a mansard roof, fish scale shingles, and gingerbread scrollwork outside, wainscoting and an elegant spiral staircase inside. Not that those amenities mattered.

The current owner, Mr. Marchant, a stuffy older gentleman, had subdivided what once was a mansion into four separate suites with front and rear common entries. Two elegant suites comprised the first level, another two the second. But as times grew leaner, or maybe because he'd become a seasoned landlord, he'd renovated the uppermost portion of the house, the attic, into what was now Tara's apartment. Only dear, sweet, irascible Mr. Marchant had called it a 'loft'—an incredibly generous description of the cramped, three-room cubbyhole with slanted ceilings and plenty of drafts on chilly days—in the real estate listing.

That was what had caught Tara's eye. She'd always wanted a loft. It sounded New Age romantic. Upbeat. Modern. In the end it was just an old attic. Not much romance about that.

There were two reasons she signed on the dotted line despite those inconveniences: the comparably safe neighborhood surrounding the old Victorian and the single rear entrance to her 'loft'. Once she parked her Honda Civic in her assigned stall in the cramped rear parking lot, there were only fifteen steps, maybe sixteen on a bad day, to the main back door. Once inside, the door to her apartment stood locked and waiting at her immediate right. She had only to unlock that door, shut it quickly behind her, engage the deadbolt, and she was safe again. Out of sight. She had her life back now. Where *he* couldn't get to her.

Inconvenience she could live with. Clanging water pipes and unreliable radiators she could work with. Bring 'em on.

As Renner turned onto the pothole-marked asphalt driveway, he looked up at the light glowing from the front dormer window as if he was studying it. Thanks to an army of timers, no one could tell whether she was home at night or not. Some turned on music. Most activated lights. But they all worked for her.

"This is it?" he asked, his brows lifted but his face devoid of expression.

"Yeah, this is me," she breathed, ready to run if he'd rather just drop her at the curb and be done with her. She wouldn't blame him. She had been rude to his boss.

But she hadn't expected to run into Kelsey's husband tonight, much less take a drive with the infamous Alex Stewart. That was an unnerving hour not well spent, and he'd been every bit as rude and condescending as the reputation that preceded him. Kelsey adored him, though why she did, Tara had no idea. Yes, he was good-looking in that crisp, silvery-gray business suit, white shirt, and red power tie. But the man was as hard as steel and he came with as much personality as some Gestapo officer. And he'd been rude to Renner. Abrupt. Good bosses just didn't treat their employees like that.

Instead of pulling over to let her out at the curb, Renner steered that massive Cadillac to the end of the driveway, then turned left into the skimpy parking lot. Angling the longer vehicle alongside the overflowing dumpster, he put it in park and turned off the key. Tipping his head sideways, he looked at her and said, "This has been quite a day. I'll bet you're tired."

She nodded, anxious to be gone now that she was almost home. Almost safe.

His fingertips landed on her shoulder, gently, like summer rain. Just letting her know he was there. "Hey, you're uptight. What's going on in that amazing brain of yours?"

"I should go. It's late." *And you turned the car off. That means you expect something. I never should've brought you here.*

Renner sighed. "I'm not going to make a move on you, Tara, if that's what you're worried about."

"I'm not worried. I'm…" What? He wasn't going to make a move? Why not? She nearly lifted an arm to smell her pits to see if she stunk after the adrenaline rush of the night. But that would've been a dumb-jock move, and she tried not to do stupid things like that in public. But once in a while, after a hard day or a close call like tonight's narrow escape, she was known to make dumb-jock moves.

He tapped her shoulder again, pulling her attention back to his handsome face and those inquisitive sad eyes. Those lips. "But I would settle for another kiss."

Tara swallowed hard. That first kiss was her fault. She never should've gotten carried away at Crazy Eights. There was just something about his smile, as if he were trying to act happy while he was really sad, that she hadn't been able to resist.

But what Renner wanted now was a nightcap. In her room. On her bed. Breakfast in the morning. The key to her solitude. Invasion. Her life. Her peace of mind. She had to correct her mistake, and she had to do it now.

'No," she whispered to the windshield. "I need to go." *Please don't make this any harder than it is.*

"Okay," he said, his voice so low it melted over her frozen heart like buttery, gooey caramel. "Mind if I at least walk you to your door?"

She shook her head. "No. I'm good. B-b-bye."

"Hey, Tara," he murmured, but by then she had one foot out the door. He leaned over the passenger seat and peered up at her, his arm extended, his palm open. "I'm not the bad guy here."

"You don't understand," she snapped, out in the open now, her heart pounding, telling her to *'Run!'*

A cat yowled from the shadows, freaking her out. And suddenly, Renner was out of the car, and she was inside his strong arms, her face plastered into his shirt, her heart hammering her insides to mush.

"You're shaking," he whispered, tightening his grip. "What's got you spooked, woman? My God, you're scared to death."

"N-no, I'm not, it's just…" Denial wasn't working. He was right, she could barely breathe or swallow. Her eyes were closed and she was afraid what she'd see once she opened them. "P-p-panic attack. I'll… I'll be fine," she lied. Once *he* was dead and buried. She'd settle for dead. Hell, she'd settle for knowing *he'd* moved out of state, maybe back to Colorado where *he* and she had lived before...

Renner bent over, settled a hand under her knees, and, as easily as if she were a little girl, he lifted her off the ground and held her tightly against him. Protectively. Tara would've argued, but he smelled good, and she'd never been more out of control. This panic attack was a monster. It sent her burrowing under his chin, one hand covering her face to hide her tears as she clung to him with the other. How embarrassing.

He angled her through the rear entrance, maneuvering adeptly past the screen door and the heavy wooden inside door. Once in the narrow hallway, Renner pressed her shoulder against the wall while she slapped the back door shut, needing to be sure her first line of defense was secure.

"S-s-stop. My key. I need to unlock m-my door." If only her fingers would stop shaking. If only she could see straight. Man, she couldn't think!

Without a word, Renner set her on her feet, took the keyring from her icy fingers, and unlocked her door with a quiet snick.

"Of course, it opens for you," she tried to tease. "I had it ready to p-p-op."

He handed the keys back. "I'm here for you, Tara," he said quietly. "You're the strongest woman I've met in a long time, but if you need any help—"

"No," she whispered, her head down, her eyes on the doorknob that meant safety. "It's just been a really long day, and I'm tired, and I'm—"

"And you're not ready to let anyone into your life, I get it. But I'm still here for you." He pulled a business card out of his back pocket. "Name's Renner Graves," he said with that same small, sad smile. "Former Marine. Still and always my mama's boyo. You need me, you call. Anytime. Anywhere. Promise?"

She nodded, calmer now because of this man and his gentle ways. He'd had plenty of opportunity. All night long he could've put the moves on her, yet he hadn't, and that meant a lot.

He turned his back on her then. Leaving her. Walking away. Renner had one hand on the painted-over rear doorknob and one boot out the door, when she breathed, "D-don't. Don't go."

That got his attention. But there was no glint in his eye that he'd won and she'd lost when he looked over his shoulder at her. Only respect. That was what Tara saw glimmering in those incredible eyes. His head dipped once. Renner closed the rear exit, stepped back inside, glanced at the ceiling and said, "You got any coffee up there?"

She nodded again, her body still trembling with fear and panic, but calmer now.

"Good. I could use a cup, but then I have to go. I can't stay all night, so don't ask. A guy like me needs his beauty sleep." He seemed to know just what to say to set her at ease.

"I've got coffee. H-hot chocolate, too. With marshmallows if you've got to have 'em."

He gave her one of his winning smiles and gestured for her to lead the way

Maybe, just maybe, tonight would be different.

Chapter Seven

Damn. This woman, this daring, outrageously brave, spit-in-your-eye acrobat who had no problem scaling tall buildings only to dive off them like a flying squirrel, was a puzzle. The closer Renner had gotten to her place, the more the tension ramped up inside the Cadillac. He'd been absorbed in Alex's obvious discomfort until he realized Tara hadn't spoken the entire drive. Then he'd kept his mouth shut, because that's what smart men did.

He'd lived with his sister long enough. He knew less was oftentimes, more. Women were the mystery of the ages. Refined and beautiful. Delightfully perplexing. Calm one moment, then out of control and temperamental the next. Prone to angry outbursts like a spring thunderstorm, just as prone to exquisite tenderness like a spring shower. But that was just his sister. This gal definitely wasn't PMSing. Tara had no trouble standing up to his boss tonight, yet she was obviously scared to death now. Renner wanted to know why.

So, he followed her up the three narrow staircases, all lined with beadboard, to an equally narrow landing, where he stood patiently while she fumbled her keys. He could've stepped in like a know-it-all tough guy and unlocked it for her. But more than anything, Tara needed to feel in control again. So, he stood back and watched until, at last, the door opened. Either she'd tell him what had her rattled or not. He was good at waiting.

She walked through her apartment like a SEAL on patrol. The place was small, yet she checked her kitchen and the opposite two small rooms, then double-checked the two deadbolts on her door. That alone spelled PARANOIA. Or fear. She was hiding from someone.

Renner stepped back and gave her more space and time to settle down. Obviously, a DIY project, he noted the bare light switches on the walls where protective plates should've been installed. There were no overhead light fixtures in this attic, which made him wonder what the wall switches were for. Maybe wall outlets? Table lamps were in abundance. A Himalayan salt rock cast a pinkish glow from the desk at the front window. That was the odd light he'd noticed from the driveway.

He still stood at her door, the only entry to her apartment. Another glaring safety hazard.

"Please tell me there's a fire escape ladder outside your window," he said as he took in the slanted walls, the single front window, itself an inconvenient dormer that jutted out from the roof like an eyesore, its only purpose to eat up more of her already cramped living space. "You do have another window, don't you?"

When she shook her head, the red curls cascading over her shoulders turned a lovely shade of copper under the dim lighting. "I don't need a fire escape. I'm fine."

Which told him Tara was desperate to control the only way in. He'd noticed she'd faced Crazy Eights' entrance like a hawk earlier. She didn't like surprises. That was a hard way to live, always watching over your shoulder, waiting to be ambushed or apprehended. Which explained her panic attack.

Renner drew in a deep breath and let her calm before he said what needed to be said. This place was a fire hazard. Treading carefully, he joined her in the kitchen. Make that kitchenette.

Tiny office-sized refrigerator and coffee-maker on a roll-about cart to his right. Built-in combination range and stove straight ahead. Sink and three overhead cupboards to his left. Which, keeping in line with the DIY plumbing, no doubt put the bathroom through the door next to the range. Want to bet the bathroom utilities were on the same wall as the kitchen sink? This place was a dollhouse, not an apartment.

Tugging one of two chairs from under the table, he straddled it, hugging the chairback while she fidgeted with the Keurig.

"Hope you like mellow roast," she muttered, flipping her hair over one shoulder as she leaned into her work. "That's all I've got."

"Coffee's coffee," he replied, watching the heart-shaped backside presented to him now, and wishing they were past this awkward, nice-to-meet-you stage. She'd come onto him back at Crazy Eights. He wished she'd kiss him again.

But yeah. Not going to happen. Rather than be caught looking, Renner took in the feminine touches throughout the place. Pristine cushions on the two kitchen chairs, dark navy blue with white dots. Matching placemats on the table. A single clean plastic plate, one glass, and a couple utensils on the drying rack alongside the sink.

The place smelled of lemon Pine-Sol. He'd scrubbed enough of his mom's floors growing up to ever forget the smell. No window in the kitchen, just a lightbar underneath the overhead cupboard above the sink. Yet green plants grew everywhere. By the sink. From a bright yellow pot on top the refrigerator. Over by the dormer. "You like green things."

"I do," she said when she finally turned to face him. "They're easy to take care of, and…" Her throat muscles worked overtime as she forced a swallow. "I'm sure sorry that I—"

He raised both hands. "No need to explain. Trust me. I've got demons, too. But if you ever need someone to scream like a little girl…"

The light came back on in her eyes. Her slender fingers went to her mouth. "I did say that, didn't I?"

"Yes, you did. To my boss, thank you very much."

She'd said a lot of things then that weren't in sync with her odd behavior now. Yet he wouldn't ask again. Some things were hard to talk about, and there were all kinds of wars. A friend didn't pry. Pandora's box was better left unopened once you'd finally nailed it shut. If you could forget the ugly things that were in it, all the better.

Tara didn't seem to be at that point in her life. She swallowed, then rolled her shoulders like Alex did when he was stressed, as if unseen demons were riding her. Running one hand over her head, she captured her long mane into a ponytail that fell like so many scarlet strands of silk when she released it over her shoulder. Her eyes closed. Her chest heaved as she drew in a long, slow breath.

Renner's heart pounded at the ethereal sight in this cramped little kitchen. He looked away instead of opening his big mouth with a cheesy, *'Hey, babe.'*

"Sugar or cream?" she asked, handing the first mug over.

He took it from her trembling fingers, nice and easy so she'd have nothing to apologize for if it spilled in his lap. "Thanks, but no. Black's good."

"But I've got them if you'd rather."

He didn't dare tell her what sweetener he preferred. Not tonight and maybe not ever. "No, this is perfect."

She joined him at the table, her long fingers curved around her mug, her lips pursed as she blew tendrils of steam away. "Tonight was crazy, huh?"

He nodded, trying not to stare at her mouth and her lips. Tara had one of those mouths that made him wonder if she'd sucked her thumb as a kid. His sister had, which had led to a pronounced overbite and braces. Not that Tara had buck teeth. She didn't. If anything, her teeth were white, straight, and picture perfect. Yet every word she spoke drew his attention to those lush full lips, and the way her mouth moved when she pronounced her consonants. God bless him if she ever pulled a spoiled brat routine and pouted. He'd be a goner, and he knew it.

"You've got quite the bat cave up here."

Tara glanced over his shoulder into her crowded living area. "It works. Less to clean."

"Your landlord needs to install fire escape ladders, pronto."

"I know it's not perfect." She shrugged. "But Mr. Marchant's been kind to me. He promised he'd add a fire escape before I moved in, but I…" She swallowed hard then.

Renner gazed into his mug. "But what? You make sure you're safe when you're working a con, just not at home?" He kept his tone steady, not accusing. This wasn't a confrontation.

She nodded. "You're right. I'll talk with him again. He needs to make this right."

"He sure does." Renner took a long, slow drink then. Giving her time. Letting her come to her own conclusions.

"It's just that..." Pursing her lips, Tara breathed on the steamy surface of her coffee. "I…"

And Renner's mind went there. To her mouth. Her lips. That kiss...

But she'd stopped talking. He thought she'd confide in him, that she'd at least finish her sentence, but the more he waited, the less likely it seemed. She'd changed yet again, back to her confident self. That was the ruse, wasn't it? Tara had no problem doing what she did best. She'd certainly held her own with Alex. She was at home on a ledge on high buildings because she was unreachable there. No one could get at her. She was free. Safe. And she'd been comfortable with Renner at her side.

It was ground level that frightened her. The shadows. The awful anticipation that someone might be waiting for her before she could get out of sight and safely inside. Hidden.

Renner wished he could stay. He could keep her safe, and he'd do it from the couch. He'd keep his hands to himself. He would. But he wouldn't ask again, and he wouldn't demand.

Finishing his drink, he pushed to his feet. "Hey, I hate to run, but I've got work tomorrow. I need to get moving."

She set her mug to the table, smiling and more like herself. "You're right. Me too."

"You have a cell number?" he asked, scanning for a charging cord, a landline, anything.

She shook her head. "Not yet. That's one of those things I can live without."

Tara didn't have to say it. Instinctively Renner knew. Cell phones enabled GPS locators. She was off the grid. Definitely hiding from someone in the hardest to reach places. Narrow penthouse ledges. Third story attics. Clouds and stars.

But the thought of her stuck in this deathtrap gnawed at him. "You sure you'll be okay?"

"Always. Like you said, I live in a bat cave. If anything goes wrong, I'll just climb into my wings and fly out of here."

Renner couldn't let that blithe, cavalier disregard for her life go unchallenged. Reaching for Tara's hand, he tugged her in close and cupped the back of her head in his hands. That put his thumbs on her cheeks right where he wanted them. Wanted her. Tara's skin was soft and pure against his tanned, stained, work-roughened fingers.

She didn't resist, didn't even struggle. Just looked up at him with her fingers on his shoulders, a trembling angel with questions in her sky blue eyes. That should've been her name. Sky.

But he had only one answer for those questions. Leaning in close, he pressed his lips to her forehead and whispered, "Keep yourself safe, Tara Tumulty. I'm on your side."

"Thanks for bringing me home," she breathed into his neck.

"Anytime." Renner could've lingered there forever with his mouth on her skin and his nose in her hair. But friends didn't do things like that, and she'd made it clear she needed space. Still, it was with great reluctance he pulled back and got his shit together.

"Lock up behind me?" he asked at her door.

She nodded, her head bobbing, her eyes bright.

"Will I see you again?" Somehow, that seemed unlikely.

Tara shrugged. "Who knows?"

And that was good enough. It had to be.

He paused downstairs at the other side of her entry door. And there it was, the snick of her deadbolt, locking her in and trapping her at the same time. He had to trust that nothing would happen to her between now and the next time they met. If they did.

But knowing someone might be stalking Tara made walking away from her the hardest thing he'd ever done.

Chapter Eight

"Alex?" Kelsey whispered as she peered through her dimly lit kitchen and into the darkened living room. Late again.

It was highly unusual for Alex not to stir when she came into the house through the garage. Their security system sent instant audio notifications, as well as vibrations to his and her cells. He had to have heard and felt that notification the instant she'd activated the garage door opener, then again when their kitchen door opened and closed.

But she was pretty sure that was him sitting in his easy chair. Who else could it be? Yet unlike her badassed husband, he hadn't moved.

Worried now, she dropped her purse beside the kitchen door and all but ran to him. He hadn't been sleeping well lately, what with the threat of Catalina Montego on the loose again. And he'd been drinking more. But nothing helped him sleep.

Alex was, and forever would be, his own worst enemy. This man was the consummate alpha, always assuming more risk and responsibility than any single man should. Always fighting the world and thinking he had to do it alone. What was it that Harley Mortimer had told her years ago? That Alex was bigger than life? Well, this bigger than life guy needed to take better care of himself, darn it. Whiskey wasn't helping him any more than stress.

Kneeling at his side now, Kelsey's heart broke at the tender scene. Alex wasn't alone and he hadn't been drinking, either. She would've smelled it on his breath. He was sound asleep with their little hobbit of a daughter tucked into the crook of his arm. Lexie nestled into her father, her thumb in her mouth and just as sound asleep. Mark and Libby must have brought her home early. That happened sometimes when Lexie watched a sad movie or missed her dad and mom. Thank goodness, Alex had been here.

"Hey," Kelsey murmured as she lifted her sleeping daughter out of his arm. "I'm home now. Let's get you to bed."

"Yeah, home," Alex muttered, his voice thick with sleep as he shrugged one shoulder, rubbing his cheek into it as if his neck were stiff.

"Another migraine?" she asked, swaying under the precious weight of her sweetest load ever. Lexie hadn't awakened, just snuggled into her mom. But the little girl was getting taller and heavier. Kelsey needed to get her into her own comfy bed.

"I'm good," Alex replied.

Kelsey caught the weary undertone to his reply. "If you were good, Lexie would be in bed and you'd be reading. Wait here," she whispered. "I'll be back as soon as I lay her down."

"Waiting," he grumbled.

She made it quick. Lexie was easy when it came to bedtime. "Sweet dreams, little one," Kelsey breathed over her still sleeping daughter. "Pancakes and bacon in the morning. 'Nite."

She had no more than straightened when Alex's arms wrapped around her shoulders. His chin landed in the crook of her neck as he murmured, "I miss us."

Kelsey smiled and closed her eyes, never more content than inside the circle of this man's embrace. "It has been a hectic couple of days," she admitted as she crossed her arms over his and held on tight to her man. "How goes the hunt for Montego? Have you talked with Jed yet?"

"I don't want to talk about Jed or her or work," Alex growled, his lips hot and moist at her ear. "Just us. Only us."

She shivered. This man knew what he was doing to her, the brat. "Shouldn't we take this conversation to our bedroom?"

"Thought you'd never ask," he said as he dipped low, reached under her knees and lifted her off her feet.

She would've giggled if not for Lexie. "You must be feeling better tonight."

That earned her a grunt as he angled her down the hall, through their door, then quietly nudged it shut with one foot. "Where have you been?"

"At work," she answered easily.

"All day?" he asked as he dropped her onto their bed.

Kelsey nodded, watching Alex strip out of his shirt, then his trousers. Of course, he spoiled the spontaneity of their impromptu rendezvous when he took the time to toss his clothes into the hamper, then took off his shoes and socks before he turned back around in his boxers. But that was her man. OCD to the core. A stickler for everything being in its proper place. And drop dead gorgeous. Undressed, Alex was all solid angles. Nothing but power and sex.

"Am I in my right place?" she had to ask, though why her voice squeaked, she didn't know.

His brows wrinkled. "What's that supposed to mean?"

"Well, you are all about law and order, stuff like that. I mean look at this room. Do you see anything not where it belongs?" Up on her elbows now, she gestured à la Vanna White to their luxurious but tidy room.

He scanned their quarters, that same weariness darkening his eyes. What was that man thinking? "No," he bit out. "Everything is not in its proper place. I can't live like this anymore. What do you intend to do about it?"

Whoa. The angst in that question caught Kelsey's heart. She had to stop and really look at him then. Something sad and terrible was going on with Alex. She could tell. He wasn't himself tonight, and it had nothing to do with the order of their house or this room. Or housework.

Scrambling out of bed, she walked into him and put both palms on his heaving chest. "You're angry."

Of course, he denied it with a curt shake of his head.

"Talk to me, Alex," she whispered as she unbuttoned her blouse. Slowly. One tiny button at a time. "You've had another hard day. I can tell. You're hurting."

"I'm fine," he growled even as he tracked what her fingertips were doing.

Off went her blouse. Kelsey maintained eye contact although he didn't. The snap on her pants drew his gaze lower, then lower as she unzipped. She'd learned early that most of their disconnects could be resolved in this room, on this bed. Yet Alex had to want this, too. As much as it was a game, it wasn't. All she could do was offer and invite. Tease and torment the worry out of him.

"We've had a lot of new kids show up this week," she murmured, keeping him aware of almost all her business problems. Her kids. Her constant worry over cash flow. Stuff like that. "Work has been kind of crazy, but it'll be over before Christmas. I promise."

With Alex's assist, she'd opened a home for runaway kids in the District, just off East Constitution, close to the Anacostia Bridge. She hadn't realized it at the time, but most of her kids came from impoverished, mostly African American, Anacostia. But like Raymond, the gentle giant she'd met and lost a couple years back, every child, teenager, and sometimes even adults, needed a safe place to run to when the streets got too hard. Only lately, she'd been welcoming more homeless men into *Raymond's Kids*, her home away from home for runaways. It was the least she could do.

"I hope so," Alex groaned, his sharp eyes intent on the way her fingers dipped into her waistband, then over her hips as she shimmied out of her slacks. "I hate coming home to an empty house."

She had to smile. Alex hated a lot of things, but her not being home when he arrived most of all. The silence made him feel hollow, he'd once said. It reminded him that *they* were gone, they being Sara and Abby, his first family. After losing them, he'd hated the entire world for a long time, but mostly, he'd hated himself for not being there when they'd died.

But Kelsey knew he adored her, though even that had taken him some time to admit. Not that he'd denied it, more like he'd fought it. Alex was so angry back then, he couldn't believe she loved him. Yet she'd eventually gotten brave and stood up to him. Today she knew the way to his heart, and it was not always through his stomach.

Kicking out of her pants, she straightened her spine and stood there nearly naked in front of him. Ready to please him if pleasing was what he wanted. It was definitely what he needed, although he might not know it yet.

His lethal gaze tracked down her centerline to her black lace panties. "Lose the underwear," he ordered grumpily.

"Lose yours first," she shot back.

He complied in a heartbeat, standing there tall and proud, at full mast, and the hottest badass on the planet. Oh, my. She'd poked the beast. Well, okay then. Let the games begin. Leaning forward, she stiffened her knees, slid the panties down her legs, and—

His resolve snapped.

Panties went flying, and Kelsey found herself face down on the bed in very capable hands. Alex shoved her hair over her head, his mouth sucking raspberries up the back of her neck to her ear. She squealed and kicked, loving the warmth and breadth of him spread out over her like a saber tooth tiger rug.

"I miss you, damn it," he breathed over those damp suction marks, chilling her with his hot breath.

"Then you'd better make it up to me," she teased, delighted when he shifted his weight to one side, while his hands roamed smoothly down her back to her backside. Cupping her. Squeezing her. Kneading the cheeks of her ass while he kissed a trail down her neck to her shoulder, then to her shoulder blade. His other hand had slipped beneath her bra and cupped her breast, pinching her nipple, playing like only Alex could.

Man, she loved this guy more than breathing or eating. More than everything except Lexie. That little girl was their one purest desire come true.

By then, Alex had lit a fire in her belly. He owned her and he knew it. He also knew how to drag out the pleasure, never letting her fall over the edge. Never letting her fly.

"I love you, woman," he breathed as he slid an arm under her and lifted her knees onto the edge of the bed. "So much. Too much sometimes."

Still face down, she waited. He started a rhythm then, slow and steady at first, then harder. Faster. His hands on her hips. Her head turned to one side. Their bodies joined in a song as old as time.

But darn him! Just as she felt the first wave of release, he pulled out and rolled her onto her back, pressing the angles and hardness of his body into hers again. His hands cupped her head. His fingers tangled in her hair. Alex groaned when he pressed his forehead to hers as he slid back into the warmth where he belonged. Where she desperately needed him.

"I can't live without you," he declared hoarsely. "Not now. Not ever."

There was so much pain in those few words. So much despair. Kelsey desperately wanted to ask him what had happened to make him unhappy. Yet she also knew he'd tell her if he could and when he was ready. Because many of his operations were top-secret classified, she never pressed or nagged. She trusted instead.

Since she had no idea what he was dealing with, Kelsey gave Alex all she had to give. "I know, sweetheart, and I love you." Spreading her legs, she settled his hips into her pelvic cradle, aptly named for the unique comfort this warrior needed. She was his home and there was nothing she loved more than belonging, in every sense of the word, to her husband. Like this. Like now.

"There's no such thing as loving too much, Alex," she whispered. "Not with us. I'm here for you. Lexie and I love you to the stars and back."

He nodded into her hair at that, and Kelsey understood. Big tough guys like Alex hid their emotions. There'd been a day when she'd been timid and easily frightened, even of him. Not anymore. With all her heart Kelsey knew she would live for Alex, but she would also die for him. She just needed a little more time. Because there were no two ways about it.

Catalina Montego absolutely… Would. Go. Down.

Chapter Nine

With Alex unraveling as fast as he was, there was no longer any choice. Renner didn't go home. Instead, he went back to McCormack's penthouse, keyed in the security code that got him into the building earlier, and then used the same code in the elevator. But he had to be extra cautious this time around. Montego was there, McCormack could be there by now as well.

The code still worked. *Thank you, Jesus.* As silently as a wraith, the elevator opened on the second level from the top like he'd meant it to. The place appeared to be empty. Though he suspected McCormack and Montego were in bed. Yet he cleared every other room as he had before. He couldn't afford to make another mistake. Alex deserved better. Then...

Quickly. Stealthily. Renner planted a host of tiny TEAM cameras known as Tattle Tales throughout Jed's apartment. Sasha Kennedy, The TEAM's previous office administrator, had been a whiz-bang technological genius. She'd gone off on some kind of hiatus after her daughter died, but before that, she invented the miniscule audio/video devices.

From what Renner had gleaned from the other agents, she'd also been a nosy busybody who'd annoyed Alex to no end. Hence her nickname: *Mother.* She'd taken that as a sweet compliment, but Renner was pretty sure Alex hadn't meant it that way. The man might have his moments, but Alex Stewart was not that sweet. Mother had to have made him plenty angry to have earned that handle.

Renner hadn't told Alex what he'd planned to do tonight. Might not ever tell him. There were times in a covert agent's life that he went rogue in order to accomplish his mission. This was one of those times. Yet Renner paused at McCormack's closed bedroom door, knowing full well Montego could kill Jed in his bed as surely as she could end him anywhere else. But she would've already done that if she'd wanted to. She'd had plenty of opportunity.

No, Renner believed that Montego was up to something. Why else had she attached herself to McCormack as publicly as she had? Why did she pander to the press for attention? Despite what the media or Tara thought, it wasn't for money or expensive jewelry. Renner felt certain of that. Montego had plenty of financial resources at her greedy fingertips. No, it had to be something else she wanted. She wanted the fame. The notoriety...

Which brought him full circle back to Alex.

Montego was a snake. Smart, evil, and twisted. She had to be behind Mrs. McCormack's sudden death, Renner just had to prove it. But Montego also had to know Jed McCormack was one of Alex's dearest friends, that he'd bankrolled Alex to get The TEAM off the ground way back when. If she could kill McCormack's sweet wife without getting caught, what would she do to McCormack to strike back at Alex? A quiet death in bed didn't seem likely. Montego wanted revenge, and the way she grandstanded for the press told Renner enough. This time would be different. She didn't want to kill Jed in his sleep. No, she wanted 'lights, camera, action!'

This death would be highly visible and highly publicized. It might even be broadcast live. But for certain, it would be an impossible thing to stop. The day she set her final scene in motion, no one would be able to rescue Jed McCormack from his own stupidity. Not even Alex.

The longer Renner stood listening to nothing but silence from behind that closed door, the more it made sense. Alex would take McCormack's death hard. He'd be inconsolable, and that was when Montego would strike. She'd get through Alex's defenses, might even get at Kelsey or Lexie. She was out to destroy him, and hurting his wife and daughter would surely do it.

Not on Renner's watch. He palmed his phone and dialed Seth McCray.

Seth answered on the second ring. "Hey, Renner, what's up?"

"Sorry to disturb you at home," Renner whispered, "but I need you to call Jed McCormack at home. Can you do that?"

"Sure, when?"

"Now. Make it good. Make something up. I just need him out of his penthouse. He's here with Montego and I've got a bad feeling."

"You and me both."

"You need his number?"

"Nope. Got it. If you're there, you might want to hide. You'll be seeing him soon," Seth whispered as well.

"Copy that," Renner replied before he disconnected.

Stepping behind wall-to-wall curtains in the living room, similar to the ones he'd met Tara behind, Renner waited. In seconds, McCormack burst out of his bedroom, still in pajamas, his silver hair mussed, his cell at his ear, and a naked Montego close behind.

"Now you listen here," he bellowed into his cell. "If you damage that headstone, if you so much as… Damn it. He hung up on me!"

Oh, crap. Seth had done it now, threatening what had to be McCormack's wife's grave.

"But, darling," Montego pitched in her gravelly smoker's voice. "It's just a rock. How could anyone possibly hurt marble or granite or whatever it is?"

"They could break it. Chip it. For the love of God! They could defecate on it! On her! It's not just a rock. It's… It's…" McCormack turned on Montego like a wild animal, his eyes wide and his chest heaving. He raked a hand over his head, and for the first time Renner could remember, McCormack looked old and tired. Confused. "You don't understand. I know sh-she's gone, b-but…"

Montego sidled up to him, rubbing her bare breasts up his chest while she lifted to her toes and kissed his chin. The elderly gentleman blinked down at her like his brain had short-circuited behind his eyeballs. And maybe it had. Montego's nude charms seemed to be working. The longer she kissed his chin, then his cheek, and the faster she stroked his manhood, the less agitated he grew until…

"You're absolutely right," McCormack breathed at the same time he sucked his gut in. "She's dead, but we're still here, aren't we? We're still alive." His head canted as if he'd just realized that.

Renner stopped breathing. *Say what? Just like that? She's dead, let's party?*

"And I have something you know you want," Montego teased in a sing-song tone that so did not gel with her rasping smoker's voice. Old man McCormack might deem that sexy, but Renner wanted to throw up in his mouth.

Montego grabbed hold of McCormack's pajama collar, turned back to the bedroom and led him away. Just like that, he gave up and gave in. He forgot the faithful woman who'd cared for and loved him for years. Yet Renner knew that Lois had stood by her husband through every battle, every heartache, and every war. They'd faced their only son's traumatic injury and then his untimely death together. What was wrong with McCormack?

Renner stayed where he was, not believing what he'd just seen or heard. For years, old man McCormack had commanded nothing but respect and admiration for his unflagging support of the military. The man was a financial wizard, a billionaire. He was no dummy. You didn't become that kind of powerful if you were. Yet he apparently still had a working dick, and…

Renner forced a swallow down his dry throat. That was it. Montego had McCormack by the balls. An easy piece of tail worked every time.

Pressing redial, he got his excited buddy back on the line.

"Did it work?" Seth all but yelled. "I knew it had to be good, so maybe I went a little overboard when I told him a bunch of skin-heads placed a burning cross over his wife's grave, but did it work? I'll bet he ran out of there like his ass was on fire, huh?"

"He's still here," Renner whispered. "He's not leaving."

"What?"

"You heard me. He went back to bed with…" Renner could barely say it, "…her."

"Well, damn. What do we do next?"

Yeah. Damn. "Not sure. I planted a couple dozen Tattle Tales throughout the penthouse."

"You activate them yet?"

Renner stepped out from behind the drapes, stunned. "That's next on my list."

Seth huffed through the connection. "You know, deploying those listening devices without Jed's knowledge is illegal."

"What else can I do? Leaving him alone with that bitch is just as wrong."

"I hear you, man, but if Montego finds even one of them—"

"Tell Alex to disavow me if this leaks to the press," Renner said quietly. He'd take the fall for his boss. Any day. Any time. Seth would too if he were there.

"Maybe you should go dark," Seth murmured. Going dark meant disappearing for a while, dropping out of sight, not contacting anyone on The TEAM. Basically, ceasing to exist on any public records or systems. He'd have to leave his apartment and go completely off-grid. It was a drastic option. Almost as bad as being disavowed.

"Not yet. She thinks she's got McCormack where she wants him, but I'm not convinced. I mean, you should've seen the look on his face when he first stormed out of his bedroom." That was what didn't make sense. Jed had been pissed and ready to act. Until she'd touched him. "I'll be in touch."

"Not going dark then?"

"Not until I have to." Renner disconnected the call. He needed to get out of there. Fast.

Chapter Ten

Instead of calling his boss, Renner hit the interstate and headed west toward the Shenandoah Mountains to talk to Alex in person. He and Kelsey lived in a gated community just short of the Shenandoah National Park. It was a good forty-mile drive, give or take, and Renner needed the music of the road to help him think. There was a day not too long ago, he would've saddled up his Harley for this kind of lonely midnight drive. But not with winter weather coming on strong. Thick gray clouds still scudded low and cold over the small towns and rural areas, heavy with snow and slush that had yet to drop. Definitely not a night for cruising.

The steady hum of tires on concrete soothed a man's brain waves like nothing else. It gave him time to think. There had to be a way to get McCormack away from Montego.

The kitchen light was on at Alex's house, which was more like a stone fortress. But that light meant someone was up. Renner called his boss to request entry. Kelsey answered instead.

"Sorry, Kelsey, if I disturbed you. I need to chat with Alex."

"No problem. I'll buzz you in."

The heavy-duty security gate slid open and Renner steered his boss's armored Cadillac onto what had to be the most secure estate in the world. Security cameras were everywhere, and didn't that speak to Alex's deteriorating sense of reality? He'd become uncommonly paranoid since Montego's return.

Renner didn't dwell on that TEAM problem for long. Kelsey already waited at the now open front door, waving him to hurry up and come on in.

"Aren't you worried some witch will fly by on her broom and cast a spell on you?" Renner meant that as a gentle jab at Alex's paranoia as she waved him inside.

She shook her head. Dressed in black running pants and a matching tank, she could've passed for Tara's twin, well, except for her chocolate brown hair, now wrapped into a messy bun. Renner had noticed her hair and her deep brown eyes when he'd been introduced to Kelsey, which proved once again that Alex was a smart guy. He'd totally scored with this beauty. *But what on earth did she see in him? That* was the real question.

"Personally, I don't think Montego has ever set foot on our property," Kelsey replied wearily. "We have dogs, remember? Whisper and Smoke would kill her before she knew what hit her."

"True." Alex did own some amazing guard dogs. "Where is he anyway?" Renner thought he'd at least be in sight, grumpy as hell, but visible.

A funny, worried, guilty smile fluttered over Kelsey's face. "He's sleeping," she whispered. "I'm sorry, but I couldn't bear to wake him, and I know you came all this way to talk with him, but he's exhausted, and I made him take Motrin and melatonin."

"You made Alex do something?"

She nodded. "Sure. He listens. Sometimes."

Renner held up a palm to stop more unnecessary explanations. That Kelsey had gotten Alex to do anything was magic enough. "No problem. I can come back tomorrow or you can pass my sitrep along. It's not top-secret, just the latest word on Montego and McCormack."

"Oh, I hate that woman. Let's retreat to the kitchen. I'll fix coffee."

Renner had to smile at that very military invitation to retreat. Everyone knew Marines didn't do that. They weren't smart enough. "Thanks, but no more coffee, ma'am. I'll never get any shuteye if I drink one more drop."

He slouched into the nearest chair, and like everywhere he went, Renner measured distance to exits, the type of glass in all windows within range, whether bullet-proof or wired to a security system, important details like that. A man didn't live months in twenty-four-seven combat zones without learning how easily a grenade could take out the fancy tilework on Kelsey's kitchen floor. Or that, no matter how hard Alex tried to prevent and control it, shit still happened. Even in the most secure places on earth, men and women still died.

It helped that Kelsey was smart enough to carry—her much smaller pistol was tucked in a holster at the small of her back. Alex had taught his wife well. Renner liked that.

Hmmm, he wondered. *Would Tara mind carrying?* A date at the range might be in order.

In minutes Kelsey presented him with a plate of steaming hot French toast slathered with butter, a pitcher of warm maple syrup, and… a big mug of hot chocolate, complete with star-shaped marshmallows.

"Thank you, ma'am," he said through a smile. This breakfast looked like something she'd make for Lexie.

"Oh, stop with the ma'am business, will you?" she asked as she took the chair opposite him, a big mug of cocoa in her hand as well. "How about I don't call you Agent Graves and you don't call me ma'am, Renner?"

He almost replied, 'Yes, ma'am,' but he caught himself in time. "Understood. I'll be Renner, you be Kelsey. Got it."

The nod she sent him was Alex all over again. Curt. To the point. And she was no doubt a lethal shot with that pistol. Made Renner feel right at home.

"So, what's going on? Why is Montego so hard to kill? Why can't you guys find her and end her?"

Also like Alex, Kelsey didn't believe in the PC rhetoric currently smothering American's freedom of speech. *Kill,* not reform. *End her,* not sign her up for a year's worth of Hollywood-style counseling because her parents were mean to her once upon a time. Wah. Wah. Wah.

Was Renner cynical? Maybe. He'd just *been there*. He'd seen firsthand what lay in store for America if Lady Liberty didn't get her act together. And it was not a pretty sight.

"She's changed," he told Kelsey honestly, pulling up that first photo taken at Arlington. "Check this out." He handed his cell to her while he finished eating. Home-cooked was always best.

Kelsey nodded as she cupped Renner's cell. He'd positioned two photos of Montego side by side, her old look and her new look. "I don't know what you're talking about. Different hair color, yes, and she's taller in this one, but a good pair of heels'll do that. It's her eyes, Renner. Can't you guys see, it's in her eyes? She hasn't changed at all. She's still a killer."

He huffed at the astute observation coming from a petite lady who ran a halfway house for teenage runaways. "Try telling Channel 13. They're the ones pushing her agenda, making her look good, lying to the public by making her seem innocent—"

"When we know she's not." Kelsey's gaze drifted to the floor. "Beau died," she said quietly. "That day. Right here in my kitchen. Did you know that? His heart stopped. He'd lost so much blood that he almost died from what that bitch did to him. She cut his finger off! What kind of a human being does that? I've seen men die before, but that..." She trembled. "McKenna had to shock him before he started breathing again. She brought him back to life, right here in my kitchen."

Renner understood Alex's paranoia, his compulsive need to protect his home. It all came down to his need to keep this beautiful, courageous, determined woman safe.

"We're getting closer," he assured her. "Trust me. I've been inside McCormack's penthouse. I was that close..." He held up two pinched fingers. "...to cuffing her—"

"So, what went wrong? Why didn't you punch her in the face and break that snooty nose job?" Kelsey sat back with a huff. "Why isn't she behind bars right now, or better yet, dead?"

Yup. Just like Alex. Renner winced as he lifted the mug to his lips, needing a taste of fortitude before he admitted for the second time today that, "I screwed up. I thought—"

"You thought what?"

Dayum, he wanted to grin. This inquisition was so much like the last. Did Alex have any idea how much he'd rubbed off on his wife? But Renner knew better than to smile when a woman had her dander up. They were, after all, the stronger sex. Even a dumb jarhead knew to stand clear of that.

"Yeah," he said evenly. "I thought I had her cornered, even had a flex cuff on her, but…" This humiliation just wasn't going away, was it?

"But what?" At least Kelsey didn't bellow and snort.

"But…" *Here goes.* "I thought I'd cuffed Montego to my wrist. I only did that to make sure she didn't get away this time. I honestly thought once I dragged her out of there, I could, you know, make her disappear for a change instead of losing more of our military guys."

"That makes sense."

Renner appreciated Kelsey's encouragement. "Well, it would've if it had actually been Montego I cuffed, but no. I ended up stuck with a burglar who was only there to pilfer McCormack's wife's jewelry, the ones Montego's been flaunting everywhere she and he go."

"A burglar? Up there? In Jed's penthouse?"

Renner nodded, his eyes on the last gooey marshmallows stuck to the bottom of his mug. "Yup. Stupid move, I know. But I'd already cleared the penthouse. I knew no one else was there. When Montego turned the shower on, I thought I had her. I mean, how hard could it be to overpower a naked woman and haul her ass to FBI jail?"

"Or throw her out the window," Kelsey muttered, her voice so low Renner cocked his head to be certain he'd heard right.

He smiled at her then. "You sure sound just like your husband."

Her lips thinned. "Alex is right. She needs to die. So, you caught a burglar instead. Then what?"

Renner cleared his throat, tired of talking about his latest, but no doubt, his stupidest mistake. "Well..." *Cough. Cough.* "Seems this burglar came prepared to fly off that penthouse like a bat. After we discussed our options… which were zip… nada…" Damn, it was harder telling Kelsey how stupid he'd been. "We decided we'd fly together."

"Not like you had a choice. Did Montego hear you? See you? Did she know you'd been inside Jed's home all that time?" Just like Alex, Kelsey didn't seem surprised by his decision to jump off a high rise.

"No. We were on the window ledge when she exited the bathroom. I'm sure of that."

It was then Kelsey's head tipped nearly onto her shoulder. "Oh, my heavens. You fell off the penthouse? Just like that? You stepped into thin air and—"

"Something like that." He was not going to tell her that Tara had pushed him or that he might've called out— something—on his way down. "My new best friend was wearing one of those wingsuits, the kind with flaps between the legs and under the arms to catch the wind. Anyway, by the time we landed, the police were there and—"

"Why were the police there?"

Renner froze. Until that second, he'd assumed someone inside the penthouse had notified the police because he might have bellowed a little too loudly on the way down. It was possible. But now... "You know, I'm not sure. Good question."

Interestingly, Alex hadn't caught that detail. An icy shiver skated down Renner's spine. Was it even remotely possible that Catalina had someone else involved, either watching Alex and his agents or watching McCormack? The woman did own her own private army, her second batch of kidnapped and tortured male slaves. What would they do to stay alive and in her good graces? Follow and report? Track and assassinate? If one of Montego's bitches had seen Renner and Tara dive off McCormack's window ledge, he could've called the police, and that meant…

Christ. Someone might have seen him with Tara. They could've been followed. And Tara was alone. The need to run to her swamped Renner. He should have stayed!

"Well, someone called them," Kelsey pointed out, her mug to her lips again, her brown eyes clear and intelligent and expecting an answer.

Renner shrugged, feigning calmness he no longer felt. His cocoa was gone. He yawned, working his way out of Kelsey's cozy kitchen. "You're right. Someone apparently called, but the police arriving might not be related to me or that woman I—"

"What woman?"

"The cat burglar. The one I jumped off McCormack's penthouse with."

A tiny light clicked on in Kelsey's bright eyes. "You didn't tell me Jed's burglar was a woman."

And he wasn't about to name names, either. "Yeah, some crazy nut job. You should've seen her, all decked out in that wingsuit. She had the damnedest tattoo. A cat, can you believe that?"

Another sip of cocoa. Another nod. Yet Kelsey didn't seem surprised at all. "Well, I guess it takes all kinds," she breathed.

"Yes, yes it does," Renner muttered as he pushed away from the table. "Hey, I really need to go. Would you tell Alex we've got eyes inside McCormack's penthouse? He'll know what I mean. If he's mad about it, he's got my number. Oh, and thanks for putting up with me tonight. As usual, it's been a pleasure." *But now I have got to get out of here.*

"You're a good man, Renner," she said as she saw him to the door. "I hope you know you're welcome here anytime. One of us is awake most nights, but tonight you got me."

He offered one last smile. "Hey, better you than that crusty old fart you married."

"You drive safe, okay? There are lots of crazy people out there."

You have no idea. "Will do. Goodnight, Kelsey," Renner replied as he turned back to the armored Cadillac. Forty miles. He had forty damned miles between him and Tara, and she had no phone. He should've given his to her. He could've gotten another at any number of stops on the road. If one of Montego's minions was on the prowl, it might already be too late. Hindsight sucked!

Renner broke all speed limits. Traffic was light this late at night. By the time he cleared Tara's street, he was coming undone. She needed protection, and by hell, like it or not, she was going to get it. He parked at the curb three houses down from her building, locked up, and did what he should've done before.

The neighborhood was quiet, a good sign. But appearances could be deceiving. Patting the weight of his pistol under his left arm for good luck, he began what he knew would be the first of many perimeter checks. He hadn't been gone that long. The sun would be up soon. Her rock still glowed in her front window. Somehow, he knew she was safe. That all was well in that POS excuse for an apartment.

He had no idea what time she went to work, so he walked and he waited, kept a sharp eye as the first two cars rolled out of her parking lot and drove off at the start of another work day. On edge, he took up his final position alongside the garbage receptacle behind her building. He knew how to keep out of sight. No one would know he was there.

Which scared the shit out of him when he found evidence that someone else had waited in the same spot, someone who smoked kreteks, a tobacco and clove cigarette, this brand particular to Indonesia. At least a dozen butts, some crushed, some nearly whole, lay scattered on the ground. Two crushed beer cans. What the hell was going on?

Chapter Eleven

The next morning Tara donned her white winter boots with fake fur cuffs over her black tights, then topped it off with a big black flannel shirt that would keep her warm at work. Snow was in the forecast, and she meant to be ready when it blew in. But snow was different along the East Coast. In her home state of Colorado, snow was light and dry. Fluffy. But here, it was either ice or slush, neither pleasant nor fun. Oh, well. There wasn't anything to be done about that.

She tied her hair back, then wound it into a sloppy bun that easily fit under her chunky knit, Peruvian skull cap, the black polka dotted one with ear flaps and dangly pink pompoms she never tied. Checking her reflection in the mirror by her door, she stuck her chin out and told herself, "You've got this, Tara. And yes, Renner is adorable, and I think he likes you."

That peppy self-talk lifted her spirits and her shoulders, which made her look younger, at least in the mirror. Sliding into her black windbreaker, she was ready to go. She had two things to take care of before going to work today. One, purchase a cell phone, the pay-as-you-go kind, in case she needed to call Renner. After all, she had his card and number. She might as well use it.

Two, speak with Mr. Marchant as soon as she had that cell phone. Renner was right. It was time her sweet elderly landlord added a decent fire escape to her 'loft.'

Feeling unusually pleased with herself, Tara unlocked her bat cave, climbed down the narrow dungeon-like stairs to her private exit, then, locking her door behind her, she sauntered over to her assigned parking stall and—

Darn. Her Honda Civic wasn't here. She'd parked it at Jed McCormack's underground parking lot. Across the Potomac. In Roslyn, Virginia. Talk about a brain fart. No matter. She had a metro/bus farecard. She was good to go. The walk to the nearest Metro station and the cold, fresh air would do her good.

Yeah, no.

Tara scurried back into the safety of her apartment building before anyone could've possibly seen her. She hoped. Her heart pounded by then. Frightened out of her wits at her foolish mistake, she called a cab from the pay phone in the front entry. Sure, she had a Metro farecard. Everyone in the District did, but she had yet to use it. Fear at seeing *him* overrode her common sense every time she got brave. Anxiety did that. But one of these days...

Yeah, no. Not today. Let's think positive. Maybe tomorrow. But maybe never...

The cabbie must've been parked around the corner, he arrived that quickly. Before Tara knew it, she was safe at work, her two most important errands now assigned to second place in her day. Maybe third. She still had to get her car.

"Hey, Tara," Kelsey Stewart called from the cafeteria where she was seated with a gaggle of the cutest little kids. "Dan the Man brought donuts. There's plenty. Come join us."

How kind was that? Dan the Man was a local mom and pop grocery store operated by a sweet older married couple who'd adopted sixteen children and had another little guy from Sri Lanka on the way. Their store was located only a block south of Raymond's Kids. Because of their big hearts, they'd adopted Kelsey and her runaways as well. Dan the Man was the best kind of neighbor. They were always dropping off boxes of foodstuffs, delicious desserts straight out of their on-site bakery, even dry goods and milk.

Tara hung her coat on the rack inside the cafeteria doors, then straddled the bench across from Kelsey.

Kelsey pushed a paper plate laden with a chocolate covered cinnamon roll at Tara. "Here. Your favorite. I saved it for you."

Raymond's Kids was Kelsey's home away from home. Originally designated as one of the District's free-clinics, Kelsey had added a privately-operated shelter where teenagers and runaways could come and stay, where they could be treated without fear of reprisal from their parents or being hauled off by police.

With an on-site staff of caregivers, counselors, kitchen and maintenance employees, her children at risk were able to hide out for a while, if that was all they needed. Confidence was the number one priority at Raymond's Kids, which went a long way to establish it as the safest place in the District for kids at risk.

But those kids were also able to reach out to any number of state, community, medical, or religious resources if they chose. Kelsey helped them contact their parents, again, if they wanted to. Some were just passing through, taking advantage of a free meal and a safe place to sleep. But others came with drug, parental, sibling, and gang problems. Kelsey worked within the law, but she never turned anyone away, not even the grumpy men who'd recently taken up residence in what used to be the big, dark, scary basement storage area.

Hungrily, Tara lifted the decadent thing to her mouth and tore off a good-sized mouthful, dodging further explanation as to why she was late. "Mmm, so good! Thanks," she mumbled. "Sorry I'm late. Any coffee left?"

"Of course." Kelsey shook her head in amazement while she filled a paper cup and handed it to Tara. "I don't know how you do it."

"Do what?" Tara mumbled through the mega-pastry that could have easily fed three people.

"Eat like you do. My gosh, you never gain a pound."

"I like food." Tara caught the gooey chocolate frosting trickling down her chin with a fingertip. It never failed. Didn't matter what she ate, it ended up on her boobs, and they weren't even that large. Just nice round C-cup babies.

She needed a napkin. Make that a bib! She licked her lips, hoping she didn't look like one of the runaways. "And I have a higher metabolism than you do." Women on the run, hiding out, and watching over their shoulders all the time tended to be skinny. But Tara wasn't about to remind Kelsey. She already knew.

That stinker Jessica pointed at Tara's shoulder, her big brown eyes bright with mischief. "You eat like a big pig. You got frosting in your hair."

Tara took another big bite and shook her head in case Jessica was right and not just spoofing her. "No, I don't."

"Yes, you do!" Jessica shrieked, grinning and still pointing.

"I do not." Darn. Yes, she did. Tara swiped the gooey flake out of her hair and flicked it at Jessica. "You callin' me out, little Twig?"

"Yes, I'm calling you out, goldfish brain. You a slob, you know that?" Jessica led with a cocky chin nod, one hand on her hip, and her customary spit-in-your-eye swagger. She hated being told she was skinny and underweight. Which she was.

And the verbal battle was on. "Least I don't blow away like a twig when I go outside on windy days."

"Ha, you blow away inside! When Jeremy farts!" Jeremy was the somewhat gaseous janitor known for letting outrageously loud—noises—at the worst possible times.

"Yeah but, you like the way they smell. I seen you and you get all dreamy-eyed when you sit next to him."

The whites showed all around Jessica's little brown pupils. "Uh uh! I do not! That's mean."

"Ha! Gotcha!" Tara smacked the table. The rule was the first whiner loses. "I win. You have to wash dishes. Neener-neener-neener."

The little girl's indignation turned to giggles. "You did that on purpose, Miss Tara. You fooled me."

"Course I did, sweetie pie. I don't like washing dishes. Makes my hands all pruny."

"Ain't no such word as pruny." Jessica folded her arms over her chest, back to stern and bossy.

Tara made bug eyes at her. "And there ain't no such word as ain't."

"Is too. It's in the dictionary, and I seen it."

Tara stuck her chin across the table. "Wanna bet?"

Jessica's shoulders lifted. Her brows dipped over her nose. Her lips pursed into a tight cinch. Then… "Nope, but you is wrong and I is right and I don't hafta prove nothin' to nobody and you oughta learn to read!"

"Are you two done teasing each other yet?" reasonable, practical Kelsey asked gently, ever ready to diffuse a tense situation. Which this wasn't. Not really.

While sweetie-pie Jessica climbed off the bench and stalked away muttering, "Dishes. I gotta do dishes again," Tara stuffed the last of the donut in her mouth and mumbled, "Yup. What's up?"

"You love that little girl," Kelsey whispered, her gaze on that adorable stubborn child heading to the kitchen.

"You know I do. I'd foster her if I could." Which was true. Before her life turned to shit, Tara had thought of retiring from skiing, giving up her Olympic dream, having a white picket fence, and all those other magical things that new wives with rose-colored glasses wanted. Didn't turn out that way.

"Why do you tease her so hard then?" Kelsey had a soft heart like no one else on earth. "You two sound so mean when you get together."

"Because she reminds me of someone I knew once," Tara replied as she watched Jessica march into the cafeteria-style kitchen with her head up, pull a chair over to the industrial-size double sink, climb up onto that chair with attitude, and crank the gooseneck faucet on like it had better do what she wanted—or else. "Jess isn't going to let anyone hug her, you know that. She's tiny, but she really is fierce, Kels. She's suffered, but she isn't ready to admit it yet. I'm just speaking her language. Hoping someday she'll let one of us in."

"Reverse psychology," Kelsey murmured.

Tara shook her head. "Nope, more like tough love." To prove it, she yelled at Jessica, "Don't forget to use the green soap! It stinks like you know what!"

Jessica shot an evil glare over her shoulder and yelled back, "Yeah, it stinks like your breath, and that ain't never no good!"

Tara laughed. Teasing the kids brought out the worst in some, but it also brought out the best in others. Jessica was one of the best. Most of Raymond's Kids had already seen the hard side of life. Some showed up in rags, some came with needle marks in various parts of their tender anatomies. Some with bruises, some so hungry they needed rice cereal and tea because anything more substantial made them sick. Some assaulted.

Yet others came in silence, unsure of who to trust, not knowing what would happen next. But Jessica was a fighter. She'd shown up parentally abused and mad as hell at the world, not afraid to take anyone on. Which was why Tara loved her so hard. That little gal with her nose stuck in the air and suds up to her elbows had actually taught Tara a thing or two.

"I don't know what I'd do without you," Kelsey said. "I'm so glad you decided to take a chance on us." Us meaning Raymond's Kids.

"Yeah, well…" Tara ran her tongue over her bottom lip, not sure how she could ever thank Kelsey enough for allowing her, an adult and a ratty, bedraggled stranger at that, to sleep on the floor in a roomful of lost kids her first night. She'd been sick, down and out. Had probably smelled bad, too. "I think it's the other way around, Mrs. Stewart. Seems to me it was you who took a chance on me."

"You were a safe bet, and stop calling me that. We go by first names here, and you know it. Can I ask you something?"

"Sure. Anything."

"Where were you last night?"

Tara cocked her head at that particular question. "Why do you need to know?"

"Because…" Most of the kids were done with donuts by then. None were within earshot. Yet Kelsey leaned over the table like she was planning a bank robbery and didn't want anyone to overhear her. Her. The woman who owned, operated, and signified all that Raymond's Kids stood for. "Because a little bird told me a story about an enchanting woman he ran into last night, a cat burglar with a peculiar cat tattoo on the back of her hand, and I thought…"

Kelsey's sharp eyes dropped to the back of Tara's right hand before she could slap her other hand over it. "You thought what? Go on. You can ask me anything. You know what I went through, and I know all the crap you lived through, so ask. I'll do anything for you."

"Even teach me how to fly off tall buildings at night without getting seen or hurt? Now?"

Oh, shit. That. Kelsey knew Renner. Which made sense, since she was Mrs. Alex Stewart, and Alex was Renner's boss and...

Tara damn near choked. "Excuse me?"

Kelsey nodded. "You know what I'm talking about, girlfriend. Agent Graves stopped by my place last night to talk to Alex, only he was already asleep. We got to talking and Renner told me part of what happened last night. He didn't mention you by name, just that tattoo."

Tara's gaze dropped to the foolish ink. Her entire Olympic ski team had gotten the same tattoo after a successful win, only they weren't Tara's team anymore. Yeah. Even that was gone. The ink was just a reminder of all she'd lost one drunken night.

"I will," she replied evenly. "But why do you want to learn how to fly off tall buildings at night? Why now? You don't skydive, and you don't take foolish chances. What's so important this can't wait until warmer weather when it'll be safer?"

Kelsey's lips thinned. "Because someone has to end that despicable woman's crime spree, and because Alex is killing himself trying to prove she's the serial killer behind those USMC murders. He's got the best team this side of the Mississippi, yet Montego's always one step ahead of them. And because she's murdering young military men. I can't let her get away with it, not anymore."

"You're planning on going into McCormack's penthouse." Tara made that a statement.

"Yes, I am. It's the only way. How'd you get in there?"

"Elevator. Like everyone else. What are you going to do when you get in there? Kill her?"

Kelsey didn't answer, but Tara could see it in her eyes. Determination. A woman protecting her man. Her family. Okay then.

"It's not hard. I have an app that, umm, helps me break into most security systems, only…" Tara sucked in a deep breath. There were things Kelsey knew about Tara's ex-husband, and things she hadn't needed to know. Until now. Maybe it was time to confess everything. Maybe Kelsey would change her mind if she knew who the friend she thought she knew, really was.

"Remember what I told you about my ex? How he beat me? How he drained my bank account and destroyed my credit after I divorced him?"

Kelsey nodded, her eyes full of confidence and trust Tara was about to destroy. "Well, he used to make me do other stuff, too. He, umm, he pimped me out."

Her throat went dry remembering… How naïve she'd been in the first place to trust that handsome, dark-skinned man with the charming British accent. How drunk. How she'd deliberately avoided her drinking buddies after she'd met him, convinced that he was the perfect, only one. That love at first sight was real and exciting.

"One day shortly after we married, I found him kneeling on a prayer rug beside our bed. He'd never done that before, but there he was with his arms raised, openly professing faith in the coming Jihad and some rat bastard in Syria," Tara explained quietly. "Until then, I honestly thought he loved me. But I was wrong. Stupid and wrong. He only needed a marriage certificate to legitimize his application for a green card. He needed an idiot like me to submit a visa petition, you know, so he could become an American citizen. And he needed a slave. In most of Indonesia, daughters are no better than chattel. They have no rights and little say in how they're married off or treated at home. Because I came into our marriage with no dowry or father's blessing, I guess you could say Jorge exacted his due out of my hide."

"Oh, Tara, I'm so sorry."

"I know. We've already talked about most of this, but I need you to know everything. One night he went crazy. He wanted me to go into this nightclub and hook up with as many guys as I could. He said American men were pigs, that I'd be perfect for them. That they'd throw money at me. That they'd be happy to do me in the men's room." She swallowed hard. "So, I umm, did."

Kelsey's grip tightened.

"It was either do what he asked or he promised a whipping, and umm… I'd had enough of those." *Man, this was a hard, ugly truth to tell.* "Because I did as he asked... I learned two lessons. A lot of American men really are pigs; I made a couple thousand that night. B-but to save myself…" Tara's throat clamped shut. "To save my physical self…" *Shit. Quit now while you're ahead. Only you're not. Tell her. Just spit it out and be done with it.* "I, umm, ended up selling my soul to the devil."

And there it was, the reason she had to stay away from Renner and couldn't hang around the District much longer. Jorge had friends everywhere. But worse, Renner didn't need someone like her in his life.

"Anyway..." Tara pursed her lips and blew out a gut full of anxiety. "He beat the crap out of me that night, all night. Broke two ribs. Kicked me. Peed on me. Even after I did what he asked, yeah. He said I proved he was right, that I was nothing but an American whore."

That seemed to break something in Kelsey. She scrambled around the table and sat alongside Tara, one arm around her waist. "I'm so sorry, sweetheart."

See? Kelsey still called her sweetheart like Tara could ever be someone's sweetheart again. But she couldn't. Not long term. Not really. Raymond's Kids was just a pitstop on the never-ending highway that was her life of keeping ahead of Jorge and his friends.

Tara struggled on. "He walked circles around me until dawn, screaming and ranting for hours that I deserved what I got. Stopping only to pray and cry and curse. When he got worked up enough, he'd start over. Beating me. Walking.

Praying. By morning I was nothing but piss, sweat, and blood. But when he went online and bought two one-way tickets to Iran…"

Her breath caught with the same fear she'd felt that morning. She could barely swallow. "Wh-when he told me to pack my shit, that he was taking me to Mecca to teach me a lesson—"

"But Mecca's in Saudi Arabia, honey," Kelsey murmured sweetly. That was the thing about Kelsey, she rarely got mad. Only gentler.

"Yeah. I know, but Jorge didn't," Tara answered, struggling to regain her tough-girl persona. "You don't have to be smart to be a terrorist. Just wealthy and evil and p-perverse." *Psychotic. Insane. Cruel as shit.*

She looked away from Kelsey to that brave little fighter in the kitchen. Jessica was still hard at work, humming some commercial jingle while she held up a plastic plate dripping with suds. She and Jessica were so much alike, and yet they had nothing in common. Jessica still had her life ahead of her. Kelsey would make sure she went into a safer home with people capable of loving her. But Tara didn't know if today was the day Jorge or one of his terrorist buddies caught up with her.

"I, umm, never told you I was an Olympic skier, either."

"You were?" Ever faithful, always loving, Kelsey cocked her head and asked, "What kind, honey?" Like any of that mattered.

"Downhill." It was always interesting how many people didn't recognize Tara even though her face had once been on every sports channel and magazine in the world. Of course, she'd been younger then. Prettier. Her eyes had been a brighter shade of blue. Filled with hope instead of worry, and without dark circles and bags beneath them. "That was when I met Jorge. Come to find out he was a scout for some ass in Syria. I was just a stupid female athlete who thought she had an Indonesian tiger by the tail. Turns out he had me."

"I'm glad you left him when you did," Kelsey soothed. "You're safe now."

Tara shook her head. "No. No, I'm not. That's the thing. He promised he'd find me if I ever left him, and he'd torture me in the most painful ways when he did. He's got friends everywhere. I made a mistake when I left him. I'll never be safe again."

Kelsey studied her for a long minute, before she whispered, "Bullshit. I have friends in low places, you know."

Okay, that was just plain funny. Kelsey in low places? Tara almost laughed out loud. But she loved this woman with her whole heart. Kelsey had been on shift the night Tara stumbled into Raymond's Kids. She'd taken her in without question. Tara had been a mess then, strung-out on prescription drugs, anything to ease the ache in her chest. Television made injuries seem sexy. Some perfectly coifed actress in six-inch heels playing the part of a tough beat cop leaned over her shot-six-times-in-the-gut-but-I'm-still-gonna-live hero partner. Yeah. Not so great in real life. Certainly not sexy. Broken ribs still hurt and those bruises would last forever. Tara still felt them sometimes late at night.

But opioids were easy to get in America, ask anyone. All the big-name pharmaceutical companies made sure they were easily available, and lawmakers weren't any good at standing in those CEOs' way, not even to protect their voting constituents. A ragged woman living on the streets had no trouble getting her hands on what she needed.

But Kelsey was different. After she'd fed Tara, let her take a nice, long, hot shower, then let her sleep in a real bed for the first time in weeks, she'd contacted her friend, Dr. McKenna Fitzgerald. Together, they'd helped Tara detox and heal. They helped her get her head on straight, and they gave her back her dignity. Kinda hard not to fall in love with friends like that. Which was why Tara would do anything for Kelsey, even teach her to fly off tall buildings in the middle of December with something better than a Superman cape.

"I already know you're physically capable, Kels. You're strong. You jog and you bench more than most the guys in this building." Which was true. That group of shifty men Kelsey hovered over like a mother hen were all missing a limb, fingers, or toes. Kelsey said they were combat vets, and that was enough for Tara. Still she asked, "Who'll watch Lexie while we're gone? Won't Alex be suspicious?"

"He will once he wakes up." Kelsey made one of her funny, guilty faces. "I might have given him a stronger dose of melatonin than I should have last night. But he's been working so hard, and he needed to rest and…" Her shoulders lifted. "Am I not the worst wife you've ever met?"

Tara leaned into her friend's motherly embrace. "Hardly. You're just taking care of your man. I met Alex last night by the way. Honestly, he looked like death warmed over, but I got the feeling he still thinks he's the baddest guy on the planet. It's a good thing he's got you to take care of him."

Kelsey nodded. "You have no idea, but he's worked miracles when no one else could, so maybe he is the baddest guy around. I just felt bad for him last night. Which is why I want you to teach me everything I need to know today, so I can get this thing with Montego over with, and we can move on.

I'm a fast learner, you'll see. Two of my staff volunteered to take over our shifts this morning. They should be here any second, and I'm not worried about Lexie. I brought her in with me this morning, so Alex could get some sleep. She's playing with Renard."

Tara glanced over Kelsey's shoulder at the focused little girl in the corner playing blocks with Renard. Renard was a high-functioning autistic teenage boy from Spain who'd arrived at Kelsey's three days ago. He'd gotten separated from his parents during their first trip to America in late November. Amber alerts went out across the nation, but things went from bad to worse.

When the authorities failed to locate him before his parents' money ran out, they'd had to return to Spain. The poor child ended up sleeping on the street, not knowing how to help himself until a worn-out Vietnam vet found him, bought Renard his first hot meal in weeks, then brought him to Kelsey. Renard's family had already paid for his way home. They'd asked that Kelsey keep him until his father arrived to accompany him.

"You trust him with your little girl?"

Kelsey nodded. "Renard's little sister is Lexie's age. He's very protective of her. Yes, I trust him."

Well, okay then. "Today, huh? I know a place where we can practice without getting caught. But I don't have a car. Can you drive me home? I've got an extra suit there that'll fit you."

"Of course, I'll drive. Where's your car?"

"I, umm, forgot it at McCormack's last night. You know, when Agent Graves got in my way."

"Tell me everything while I drive. When can you be ready?"

Tara lifted to her feet, headed for the kitchen. "Right after dishes."

Chapter Twelve

Once the cab had driven away with Tara tucked safely in the back seat, Renner breathed easier. He still needed to check in with Alex. A little one-on-one facetime with the boss couldn't hurt after last night's fiasco.

But Alex wasn't in when Renner arrived at TEAM Headquarters. He double-checked his cell. It wasn't yet eight am. That was odd. Alex usually arrived earlier than everyone else. Stranger yet, the light in Senior Agent Mark Houston's office was on. Renner crossed the quiet work area and knocked before he entered.

Mark looked up. "Hey. How's the hunt for Montego going?"

"Where's Alex?" Renner asked as he took a seat in the chair next to Mark's desk.

Mark's office wasn't the OCD wasteland that Alex's was. He had more framed family pictures on his desk than most agents. Little knickknacks his girls made for him. A red and black lump of clay that was supposed to be a ladybug pencil holder. A popsicle-stick piece of unidentifiable artwork. Other stuff. But the black folder he'd just slapped shut meant either an agent was already deep undercover on some classified operation or soon would be. There was a day not too long ago that Renner would've thrilled at the chance to be that guy. Not anymore. Black ops usually meant someone had to die. Renner preferred to stick close to home instead of sticking his neck out.

"Alex won't be in today if he knows what's good for him," Mark answered easily. "Kelsey called, said he's pretty sick. Nothing serious, just the flu, but she called Doc Fitz to make sure."

"Good on her. He looked like shit last night."

"He did?"

Renner hooked one arm over the chairback. "Yes. I was in late, talked to him on the way to Reagan, maybe ten, ten-thirty. Never seen him so, I don't know, off. Is there something going on besides this thing with Montego that I should know about?"

"Frankly, that's enough on his plate for now," Mark answered. "Just glad Kelsey knows how to handle him. I've been trying to get him to back off for months now, but you know Alex."

Renner grunted. "Yeah, he's a ball buster, but that's what makes him a good boss. I've worked with plenty of LTs who cared less about their men and women and more about getting their captain stripes. Alex isn't like that. I thought Kelsey had the wives and families handled as well?"

"That woman…" Mark shook his head, smiling. "She never ceases to amaze me. Yes, she's gone and organized daycare and babysitting, shifting the workload from home to home like a professional. She's even scheduling the agents Alex assigned to help her now, so they know when and where to be. We took our turn yesterday. Only had Kelsey's, Adam's, Hunter's and David's kids, so we got off easy."

"Sounds like a nightmare to me. All those kids…"

Mark barked a laugh. "That's because you're still single. You don't have any kids. But trust me. It's easier when your kids get older. My girls and David's boys just naturally watch over the littler ones after school. Only had a minor bump with Lexie last night. She wanted to go home early. No big deal. Think she was coming down with something. It happens. Anything you need to tell me?"

"I could use some sleep is all," Renner admitted. "Who's covering the women and kids during the day?"

"This week, Lee and Jake. I may have to get creative over Christmas vacation, though. That'll be two weeks of no school, and kids get antsy when they're cooped up too long. I'm thinking we take everyone out of town. Gabe's folks in Texas invited all of us to their ranch. He says it's large enough. Might be fun."

Renner nodded at the prospect of spending Christmas in Texas. "We now have eyes and ears inside McCormack's penthouse."

Mark's brows lifted. "You're spying on Jed? Inside his personal residence? Why? Did Alex authorize that?"

"No, but disavow me if you need to. I won't sit by and let her kill him on my watch," Renner said evenly. "Sometimes the moral imperative takes precedence."

"Agreed." Mark was a big guy, broad at the shoulders, thick-necked, but as fit a man as Renner had ever met. Like Zack Lennox, Mark could pass for a heavyweight champion any day. That he didn't climb across his desk and wring Renner's neck for breaking the law spoke to his utter respect for the men and women who served under him. "Go on," he said quietly.

"I know Alex just wants me to stick close to McCormack, but it didn't feel right walking away from him last night."

Mark offered nothing more than a nod, so Renner kept on explaining. "Something's going on that we're not seeing, Mark. I had Seth place a harassing call because I needed McCormack out of bed and away from her. The man who came charging out of his bedroom was the old McCormack, pissed that someone would dare violate his wife's headstone and ready to fight. Wish I'd had those Tattle Tales activated then, you could see what I'm talking about. But once she started rubbing up against him and talking…" Renner scrubbed a hand over his face, wishing he could bleach that memory out of his mind forever.

"Yeah, she was nude all right, but it was like he snapped into a trance. One second, he looked like he was having an apoplectic stroke, but the next…" Renner snapped his fingers. "…he shrugs his shoulders and says, *'She's dead, but we're still here, aren't we? We're still alive.'* It was like Montego flipped a switch or something. McCormack stopped ranting, in fact he calmed right down. It was… weird."

By then Mark's elbows were on the desk, his chin resting at the peak of his steepled fingers. "You think she's drugging him?"

"No, I don't. I mean, I did find a hypo at his place, but…" Renner slapped his pockets. Damn, last night was one for the books. Not only had he done the stupidest thing ever, he'd also lost a critical piece of evidence, most likely during the fall. Anyway… "You've seen him on live TV. Montego's always at his side. I guess it's possible she's using some kind of mind-control on him, but he always appears alert and sharp when he's dealing with reporters. He fires probing questions right back at them when they ask something stupid. That's what doesn't sit right with me. I've worked with him. I've seen him with Lois. That man adored his wife. Unless he's been a pathological liar all these years—"

"Not Jed," Mark stated unequivocally.

"Copy that," Renner breathed. "But yeah. I don't know what's really going on. Nonetheless, a dozen Tattle Tales are now planted and ready to go live inside his penthouse. Maybe they'll tell us something. You tell me. Do I activate them or not?"

Mark didn't hesitate. "Light 'em up."

Words Renner lived for. It took seconds to open the app on his cell and activate McCormack's newest in-house security system, the one he didn't know he had. Thumbing the down menu, Renner could now view or listen in on any of the multiple frames the app displayed. He wouldn't have needed so many if the rooms in that penthouse hadn't been so large. Tattle Tales only captured a radius of ten feet or so. "Another thing. I'd rather our new employee not have access to this app or this intel. Not sure I trust her."

Mark grunted. "Don't worry. Right now, we can't even get Camilla to type a memo. On her computer. Using a word processing app."

Which was just plain wrong. There were plenty of good workers who'd kill for the chance to work with The TEAM. "Then why hasn't Alex fired her?"

Mark shrugged, his dark eyes bright and intelligently assessing everything Renner said. "You know why. FBI Director Chase might've unloaded an unwanted employee on Alex, but Alex doesn't back down from a challenge, and he doesn't quit."

Renner couldn't help that his face wrinkled into a WTF grimace. "You think he sees something in Brinkman? Like what?" All Renner saw was a snotty teenager dressed like a professional woman in six-inch heels and claws. And therein was the rub. Camilla Brinkman was smart. He damn well knew it. She was also the most insensitive, entitled, rude brat he'd ever met. Frankie, his four-year-old niece, had more manners in her little finger than Camilla had in her whole privileged body.

"He saw something in us, didn't he?" Mark asked.

There was that. But man, Brinkman was a challenge like no other. That woman had a mighty high opinion of herself, yet treated everyone else in the office like dirt. Including Alex. Either she hated men in general or military members in particular. "I might know someone if he decides to let Brinkman go. Just saying."

"So noted," Mark replied.

"Another thing. I need information on a Tara Tumulty."

"How's she figure in the Montego case?"

"She doesn't, other than I bumped into her inside McCormack's penthouse last night, and she can see right through Montego. But Tumulty's got some creep stalking her. I'd like to help if I can. That's all. Might ask Ember to assist. Okay with you?"

"You bet. Alex doesn't care who we help as long as we follow through on our assigned missions. Anything else?"

"Not at the moment." Renner couldn't help but notice how Mark's fingertips worried that top secret folder.

"Stay in touch."

"Copy that."

Chapter Thirteen

The derelict high rise across the Anacostia River in Hillcrest Heights was made for practice jumps. A multi-building complex of apartment buildings, its owner had filed for bankruptcy. A city cease-work order rendered the property off-limits to investors, contractors, and public alike. Yet here they were, two crazy women on the thirty-fifth floor. Kelsey only wished it weren't so cold when she stepped toward the windowless opening and the steep, vertical drop it framed. Down was a loooong way—down.

"Come on. You know you can do this. It'll be fun," Tara encouraged, grinning and bouncing like a jumping jack at her side. Of course, she was excited; she'd done this before. She was good at it. As a former Olympic hopeful, she'd probably thrived on the adrenaline rush.

But Kelsey did not. Decked out in skin-tight thermals beneath her wingsuit, she could only nod because if she said anything, so much as one word, she'd chicken out. It was cold up here, and she kept shivering. Alex would laugh if he were up here, and she wouldn't blame him. Jumping out of a perfectly safe wooden and steel structure had to be one of the craziest things she'd ever thought of doing. And she'd asked for this? Yup. Crazzzzzzy!

A dismal gray landscape faced her from the east. The last time she'd looked, nothing but cold hard concrete waited for her below. The full force of the forecasted weather front had yet to make land. For now, old man winter had stalled over the Atlantic, where it was churning whitecaps, gathering moisture, and gaining velocity. A blizzard might've hidden her disastrous descent if things went awry, but Kelsey didn't need inclement weather complicating her first, maybe once in a lifetime, jump.

Tara had assured her multiple times she'd be fine. She'd instructed Kelsey on how wingsuit flying was the best of both worlds, those worlds being skydiving and hang gliding, two worlds Kelsey had never wanted admission to, not even once in her practical, ordinary, somewhat boring life. She'd suffered through enough excitement during her first marriage. Normal and boring were solid career goals, though living with Alex had proven to be anything but boring. Yet here she was, branching out. Doing ridiculously scary things.

Adrenaline was not her friend right now, and her heart wouldn't stop climbing up her throat. Breathing evenly was nearly impossible to do. Staying calm was a whole different problem. Even something as simple as swallowing took effort. She hadn't a drop of saliva in her mouth to moisten her poor parched tongue or lips.

But she wasn't doing it for the adrenaline high or the thrill. This was for Alex and Lexie. For all those poor homeless men she now carefully tended at Raymond's Kids. Okay, so they weren't children, yet in a way, they very much were. They were all homeless, most by choice. Each of them had been betrayed and seduced by Montego, all of them tortured. They would struggle for the rest of their lives adapting to their physical impairments as well as their confused mental states.

They desperately needed someone to care. She'd taken most of them in after Alex, Beau, and Maverick discovered

Montego's gruesome pit. There were sixteen left of the nineteen original survivors. Three had already committed suicide, and Kelsey was darned if she'd allow the others to go that route. They'd been in shock when they were finally rescued. Some had suffered for years, others for less than a month. Some went home, but all returned when home became too much or too little to endure. One by one, Kelsey had opened Raymond's Kids' doors to them. She gave each a private room to recover, hide, or heal in. She enlisted the aid of psychologists, surgeons, and the Veterans Administration. Anyone who would listen to their cries for help, she now knew by name, office symbol, and phone number.

But in the end, it all came down to her, a simple housewife who loved children, reaching out and doing what little she could to right a terrible injustice. It wasn't a great leap to go from loving children to helping young men. Montego's barbaric form of torture had reduced all her victims to frightened little boys, who now dreamed horrific nightmares they couldn't escape and battled demons most people could never imagine. They were shattered men who cried at night for their mothers. Who drank too much, cursed vehemently, or self-medicated any way and every way they could.

Gone were the dashing braggarts intent on saving the world. In their place remained young, vulnerable soldiers, airmen, sailors, and Marines, who, because of their extreme injuries, could no longer serve. Forced out of the military, they felt impotent and useless. Powerless. Which one by one, had led each of them to Kelsey. They needed someone to stand for them, to scream, 'No more!' And that person was her.

Today was as much for those wounded warriors as it was for Alex and Lexie. Kelsey absolutely had to know how to fall safely out of Jed McCormack's penthouse window. Because Catalina Montego needed to die.

"Pretend I'm Yoda," Tara quipped at her side, bouncing on the balls of her feet, slapping her thighs to keep warm, and blowing great puffs of frosty white into the void where Kelsey was soon to go. "Remember what he said?"

"W-who?" Kelsey didn't have a clue who Yoda was at the moment. She'd lost all ability to think coherently the moment she'd looked down. Which was her fault. Tara told her not to do it, but of course, that only meant she would most certainly look down. Not smart.

Tara's palm on her back was soothing, though. Warm. Sisterly. "He's the little green guy in Star Wars. Tell me you've at least heard of him."

"If you say so."

"Anyway…" Another billow of crystal breath wafted out into the frigid air, hovering there, daring her to be as brave as she'd thought she was. "Yoda was very old and very wise. He told Luke Skywalker something like *'Don't just try. Get it done.'*"

"Ah huh," Kelsey murmured, her heart pounding so hard she was beginning to see little black dots at her peripheral.

"So, let's do this!" Tara yelled as she pushed Kelsey out the window—to her death!

Okay, not to her death, but she *was* falling with her eyes closed and—

"Son of a bitch!" flew out of her mouth. She was channeling Alex! But what else had Tara said? Oh, yes. *'Pretend you're a bird. Spread your wings and legs to catch the updraft.'* Only she'd also warned that there'd be less updraft today due to the cold weather, which Kelsey only now realized had been a warning to maybe not try this crazy stunt in December.

Here goes. Kelsey stretched her arms as wide as they would go, her legs too, and…

WHOOSH!

What do you know? It works.

She ceased falling like a rock the second her wings caught the wind. Okay, that was kind of cool. She was nearly at ground level by then and floating. She and Tara were close to the same distance from the ground. Both hovering. Both falling. Earth was still coming up fast. *Bend my knees. Hold my breath. Tuck, roll, and… what was that other thing?*

Touchdown!

Glory, glory halleluiah! Kelsey lay still as death while her pulse stopped thundering through her veins. The enormity of what she'd just accomplished flooded her timid self. There was a time she'd been afraid of her own shadow. Not today. She'd been brave. Courageous. She could do anything!

Scrambling to her feet, she was amazed at how much she'd actually loved flying. The rush. The sensation of being free and scared, but mostly, free. She'd conquered fear, damn it. "I did it! I did it!" she called out, dancing like an idiot.

Until she remembered. "You pushed me! Off a building! You brat!"

Tara grinned that big beautiful smile of hers. "Would you have taken that last step if I hadn't?"

All straight white teeth and blue, blue eyes, she really was a knockout when she wasn't glancing over her shoulder, looking for that despicable creep she'd divorced. Jorge… Jorge… What was his last name? Couldn't be Tumulty.

"Maybe, but you didn't know that. You owe me, girlfriend," Kelsey all but squealed, her adrenaline still on high and her heart pounding at her success. "After you pushed me off that building, you owe me."

"Who, *moi*?" Tara asked innocently, her brows lifted in play and those bright eyes sparkling.

"Yes, you," Kelsey declared with gusto. "What's your real name anyway. Your married name."

The second Tara's lashes dropped, Kelsey knew she'd asked too much. The day turned back to dismal and gray. The muscles in Tara's slender neck contracted as if swallowing were impossible. Instantly repentant for outing her friend, Kelsey said. "Forget it. You know I love you no matter what name you go by. You're still you."

A big sigh. More frosty vapor. Tara's chin came up. "You're right," she said quietly. "My married name was Poerbatjaraka. I haven't had time to get it legally changed yet. Yeah, I know. Try saying that ten times real fast. But I couldn't go back to using his name. It was never mine to begin with. Does Tara Shanahan ring a bell?"

"Oh, my. You're her. But she was…" Kelsey bit her tongue instead of saying 'happy.' Her heart broke remembering that once sassy, vibrant young woman who'd turned America on its ear on her way to the Olympics. The darling who'd once danced in skis on the slopes was a shadow of the gaunt woman with dark shadows circling her eyes standing before her now.

Kelsey asked what she asked every child who showed up at Raymond's Kids. "Do your parents know where you are? Do you want me to call them for you?"

Tara shrugged. "It's too late. They weren't happy when I married Jorge. My fault. I was drunk, kind of didn't tell them their only daughter was a slut, ran off and had already eloped."

"Don't call my BFF names. You're not a slut," Kelsey murmured as she grabbed hold of Tara and pulled her in for a hug. "You should call them. Parent's don't forget their babies. They still love you."

"I can't. He'll hurt them."

"Honey, he'll hurt them anyway if he thinks he can use them to get at you. They need to know. Tell them what happened and where you are. At least warn them what you've gotten yourself into."

Tara sucked in a harsh breath. "You're right. I never thought—"

"Because he's only threatened you so far, but trust me. Cruel men will do anything to strike back." How well Kelsey knew. She'd lost her two tiny sons to the same kind of brutish man.

"I… I have to go."

"Where?"

"To Colorado. That's where they live." Poor Tara was coming undone.

Kelsey handed over her cell. "Then take back your power and call them right now, Tara Shanahan. Here. That bastard doesn't have my number. He can't track me."

In a heartbeat, Kelsey was smashed into a teary hug. "I'm so sorry," Tara cried, "for all that brought us here together, I'm so sorry for what you had to go through, but I'm so thankful at the same time. For you, Kelsey. Every time I turn around, you're saving me."

Which wasn't exactly true, but Kelsey would never correct her friend. But if not for Alex all those years ago, there'd be no Kelsey, Lexie, or Raymond's Kids. There would only be two stone markers in a far-off place called Lakewood, Washington. One to mark where her boys were buried together, the other for a grieving mother who'd lost her mind to suicide.

Kelsey had been that close to ending herself back then. If the cantankerous Marine she'd married hadn't gotten fed up with the world, himself in particular, at that same time, she wouldn't be here today. Alex was her miracle in a world gone dark as sin back then, so dark and bleak she hadn't known who she was. Oddly, it was his initial unwillingness to help that motivated her today. Because in the end, that recalcitrant jarhead who thought he knew everything, had thrust himself squarely between Kelsey and the bullets of her murderous ex. But that was a long time ago. A lesson learned...

Trembling now, Tara grabbed Kelsey's cell. Hurriedly, she thumbed in a number and the best word in the world tumbled off her chapped lips, "M-M-Mom?"

Kelsey turned away to give her emotional friend privacy. Scaffolding still climbed a good portion of the building she'd just conquered. Tattered plastic sheeting billowed off several lower levels. The structure stood tall, but she was certain that she, Kelsey Stewart, wife to the sweetest husband in the universe, stood taller. It was just steel, mortar, and two-by-fours, but she was a married woman, a survivor. Because of Alex she was alive and all but glowing at the incredibly brave thing she'd just done. And all because a crotchety jarhead had suffered the unexpected visit of a sickly, battered woman that day in the woods, and in doing so, in taking her in when all he'd wanted was a quiet vacation, Alex had given her everything.

Some might call jumping off this building stupid, especially in cold weather. Others might call it brave, Kelsey certainly did. But she'd done it in spite of herself, and she could do it again. Only next time, she was taking Montego down with her.

Chapter Fourteen

"Hey, Ember," Renner called out as he closed Mark's office door.

She waved back from her seat behind The TEAM customer service counter, her cheeks pink from the cold. "Hey yourself. Aren't you supposed to be watching Montego?"

He patted his butt pocket where he'd stuck his phone. "I am."

"Ah. You've deployed Tattle Tales." She fluttered her fingers at him. "Hand it over. You've got plenty to do without monitoring them. Let me be your eyes and ears while you do whatever else you should be doing."

Ember Dennison was one-of-a-kind gorgeous and twice as smart as most agents. Blonde and built, she made everything she wore too sexy for the work place. Today she'd dressed in black slacks, flat-heeled shoes, and a red sweater, one with a sagging rolled collar that didn't need to dip low to enhance her full cleavage. Ember had assets. The clothes didn't make her; she made the clothes. And she made them all hot-damned attractive. Rory Dennison was one lucky bastard to have convinced her to marry him.

Without a worry, Renner handed over his cell and watched her extract whatever codes she needed to copy data from the app on his phone to her network. She did have a nice setup. Banks of monitors lined the wall between her office space and other TEAM work stations. Multiple printers, CPUs, and towers were already booted up and humming.

The entire station where she spent most of her days looked like something out of Star Trek, with more technical gear than Renner could name. But then his MOS, military occupational specialty, had never been techie or genius related. Not unless dialing in precise minutes of angle to tighten the point of impact with his target put him in the same league as Ember. Which it did not. She was the brainiac behind The TEAM. He was just a grunt who knew how to shoot and follow orders.

"Mark authorized this?" Ember asked, her finger on the RETURN key, ready to activate the Tattle Tales.

"Yes, he did."

With one tap of her finger, the views from inside McCormack's penthouse displayed inside a grid of windows on Ember's private, big-screen monitor. She handed a pair of dark glasses over her counter. "Here. Put these on. I'm going dark."

Apparently going dark meant something different to Ember than it did Renner. Her monitor flickered, then went blank. He slid the ordinary looking glasses onto his nose, and... All those little boxes of confidential information reappeared.

"You're amazing," Renner breathed as he studied the lack of movement at McCormack's place.

"Yeah, I know. I keep privacy filters on all my other screens. Never had to worry about that until Miss Know-It-All showed up."

When Renner had nothing to say about Brinkman, Ember inserted an earbud and asked, "So where's Jed?"

"Still sleeping," Renner replied, tapping his own earbud in case something he couldn't see was happening at McCormack's.

"You didn't put anything in his bedroom?"

Renner shook his head. "Didn't think we needed to. I'm no perv."

Ember grunted. "Understood, but if I was going to kill someone, that's where I'd do it."

He had to smile. If she killed a guy in bed, he'd die happy.

"And he wouldn't die by sex, either, Renner. Get your mind out of the gutter." She hadn't looked away from her screen when she said that. Which was good. He didn't need her reading his eyes like she seemed to be reading his mind.

Ember wasn't one of those women who flirted or trolled for action, then cried sexual abuse when a guy came onto her. She'd worked with enough sailors to understand how to talk with them as well as how to put them in their place. That she knew how to shoot and controlled monthly weapons certification was also no small thing. The woman could take care of herself, and she didn't need the Equal Rights Amendment to do it for her.

"Anyway…" Renner ground out. "Exactly how would you kill a guy in bed?"

"Easy. Once I warmed him up, I'd cut his femoral artery and leave him there to bleed out."

Renner shook his head at the image of her anywhere near a guy's femoral artery. *Was it hot in here?* "I need to go," he said before he dug a hole he couldn't climb out of.

"Was that all you wanted?"

Oh, yeah. "Thanks for reminding me. Can you run a lowdown on a Tara Tumulty? She was at McCormack's last night and I picked up a vibe from her that she might be in trouble."

"Sure. What else do you know about her?"

"Just her address and that she might be an adrenaline junkie."

Ember made a funny face. "I need more to go on. A picture or something."

"Hold that thought," he told her as he texted a quick note to his mother.

You wouldn't happen to have a shot of the girl I was with last night on your security camera, would you?

It took a minute before his mother answered. You betcha. I was just telling Mr. Duggan how pretty she was, and how good you and she looked together.

Stop matchmaking, Mom. Send the pic.

Aye, I suspected you'd be needing one. Should be in your inbox, luvvie. You get it?"

Easing back from his cell, Renner checked his email, then sent a reply.

Got it. TY.

Will you be wanting a glossy next?

She's a client, not a friend. Talk to you soon.

Renner disconnected before his mother turned into her busybody self. "Here, Ember," he said as he transferred the file to her inbox. "Mom caught this shot on her security footage last night. Maybe you could run it through facial rec?"

"Will do. I'll contact you when I have something." Ember cocked her head in that inquisitive, knowing way she had, her green eyes glimmering, asking questions he didn't want to answer. Yet he said, "She's a client. Just like I said."

"Oh, really?"

Renner turned away, headed for the elevator and a quick way out. "Thanks, Ember," he called over his shoulder.

"Anytime," she sing-songed back.

Renner hightailed it out of the office to parking at ground level. He had one more thing to do this morning. Feed his dog. Make that two things. Three. A shower and nap would've been nice. Until his cell buzzed. Without checking the caller ID, he answered, "I said she's a client, Ember."

"Renner!" Kelsey screamed in his ear. "He's got her! He took Tara!"

"Kelsey? Who took her? Where are you?"

"Don't worry about me. She's still got my phone! Track her, Renner! Find her! He'll kill her!"

She didn't have to ask twice. "I will," he said as he disconnected. All agents' wives were protected under the same protocols that ruled The TEAM. Renner thumbed the app that would allow him to hone onto any TEAM member's GPS signal. Including Kelsey's.

Pissed that he hadn't been there to keep Tara safe, he promised her now, "I'm coming, baby. Be strong. Hold on for me. I'm coming." *And when I get there, I'll kill the son of a bitch who kidnapped you with my bare hands.*

Chapter Fifteen

She couldn't breathe. Couldn't think.

God, please let Kelsey be safe. Let her be alive.

The dark place she found herself in smelled like blood. Probably hers. As much as she wanted to scream, Tara lay still, listening to the sound of tires humming on the pavement. Her head hurt and a couple teeth were loose. Crap. She was in a trunk with her hands and feet bound and a bag over her head. A plastic bag that sucked against her nostrils every time she inhaled too hard.

Tara had no recollection of what happened, not to her or to Kelsey. Kelsey had just made her first successful flight. She'd stuck the landing. It was a great morning. Tara had just finished her first phone call home in nearly two years. Mom had sounded so happy. Tara hadn't understood what Kelsey said. Until now. She'd screamed, "Run!"

It had finally happened. Jorge had found her. And now she would die.

Shaking with fright at the nightmare that lay ahead of her, Tara forced her mind to Colorado and her favorite ski run at Breckenridge. Crazy Ivan2, so named for its forty-nine-degree slope. Man, she loved skiing. The cold. The thrill of launching off a deceptively smooth cornice, dropping straight down. The icy wind in her nose and her hair. The shit-eating grin on her face. The sure knowledge that she'd faced danger and death and spit in their eyes—once upon a time.

The vehicle taking her to hell slowed and then turned left. Tara straightened her legs and braced her head against one padded trunk wall, her boots against the other, to keep from being tossed around. Jorge had struck her head when he'd captured her. She'd never seen him coming.

Tears sprang to her eyes. This was not the way she'd envisioned her life ending. Back when she'd been an Olympic hopeful, she'd lived for the adrenaline rush during the day, the bars, hot-tubbing, and beer parties at night. Yes, she'd been wild, but she'd also been sure she'd die on the slopes after any number of disastrous falls. Maybe from a concussion or some other bizarre injury. Reckless skiers courted death, and she'd been one of the most reckless. Brash. Arrogant. Stupid…

The vehicle jerked to a full stop. The engine died. Tara shook her head to buy some room to breathe. But the plastic bag seemed to have a life of its own. It clung to her cheeks and nose. It covered her nostrils.

And then it was gone, jerked away, and Jorge was breathing in her face. "You think you can run?" he hissed. "From me?" He reached in and grabbed her jacket collar. "What did I tell you would happen?"

She would've answered if he'd removed the tape over her mouth.

He slapped her face anyway. "I will kill you!" he spat, his eyes wide and his mouth twisted with venom. "That's what I'll do! Only first we'll play games, you and me." He had her hanging half-out of the trunk by then, still fisting her collar. "And when you're done entertaining me, when I'm good and sick of you, only then will I let you die. You hear me?"

Tara nodded through the brain-rattling shake he was giving her, his fist hard against her throat, and her heart clamoring like a gong in her ears. Man, he'd gotten uglier these last few months. His black beard was long and shaggy, filthy. His hair was the same.

"Speak, you disgusting whore!" he commanded like an idiot. Another shake. Another slap. He banged her skull on the trunk edge.

Yet she tried, mumbling through what felt like duct tape covering her lips.

It must have registered with the dumbass that she couldn't answer. Growling, he lifted her head and tore the tape off, taking a snarl of her hair with it. Another shake. Another vicious slap. And she would've told him anything if he'd just stop battering her.

But she'd been here before. Jorge didn't want answers. Wouldn't matter if she told lies or truths. All he wanted was her pain and her blood.

"I'm sorry," she cried out.

He almost looked surprised, like he actually believed her.

"I'm sorry I ever met you!" Why lie?

He dragged her out of the trunk then, dumped her hard onto her shoulder on the ground and slammed the trunk lid closed. Tara rolled to keep from breaking her neck, then sucked in a gut full of cold air, thankful for that smallest of small things. Until he knotted her hair in a fist and dragged her backward through the dark alley like a bag of garbage, and into the back door of…

Oh, shit. A butcher shop. Heavy wooden chopping blocks. Long stainless-steel countertops. All dirty. All previously used and worn and… *Shit.*

Her stomach pitched at the smell of rancid meat and decay. This wasn't just any butcher shop. This had to be where all bad wives of terrorist assholes ended up. Dead. Chopped. Flushed down the sewers.

Lifting her onto her feet, Jorge balanced her on a tall wooden stool with no back. More duct tape fastened her already bound feet to the bottom rung. Another half-dozen layers fastened her thighs to the round wooden seat. And Tara was thankful she still had her clothes. She hadn't always been allowed that small privilege.

At last, Jorge stood before her, his hands on his hips and an evil light in his eye. To think that she'd once thought him handsome. All that dark wavy hair. His dark skin. Those full lips that had once tasted of decadence, rebellion, and the clove cigarettes he favored. He'd been a striking male the first time she'd seen him, ultra-polite and gentlemanly.

Man, she'd been wrong. So damned foolish.

Slowly he turned to the counter at his left, drawing her attention to what lay in store for her. Large metal hooks. A gleaming set of polished knives, all sizes. A drill. Drill bits. Other things she couldn't name. "We start now, heh?" he asked, grinning like this was going to be fun.

Tara could barely sit upright by then. But when he stepped into her space with a knife in his hand and cut the jacket off her shoulders... When he smiled as the blade slithered under her sleeves and reduced them to nothing... When he set the knife aside and put his hands on her Under Armour t-shirt and ripped it down the center, baring her bra and her breasts...

She let her tears fall. It wouldn't matter if she screamed or begged or cried for her life.

By the end of this day, she would be dead.

Renner pulled into the alley in Deanwood, one of the worst neighborhoods, located in the Northeastern part of the District. The app on his phone pinged loud and clear that he was within twenty feet of Tara—if she still had Kelsey's phone. If only he could see through walls. It was early afternoon, yet this alley was dark, closed in by project apartments built back in the 1980s. No lights glimmered from windows or doors on the solid brick walls to his left or to his right. No dark sinister figures skulked in the shadows. His only lead was the rusty Ford sedan parked alongside a row of industrial-sized trash receptacles up ahead. And that was good enough.

Renner left his leather cut behind. He needed to be able to move fast. Out of his vehicle now and on his feet, he didn't waste time looking over the Ford, searching for clues. Clues had nothing to offer. Not now. Whoever had taken Tara might've left evidence of her abduction behind, but that wasn't what Renner wanted now. He had a woman to rescue. Once she was safe he'd call for reinforcements. They could bag the evidence.

His soul came to scary, brilliant life at times like this. His cell still pinged in his rear pocket telling him he was on track. And now the weight of cold hard steel graced his dry palms. His body hummed, drawing on all five heightened senses, as well as his sixth—his sniper sense. Self-reliance kept a man alive. But those uniquely sharpened senses made him the hunter/killer he needed to be.

Renner became the night as he advanced toward one of two metal doors, spaced twenty feet from each other, on the brick wall to his left. What'll it be? Door A or Door B? He zeroed in on Door A. Most thugs were arrogant assholes who thought they were invincible. They didn't think they'd get caught, so they didn't take precautions, like parking a car full of forensic evidence farther from their man cave—or whatever this place was.

Ember's voice crackled to life inside his head the second his palm hugged the rusty doorknob. "Hey, Renner. I've got news on that Tara Tumulty."

"Speak," he whispered.

"Are you okay?"

"Just tell me what you've got."

"I ran her through facial rec like you suggested. Her name's not Tumulty. It's Shanahan, as in Tara Shanahan. As in Olympic hopeful, downhill skier, Tara Shanahan."

"Copy that," he answered, his brain filtering, sorting, and judging all he knew about Tara Shanahan. Not much. He tended to follow Olympic shooting events. Air rifle, rapid fire pistol, skeet, and trap. Summer sports.

"She's lost weight and her hair used to be short and bleached blonde. Another thing. She married a man from Indonesia, Jorge Poerbatjaraka, over a year ago. But this is where it gets really bad. He's got ties with ISIL, specifically Ahmed Al-Yousif in Syria. I'm tracking the money trail between the two, as well as their latest texts. He's a recruiter. He funnels angry, impressionable young men and women to Al-Yousif, and Al-Yousif makes sure he stays in business. They've worked together for years, Renner. Years."

"Shit," Renner hissed under his breath. "What else?"

He knew about Al-Yousif. The bastard was the infamous former NFL running back Anderson White. Born in New York City to hardworking, African American, middle-class parents, he betrayed his country and his family when he'd joined ISIL. Hit all the international ten-most-wanted lists. Made a name for himself by kidnapping two Kuwaiti politicians, then bragged via live-streaming egotistical rants that every nation had twenty-four hours to release his imprisoned ISIL brothers and sisters, or he'd execute the politicians. Which he'd known would never happen. The man was a flaming narcissist. Twenty-four hours later Al-Yousif filmed two cold-blooded beheadings, then wiped his bloody sword on his robe and laughed into the camera.

"She divorced him seven months ago and disappeared off the grid until the security video from your mom's place surfaced."

"What do you mean surfaced?"

"It's on YouTube, Renner. Produced by anonymous. It claims to have located the missing USA Olympic hopeful, Tara Shanahan. It's already gotten over fifty-thousand hits."

Ouch. Renner bowed his head at what he'd done. He'd outed Tara. Not intentionally, but by taking her to what he'd thought was a safe place. Apparently, her buddy Jorge had the means to hack into Crazy Eights' security cameras. Or someone did.

That frightening detail had Renner rethinking his strategy, which until Ember's call, had been to kill the bastard, call for clean-up on aisle Jorge, and whisk Tara off to safety. Only now, the better way forward might be to take Jorge into custody in order to glean additional information on Ahmed, aka Andy White.

"Are you still there?" Ember asked quietly.

"Yeah," he answered, his voice stuck in his throat and his common sense online. "Listen, I've got to go. I'm in the middle of something."

"I can send help," she told him. "I know where you are."

Of course, she did. Ember had her pretty fingertips on the pulse of every TEAM agent. She knew exactly what he was doing and where he was.

"No," Renner ground out, his ear to the heavy steel door, but no sound came from within.

"Copy that," she whispered before disconnecting.

Tara Shanahan, huh?

Chapter Sixteen

Tara sagged on the stool, fighting to stay upright, dizzy and beaten and bloody, but not out, not by a long shot. At least not yet. Jorge wanted from her what every conceited man wanted from a woman, for her to grovel at his feet like some lovesick idiot and beg his forgiveness. Like she was the bastard in this twisted relationship. He kept calling their marriage 'sacred' as if he were the saint. As if she'd forsaken her vows, and he was the poor innocent slighted one she'd left behind. As if he hadn't made her married life a living hell.

He had hold of her hair again, twisting his fist, pulling her head back and threatening to cut her neck. He had yet to stab her with that curved blade he seemed to favor, but he'd done enough cutting to keep her on edge. She could tell he'd sliced her throat, but just deep enough to scare her into submission. Just enough she felt her blood trickling down her chest.

But the small surface slices he'd traced down her arm to her tattoo stung worse. He'd said ink offended his higher sensibilities. As if a man who cut women had any.

"No proper woman would adorn herself with such disrespectful art unless she wants her husband to beat her every day for the rest of her worthless life," he told her again. "Is that what you want, wife? A whipping every day?"

"I'm not your wife," she rasped. "Divorced, remember?"

"I never signed those piece of shit papers your lawyer sent me!" he spat into her sweaty face. "It was not true! None of it! You told them lies! All lies!"

"It was legal," she shot back at him, wincing as the knife lanced her bicep, shaking to keep from screaming. Whimpering excited Jorge, but she couldn't help it. She cried, choking on her real crimes. Wishing she knew what happened to Kelsey and hoping her mother could forgive her wayward daughter for always thinking she was smarter than she was. Smart women didn't end up married to ISIL operators, did they?

Blood trickled down Tara's arm to the floor, and it was hard to keep her eyes on the prize of dying with dignity. This was torture, and yeah, there was gallows humor in this rat bastard's ranting while he scraped her beloved cat tattoo off her skin. Which hurt!

A hysterical laugh bubbled up from her gut. *Don't laugh! Don't giggle!* And now she was talking to herself. Which meant she was dehydrated and losing more blood than Jorge realized. She wouldn't last much longer. He'd either have to get serious about the torture schtick he kept bragging he was so good at, or he'd have to do something to keep her alive, so he could… yeah. Kill her slowly.

"Oink, oink," she breathed at the man she hated.

"You dare insult me?" He bellowed like an animal in pain. "Your husband!"

"I dare insult Porky Pig…"

The knife bit into her throat. Finally. He was angry enough to kill her. *Okay, good.* The words Yul Brenner said in that old-time movie about the ten commandments flashed out of the archives of her dizzy mind. *'So, let it be written. So, let it be done.'*

Yeah. That. I'm ready.

"I hated you then," she whispered, the sweat dripping in her eyes making it hard to see his ugly face. Or maybe it was her blood. Could have been. She'd been slapped and punched enough. It was getting hard to tell. "B-b-but…"

He leaned in closer like he expected a confession or something.

She let him have it. "But I hate you more now."

"No!" Jorge roared again, but who cared? Not—

BANG!

He let loose of her, and because Tara was weak and unprepared, her neck snapped backward. Still taped to the stool, she fell. There was no way to keep from hitting the floor. She landed hard. Oomph! The fall knocked the wind out of her. Her poor head bounced. One big star exploded into a thousand smaller streaming stars that seemed to be falling over her. She blinked when the fireworks faded, but there she was. Still in the same dark place. Her eyes crossed. Her head split open, and damn… *Just let me die.*

She turned to the side when he bellowed another dramatic, "No!" All she could see was Jorge's legs and boots. But yes. Tara could also see someone else across the room, someone facing Jorge. A man. How had he gotten inside this hellhole? Was he stupid? She blinked, trying to clear her vision. It couldn't be.

"Renner?" she breathed, her voice lost as Jorge bellowed, facing Renner like an angry bear protecting his kill. Scraping his boot soles on the floor like a bull. Snorting like a pig. *Jorge always was an ass…*

Tara would've laughed at the imagery her scrambled brain had just conjured up—if she could've seen through her tears. "Don't kill him," she cried from her front-row seat of what would surely be Renner's death. "Please. Don't kill him..."

Jorge was a massive monster. Yet while he ranted, Renner stood there poised and lethal. He wasn't wearing his leather jacket, and his skin-tight t-shirt looked lacquered to his chest. She'd never noticed before how his biceps bulged, nor how thick veins roped up the muscled granite of his arms to the tight edge of his sleeves. How black his eyes were. How his lip curled. How his nose flared. Heat curled around him. Fire and death and revenge.

Renner wasn't as big a man. Jorge outweighed him by a good hundred pounds, but Renner still struck lightning fast. So fast Tara didn't see him move, but then he was in Jorge's face. Smashing a fist into Jorge's eyes. Chopping his throat. Slapping his ears.

Jorge screamed as bodies collided. Renner's lightning fast rabbit punches connected with Jorge's thick gut in a blinding sequence that dropped him to his knees. He'd barely scrambled to his feet, when Renner leaped sideways at him. His powerful kick sent Jorge backward into the concrete wall.

Yet Jorge used that for leverage. Bleeding profusely, he shoved off the wall and caught Renner full in the chest with a fist, sending him flying backward over the carefully laid out table covered with instruments of torture.

Instead of ragdolling out of control, Renner performed the most perfect backflip. He stuck a three-point landing. What a magnificent sight. Sweat drenched his short hair and face, but when he lifted his head to face Jorge down, when he glared through his brows—the harsh, dark light in his eyes told a story all by itself. Renner was military trained. He was primed and he was lethal.

Jorge was already dead. He just didn't know it.

The fight to the death became a slow-motion dance of one-two-three punches followed with slicing uppercuts to Jorge's throat. He reeled back. Blood gushed from his nose and open mouth. It poured out of the cuts over his eye. The big baby whined, and Tara wanted to spit in his face. But Renner was the master assassin here. He kept dishing out punishing blows and brutal kicks. Slapping Jorge, egging him on, until suddenly the world went wonky and everything dissolved into slo-mo.

Tara knew it then. Renner had come too late, and she was so, so tired. It was time to let go.

With her cheek to the dirty concrete floor, she whispered the softest, "Love you," into the universe. She meant it for her mom and her dad and for sweet little Jessica. For Tyrone and for Kelsey. For everyone she'd disappointed in her short, worthless life. For everyone she'd let down. For herself, and now—for Renner. Her savior. Her knight in shining black armor.

She hadn't known him very long, but she wanted to. She already liked him. His mom. Crazy Eights. But now he'd never know.

He nearly snapped his neck looking back at her when Tara sighed. *What'd she say? Sounded like 'love you.'* It was time to end this battle. She was all that mattered, not him. Certainly, not Jorge.

Renner fingered his blade up from his boot sheath and cursed Jorge What's-His-Fuckin'-Name back to hell with it. Of course, the knife flew true and, like the perfectly balanced weapon it was, it landed where Renner intended. In Jorge's thick meaty thigh instead of between his beady eyes. The guy dropped to his knees howling.

Renner's pistol came up then, pointing at the asshat who'd hurt Tara. "Get on the ground! Face down! Now!"

"You stuck me," he hissed. "I can't."

"Find a goddamned way!" Renner ordered.

Sniffling, Jorge complied, twisting one knee to keep the knife from going deeper. With his knee in Jorge's back, Renner jerked his arms behind his back, and snapped flex cuffs on his wrists. He logrolled his prisoner onto one side, then cuffed his ankles.

"Make one move and I'll kill you," Renner whispered as he kneed Jorge one last time before lifting to his feet.

Jorge seemed inclined to want to live and breathe. Renner stepped away from him to tend to Tara. She lay taped to a stool, for fuck's sake, and the bastard had beaten her. She was bleeding from multiple wounds. Her poor face. Her arm. Her hands.

Renner shot Jorge a dark look and a promise of death as he sliced through the tape that held her and gathered her limp body into his arms.

"You beat a defenseless woman," he hissed, angry enough to shoot the bastard in the face.

"She's my wife!" Jorge bellowed. "I do what I want!"

"Not anymore," Renner whispered to the valiant woman in his arms. "Hey," he breathed even as he thumb-dialed Ember.

"Don't die on me, Tara Shanahan. I know who you are now. You got some 'splaining to do, babe, and—"

Ember interrupted with a steady, "Help's on its way, Renner. Do you need medical?"

"Yeah," he cried, suddenly overcome with all he stood to lose, tears and sweat and blood running in his eyes. "I need EMTs. She's hurt, Ember. Bad. Send EMTs and the Life Flight guys. Send everybody! H-Hurry."

"Copy that," she murmured kindly.

He lifted Tara into his cheek and pressed his mouth to her temple. "Please stay with me. I don't want to lose you now that I found—"

The door burst open. God bless Ember. Mark and Harley were already here.

"Kill him," Renner begged his senior agents, nodding at Jorge and meaning it from the depth of his soul. "Please. Kill the bastard, so Tara can live in peace. He'll never let her go. End the son of a bitch! Before anyone else gets here. Do it! God, please."

Mark's dark somber gaze flittered over Tara, to Jorge, then back to Renner. "How about we make sure she lives instead?" he asked as he jerked the first aid kit out of his gear bag and knelt with Renner. Antiseptic wipes came first, then butterfly bandages on her cheek and forehead.

Snapping the endothermic icepack he'd unwrapped from his own gear bag, Harley applied it gingerly to her forehead and told Renner, "Can you hold her steady?"

"Yes," Renner answered, frightened at the depth of his feelings for this woman he really didn't know. His chest still heaved like a blacksmith's bellows at the thought of losing her, and droplets of his sweat were splashing onto her.

For the first time, he doubted himself. He should've ended Jorge the moment he laid eyes on the bastard instead of slapping him around, keeping him alive to get to the mastermind behind him. He could've at least wounded Jorge, taken him out with a non-lethal shot instead of wasting precious time. He should've rescued Tara first, and only Tara! She was the prime objective. Not some egotistical asshat out to kill her.

"I should've just killed him, but I was so mad," he explained to no one. "I knew if I even touched my piece, I would've shot him in the face first and asked questions later."

With every drop of his sweat that splashed onto her sweet face, Renner cursed himself for being too late and being less than what Tara deserved. She had yet to moan or sigh, but she was alive, and for that, he thanked his lucky stars.

The EMTs had arrived with flashing lights, howling sirens, and a police escort.

"Renner," Mark said, snapping his fingers. "Hey. Renner."

Renner hadn't realized Mark was talking to him. "Yes?" he asked as the EMTs lifted Tara out of his arms and gently placed her onto their gurney to begin their assessment and treatment.

"The police will need you to stay and answer questions."

"Will you go with—?"

Mark shook his head. "Not me. Harley will accompany Miss Shanahan to the hospital, and he'll stay with her until I can get there. In the meantime. I'll post around the clock guards at her room. No one gets in to see her but her doctors, namely McKenna and Libby, and her nurses, do you understand me? Are you listening?"

"Your wife's going to be her doctor?" Renner asked, incredulous. "You'd let Libby do that for someone you don't know?"

Mark sent Renner a brotherly nod. "Hell, yeah. This woman's important to you, right? Anytime. Anywhere."

It was enough to make a grown man cry, but Renner swiped the moisture off his brow, sure most of it was sweat anyway. "Thanks," he told his friend hoarsely as he tugged his phone out of his butt pocket. "I'll be there as quick as I can get away."

Renner had to know what happened to Kelsey after she'd called. Now that he had time to think on it, he hadn't even asked her if she'd been injured, and he should have. Yet something told him to keep that conversation private. Else why had she called him instead of Alex, Mark, or Ember?

Turning his back on Mark and Harley, he sent Kelsey a text.

U OK?

Her answer came back instantly.

Thank God! I've been waiting. Did you find Tara? Is she OK?

Got her. She's on her way to the hospital. She's been roughed up a bit, but she's tough. She'll be OK.

And U?

Better now. U?

Fine. On my way home. Thx Renner!

We need to talk.

He got a smiley face back for that instead of an answer. But yeah, Renner had questions, and if Tara couldn't answer them, by hell, Kelsey would.

Chapter Seventeen

Alex woke groggy as shit. Stiff. Sore. And still at home in his son of a bitchin' bed.

"Kelsey!" he barked, as in truly, like a dog barked. Not only did he feel as if he'd been run over by an eighteen-wheeler, but his throat hurt like a mother. But Alex was not one to lay around. He lifted to his elbows, assessing how much he ached and where. Damn. Everywhere. Head to toes. But ready to forge ahead nonetheless. Rest was not on his schedule. It could wait.

Someone knocked at his door. "Who is it?" he snapped, instantly regretting the vehemence in his tone while pulling the blanket over his naked ass at the same time.

"Well, I'm not Kelsey," Doc Fitz said as she opened the door and peered into the room, looking every bit like the physician he'd hired her to be. Only she was supposed to be at the office, not here. She worked for him now. "And you, sir, aren't going anywhere, so lay back down and let me take a look at you."

Many tried to boss him around. Few succeeded. But no one called him 'sir.' With the blanket secured at his waist, Alex swung both feet to the floor and growled, "Like hell I'm not. What are you doing here?"

"Kelsey asked me to stop by." She crossed both arms over her chest. "You're running a fever and that usually means you're contagious. Do you want your agents sick on the job? And what about Kelsey and Lexie? Should they feel like crap just because you're too hard-headed to listen to your doctor and stay home?"

He waved her off. "Knock it off, Fitz. I haven't been sick in years. You'll see. Coffee. Then I'm out of here. Where's Kelsey?"

"I'm not leaving until I'm finished."

"Where is my wife?"

"I heard you." McKenna used her doctor voice on him. "She's on her way home with Lexie, who is also running a fever."

"My daughter's sick?" That got Alex's attention. "Since when?"

"I assume since last night. Kelsey said Lexie was fussy this morning. She wasn't running a temp then, but she is now."

Well, damn, that changed everything. "Did I make her sick?"

McKenna shook her head. "More likely, it's the other way around. Two of David's kids have been down with the flu."

Alex stared at the floor, unashamed at his nudity but not willing to share any more with McKenna than he already had. His bedroom was off limits, and he was a Marine, for hell's sake. Not one of those namby-pamby snowflakes who crawled under their desk to whine and cry when things didn't go their way.

"Give me a minute," he murmured.

He liked McKenna fine, but he didn't care to be alone with other women. Call him old-fashioned and he'd kick your ass, but he had a code, damn it. One woman, ever and only, and that woman was Kelsey. Maybe she and Lexie would be home after he showered.

McKenna was smart enough to back off her high-and-mighty doctor schtick. "Great. I'll make coffee."

"I'll make it myself."

She closed the door without arguing, though Alex knew well she'd have a cup waiting for him when he showed his face. Okay then. Shower first. Coffee and a handful of ibuprofens next. That ought to do the trick.

He doffed the blanket and made it to the en suite bathroom on shaky legs which didn't get much steadier after a good hot shower. Too bad. He had work to do and a thriving business to run. Although now that he knew Kelsey and Lexie were on their way back, he considered working at home for the day. What would it hurt? Mark and Harley handled TEAM business whenever he traveled. They were better at some things than he was. But Montego was still at large, dangerous. Today could be the day Renner ended her...

That made up his mind. Alex brushed his teeth, rinsed with mouthwash, and spritzed the men's body spray Kelsey liked over his chest before he hung his towel on the hamper to dry. Striding back into the bedroom, he headed for his closet.

Choosing attire for the day was a no-brainer. He organized his life to be ready for anything at a moment's notice; his closet was the same. Laundered and pressed dress shirts and suit jackets on one side; slacks on the other. Ties arranged by color on the tie rack hung on the door. Socks neatly rolled and ready in the top drawer of the built-in dresser that he'd made by hand. Underwear in the next drawer down. Shoes polished as they should be, arranged by color on the rack beneath the slacks.

Alex selected a silvery-gray shirt, red tie, black slacks with matching jacket. Eagle tie tack. Matching cuff links. In seconds, the closet door was shut, he was dressed, pressed, and ready to take on the world.

All he needed now was to lose these ungodly head- and body aches. Back at his bed, he shook the blanket out, smoothed the sheets, squared the corners on the duvet, and tossed Kelsey's plethora of pillows back where she liked them. With the bed now tight and proper like it should be, he lifted his cell from its bedside charger, stuffed it in his inner jacket pocket, and beelined for the kitchen.

Only Doc Fitz was there instead of Kelsey. Problem easily solved. He palmed his phone and called his wife while McKenna dared him to leave. Only Kelsey didn't answer.

"Kelsey Stewart's phone. Renner Graves speaking."

"Renner? What the hell? Where's my wife?"

"Ah…" Sounded like Renner put his palm over the mic.

Alex strained to hear over his junior agent's poor attempt to shut him up. A different voice on Renner's side of the call declared, 'Dr. Smyth, please come to radiology.' "Are you in a hospital?"

Renner blew into the phone. "Umm, yes. I'm at MedStar Georgetown with Tara. Her ex beat the crap out of her. She's still unconscious."

"When did this happen?"

"Hold on a sec…" Renner mumbled to someone else, "Yeah, he's on the phone now. You want to talk to him?"

The phone got passed and, "Hey, Boss," Mark said evenly. "I've got two agents posted at Tara Tumulty, er, umm, what? Shanahan?"

"Damn it, will you tell Renner to shut up and let you talk? Is that the same woman Renner was with last night?"

Mark chuckled. "Sure thing, but here's the deal. Tara Tumulty's real name is Tara Shanahan. She's been hiding from her ex, and I've placed her under TEAM protective custody."

"Good job," Alex answered. "Did you get her ex? Is he dead? His name?"

"Yes, Renner apprehended the douchebag. Name's Jorge… What?" Again, with the side chatter. "I can't pronounce that. You tell him."

Renner came back on. "He's an ISIL militant from Indonesia, Boss. Name is Jorge… shit. I can't pronounce his last name, either, but he's an asshole. He abducted Tara from Hillcrest Heights this morning. Drove her over the river to what looked like a butcher shop in—"

"What was she doing in Hillcrest Heights? And why do you have Kelsey's phone?"

More humming. More hawing.

"Renner?" Alex growled, not sure who he'd end up talking to next and getting damned tired of being passed around like a hot potato.

Sure enough, Mark came back on the line. "Details are still sketchy as to what happened, at least until Tara wakes up. The man who kidnapped her is Jorge Poer-bat-jar-aka." That was a mouthful. "And he meant to kill her, that much is fact. Renner caught up with him at a rundown butcher shop in Deanwood, only it looked more like a clean-up shop where Poer-bat-jar-aka made people disappear."

"How the hell'd she get tangled up with an asshole like him?"

"Not sure yet, but like I said, we'll know more when we can finally talk to her. You're not coming into the office today?"

"Yes, I am. Later," Alex bit out, tired of talking and his throat raw. "Put Renner back on."

"You bet." Mark handed the phone over.

"Yeah, Boss?" Renner asked.

Alex paused, not sure what was going on, but positive he wasn't getting the whole story. "What were you doing in Deanwood? Or were you also at Hillcrest Heights?"

"Just following a hunch. Had one of those gut feelings Tara might be in trouble, so I, ah, tracked her GPS signal and… Is she awake? Great. Hey, listen, Boss, I've got to go. Call you later."

And the phone went dead as Alex's last frayed nerve sprang to life. Something was up and his men were not giving him the full story. But by then, McKenna leaned her hip into the counter, watching. Her light yellow scrubs made the raspberry streaks in her blonde hair softer. More golden. She really was the prettiest doctor Alex knew, and the best wife for Beau. Until she'd come along, he'd been a royal pain in the ass and on his way off The TEAM. Now Alex was glad he'd kept the young man.

"Don't you have somewhere else to be?" he hinted, his voice gravelly and his throat sore as hell.

She fluttered her lashes as she handed over a steaming cup of coffee. "I'm already on the job. Sometimes I make house calls when stubborn patients refuse to come to me."

Scowling, Alex took the cup, then settled at the table, between Kelsey's chair and Lexie's booster seat. A bottle of ibuprofen sat on the table along with a tall glass of orange juice, a plate of toast and bacon. Damn. McKenna'd thought of everything.

Taking the chair opposite him, she folded her hands in front of her. "Tell me about your headaches."

He would've argued, but if Kelsey was worried enough to have called McKenna, well... *Shit.* She'd already told Doc Fitz everything.

"Migraines," he corrected, swallowing past the steaming lumps of coal in his throat. "I've had migraines for years. Mostly left frontal lobe. Always stress related." He rattled the green plastic bottle of two-hundred-milligram pain meds. "These help." *Now leave me alone.*

"But I'll bet more often than not, they don't." McKenna dipped into her pocket and drew out a prescription pad. "I'm writing you an order for anti-seizure meds. Not that you're having seizures, but this specific drug will ease those migraines. You have how many stents? Two? Three?"

He shrugged. "Enough."

"Hmm. I already know the major stressor in your busy life is your business." Her hand came up, her index finger displayed. "Count with me, Alex. High blood pressure. That's one. Tension-induced migraines. Two. Chronic fatigue. Cardio-vascular issues. Problems sleeping. Probably upset stomach or gut-related issues on a twenty-four-seven basis, an ulcer you won't admit you have, and constant backaches. Am I missing anything?"

By then she showed all ten fingers, which either meant she couldn't count or a couple of those items counted double. There was no sense answering. She'd hit all the high points— or low points, depending on which side of the table you were sitting on.

"Stress is a killer, Alex."

No shit. "Tell me something I don't know." He stared her down. "None of us are going to get out of this alive, Doc. What do you expect? Me to call in sick every time I wake up with a sniffle? Sorry, not happening."

"You've got the flu, Alex, not just a cold, and because of your heart issues, you're a patient at risk. You're running a fever, I can see it in your eyes. Take your ibuprofen now, but I'll have your pharmacy deliver what you need. Which do you deal with?"

Alex shrugged. He didn't have a pharmacy. "Kelsey would know that."

"Of course, she would. Did you ever stop and think that she worries herself sick about you? That maybe you expect too much of her?"

Damn, this woman of Beau's was bossy, and staring her down wasn't working so good. Alex rolled four of the pain meds out of the bottle and into his palm, tipped his head back, and swallowed them with the OJ chaser.

"There," he ground out, wishing to hell the rasp in his voice didn't make him sound like a liar. *Cough. Cough.* "Problem solved. Now if you don't mind, I'm going to work."

"After you eat breakfast. It's the most important meal of the day."

There went those lips again, only McKenna'd pursed them like she was thinking what to say next. Goodbye would've been nice, but Alex knew he wasn't going to get that lucky. Not this time. He really was sick, damn it, with one of the many strains of damned inconvenient flu caused by an insignificant, microscopic bug that doctors and researchers should've found a way to eradicate years ago. But they hadn't, and he felt like shit. That was enough to make him reconsider the home office Kelsey kept hinting they should organize.

Maybe it was time to step back and let younger men play god. Mark and Harley surely handled more than their fair share of meetings and deployments already. Beau had stepped up to fill Mother's role. He and Ember worked together well. She kept him busy and engaged in learning The TEAM's inner workings, when he might have withdrawn into his surly shell again.

Which was more than Alex could say for that ship anchor Tucker Chase had offloaded on him, that Camilla *You-Pronounce-It-Kah-Me-Ah* Brinkman. Ugh, his brain spasmed just thinking about her snotty *I-am-better-than-everyone-in-the-goddamned-universe* attitude.

If she'd been military, he'd have already dressed her down and ripped her a new one. But she was young and somehow fragile and... *Shit.* The woman was a freakin' puzzle he hadn't yet had the time nor the compunction to figure out. People weren't born rude, and Alex knew she was smart. He wasn't about to throw her back. Not yet. He didn't give up on people, damn it. But if things didn't change... If she didn't pull that stick out of her ass and straighten up...

Ping!

The security app on Alex's cell interrupted his mental rant, notifying him that the love of his life was home. Alex sucked in a gut full of relief. Until said love of his life burst through the kitchen garage door with Lexie in her arms and growled, "Don't you dare think of going to work today, Alex."

"But, sweetheart..." He still planned to blow off this temporary illness—cold or flu, it didn't matter. Until he caught sight of his little girl's red face.

Lexie looked like she'd been crying. Her eyelids were puffy and the whites of her eyes were pink. She stretched her arms out for him to take her.

"I want my Daddy," she cried, her voice as scratchy sounding as his. "I sick. My froat hurts and I runnin' a temper-ah-chur." She said that big word like the big girl she was trying so hard to be. "And Mama says we gotta take a nap together or we gonna be gwounded for a week. She mad at me, Daddy. A whole week." Lexie broke into tears the moment he cuddled her inside his arms.

"Mama's going to ground us?" he asked, going for gentle, but he ended up growling like a bear.

Lexie leaned back away from him, her big brown eyes wide and glistening. "I don't wanna be gwounded." She hiccupped. "What's a matter, Daddy? You sound scawy."

Well, yeah. Alex cupped her sweaty head and leaned into her forehead. "That's because Daddy's sick, too," he finally admitted. "Come on, tiger. Let's go find Beagle Boy." Her stuffed, plush raccoon.

"But I want Mommy," Lexie sobbed even as she nestled her sweaty little body into him, her arms tucked between them and her head under his chin.

Man, this was everything Alex had ever wanted when he'd come home all those years ago to an empty house, his first wife and daughter dead and gone forever. Lexie was burning up, and he was such an ass, forever running off to work instead of watching his one and only baby girl grow, eating Oreo cookies with her in the kitchen… Doing all the things he missed doing with Abby. Kelsey was right. Of course, she was.

"I know, baby," he whispered to the child he adored. "I want Mommy too, but she needs to talk with Doc Fitz right now. You want to sleep in Mommy's room with me, or should I bunk with you?" For some reason Lexie had always called his and Kelsey's bedroom 'Mommy's room'. Why wouldn't she? Kelsey was usually the only one there when Lexie had a bad dream or a tummy ache.

"My bed's too widdle!" Lexie bawled. "I wanna sweep with you and Mommy!"

And there it was, as plain and as simple as the cute little runny nose on her adorable red face. Lexie needed her dad, and Alex needed her more than he'd been smart enough to realize. That made his decision easy. Mark could handle Montego. And Montego? Well, she could go to hell.

Kelsey shot Alex a funny look when he lifted to his feet without further argument and retreated to their bedroom with Lexie tucked against him.

"We're, umm, going to go nap, so we don't get *'gwounded,'*" he told McKenna at the entrance to the living room. "Bring baby aspirin when you can get away from Mama Bear over there." He nodded at Kelsey. "Two OJs would be nice. On the rocks. With those cute little bendy straws. You know how we like 'em."

"I do," Kelsey said quietly.

"And something to soothe that sore throat," McKenna added.

"Yeah, well, okay. You're the doctor. Kelsey, McKenna needs to call something into our pharmacy. I told her you handle important stuff like that."

Kelsey broke into a sad smile. "I'm on it, sweetheart. Thank you."

Alex nestled his chin into Lexie's little neck, sick and tired but doing it at home for a change. He and Kelsey would talk later, after Doc Fitz left. He would ask how she'd gotten that dark bruise on her cheek. It wasn't there last night. *What'd she run into at work? A wall?*

Chapter Eighteen

Renner leaned over Tara, needing to see those pretty eyes open again and clear. Needing to hear her tell him that she would be okay even though he knew she wasn't. The slice on her neck was long but minimal. Her ex had only made a superficial cut. The ER doctor had glued it shut, but the others on her arm were deeper. They'd required stitches. Over a hundred. Her bastard ex-husband had scraped off a good portion of her cat tattoo as well. That couldn't be stitched but was sealed at the moment with the same kind of glue. As a result of those combined injuries, she'd lost a lot of blood. For now, bags of saline and type-O IVs hung at her bedside.

Besides being dehydrated and hypothermic when she'd arrived, she had a concussion. The side of her head was swollen and bruised. Renner felt like shit that he hadn't taken Jorge down quicker, especially after he'd seen the clear signs of torture. He should have. Tara's ex was not only a dangerous man, he was a sadist. And he would die in the near future for what he'd done to Tara if it was the last thing Renner did.

But now, like Alex, Mark wanted specifics. He started out slow and kind. "You need stitches."

"Nah, I'm good."

"You want anything to drink? You hungry?"

Renner shook his head. Mark was just making small talk before the inquisition. Warming up. *Batter, batter, batter…*

"Precisely how long have you known Miss Shanahan?" And there it was. The sneaky fast pitch.

"Already told you. I bumped into her at McCormack's last night shortly after sundown." Renner tapped at his cell screen for the current time, realizing it had been another long day without sleep. Not that he was worried. Days like this one were a given in the Corps, especially for scout snipers, when a guy laid for days in the sand or the mud just for the chance to end a designated tango. "That makes it a half hour later than the last time you asked." He didn't look at Mark when he said that. Either Mark believed him or not.

"She's not just a cat burglar, and that man she married on a drunken whim in Colorado is not just *some* terrorist." The big guy sucked in a belly full of air, then slowly blew it out before he said, "Jorge Poerbatjaraka is a recruiter for ISIL. Right now, he's working for the American turncoat who changed his name to Ahmed Al-Yousif, and who now lives in Syria under the protection of the current POS regime."

"Yeah, I know. Ember told me."

Mark leaned into Renner's space. "He's in Washington, DC, Renner. Right now. Al-Yousif is in our town, only he didn't arrive on any transatlantic flights that we know of, which means he either came down through Canada or up from Mexico."

That got Renner's attention. "Are you thinking he's planning an attack?"

"That's exactly what he's planning, but before you run off and do something stupid, relax. The FBI's got this one and, just in case, I've also got Connor and Hunter watching him."

"You know where he is?" Incredible. Some terrorist from the Mideast came to town and The TEAM was on him like white on rice. But Renner couldn't catch a blood-thirsty serial killer from Cuba on her second whirlwind tour of the District.

"Of course, we know where he is," Mark continued in that calm, calculating tone he used when he talked to Alex. "I'm going out on a limb here to say something I never thought I would or could say about the FBI…" He cleared his throat. "But I trust the particular FBI office that's handling Ahmed Al-Yousif's threat. Director Tucker Chase is all over this creep's ass, and his people have already taken custody of Jorge Poerbatjaraka. We are officially off the case. I understand how you feel. I'd want to kill the guy if he hurt Libby, too. But you are not to go after him for any reason, understood?"

That was another thing. Mark now pronounced Jorge's surname easily.

"Good, because tonight I've got better things to do. I'm going after Montego. Once and for all, that bitch is going down."

"What I don't understand…" There went that steady, patient tone again. "… is how you knew where to locate Miss Shanahan."

"Because she called me," Renner said to the empty space between him and Tara. Which wasn't true at all. Kelsey was the one who'd called him, and she'd been frightened enough for Tara that she'd screamed in his ear. Renner'd never heard a woman scream like that. But he wasn't about to tell Mark anything that would lead back to Kelsey.

"Okay, but then what? She didn't know where she was. The police found blood evidence that she was inside Poerbatjaraka's trunk. There was no way she could've known where he'd taken her, and…" Mark held up one hand. "…before you tell me you tracked her GPS signal, understand that I've already spoken with Ember. You did not request an assist from her to track any cell, and it can't be done with a random third-party number you pulled off your caller ID. You know the technology behind GPS tracking, the network of twenty-four USA global positioned satellites transmitting information back and forth to receivers on earth. Triangulation, Renner. Zeroing down on one specific cell number is all about latitude, longitude, and altitude—but that's only if four or more of those government operated satellites just happen to be in view of the designated cell you want tracked at the same time. Maybe Ember could pull off something like that, but you plain and simply do not have high enough Department of Defense clearance, her network of contacts, or her level of expertise, to get it done."

Renner turned a half-smile on Mark. By expertise, Mark meant Ember's ability to hack into most secure sites on the entire planet. "I'm insulted. You telling me I'm technically challenged?"

"I'm telling you I need the whole story."

And there it was. The real reason Renner couldn't leave Tara. She didn't need some gentle, good-looking giant coaxing the truth out of her when she finally opened her eyes. Renner didn't yet know what that whole truth was, only that he needed to talk with Kelsey before Mark talked with Tara.

Because things weren't lining up. Kelsey had been with Tara at Hillcrest Heights, and Tara had been using Kelsey's cell phone when Jorge struck. But why were they there and who were they meeting? For that matter, why wasn't Kelsey at Raymond's Kids home for runaways like she should have been? He'd checked. That was the first place he'd called once Tara was safely in the ER. He'd had questions for her then, but her staff said Kelsey had left early, that she had a pressing engagement that couldn't wait. Somewhere between eight-thirty this morning and noon, Kelsey was not where she should've been. Instead, she was across the Anacostia River in a mostly African American, rundown section of Maryland. Doing what?

He now knew Tara worked for Kelsey, a tiny piece of intel Tara could've shared with him last night, yet hadn't. Why not? Yes, she'd admitted she worked at a halfway house for runaways, and maybe she hadn't intentionally concealed who her boss was, but most people would have been forthcoming about insignificant details like that. Unless...

Was it possible Tara was not who she said she was? Could she be part of her ex-husband's terrorist scheme? Was the beating he'd given her a clever misdirect? A ruse? Just part of their plan to gain Kelsey's sympathy? To get inside The TEAM?

Weary, Renner ran a hand over his face, scrubbing extra hard to get the cobwebs out of his mind. No. He'd seen the real Tara last night. She was no terrorist, and he was an ass, a tired ass, for letting his cynicism run away with him. Not every shadow was an assassin in waiting, and not every pretty woman had a bomb strapped to her belly.

But until he knew precisely what Tara and Kelsey were mixed up in, Renner refused to out them. Neither of them were idiots, nor were they untrustworthy. Besides, Kelsey was not one to take risks. That she'd put herself in harm's way to protect Tara from her ex said a lot about her. Kelsey was loyal to a fault. Unfortunately, the window to contact her at home and ask those questions had come and gone. Renner wasn't about to disturb Alex. Uh uh. Let sleeping dogs lie and all that…

Yet Renner couldn't stay with Tara any longer. He needed to check in with Ember on Montego's whereabouts. That was his primary mission. He needed to get back on the job. Mark had made a sound decision assigning Junior Agents Seth McCray and Beckam Garner to watch over Tara. Renner liked and respected those men. Seth was a man you could always count on to always do what was right. Beckam had only been with The TEAM two months. The former Army Ranger was green to the ways of civilian life, yet eager to work with the legendary Alex Stewart. Seth and Beck were a good match. Both Army, and both rock solid.

Yet he didn't want to leave.

"You're not going to tell me, are you?" Mark asked quietly.

Renner shook his head. "To be honest, I'm not sure I know. But I need you to trust me."

"Never said I didn't. Just wish I knew how to help."

"Then don't let Tara out of your sight for a minute," Renner said quietly as he lifted to his feet and watched her breathe. Man, her poor face. "She needs an ice pack."

"You're right, I'll talk to the nurse and make sure she gets one."

"Keep her safe."

"Copy that," was all Mark replied. "We're in the home stretch, Renner. It's up to you now."

"Great. No pressure. Thanks for that."

"I'm serious. You're the only one who can bring Montego down. So do it."

Renner looked into Mark's eyes then. "Thanks, Boss."

Yeah, Tara couldn't be safer.

Chapter Nineteen

With Tara under armed guard, and Alex out of his way for the day, Renner aimed for Roslyn and McCormack Industries once again. But traffic on the George Washington Memorial Highway was thick. He was barely within sight of the Lincoln Memorial on his right when Ember's call came over his hands-free.

"Renner," he answered, braking as traffic ground to a full stop yet again.

"I couldn't disobey Mark," she led with.

"What are you talking about?"

"About you not asking me to track your friend-who-is-not-a-client's GPS. If I'd known what was happening..." She choked. "If I'd known she was in trouble...I'm so sorry. I would've helped. I would've covered for you."

"Stop. How could you have known what I didn't even know?"

A sniffle came over the connection. "I will always help you, Renner."

"I know. Anything else?" Some disgruntled driver had just careened into Renner's lane. He didn't mean to sound curt.

"Yes. Jed's holding a press conference in an hour at the Russell Senate Rotunda. Can you be there?"

Renner growled. "I'm headed in the opposite direction. It's a parking lot, but yes. I can be there. What the hell's going on in this town today?"

"The usual. A three-car accident with a bus south of the Lincoln Memorial. A peaceful demonstration on immigration in front of the White House." That explained the traffic.

"A demonstration this time of day?" It was late afternoon and already getting dark with the approaching storm. What were those people thinking?

She chuckled. "Hey, I just pass the news along. It's not like I approved the permit for that parade."

Unfortunately, Washington, DC attracted every agitator and do-gooder in the country, and they all wanted to be seen, either by the press or the president. Hopefully, this demonstration stayed peaceful. Which meant the Mall would still be overrun with thousands of people and the streets choked with vehicles. Trains would be jam packed and buses overflowing. Metro PD would have roads closed and enough on-site police presence to choke a horse.

Dodging another belligerent driver, Renner cranked the wheel and performed a lightning-quick illegal U-turn that led him to the roundabout on the Virginia side of Arlington Memorial Bridge. There was more than one way to get into town. "I'll be there," he told Ember as he headed southwest. "Any more missing military I need to know about?"

"Yes," she said somberly. "Another Marine from LeJeune last night. He's just nineteen."

Renner's fist hit the steering wheel. "Damn her. You know what we're dealing with, don't you? Montego's a son of a bitchin' reincarnated female version of Ted Bundy. She's just like him, doing the most despicable things and then laughing in our faces!"

"You're right. She is a sadistic sociopath. Did you know Bundy confessed to committing thirty homicides inside of four years back in the seventies? But authorities believed he killed more. We'll just never know all of them."

"Bundy didn't just kill women," Renner murmured. "The creep decapitated at least twelve of his victims. They found a dozen severed female heads in his apartment."

"And he revisited his victims' decomposing bodies—"

"No," Renner hissed. "He didn't."

"Yes, he did. Until putrefaction made it impossible for him to… you know… those poor women. How on earth do people stoop that low? How do they get so sick to even think of something like that? I don't understand."

"I honestly don't, either." Renner sighed as he bypassed the I-395 turnoff into the District and headed farther east for the next bridge across the Potomac. It was plenty congested as well, but flowing smoothly at the moment. In minutes, he'd be at the Russell Senate office building on Constitution Avenue and C Street—unless a demonstration was happening there as well.

"Oh, oh, Alex is on my other line. Talk to you later. Bye."

"Copy that," he replied as Ember disconnected. The farther from the mayhem at the White House, the less traffic. Renner parked on the street east of the Russell Senate Building, then walked the rest of the way. He arrived just as McCormack's sleek black limo pulled to the curb on Constitution Avenue.

Most days, McCormack would have waved a cheery hello and headed straight over to shake his hand and ask after his mom. Jed was like that. He knew all Alex's agents by name and he treated them like friends. He considered himself one of the guys.

Not today. The second he spotted Renner, he jerked his head in the opposite direction. Yet Renner knew he'd made eye contact with the guy. The clever witch at McCormack's side hadn't seen him, though. In fact, it seemed McCormack had purposefully positioned himself between Renner and Montego, she on his left, Renner still walking distance away at his right.

He hung back and blended in with the frantic mix of reporters, cameramen, and assorted media hounds that attended press conferences like this. To keep on his senior agent's good side, Renner tapped his Bluetooth earpiece and phoned Mark. A sitrep ought to make him happy.

"Houston."

"I'm following McCormack into the Russell Senate Building. He's holding a press conference. You know about the kid Montego abducted last night?"

"I do. We're not certain she's behind Private Demarais' disappearance, though."

"You're kidding me, he's just a private? Not a stripe? Not an E-3? Did he just step off the bus?"

After arriving at LeJeune on said bus, the young men and women who joined the Marines attended basic training. By the time they graduated, they'd earned their rank of private, E-1, no stripe, no rank insignia. At that point, they were the lowest grunts in the Corps. Their one and only job was to do what they were told, how they were told to do it, and when. Most automatically advanced to PFC, private first class, E-2, one stripe, within a month, then onto lance corporal, E3. But some did not…

Mark sounded weary. "That makes seven since Montego returned."

"This kid's disappearance fits her MO though, right?"

"Yes. He went out drinking last night with his buddies. Didn't show at reveille this morning."

Renner knew the USMC CID, the Marine Corps Criminal Investigation Department, was deeply involved in tracking Montego, as well as NCIS, the Naval Criminal Investigative Service, the FBI and Homeland Security. That a smaller business like The TEAM had been called in to assist spoke to the desperateness of the situation and to their reputation for getting the tough jobs done. But Montego had to be stopped sooner rather than later.

"You heard from Alex again?"

"Not since we last talked. Kelsey said he and Lexie are down with the flu, that he won't be in at all today."

"Good. You do realize that I could end her here and now. Montego," Renner murmured, tracking the seemingly happy couple past the media gaggle, through the lobby and toward the rotunda, his sight on the killer at McCormack's side. "Just say the word, Boss, and America's latest serial killer will be red mist."

"That's twice you've indicated you'd end someone without due process," Mark replied testily. "Are you telling me you're ready to be judge, jury, and executioner? Have you acted on that impulse before?"

"No, but I am here," Renner drawled, "and we both know—"

"We both know America is founded on the point of law, junior agent. On law and order. We are better than scum like Montego. That's what sets us apart from every other country on earth. We do this by the book or we don't do this at all. Am I clear?"

Renner nodded, undisturbed by Mark's vehemence as he ducked out of sight from Montego's piercing, roving gaze. The woman certainly had her head on a swivel. It was as if she were expecting someone. Her sharp black eyes were surely searching.

"See, that's the difference between you and me, Mark. Some victims can't wait for justice to get around to serving them, and I will do what needs to be done even if it lands me in prison."

"You're off the case," Mark snapped. "In fact—"

Renner interrupted with a chuckle. "Not yet, I'm not. Hang on. McCormack's got the mike." Whether Mark liked it or not, Renner disconnected, but kept his finger on the call button. Mark would be back online any second now. He'd be pissed, but Renner had pissed off higher ranking officers before.

Jed McCormack stepped up to the podium amidst glaring lights on tripods and into the media frenzy just as a ballsy male reporter called out, "Hey, LuAnn! Look this way! Smile for the camera! That's it. Yeah!"

Damned if she didn't smile and parade-wave back at them as if she were the First Lady. Strings of jade gems glistened around her neck, drawing attention to the plunging neckline of her shimmering green gown. Renner couldn't see through the crowd to identify her style of footwear for the occasion, but he guesstimated platforms or stilettos since the top of her head usually met Jed's shoulder. Flat-footed, she stood a little over five feet tall and would be hard to keep track of in this crowd. But damn, could she preen.

That a woman as small as she was had performed heinous tortures against more than a couple dozen men, only illustrated the strength of the army behind her. During her last visit to the States, she'd brainwashed nearly twenty men. Some young. Some older. But all military and all tortured until they believed everything she said and did what she told them to do. They were the manpower behind Beau's kidnapping. An old friend of Alex's had been involved in that crime. Gave an entirely different slant to the phrase 'power of a woman'.

McCormack tapped the mike, lifted his chin, and looked into the camera. "Thank you for joining me here today," he said. "Sorry for the last-minute invitation, but I wanted you here as I announce what I hope will be a long and fruitful association with one of my dearest friends. Please help me welcome Mrs. Kelsey Stewart, the woman behind the District's successful home for runaways, Raymond's Kids."

A smattering of applause followed Kelsey as she stepped out of an adjoining hallway and up into McCormack's extended arm. Dressed in a simple black dress with a classic string of white pearls on her neck and matching pearl studs in her ears, she smiled shyly at the reporter.

Renner tapped Mark's cell number and got a terse, "Damn it, Graves. If you ever hang up on—"

"Did you know Kelsey was going to be here with McCormack today?" Renner asked.

"Kelsey's there? Why?"

"Not sure. He said something about a long and fruitful association. It has to do with Raymond's Kids. Hold on…"

"Mrs. Stewart has never once flagged in her support of the District's most vulnerable runaways," McCormack declared. "As you can imagine, many homeless have flocked to her, and

I can safely assure you, they chose her because of her open-door policy and because of her kind heart."

McCormack paused and straightened his tie. "She has never turned anyone away nor will she. Kelsey is the epitome of what America used to stand for. She has welcomed the weak and the lost, the destitute and the frightened, and in doing that, she's accomplished what each and every one of us should have done. It is with pride and, dare I say—love?" He looked down at the woman on his right. "I do love you, you know."

She glanced up at him, nodded.

Jed continued, "Today I'm donating five million dollars to Raymond's Kids. I sincerely hope this small gift will ease, if not eliminate, every last one of Mrs. Stewart's financial woes."

Montego craned her neck to see around him to the woman Renner suspected she saw as her competition. Either that, or she knew precisely who Kelsey was. But Kelsey faced forward, never acknowledging Montego was in the same room.

"He just gave Kelsey a hefty donation. Five mil," Renner told Mark.

"But why? He already supports Raymond's Kids," Mark said. "He's her biggest donor."

"And now he owns the place," Renner muttered, still out of sight behind an array of bright lights focused on the podium.

"Will that money help you stay afloat?" McCormack asked Kelsey.

She blinked up at him. He gazed down at her. For a moment there, it seemed time stopped. The press waited. Montego glared past Jed's broad shoulders again. He stood there with both Kelsey's hands in his, his eyes bright and clear, looking like the gallant billionaire he used to be.

Poor Kelsey honestly looked as if she'd been crying. Her tongue slid over her bottom lip. She blinked up at him, then said, "I miss her, Jed," quietly, but loud enough every microphone in the place picked it up.

The room stilled, and Renner held his breath. McCormack shook his head, the movement almost imperceptible as if he were shaking off a gnat, as if he hadn't understood what Kelsey was talking about. Either that or—he had.

Once again, the giant of a man seemed to age before Renner's eyes. His lips thinned and his energetic demeanor flagged. He paled, and the wide gregarious smile he was known for, faded. He coughed, broke eye contact with Kelsey and stared over her at the audience.

"Which is why I'm doing this. My wife adored Kelsey Stewart. Lois always wanted to throw her support behind Raymond's Kids. We've… we'd talked about opening a halfway house to help those lost kids for months before…" The muscles in his jaw ticked. Jed seemed to be struggling to stand upright, and for a moment, Renner thought he teetered. But then he gripped the podium, cocked his head, and murmured into the mic, "I'm just sorry Lois couldn't be here to see this today. She'd like to know all of you care about the homeless as much as she does, ahem, I mean did."

Kelsey ran her index finger under her eye, and Renner knew she was crying. It was strange seeing her up there by herself, the timid housewife without the fearsome bodyguard she'd married hulking at her side, ready to rip apart anyone who dared come too close to her. And God help them if they hurt her feelings. Alex would waste them. She seemed so much frailer without him at her side. So small. So pure in comparison to the skank at Jed's other side.

By now Montego's bright smile to the press seemed strained, as if she'd had enough of this charade.

"Th-thank you, Jed," Kelsey said humbly while she turned to face the television camera. "On behalf of all my runaways…"

Jed adjusted the mic so everyone could hear her. She cleared her throat and tried again. "I'm sorry. I'm not usually the one who gets to talk to you guys. That would be my husband. You remember Alex?"

"Yeah, but we'd rather listen to you!" some brash reporter bellowed amidst the guffaws and murmurs that broke out in the rotunda at the mention of her proud man's name.

Everyone laughed. Everyone but Kelsey. She looked like a bird caught by a bunch of hungry cats.

"Ahem…" The poor thing cleared her throat again. "Thank you so much, Mr. McCormack, for always supporting me and my work. And thank you all from the bottom of my heart for giving Raymond's Kids a chance. I love all my kids, and I know you do, too."

Damn, that woman had Alex beat when it came to courage. Renner swiped the corner of his eye when Kelsey bowed her head. Her cheeks were bright red by then, and he was pretty sure she was hyperventilating. She was so out of her league.

McCormack hugged her into his side, and whispered into her ear. Several cameramen stepped in close, capturing Jed with Kelsey while Montego gazed up at the ceiling like she had better things to do.

Kelsey nodded at whatever McCormack was telling her.

"Well?" Mark asked.

"Well, shit," Renner hissed. "I know damned well something's up now. Kelsey just told McCormack she missed his wife. He damned near lost it. He loved his wife, Mark. I know he did. It's written all over his face."

"Then why's he sleeping with that bitch?"

"Good question. Just a sec…"

Kelsey had just retreated down the same hall she'd come from. Montego's lips were twisted. Her eyes were hard and bright, and McCormack's hands were palms forward to the press.

"Don't go, there's more," he exclaimed. "You're all invited to the official ribbon cutting ceremony tomorrow night at Raymond's Kids. On top of that little donation, I'm building a new wing for Mrs. Stewart. You can see the complete scale model. It'll be fun!"

And just that fast, the last of Renner's faith in Jed McCormack evaporated. He'd just transformed from a savvy businessman who missed Lois, to a wild-eyed octogenarian with dementia—or something—coming on strong.

"What do you say to that?" he asked the media, his eyes as bright as a five-year-old's on Christmas morning. "I'm in the mood to play Santa. There's your byline, people. Kris Kringle strikes the District!"

Renner looked away, sad to be witnessing the decline of a giant like McCormack. America was losing another hero.

"She's awake," Mark said quietly.

"Tara?"

"Yes. She won't talk to me, just keeps asking for you. When are you coming back?"

Renner could not help the smile that creased his lips at that info byte. Go figure. Tara wanted him and only him. *Atta girl.* "Not sure. I've got something to do tonight, and it can't wait. But I will stop by as soon as I'm done. Tell her that, would you? And just so we're clear, I'm not going rogue, Mark, and I'm no vigilante. My mouth just gets away from me sometimes."

"Mine too," Mark admitted. "Trust me, I've wanted to end a few bastards in the past, too. I've had a couple in my sights. We've just got to be better than criminals like Montego, Renner. We owe all the men she's killed that much."

"You're right." Renner blew out a sigh. "That's why we do what we do."

"Stay in touch."

"Always, Boss. Always."

Chapter Twenty

The things Renner most loved about Washington, DC, were the steady magnetism of the world's most dynamic city, the draw, the allure, and the drama. The twenty-four-seven lights and the Black Hawks flying stealthy and low, perpetually on the prowl overhead, ever faithful as they protected their president and the capital. The energy that emanated from thoroughfares and by-ways, even after business hours in December. And the winter weather. One year it might be seventy degrees at Christmas time in the District, the next year could bring a white-out that shut the city down.

By the time the reporters stopped asking McCormack questions, Kelsey was long gone. Renner headed to his car. The last glimmer in the sky to the west had turned dark, and the storm that had stalled off the East Coast had finally arrived in all its wet, soggy glory. Snow covered his windshield, but it was a mantle of slushy gray instead powdery white. He scraped it off with the edge of his hand, climbed into his car, and pulled away from the curb.

Cranking the defrost to high, he watched through his rearview mirror as McCormack's limo turned north, headed toward the Union train station—or wherever. As long as he and Montego weren't going straight home. Renner needed another stab at that penthouse and a look inside McCormack's bedroom, this time without the interference of a certain cat burglar. Only then would he allow himself a quick combat nap, preferably at Tara's side. Maybe some bland hospital food, too.

Back on the GW, he made good time. Traffic was light this time of night and in this weather. Across the river, Jefferson's Monument glowed like a golden sentinel. Beyond that masterpiece, the Washington Monument declared America's rebellious spirit for the world to see. Further along the riverbank, the John F. Kennedy Center for Performing Arts was dark for a change.

Hooking right onto the exit for I-66, he coasted off the overpass and into Roslyn. The roads weren't slick, just wet and messy, but it was enough to discourage other drivers. When Renner passed McCormack Industries, a touch of melancholy sneaked up on him. MI was still the lighted complex of a proud, patriot. Jed had always been the common man's best friend. He'd only ever advocated for stronger armor, better weaponry, had even dabbled in CGI-type outfits that could make every soldier and some combat vehicles, invisible. Every grunt knew his name and his rep. He should've run for office; he would have won.

But now…

The lights that used to glitter at MI's grand entry seemed dim tonight. It would be a sad day for civilians and military alike when McCormack stepped down. Witnessing the slow demise of a great man was just plain distressing. Renner parked his ride a block south of Crazy Eights, disgusted all over again at Montego and what he was sure she'd done. The woman seemed invincible, as if she were not only above the law, but as if she delighted in destroying one of America's heroes. And his wife…

Renner hurt for his friend. McCormack was just a tired old man being used by a twisted witch. Renner wouldn't be surprised if Montego sacrificed babies in some kind of devil worship ceremony. She was that kind of ugly, evil, and cruel.

Renner passed the street that led to his mother's place. He didn't have time for dinner tonight. Come to think of it, he hadn't eaten all day. What he had to do couldn't wait. Like before, he easily accessed McCormack's high rise, then took the elevator up to the penthouse. He wasn't certain what he was looking for, but he knew he had to try. Mark was right. Everything depended on him.

Unfortunately, he found himself in McCormack's Japanese garden again. Yeah. Lack of food and sleep did that to a guy. He'd no more than turned on his heel to go back down a level, when he heard a noise somewhere off to his right. The trailing vines hanging from every branch in the place shifted in the now chilly breeze, casting shadows from the soft glow of the pagodas. Someone had opened a window. WTF?

Stealthy now, he crept toward that singular sound, his senses on high alert and his pistol in his hand. His boots made no noise. He stepped around one of the palm trees and...

There she was. Tara. Damn it. All decked out in her black wingsuit. One foot planted on the windowsill. One hand palming the window. A bag strapped over her shoulder.

He lowered his firearm. "What the fuck are you doing here, woman? Are those diamonds and crap that important to you?"

She whirled on him, her usual tight black cap concealing her hair. Tiny black climbing shoes. Velcro straps instead of laces. The only thing different tonight was the Lone Ranger mask and the whites of her eyes staring out from it.

"Damn it, this has got to stop, Tara. You… Wait a minute. I just talked to Mark and…" *Tara's in the hospital.* His pistol came back up. "You're not Tara! Who the fuck are you?"

Her chin came up—just like Tara's. Whoever she was, she turned her face into the breeze coming through that open window—just like Tara. Still no answer. But then she looked down...

Tara would not have done that.

"Move away from that window," he ordered, advancing one cautious step after another, his boots positioned sideways, not making himself a bigger target than he had to. "Give me the bag. Hand it over."

She made no move to comply, and he had to assume she was armed and had already pilfered McCormack's penthouse. But what were the odds that two cat burglars would have come after those jewels within a day of each other? The coincidence didn't gel.

Renner cocked his head at what he thought he was seeing. What he thought he knew. Same outfit. Same measurements. Same height, weight, same everything. Hillcrest Heights. Tara's borrowed phone. The odd coincidence of Jed's gratuitous donation, Kelsey's unexpected appearance at the Russell Senate Building. Her quick retreat. It couldn't be...

"Kelsey?" he asked, not believing it, but yeah. Who else could it be?

The cat burglar balanced on her perch, ready to fly, and Renner knew in one second, he could lose her. He holstered his weapon. "Does Alex have any clue you're up here?"

She no longer needed to deny or confirm. He knew she was as scared now as he'd been last night. That was why Kelsey looked down. She wasn't good at just dropping off tall buildings and flying away, either. Damn. That happened just last night. What a day.

Renner offered his hand and lowered his voice. Smooth and easy. "Come on, Kels. Hop down. I'm not going to tell Alex. Maybe I can help."

She hesitated.

"Come on, don't cry. Stop biting your lip." He fluttered his fingers at her, not daring to take his eyes off her for a second. "And were you born in a barn? Shut that window. You're freezing Jed's pretty garden, and you're letting snow in. You're also scaring the hell out of me. Come off that ledge. Please? Get down, honey. I do not want to be the one who gets to tell Alex I let you fall to your death. That's what you're afraid of, isn't it? Dying? That Tara's stupid wingsuit won't work in this cold weather?"

Her fist went to her mouth, and Kelsey slinked off the ledge to the floor.

Renner ran to the window and closed it, bolting the decorative handle before he turned to her in the dark and blew out a breathy, "Jesus Christ, you—"

She crashed into him, her arms around his neck and her heart beating like crazy. "I had to do it," she breathed.

"Do what? Scare the shit out of me?" he half-chuckled even as he held onto his boss's sweet wife. She was freezing. Shaking almost as much as he was. Jesus! "What the hell, Kelsey? What are you doing up here? Does Jed know? Is that why you're here? Are you trying to save him or something?"

She shook her head, panting, her mouth opened into an 'O' as she sucked in breath after breath, trembling with adrenaline. "I... I..."

"Settle down," he said encouragingly. Gently. "It's okay. It's just me and I don't bite. Take as long as you need to catch your breath. We are in a meditation garden after all."

She stepped away from him then, her fingertips tapping her chest. Off came the cap, releasing her chocolate tangles. Damn, it was hard not to fall in love with this daring woman.

"I'm so glad it's you," she finally said. "I thought maybe it was…her."

"Who? Montego? Nah, she and McCormack took off together after the press release ended." Which left Renner with an ugly taste at the back of his throat. McCormack was once again alone with that bitch. Tonight could be his last. Maybe Renner should've been tailing him instead of sneaking in here again. Yeah, no. Kelsey might have done something really crazy stupid then—like fall.

She turned on her heel to the still waiting elevator. "Quick, Renner. We have to get out of here."

"Then let's go," he agreed as they ran onto the waiting elevator. "How'd you get up here?"

"I have Jed's code."

Renner smirked to himself at that. Didn't everybody?

He pushed the button for the ground floor and the doors closed.

"Oh, hurry," Kelsey breathed, watching the floor numbers diminish as they dropped lower and lower. "Hurry. Please hurry."

"Only a few more to go."

"I've never done anything this stupid in my life," she hissed. "Oh, man, hurry!"

Renner put a hand on her shoulder. "Not stupid. Maybe brave, maybe daring." She shot him a wild look and he had to laugh. "Okay. You're right. Stupid."

"But I had to do it. You'll see. It had to be done."

"And you are going to tell me precisely what had to be done as soon as we get out of here, understood?"

Her head bobbed. "Yes. Oh, yes, yes, yes."

The poor thing was close to hyperventilating. "Breathe, Kelsey. Just breathe."

"Can't this elevator go any faster?"

They were on the ground level by then. Renner put his hand on her back as together they hightailed it out of the elevator and away from the penthouse. She all but ran across the street, and Renner followed close behind, keeping watch on his surroundings. Not going to lose track of Kelsey. "Three blocks east, take a left," he called to her.

She nodded as she began jogging in that crazy wingsuit. Had to be Tara's. That had to be what was in her bag also, a change of clothes. At last out of sight and safe inside Crazy Eights, she headed for the women's restroom with her bag, then returned wearing just a sleek black tank and matching running pants. No jacket.

"Man, you look like someone I know."

She nodded. "Yes. Tara Tumulty. She's just my size."

He frowned then. "Except for that bruise on your jaw…"

Kelsey pressed her palm to her cheek but offered no explanation.

"You were at Hillcrest Heights with her," he stated, now sitting in the same back booth he'd shared with Tara only the night before. "And lose the act, Kels. I know she's Tara Shanahan. Tumulty was just a good Irish name."

She nodded. "Oh, good, I'm glad you know. Yes, I was with her at Hillcrest Heights. She had my phone because we were talking, and she needed to make a call, but then…" Kelsey licked her lips, then pursed them, still breathing hard. "All of a sudden, her ex showed up. He must've been following her, but he hit her, and when I tried to stop him, he punched me and…" Another trembling breath. "He had a gun, Renner. I thought I was going to die, but by the time I got to my feet, he and Tara were gone. I had to run to the strip mall on the highway to use their phone to call you."

"The creep who took her is a very bad man, Jorge Poerbatjaraka." Renner signaled his mom, holding up two fingers for two glasses of water—or beer. He was okay with whatever she brought, but he suspected after the way he and Kelsey had run past the bar to the very back booth, his mom would know what they needed.

"You're right. It was Jorge." Kelsey dropped her head onto her folded arms on the table. "Oh, Renner, what am I going to do? Alex already knows I've been up to something. I can't hide this mess from him forever."

"Speaking of Alex…" Renner debated asking. He already knew the answer, just not all the details. "Wasn't one of his USMC buddies caught up in this mess with Montego way back when?" Better question, had Montego contacted the guy since she'd come back into America? Was he assisting her now? And just how much did Kelsey know?

"Yes. Aaron Pope. She took off the fingers on his left hand. Left his thumb, that poor man."

"What happened to Pope? Wasn't he charged as an accomplice?"

Kelsey shook her head vigorously. "Oh, no. Alex retained a good lawyer, and Aaron ended up on probation for a year, and I…" Her tongue ran a quick lap around her mouth. She sucked her bottom lip in, then licked it before she bit it and said, "I gave him a job. No one would hire him, Renner, and he's suffered so much. He didn't want to stay with his parents, and honestly, they didn't know how to help him. So yeah… I gave Aaron a full-time job. He's not a convicted felon and…" Her head was bobbing by then, either trying to convince Renner or herself, he wasn't sure which. "He's, umm, seeing a good counselor at the VA, and he's honest. He works hard. He stays in one of the dorms that we, that I—"

"Well, be still my Irish heart," Renner's mother drawled as she offloaded two glasses of water, two mugs of beer, and her usual giant bowl of pub mix to the table. "'Tisn't often me boy visits me two nights in a row, and with two different but very lovely ladies at that. Good to see you again, Mrs. Stewart."

"Brenda. You run Crazy Eights?" Kelsey fussed with her hair like women were prone to do. In a bun, it had more tendrils spiraling out of it than pins could hold together. "I had no idea. I must look a wreck."

"You look as pretty as ever," his mother said, "and yes, I actually own this place. It keeps me busy now that the kids are grown and on their own. What'll you be eating tonight, me darlings?"

"Thank you, but nothing for me," Kelsey answered. "I have to get home."

"Just the drinks, Mom." Renner made a sweeping gesture with his fingertips, hoping she'd take the hint and walk away before she started asking questions he wouldn't be able to answer.

"But you haven't been eating right, son. I can see it in your eyes."

Which he rolled to high heaven. There was nothing to do but match her nosy questions with dead silence. After a few seconds of that, she knew to mind her business. Brenda sauntered away, grumbling about wayward sons and disobedient children, lucky stars and Killarney, though what one had to do with another, he never knew.

"She's worried about you," Kelsey whispered once they were alone.

"Yes, and she's a good mom," he admitted as he sipped from the nearest frothy mug. "Just a little bossy sometimes and wishing she had a dozen grandchildren, which isn't going to happen unless Mo gets married again. Now talk. You had to do what?"

"You'd make a good father," Kelsey whispered, her gaze off-track on his mother at the bar, listening to some other more obliging, weary soul's problems.

Renner huffed and held up his left hand. "In case you haven't noticed... No ring. No girlfriend in sight. Not going to happen."

"But I am right. I can tell."

He shrugged at that womanly prognostication thing that all women did. "Stop distracting me. Come on. Out with it. Why were in you Jed's penthouse?"

She tugged her bag off her shoulder, unzipped it, and pulled out a large, flowery cosmetic bag. "Here," she announced like he already knew what it was. "This is all the DNA you need."

He opened the zippered bag. "This is Montego's? You were in Jed's bathroom? You took her... her..."

"The bag's mine, but I took some of her stuff, yes," Kelsey murmured. "There's hair from a brush in there, old lipsticks and tubes of face cream, deodorant, a toothbrush. I even dug used tissues with lipstick on them out of the waste can. Cotton swabs, soiled fresh wipes, and icky cotton balls. Even nitrile gloves in one of the bottom bathroom drawers. I'm sure there's plenty of dead skin cells inside those fingers, maybe more. How much DNA do you need to convict her?"

Ah, so that's what this was about. Renner hated to let Kelsey down, but he told her anyway. "That's not how it works. This is all fine and good, and I'm sure there's plenty of DNA on everything you collected. Most of it might even be Montego's, but now of it's admissible in—"

"Stop it," she snapped. There was fire in her eyes. "I know the laws on illegal search and seizure, Renner. Don't patronize me, and don't treat me like I'm stupid. Don't you get it? This alone isn't good enough. I know that, but I have faith, and now you guys have got something to compare against the real evidence you're going to find. Most of this is garbage. You can say you dug it out of the trash receptacle; I certainly did. I have faith in you and Alex and everyone on The TEAM. You guys are the best. You *are* going to find evidence to link Montego to every despicable thing she ever did. You *are* going to bring her down. And when you do, this—" She held the bag out to him and shook it. "—this will help you nail her skinny ass to the wall."

It was hard not to grin at this ferocity of Alex's woman. What he wouldn't give to see the day Montego got what she had coming to her. Better yet if it came at Kelsey's hand.

"She does have a raunchy, skinny ass," he deadpanned.

But all this DNA was useless. It certainly proved Kelsey's heart was in the right place, but there'd be plenty of time to get Montego's DNA after the medical examiner picked her brains off the sidewalk—or wherever she was when Renner ended her. Which he meant to do.

DNA was not the problem. Everyone had it. Finding it at her crime scenes was the challenge. And now that she'd moved in with McCormack, she'd isolated herself yet again. Her DNA was all over his suite. Even in his bed.

"She's an asshole," Kelsey shot back at him, "and I'm sick of people like her using America's courts and justice system to hurt good people. For all we know, she's torturing another Marine or soldier right now, damn it. It's not right, and this whole ugly mess is killing Alex. You may not know it, but he blames himself every time anything goes wrong. That's why he's sick. He's wearing himself out trying to fix everybody. If I could... Oh, I'd strangle her myself before she hurt anyone else."

Renner had to smile. It was only hours ago that he'd offered to shoot Montego on sight, legal or not. Made it difficult to fault Kelsey for her energetic belief in her husband and in him.

"You're something else, Mrs. Stewart," he said evenly.

She shook her head, sending more tangles cascading out of that messy bun onto her shoulders. Alex lived with a queen. There was no other way to describe her. Made a man humble and proud to be serving good people like Kelsey.

Her eyes brimmed. "I'm an idiot is what I am. I've used my husband's business helicopter without his knowledge. I've told him more half-truths this last week than I have in our entire life together. And my baby's sick. I should be home taking care of my family instead of up on some high-rise playing *Wonder Woman*."

Which reminded Renner. "Tara taught you to fly, didn't she? That's why you two were over at Hillcrest Heights. You were practicing—"

"Ha! Practicing, nothing. She pushed me! From the top floor of that derelict building!" Kelsey leaned over the table toward Renner. "Can you believe that? I'm not sure I would've been brave enough to try that wingsuit if she hadn't pushed me, but still. It was a loooong way down, and I'm such a chicken when it comes to flying. I think I screamed. I still can't believe I did it."

Renner leaned over his clasped fingers. "I'll tell you a secret. She pushed me, too."

"She did?"

He nodded. "Yes, she's gutsy, I'll give you that. And there was no way I was taking one step off that building. I hate flying, too."

"Oh, what am I going to do?" Kelsey wailed. "I've lied to Alex. That alone will crush him."

"You haven't lied. You've protected him the same way he protects you. Stop worrying, Mrs. Stewart. And may I say you handled the press today like a polished pro?"

She had the grace to blush. "They're not so bad."

Renner had a different opinion, but, good enough. If Kelsey liked the press, so be it. "Now let's get you home before the boss realizes you're gone and calls in the Marines to come find you. For today, just tell him about McCormack's generous offer. Alex knows about that, doesn't he?"

"There is that," she agreed. "But no, I just found out about it today, and I didn't call Alex to let him know, in case he or

Lexie were sleeping. But now I have to be back at work first thing in the morning to get everything clean and ready. Jed's planning a bigger presentation at Raymond's Kids tomorrow afternoon. The governor will be there, more national news outlets, and…" She rolled her eyes. "I have floors to wash. I don't know how Alex deals with all this stress."

"He doesn't. That's why he's got migraines and the flu. His body's trying to tell him something. Let's hope he listens this time."

Kelsey's head bobbed. "You're right. Oh, Renner, thank you. Like you said, I don't know if I would've jumped tonight. But that witch might have caught me in the act if I hadn't. I'm glad you showed up."

He shrugged. "Showing up's just part of the job, ma'am. But Kelsey…" He needed her to look at him.

She did, her brown eyes still full of worry for all the things she couldn't keep from happening. "Yes?"

"Your secret's safe with me, understood? You tell Alex in your own way what you've been up to. If you decide to never come clean, trust me. I've got your six. I won't tell."

Her lower lip quivered. There was that tender, frightened look in her eye again.

He frowned. "Don't do that, *Wonder Woman*. Please, don't cry. Be brave just a little longer. This'll be over soon."

"I'm not brave," she whispered tearfully. "All I wanted to do was help Alex and you."

"And you have," he insisted. "Now let's go home. Do you want to keep your bag of evidence with you or do you want me to hang onto it?"

Her fingers hadn't stopped clutching the bag since she told him what she'd done. "Would you?"

"It'd be my pleasure," he replied as she handed it over. "Now where'd you park?"

"I didn't. My car's still over in Hillcrest Heights. After I finally found a phone, I didn't want to walk all the way back, so I called a cab to drop me off at Reagan where I could fly home."

He didn't so much as smile, wink, or frown at that very illogical line of reasoning. She'd been back and forth between the District and home twice today? Here was a woman intelligent enough to tangle with Montego without getting caught, yet she hadn't realized it would've been easier if the cabbie dropped her at her car back in Hillcrest Heights instead of driving her across the river to Reagan National Airport where she had no vehicle.

By then Kelsey was chewing her cheek. "I know what you're thinking."

"Don't know what you're talking about." Renner lifted his brows, not thinking anything, not admitting nothing. No ma'am. No way. Just waiting to find out if he and Kelsey were the same kind of dumb. After all, the same woman had pushed both of them off very tall buildings. He was smart enough not to point that out, either. Big sister taught him well.

"You're just like Alex. He knows when to keep his mouth shut, too." She almost sounded wistful. "That was pretty dumb, me going to the airport instead of back to my car, huh? But I was upset, and I was worried about Tara and, oh, hell…"

Renner understood perfectly. Post-traumatic stress victims, like Kelsey, tended to live with bouts of anxiety that short-circuited their logic cards. He would know.

"My car's near here," he interrupted before she teared up again. "Let's walk. And while we're walking, I'll have Ember do her thing and delete any trace of that cab ride."

For the first time, Kelsey drew in a cleansing breath and blew it out through her mouth in a big sigh. "Wren? Is that what your mom called you? Wren, like the bird?"

He smiled at the sound of that endearment on her lips. "Yeah. I was a preemie. Wasn't supposed to live. Only weighed a pound and two ounces when I was born. Doctor told Mom I wasn't going to live, to make burial arrangements. She told him to go to hell. Said I looked like a tiny bird. All mouth. That a kid with a mouth as big as mine was definitely going to live."

Kelsey didn't get the joke. "And look at you now. She must be so proud."

He nodded, embarrassed, but yeah, just as proud of the feisty, Irish woman who'd only ever had his back as his mother was of him. "I lucked out," he admitted. "Now let's get you home. If you want, I'll go inside with you in case Alex has questions."

Kelsey shook her head, the stress gone from her face and the glow back in her eyes. "Thanks, but I'm not afraid of Alex. He's my best friend. Let's go."

Chapter Twenty-One

Tara blinked up at him, biting her lip and determined not to let this hulking brute make her cry. He'd introduced himself as Renner's friend, Senior Agent Mark Houston. He did have kind and gentle brown eyes. But she didn't know him, and she didn't care how important he thought he was. Senior agent, huh? Like that was supposed to mean something to her? It didn't.

She was done trusting men she didn't know. That and he kept asking her probing questions about Jorge. He wanted names and details, who Jorge worked with, and if she knew where he'd been staying in the District. He wanted numbers and addresses, descriptions of known associates, all that stuff. As if Jorge would've told a mere woman anything.

Tara knew she was in bad shape, but this guy made it sound like she wouldn't be allowed to leave the hospital unless she cooperated, and that wasn't fair. She hadn't done anything wrong, other than marry a bastard and then get caught and nearly killed by him. But Mark What's-His-Name was big and imposing. The sheer size of this guy intimidated her, and Tara didn't know why. He hadn't hurt her, and he hadn't actually threatened her, and…

Oh, hell. Renner. She wanted Renner. He'd know what to do.

"Can I get you anything?" the gentle giant asked from the chair across the room where he'd taken up residence.

"Kelsey," she murmured. "Is… is Kelsey okay?"

"As far as I know. Why wouldn't she be?"

"Just…" *Just what? Wondering? Blowing Kelsey's cover? Just giving her secret away to the first guy who comes knocking?* "Just, umm, need to tell her I won't be in today."

"You work for her?"

Why couldn't he just leave her alone?

Kelsey leaned back into the passenger seat and closed her eyes. Renner turned on his favorite guitar instrumentals and let her sleep the entire ride west. By the time he pulled up to the Stewart's security gate, she was awake, if she'd slept at all. Her evidence bag with all her stolen DNA lay on the back seat, but Renner was dog-tired.

"We're back. Nice digs," he offered as she opened her door and put one foot to the ground.

Kelsey grunted. "Nice? You've been here before. It's a mansion, Renner. A big stone mansion."

He had nothing to say about that. Most folks worked all their lives to live in a grand mansion. Kelsey didn't seem to be one of them. She made it sound more like a prison.

"You still sure you don't want to be inside the gate where it's safe before you get out of the car? It's only fifty more feet."

She shook her head. "Like I told you last night, I'm plenty safe. Besides, I'm sure you'd jump out and save me if someone tried to grab me before I made it to my front door."

"'Course I would. Now go put some ice on that pretty face. It'll help keep the swelling down."

Kelsey huffed. "But it'll never hide the bruise. Thanks for the ride. For everything else, too."

"You bet," he replied as she closed the car door and approached a smaller gate to the right of the drive. The gate opened at her approach, which meant there was some kind of security app behind the locking mechanism that identified her biometrics—or something.

Once at her door, Kelsey didn't look back at Renner or wave, just opened her home and entered with her head held high. He wished her luck with her devil dog husband. But if Alex ever caught Jorge, there'd be hell to pay.

The drive back to Tara seemed long and tiresome. Renner stopped for a bottled water and a footlong at an all-night sub-sandwich shop before he hit the hospital. By the time he spotted Seth and Beckam in the hall outside Tara's door, it was early morning and he was pissed all over again at McCormack. The man was a moron to have fallen for Montego's lies. Jesus. Even Tara could see through her. Why couldn't Jed?

"Hey," Seth said. "You look like shit warmed over."

Renner lifted both shoulders when Seth's eyes scrolled over his arm to the sandwich shop bag. "Sorry, I should've brought something for you guys."

"No need," Beckam replied, nodding to the nurses' station three doors down. "They've been taking good care of us."

"Mark still here?"

Seth nodded. "He's inside with your girl."

"She's not my girl, understood?" Renner needed that out in the open.

"Ah huh. If you say so."

He would've argued, but what was the point? Seth jumped up to get the door, and there she was. In bed. Sound asleep. The lights were turned down low. Her monitor beeped, quietly tracking her stats. Mark Houston lay sprawled out, sound asleep in the recliner in the corner, the footrest up and his head back.

Renner set his meal for the day on the table beside the recliner. "Hey," he whispered as he bumped Mark's shoulder. "You're sleeping on the job."

"Yeah, well…" Mark stretched and yawned. "I've got serious back-up in the hall, so I'm not worried. You here to stay?"

"Yes, for a couple hours."

"Good, I'm outta here." Mark stood with another yawn, his arms over his head aas he arched his back.

"Your wife been in yet?"

"Yes, but Tara was still out then. Libby will be back first thing in the morning."

"She say anything?"

He shook his head. "Only that she wants you."

"I get that a lot," Renner deadpanned, his gaze on the too quiet woman lying on the bed. Tara seemed pale. He'd expected more color in her cheeks, not that ghostly pallor. "She on pain meds?"

"Won't take them. Libby ordered something to help her sleep, though."

"Good. She's had one helluva day."

"You too," Mark pointed out. "Want me to call a doctor for that bruise on your cheek?"

"Nah, I'm good," Renner said because, well, he was good now that he was back with Tara. He hadn't known he had a bruise until then. "McCormack's holding an official ribbon cutting ceremony at Raymond's Kids later this afternoon. Governor's supposed to be there. National news outlets, too."

"Great. Did he invite the damned president, too?"

"Why not?" Renner muttered as he dropped into the recliner and flipped the footrest up. "Seems like he's invited everyone else. We need to be prepared. I've got a gut feeling. Montego's been quiet too long. She's going to make her move soon. Might be today."

Mark stopped with his palm on the door. "And…?"

"Like I said, it's just a feeling. But think about this. In the last twenty-four hours, I've watched McCormack come undone when he thought vandals were messing with his wife's grave, then again when Kelsey told him she missed Lois." Renner blew out a long sigh as the hard day caught up with him. He leaned his head back into the padded recliner pillow. "Honestly, for a second with Kelsey, I thought he was going to fall apart. You should've seen him. It was like the world stopped or something. As if…"

Renner stopped talking then, but yes. Jed had looked into Kelsey's eyes as if he'd wanted to tell her something. And he had told her something, something confidential that not even Montego could've heard. Renner just hadn't remembered to ask Kelsey about it until now. He scratched the headache blooming between his eyes, pissed at his forgetfulness but intent on keeping his promise to her if it killed him.

"Where is Kelsey now?" Mark asked.

Which struck Renner as oddly amusing. Both he and Mark seemed more worried about Kelsey and Tara than the elderly man they'd been assigned to protect.

"Home," Renner said before he had a chance to think twice.

"And you know that how?"

Oh, shit. "I know that because where else would she be this time of night?" Renner growled back at his Senior Agent. "What do you think I am, a mind-reader?"

Mark shook his head, then wiped a hand over his eyes and yawned again. "Where's Jed?"

Renner shrugged. "How would I know? The dumbass ran off with Montego as soon as the media circus ended."

"You didn't tail him?"

"I can't very well get into his penthouse if I'm tailing him all over town."

Mark huffed. "But he knows we're there to help him. Alex told him."

"Then why doesn't he keep us better informed? I've wasted most of my time tracking his sorry ass and waiting for him to show at McCormack Industries or at his penthouse. Hell, it's easier to follow Montego than him."

"So why aren't you?"

Renner cast his eyes over Tara. "Because Jed isn't the only one in trouble, Boss, but he sure as hell is the only one who seems intent on dodging us."

Something wiggled to life at the back of Renner's mind at that very obvious fact, but before he could grab onto the gist of it, before he could make it real and tangible, the thought slipped away into the fog of too many hours without enough sleep or food. Shit. He hated losing a hint or whatever that feeling was. But yeah… A clue… It might've been a clue.

He'd almost conjured the slippery thing back into his higher consciousness again when Mark said, "I'll be working the event at Raymond's Kids with you this afternoon. Get some sleep. Shave. Grab a shower. We'll need to dress appropriately."

"You mean in a tux?" And flash. The elusive clue—or whatever it was—vanished for good.

"If the governor's going to be there, yes. You do have one, don't you?"

"I can rent one."

Mark rolled his eyes. "You don't own your own?"

Well, that was just plain rude. But Renner let it go. "Later," he said to hasten Mark's departure. "Yeah, don't worry. I'll be there in a tux. You want tails with that?"

Mark shook his head on his way out. "Hell, no. Night, Renner."

After the door hissed shut behind him, Renner climbed to his feet and doffed his biker jacket. He took a quick hit off that flask, then pocketed it and went directly to Tara.

With all that red hair tumbled over the pillow around her, she looked like a pale, fragile, and very battered angel. Exquisite brows arched over closed eyelids that were now bruised and puffy. Long, lush lashes lay like velvet on her colorless cheeks. Yet even with the butterfly bandages over her brow, this was the most peaceful she'd looked in their twenty-some hours together.

He tipped his mouth to her poor forehead and murmured against her skin, "I'm back, babe. You're still safe. No nightmares tonight, okay? Sleep easy."

She groaned as if at some deep level she'd heard him.

Renner went back to his post, popped the cap off his water and settled down to his one meal of the day. Pastrami on rye never tasted so good. He'd barely crumbled the wrapper and stuffed the debris from his midnight snack into its paper bag when his angel stirred.

He hunkered low in the chair, needing her to go back to sleep. They both needed rest.

Tara lifted to her elbows. "Renner?" she whispered in his direction.

"Yeah, it's me." Hurriedly, he dug for a mint from his pants pocket, then brushed the crumbs off his lap in case she needed anything.

"Is Kelsey safe? Did he hurt her?"

"I just drove her home. She's fine."

"No, she's not. She's going after that Montego woman. You have to stop her. Hurry. Please. She can't fly tonight. It's too cold and the storm... Wait. You did what?"

"I drove Kelsey home," he said more deliberately. "Your ex punched her, but she's not hurt, and trust me, she's not going anywhere but to bed."

Tara pushed the blanket off and swung her legs over the edge of the bed.

"Hey, hold up. Let me—"

"No," she told him. "Stay there. I'm... coming."

Renner did as she asked, aching to help her if she'd let him get close, yet willing to let that decision be hers. Abuse victims could be touchy about, well, being touched. He didn't want to force her to do anything until she was ready.

But come to him she did, dragging her cords, wires, and IV tubing with her. He lifted his hands when Tara cocked one knee on his thigh, then climbed over the armrest and onto his lap. The bed was close enough he was able to stretch over her and grab her blanket. And there he was, a tired but happy man with this particular woman in his arms again, her bare bottom warm on his thigh and her breath in his neck.

"There," she breathed softly. "This is better."

"Your nurse won't like it," he told her quietly. "You should've stayed in bed."

Tara made an odd crying sound in the back of her throat. "Who cares? I don't like hospitals. Guess that makes us even."

Renner spread the blanket over her long, bare legs and under her butt. He tucked it around her shoulders and draped it under her chin. "There now. You hungry?"

Her head bumped a definite 'no' under his chin. "You… you were there. You saved me."

"Yeah, well. Wish I'd gotten there sooner." He smoothed a hand lightly over her shoulder, careful not to hurt her, but firmly enough she knew that he knew where she'd been injured.

Her fingertips tapped nervously on his collarbone. "Never thought anyone would find me. Thought I was going to die. He was so mad. I was scared."

Renner debated how much to say, but figured Tara already knew how things went down. "Kelsey called, and said you had her phone, and, well, I tracked her GPS signal. Thank God for that, or I never would've found you."

"He was going to kill me."

Renner nodded. "Yes, he was."

"Did you kill him?"

The pain in that question crushed Renner all over again. "No, FBI has him in custody."

She buried her face in his neck and cried, "You should've killed him."

And Renner wished he had. Encircling Tara inside his arms, he cradled her shaking shoulders against him, rocking to soothe her. To stop the crying. He'd do anything to end the nightmare she was caught in.

"It's a good thing I didn't kill him like I wanted to," he murmured, keeping his voice soft and low. "Now we can catch the mastermind behind your ex. Jorge has something to do with a terrorist threat here in the District."

"But I hate him," she whined like a sad little girl who just wanted her way. Which was what she'd probably been long before Jorge-the-bastard came into her life and crushed her under his boot.

Renner closed his eyes. He was fast falling for this spoiled princess who'd learned one helluva lesson at the hands of a murderer. But because he was his mother's son, Renner gave Tara what she needed more than that rat bastard's death. He gave her hope.

"Soon, baby," he crooned, his lips in her hair and his honor at stake. "As soon as this thing with Montego's over, I'll go after What's-His-Name, and I'll end him. I promise. For you I'll do anything."

"Jorge," she cried as if Renner didn't already know, "his name's Jorge Poerbatjaraka-ka-ka."

Which wasn't precisely accurate. But close enough. "I know, baby. Trust me, I know."

Renner nearly smiled at the petulant woman falling quickly back to sleep in his arms, and at the *'ka-ka'* she'd ended her weary rant with. Jorge most definitely was a piece of shit.

She might not remember this conversation or climbing onto his lap. But Renner would. Because he never—ever—made a promise he couldn't keep.

Chapter Twenty-Two

Tara snuggled into the heat of her all-male comforter, loving the feel of Renner's powerful arms around her sore body, the hard man beneath her bruised rump, and the scent of his breath in her face. But she loved the other scents that came with Renner as much. Leather. Whiskey. Mint. And ever since that first chance meeting—wind and freedom.

What she really wanted was to sneak out of this hospital room and run back to her loft. She didn't have a catheter, but her body aches kept her from being crazy. Resisting the urge to run home, she burrowed under the blankets to that warm dark place where she could hear Renner's heart beating. It never faltered, never skipped a beat. Just kept her anchored. Grounded.

For the first time in a long time, she was comfy warm and truly safe. Secure. She'd met Renner's friends who were guarding her door, Seth and Beckam, both big, strong, and handsome men. They'd come into her room and introduced themselves last night when she woke up. But they would never let her leave this morning. And Mark? Tara was sure he was still in the hospital somewhere waiting for her to make a break for it. Watching her. She didn't really mind. Now that she'd knew her doctor Libby Houston was his wife, Tara realized Mark wasn't so bad. He was just being annoying in a big brotherly way.

Inhaling a deep cleansing breath, she let it out slowly. She relaxed. She finally had what she'd been searching for all those hard years of early morning practice on the slopes, all those twisted knees, bruised buttocks, sore throats, and long cold days. She had a guy who loved his mom and who treated Tara like a lady. Even when she pushed him off tall, tall buildings…

The corners of her mouth quirked remembering. Her tongue slid over her lower lip recalling the heat in that first kiss. Renner did know how to kiss, and he'd tasted male and delicious, of beer and pub mix, steak and more beer. Tempted, she ran the tip of her tongue up his throat, breathing the musky, sweaty heat of him in. She closed her eyes, wondering where her clothes ended up. She vaguely remembered the emergency room. Flashing lights. Worried voices. And then she woke up to Mark Houston. Not her finest moment.

But then, he wasn't her favorite guy, was he? There was still Kelsey to think about though. She'd go after Montego, but to do that and be successful, she'd need Tara's help. Kelsey was not ready for a solo flight. Even if she were, it would be smarter if she had a partner at her side in case anything went wrong. Not that Tara followed her own advice, but the world wouldn't miss an Olympic wannabe. They would, however, miss the savvy woman who ran Raymond's Kids.

So yeah. Tara eased away from her happy, safe place and—

"Stay," Renner ordered groggily, which had a surprising effect on her body. Ordinarily being told what to do turned Tara's stubborn spine to titanium. But the way Renner said it, all soft and deep and achingly slow, slipped straight to her core.

She melted onto his chest again, loving the feel of his muscular arms tightening around her, wishing she could simply stay inside his embrace and forget the rest of the world. This was why she liked him. He made her believe in herself again without pushing too hard. He made her hope. And she'd rewarded him by shoving his cute ass off a building... Yes, she'd noticed. He might have been scared, but he'd also listened and did what he needed to land safely. And he did have a nice taut backside.

Tara drew in a deep breath. "I have to go to work today."

"Oh?" he asked, his eyes still closed. "You mean at Raymond's Kids? With Kelsey Stewart?"

She turned coy. "You knew?"

His shoulders lifted. "Course I knew. But no, you're not going anywhere. You have one more day of hospital time. They're keeping you for observation. Twenty-four more hours... if you're good."

"If I'm good?" That made her smile. She let her fingers walk up that magnificent chest. To his neck. To the scruff on his chin. Man, just breathing him in was turning her on. "When did you figure it out?"

"Ah, let me think." His big, capable hands slid down her back, tangling with the ties at the back of her—

Oh, no! I'm in a stupid hospital gown. Naked!

Tara stiffened, but Renner must've sensed her unease. Of course. How could he miss? She'd all but turned into a board that he was even now massaging into compliance and warmth and... lust? The way his fingers cupped the cheek of her ass— helped. Tara tipped her upper body into him, rubbing against his pecs. His belly. His cock.

From that once in a lifetime moment at McCormack's penthouse window, she'd been attracted to this guy. He'd been a virgin to windsurfing then. Yes, he'd certainly thought he was going to die, but now... here... Tara wanted to lay down and die with him. Wasn't that what an orgasm with the right man was called, a glorious mini-death of meteoric proportions? A bright and sizzling star in the darkest night? Wasn't that what happened when two people fell in—

No. This was not love. She'd been dumb once. Never again.

Until he growled, "Come here, you," and tugged her into his mouth.

Tara wanted him. There. Now. It might not be love, but with all her cuts and bruises and sins and crimes, she still wanted him. The only thing standing between them was…

"Kelsey," she murmured into his luscious open mouth. Against his lickable lips. Breathing hard, she told him what she had planned never to reveal. "Kelsey's in trouble. She's going after Montego, Renner. She means to kill her."

His hands never hesitated, never loosened their tight grip on her ass. "Kelsey's fine. Trust me. She's good."

"But how…?" His tongue arrowed along the seam of her lips and she opened, thrilled at the gentle but thorough way he took over the kiss, one hand now circling her neck, the other palm still warm and firm, kneading her rump as he made love with her mouth. Her tongue. Oh, man, yes. "How…? But Kel… Kel…"

Ah, he was kissing the hell out of her. She couldn't think! But when his hand slipped from her butt to her core… When his fingers slipped between her legs… Into her body… When he found that tiny spot of sweet release…

When he groaned…

Tara gave in to the fast-as-lightning spike of crazy hot pleasure spiraling through her battered body. "Renner," she gasped, not thinking, just feeling. The pinch where it mattered.

The nibble of his teeth on her chin. The rub and friction of his whiskers against her sensitive skin. The wet gush of heat and heaven and bliss and...

"Ah," she growled into his neck, wanting to scream his name without his friends in the hall hearing. But yes. Shouting 'Renner!' to the stars was all she wanted to do. He held her a little tighter as she drifted back into herself. Still clenching. Still throbbing. Still aching and wanting so much more than this singular, stolen rush of two hearts beating as one.

Strung tight, she let the shock waves coursing over her body hold onto his fingers even as she knew this was not the time or place to return the favor. But man, oh, man, oh, man. He had no idea what this little petting party meant to a woman who'd been raped and forced to endure the vilest humiliations under the guise of sacred matrimony. She'd honestly never wanted a man to touch her again. Yet here Renner was. Ever gentle. So careful. He'd slipped past her defenses like the wind. There'd been no time for worry or all those awful what-ifs. He'd given only pleasure. And not once had he hurt her during her quick rise to the stars.

"You're crying," he murmured, his head ducked low to peer into her face.

Tara shook her head, embarrassed yet thrilled, shocked yet infinitely serene. How all those contrasting emotions fit together had her wondering if she'd gone bi-polar overnight.

She ran a finger under her leakiest eye, wiping the drip before it got away from her. "It's just that..." How could she tell Renner how much this small indiscretion meant? That he'd given a measure of her femininity back. That maybe she wasn't broken or ugly or a worthless whore after all. That she could finally face her demons and heal. Maybe even—live. Look people in the eye again. Did she dare? "It's just that you seem to see right through me. All the time. You know what to say."

By then she was face to face with her gorgeously handsome male *friend*. Renner cut a dashing figure after sex, or whatever this was. His mussed hair was even more mussed. His face glowed. She wanted to run her fingers over his head just to watch him smile. His five o'clock shadow gave him a rugged, dangerous appeal. But the soft light in those dark blues... The small smile quirking his lips... Lips she wanted to bite and lick...

"Are you going to live now?" he whispered, his voice the soft, sexy purr of a contented man who knew how to take care of his woman. He *had* hit all the high spots. She wasn't anyone's woman, yet she could see this man being in her life. Somehow. He would be a hot mess to wake up to every morning. Under the covers. Or on top. Maybe just for as long as it took to bring Montego down. That'd be nice. Maybe longer. But maybe not.

"Are you?" she asked, ashamed at the quivering fear in her tone instead of the bolstering confidence he'd given her.

Renner nodded, never blinking. "Yes, ma'am."

That was all. Just *'yes, ma'am.'* Just ultra-polite and genuinely tender. Even falling to what he'd thought was his death, he'd never cursed, fought or denigrated her. He'd simply grabbed hold and he'd held on. He'd fallen with her.

Tara smiled then. At last, it felt like she had her life back.

Chapter Twenty-Three

Alex wouldn't wake up. Kelsey held her palm to his chest. He was barely breathing. Her worst fears were coming true. Frightened now, she placed a quick 911 call, then rang McKenna, all while she planted Lexie at the kitchen table in front of a bowl of cold cereal. With her cell phone tucked into her neck, Kelsey listened to McKenna's voice mail, then left a panicked, "I need you. Hurry! This is Kelsey. Something's happened and Alex isn't breathing right or enough. He won't wake up. I don't know what to do."

"I hewped Daddy," Lexie mumbled proudly around a mouthful of something fruity and probably loaded with too much sugar.

"That's nice. You're such a big girl," Kelsey answered, her mind on Alex and her heart pumping furiously even as she forced a calm demeanor for her daughter's sake. "Stay here and eat. I'll be right back, okay, sweetie?"

"Ah huh. I a big girl cuz I hewped Daddy." She'd been saying that a lot since she'd helped Alex at Arlington. Lexie adored her father, and no, just no! This couldn't be happening. It was too soon! He was still young and virile and… "No!" Kelsey growled at the heavens as she flew back to his side. "No! I refuse to let him go. Please don't take him from us."

Alex lay silent on his back on his side of their bed, still in a ratty old USMC t-shirt and gym shorts, his usual pajamas, one hand on his chest. Still not drawing in air like he should. He looked peaceful enough, but the dying were just as peaceful and quiet.

"God, Alex, not you, too," she cried as she pressed her ear to his chest, tears flooding her vision. He didn't seem to be in any pain or distress. He just wasn't breathing right. Too slow. So shallow. She could barely hear him. "I need you, baby. Please! Don't die!"

She couldn't beg hard enough. Her tears fell like rain. When she'd come home last night, Alex had already been asleep. But he'd been sick, so she hadn't worried. He was a stubborn man, and he always refused to rest when he should. It was bound to catch up with him.

Diligently, she'd checked his forehead for a fever, put Lexie into her own bed, then snuggled into bed with Alex, spooning like they always did. He'd grumbled something about Renner, but then he wrapped an arm around her, again, like he always did. Kelsey told him she loved him, that they needed to talk, and they both fell asleep.

But when her alarm rang this morning and Alex was still in bed…

When he didn't answer when she asked him if he was going in late…

When she couldn't wake him…

She ran her fingers over his hard head and through his hair, measuring the loss staring her in the face against their too few years together. They needed more time. More lovemaking. More everything!

It seemed like forever before her security app pinged a notification. Thank God! McKenna was here. Kelsey ran to let her friend in.

"Tell me what you know," McKenna ordered, her voice stern and professional as she marched down the hall to Alex.

"Alex doesn't seem to be in any pain. He's not pale. No temp this morning or last night. He just won't wake up and he's not breathing right."

"Has he fallen lately? Any head injury I don't know about? Dizziness? We need to talk about concussions one of these days. Has he had any?"

"None that I know of, not that he'd tell me. Usually, it's the other guy who gets concussed."

"Could be nothing," McKenna assured her before she palmed the bedroom door and strode purposefully to Alex's side. "Let's not panic, okay?"

Kelsey bit back a cry. She was way past the point of panicking. This fierce, bossy, arrogant man was everything good in her life. Alex and Lexie. If she lost either of them...

McKenna had brought her doctor bag with her, which caught Lexie's eye. She scampered in and right away climbed up beside Alex and told McKenna, "I hewped Daddy," in her big girl voice.

"You did? Well, aren't you the good girl?" McKenna asked as she checked his eyes, ears, nose and mouth, then told Kelsey, "No sign of blockage. Airways are clear."

Lexie nodded, her cute little lips puckered into a pout. "He was firsty and I hewped." She wiggled when she said that. So proud. So much the light in her father's eye.

"Oh, that's nice." McKenna's stethoscope centered on Alex's chest, her head canted as she listened. "Kelsey, please hand the pressure cuff to me. Should be at the top of my bag."

"And Mommy says always hewp Daddy cuz he's the best Daddy I got."

"I called 911," Kelsey breathed as she handed the cuff over. By then her hands were shaking. This couldn't be happening! How would she live without Alex?

Lexie craned her sweet little head, peering sideways at Kelsey. "You sad, Mommy? You wanna dwink?"

"Yes, baby. Mommy's thirsty. Run and get me a drink." Kelsey ran her fingers through her hair, frantic to help McKenna but not medically trained. She felt so helpless!

"You're going to pass out if you don't settle down," McKenna warned as Lexie toddled off. "Honestly, I'm not hearing a heart arrhythmia, there are no signs he's had a stroke, which, and I have to be honest with you, was my first suspicion. But now that I see him…" McKenna ran her practiced hands over his forehead and down his neck. Over his shoulders, pressing the glands under his arms, then his spleen. "I'd say we're looking at a terribly fit, healthy man, who's worked himself to a state of exhaustion. Course he'd argue that diagnosis if he were awake."

"Here, Mommy," Lexie announced, a glass of orange juice in her hand. "I hewpin'."

"Oh, yes, baby, you're Mommy's best helper." Kelsey tossed the drink back, then choked. She couldn't get into the bathroom fast enough.

"What's wrong?" McKenna called as she followed.

Kelsey couldn't speak. She was leaning over the sink with two fingers stuck far into her throat until… *Cough, cough. Choke, choke.* Up they came. Two orange juice tinted tablets hit the porcelain.

Breathing hard, Kelsey picked them out of the sink, then dropped her backside to the edge of the tub, her eyes watering as she stared at those tablets in her palm. Suddenly everything made sense. "Lexie. Come here, sweetheart."

"Okay," Lexie called out in her innocence. "I coming!"

McKenna frowned at the damp tablets in Kelsey's palm. "Do you know what those are?"

"I think so," Kelsey replied as she pulled Lexie onto her knee. She surely hoped so. "Did you give Daddy medicine today?"

Her bright brown eyes lit up. "Yes! I hewped him. I'm a big girl."

Which was probably exactly what Alex had told her. They both praised Lexie when she followed through and when she thought of others.

"Oh, baby," Kelsey cried as she hugged her precious little girl. "Yes, honey, you are such a good big girl for helping Daddy, and I know he's proud of you. When did you help him?"

"This mornin'," Lexie announced proudly. "He was coughin' and he was firsty and I hewped."

"Did you give him the same medicine you gave me?"

"Ah huh."

"How did you reach the bottle these tablets were in?"

"Wiff a stool. It's easy. I show you."

Kelsey followed her precocious daughter out of the bathroom and back into the kitchen. She and McKenna watched while Lexie pushed the stool against the counter, climbed up, then walked carefully across the marble countertop to the cabinet alongside the refrigerator—where Kelsey and Alex kept all medicine, vitamins, and over the counter drugs. Which, until today, they had both considered childproof. Not anymore.

Teaching moment. Kelsey lifted Lexie off the counter, her heart still pounding but relieved now that she knew what happened. "Sweetheart, this cabinet is only for Mommy and Daddy, okay? Remember how only big people can drive cars and take the dogs for walks?"

"And buy peppamint ice cweam?" Lexie beamed, bouncing in her mother's arms.

"Yes, big people like Mommy and Daddy can buy peppermint ice cream. Well, baby, this cabinet is also only for Mommy and Daddy, okay? You mustn't touch anything in it again."

Lexie frowned. "But how kin I hewp Daddy if it's only for big people and he's firsty and I not a big person yet?"

This little girl was always thinking. "Then you come and tell Mommy that Daddy needs something, and I'll help you. That way we can both help Daddy."

She shrugged. "Okay. Kin we get ice cweam now?"

"Maybe when Daddy wakes up." Kelsey wanted to cry. If only the world's problems could be solved with peppermint ice cream. "Do you remember how many tablets you gave Daddy?"

"Fwee." Lexie held up three fingers.

"But you only gave me two," Kelsey said, needing to be absolutely sure.

"But he's my Daddy, Mommy, and he's bigger than you and me." Lexie shook her head like that was a no-brainer, and Kelsey should already know that. "He needed more than just two, Mommy." Was there a hint of condescension in that three-year old's sassy answer?

McKenna's toes were still tapping. She did not look amused.

"Melatonin," Kelsey said just as her security app sent another notification that she had more company, most likely the paramedics. "Lexie gave Alex melatonin, and knowing him, he knocked it back without realizing what was in his orange juice. Like I almost did."

"Ah, huh," Lexie confirmed. "An' he told me I was a real good girl, too."

McKenna held out her palm. "Where's the bottle?"

"Right there!" Lexie pointed. "I put 'em back where they belong like good girls should."

Kelsey rolled her eyes, trying not to cry as Alex's and her words came back to bite her. "We taught her to do this," she murmured to McKenna. "This is our fault. We've taught her to clean up after herself and put things back where they belong."

"You're right," McKenna said after she used a steak knife to half one of the tablets Kelsey had coughed up. "Same shape. Same color inside. Same letter on what's left of the icon on the exterior. Thankfully you threw them up."

"And now I have an ambulance and paramedics in my driveway." Kelsey felt like she was the one who needed emergency first aid.

"I'll deal with those guys," McKenna offered. "You two *big girls* go take care of that sleeping prince in there."

"He's not a pwince, he's my daddy."

"Trust me, sweetheart," McKenna told Lexie. "That daddy of yours is one in a million. You look like you're over the flu. How are you feeling today?"

"I good," she cooed, sounding just like her stubborn father.

"She is feeling better. She was up bright and early," Kelsey confirmed. "But how long will he sleep?" She had a nightmare of a day still ahead of her.

"Since we now know he only took thirty milligrams, I'd guesstimate the rest of the day, but melatonin affects everyone differently." McKenna blew out a long-suffering sigh. "And knowing Alex, he'll prove me wrong. Heck, he's probably in the shower shaving right now."

Kelsey drew McKenna in for a quick hug. "Thank you."

"No, thank you. This is actually hilarious. A three-year-old got one over on Alex Stewart."

Lexie laughed like it was a funny joke. "I did!" she squealed. "I got one daddy!"

Oh, hell. Kelsey had to smile at Lexie's innocent version of what McKenna said. It was funny. She hoped Alex thought so when he finally woke up.

And then it got funnier. Kelsey laughed until she cried, tears running down her face with relief, and… *Oh, my gosh, joy.* Her terrible day had turned into the best. Alex was finally sleeping soundly, untroubled and unaware. A doctor had checked him over, and for once, he hadn't grouched his way through the exam, complaining he had better things to do. He was healthy, but exhausted, darn him. God willing, by the time he woke, he'd be himself again.

Best of all, Lexie was a good and thoughtful little girl who'd only wanted to help her father. Kelsey still planned to buy a lock for that medicine cabinet to make sure Lexie stayed that way. And then… Lexie was going to take an IQ test. Three-year-olds were supposed to be precocious, not observant enough to pick a particular bottle out of a line-up of ibuprofen, vitamins, herbal supplements, and blood pressure medicine bottles. Lexie was her father's daughter all right. Too smart for her own good.

Chapter Twenty-Four

Renner held Tara carefully as she snuggled into him, warm and soft. Perfect. They'd both needed this connection. This genuine oneness that came out of nowhere. That he'd slept for the first time in days hadn't hurt, either. That she'd slept with him instead of climbing back into her bed was absolute heaven.

He was awake when the night nurse came in to check her stats. He'd caught her look of disapproval, but disturbing Tara to satisfy some by-the-numbers hospital protocol? Not happening. The same nurse surprised him when she returned with two breakfast trays, juices, and coffees just a moment ago. Yes, she'd also still told him to be sure and hit the call button the second Tara opened her eyes. Maybe he would. But maybe he wouldn't.

Trying not to wake her, Renner managed to reach one coffee without spilling it, and ahh… *Best part of waking up…* Well, almost. Renner smiled down at his very own sleeping angel. Holding her filled some indefinable hole in the well of his soul. It'd been empty a long time. Now it felt full. At least, fuller. And breathing her unique scent in at the start of his day was a helluva lot better than coffee.

Tara's lashes fluttered. The paper coffee cup was in his way. Still careful, he set it back in its round little divot on the tray. "Hey," he murmured as she came to.

Her drowsy gaze stopped roving at his mouth.

Automatically, he zeroed on her lips. Still slightly swollen. Slightly curved at the corners. Contentment looked good on her. Pure male satisfaction warmed his gut. If possession were nine-tenths of the law, then right now, right here, Renner had everything he wanted.

"Mornin'," she murmured, her morning voice sultry and sexy as hell. "Thought you'd be gone by now."

"And miss this?" He planted a kiss in her hair. "Mom didn't raise any stupid boys."

That brought out the glow in Tara's eyes. "I like her. She's always smiling."

"Yes, and she's bossy, or didn't you notice?"

"But you love her, I can tell."

"That I do. How about your mom? She's still alive, isn't she?"

Tara sat up straighter. "Yes, and I called her yesterday, and she and dad are okay, and that means I'm okay."

"Why wouldn't they be?"

"Because I haven't stayed in touch. After my marriage—"

"He wouldn't let you call. I get it." The rat bastard.

"No. Not exactly. You have to understand, I was a different person back then. I partied a lot and…" She ran a quick hand over her head, ruffling layers of silky red. Rubbed the sleep out of her eyes. Licked her lips and sighed. "I… oh, damn, Renner. I was drunk the night I met Jorge. He asked me to marry him, and I was young and dumb, and I thought, sure, why not? I was too buzzed to care, and I wasn't thinking clearly, and he… and he…"

Shit. Not what Renner expected, but he knew about getting buzzed and the stupid that followed. "And…" he prompted patiently, willing to hear her out.

"And Mom and Dad were upset when I told them I'd run off and got married without them." She huffed. "Actually, they were angry. I don't blame them. We had words. I was a drama queen back then, think I said something like 'fine then this is goodbye.' I hadn't talked to Mom since, not until Kelsey handed me her phone and told me to call."

"But she still loves you," he persisted. "Mom's don't give up on their kids." How well Renner knew.

Tara swallowed hard. "Yes, she and Dad both love me. I'm just glad I was off the line when Jorge showed up. Hearing that screaming would've destroyed her."

Renner tipped his head and kissed Tara's mouth. "I'm glad you're as strong as you are, Tara Shanahan. Nice name. It fits you."

She hmphed. "I've been such a liar. You might as well know all my secrets. I'm a recovering alcoholic, and I'll bet I've done more prescription drugs than you've ever heard of."

"Wanna bet?"

Tara really looked at him then. "You too?"

"Yeah. Not proud, but when I got home from Saudi…" Now it was his turn to hum and haw. "Went a little sideways. Didn't want to be around people. Too much noise. Too many selfies and too many stupid people. Took off for the West Coast." *Cough. Cough.* "Folks don't realize we all come home… I don't know. Depleted is the closest word that explains it. If we're CA, we're either—"

"CA?"

"Combat Assault. It means direct action. We've been *there.* But yeah. You know that glass half-empty, half-full thing?" He stalled, not sure he wanted to share how broken he'd been back then. But what the hell. "Well, I'm pretty sure I came back all empty. Pretty much needed more space than my old life could give me. I was selfish. All I wanted was to get away, to have more time to myself. Just more."

She traced her fingers up his throat to his chin, petting him. Gentling him. "That must be when you bought your bike."

Renner cocked his head at her, wondering how she knew that.

A half smiled curled her lips. "You wear an MC cut, a dead giveaway you were in a motorcycle club."

He nodded. "You're a smart woman. I'm still not convinced I need AA though, but—" He snapped his big mouth shut. *AA? Really? Way to go, Wren. Open your big mouth.*

"Oh, I can help you with that," she murmured, "but only when you're ready. Does your mom know how much you drink? That you've got a problem?"

"No, and I'd like to keep it that way. She'd cut me off." And this conversation had gone way off-track. Absentmindedly, his hand went for the inner pocket of his jacket, now hanging off the back of the recliner. A hit of liquid courage would help.

"You've got a flask," Tara told him. "With you. It's in your cut. Right now, don't you?"

Renner nodded, his hackles rising. "Always."

"What's your poison?"

"Whiskey. Jameson when I can get it."

"Hmmm, my favorite." Tara closed her eyes when she said that, her tongue skimmed over her bottom lip, and for a split second, Renner had himself convinced he really could lick this habit if he could lick her lips.

But, yeah. No. He needed a drink now and then. What the feck did it hurt? One drink did not make him an alcoholic. Only he knew better. One drink led to two, and before he knew it, the bottle would be on its side and empty. He'd be pretty much the same way, face down on a dirty bathroom floor of some bar with his tongue hanging out. Like a pig. He wouldn't remember how he'd gotten there and his wallet would be gone.

Tara opened her eyes and smiled up at him. "It's not my decision to make for you, but know this, Renner Graves. I've been where you are, and I'll be here for you when you're ready."

Okay, fine. Good to know. Time to move on. "You work with Kelsey. Mind telling me what you know about Aaron Pope?"

"He's nice. Quiet. Doesn't like closets or loud noises. Why?"

"Just wondering if he's gone back to his old ways."

"You think he might be helping Montego?"

Renner nodded. "Someone is. Another kid went missing yesterday. But Montego was with Jed the night before and yesterday afternoon. I hardly think she had time to kidnap anyone." But it wasn't impossible. She'd tortured nineteen young men her last time in the States, and those were just the ones who'd lived. God only knew how many others she'd left in her bloody wake.

"Not Aaron," Tara said firmly. "He's a nice man, and he detests that bitch. You should see him with the teens. They come to us acting tough and in your face, spouting gang-speak like they're so bad. But they're really just lost little boys, and some of them have been molested, Renner. Prostituted. You can see it on their faces. It's in their eyes. They're scared and ashamed, and they don't know who to trust. But Aaron sees through that. He doesn't take any bullshit, either. I think that's why they gravitate toward him. They can see he's missing a few fingers, that he's been through some shit. He doesn't hide his handicap, but he's still a badass. He's straight with them and he expects something of them. You'd like him. I can introduce you."

"I'd like that."

"Maybe today?"

He should've known she wanted to leave. "Breakfast first. Then I'll see about getting you discharged. Deal?"

Tara chose that moment to climb onto him, straddling his thighs, and damn… She was feeling better this morning. Quick as he could, Renner tugged the blanket to keep her bare derriere out of sight.

"You're killing me," he murmured, his voice hoarse and gruff. He couldn't see everything beneath that simple cotton gown, but he could be inside those shoulder snaps in seconds.

Now she was looking down at him. "I don't love you," she said quietly. Thoughtfully. "But I'd like to get to know you better, Renner. I mean, if that's what you want. Umm, if you're not too busy or—"

"I'll never be too busy for you," he told her, his resolve to be a better man slipping away. She was so warm. So willing. "But your door's unlocked, and now is really not the best time for us to   "

She collapsed, her mouth to his mouth, her breasts to his chest, kissing the life out of him. His hands went to her backside as hunger for this timid yet wild, wonderful woman roared to life in his veins. The way she moved her core against him. The way he sprang to life with every wet kiss and every dry rub. My hell, he wanted his hands and tongue all over her.

In an instant, she drew back and left him with his mouth wet from her kisses and his body in flames. Tara settled her ear over his hammering heart. One firm, feminine hand cupped the steel spike beneath his zipper. "Take me home with you, Renner," she purred. "I'm scared to go back to my place. Please. Take me home."

Oh, man, did she know how to get her way.

"You bet," he replied gruffly. "Get your stuff. We're outta here."

Chapter Twenty-Five

"Let's stop at Raymond's Kids first," Tara suggested.

"Good idea," Renner replied as he executed a left turn onto Pennsylvania Avenue SE. It hadn't taken any time to get the doctor on staff to sign her discharge papers, not after Renner promised he'd keep her quiet the next couple days. He knew he'd jumped the gun. Mark wouldn't be pleased that he'd ended Seth and Beckam's tours-of-duty without checking first. But these were the proverbial *'times that tried men's souls.'* Or so Renner planned to tell Mark.

They hadn't time to waste. Renner's gut kept twisting. Montego was up to something, and whatever it was, it would happen soon. Maybe today. He needed to talk with Aaron Pope and get a feel for the guy, the sooner the better. Because someone was behind the scenes helping Montego. If not Aaron, then who? One of the other men she'd tortured before? One of the last sixteen? Or her new batch of recruits, one of the seven missing young military men?

"If you turn right at Potomac, you'll intersect with Fourteenth," Tara offered. "It's easier to get into the back parking lot that way."

Then Potomac Avenue SE, it was. Renner followed her instructions, and soon they were parked behind a decades-old brick building that had once been Lincoln High School. Most of the lawn around the parking lot had been replaced by heavy construction equipment, most likely there to begin what, by the end of the day, would be McCormack's renovation to Raymond's Kids. It was a good thing that Jed was doing, but something about it still niggled at the back of Renner's mind.

"Pull up and park next to Kelsey's car," Tara directed, pointing at what Renner knew was the armored SUV Alex had reinforced for his wife, fully equipped with as much, if not more, security gizmos than the president's limo. If that didn't scream OCD, nothing did. Several other cars and SUVs were parked in what remained of the parking lot, none Renner recognized. But it was good to see that Kelsey had her vehicle back.

Tara grabbed hold of his hand and they walked up the rear steps and into a long hallway that still smelled like schoolbooks and glue sticks, chalkboards and mac-n-cheese. On his left, the men's and women's restrooms and the rear kitchen exit. To his immediate right were stairs that led up to the children's sleeping quarters, and down to individual bedrooms that, as far as Renner knew, were still vacant. He and Tara passed the supply cabinet, Kelsey's office, and finally came to the front lobby and entry. Hunter-green-and-white-checkered linoleum covered all the floors, and in the cafeteria across from the entry, kids were singing *God Bless America.*

A portly janitor dressed in brown coveralls pushed a four-foot wide dust mop across the floor, swooshing dust bunnies and dirt from the corners as he headed their way.

"Hey, Jeremy," Tara called to him. "What's up with all the music?"

"Hi, Killer Tara! Miss Kelsey's teaching a couple songs for the presentation tonight. Y'all heard, din't you? Mister Jed McCormack's building us a new wing. Ha!" Jeremy said that with pride, grinning his usual innocent jack-o-lantern smile that covered his entire face. "Hey, Mister Renner Graves. Whatcha doing here today?"

Everyone received a proper salutation from Jeremy. Renner always suspected Kelsey hired this middle-aged man because he reminded her of Raymond, the man/child she'd found and lost a couple years back. From what Renner knew, Jeremy was as guileless as Raymond had been.

"I thought I'd stop by and see Aaron for a minute. Is he around?"

"Ah huh, he's helpin' Miss Kelsey. Some of the boys din't want to sing, but he talked 'em into it. Ha!"

"Thanks, Jeremy," Tara said.

"You're welcome," he replied with unabashed cheer as he ambled by. "Catch ya later, alligators. Ha!"

By then her hand rested on Renner's forearm, and br-r-r-t…

Renner looked over his shoulder. "Did he just—?"

"Yes." Tara giggled. "He does it all the time. Just keep walking. It'll pass."

"I think it already did." Renner was still shaking his head when they walked into the cafeteria, where Kelsey led her chorus through the final burst of musical patriotism.

She did have a way with kids, even directing choir. Most of them actually sang and looked like they were having fun. But Kelsey looked tense. Most likely because of the several utility carts loaded with stacks of folded chairs, the two industrial floor scrubbers, a raft of buckets, and cartons of other cleaning supplies lining the far wall of the cafeteria.

The floor plan was your everyday simple cafeteria. To Renner's left lay the kitchen, its door to the left of a long serving counter that could be closed off with a drop-down aluminum screen. Stocked with modern industrial appliances and everything necessary to feed a small army, Kelsey's two kitchen helpers were busy doing dishes.

To his right, a wooden podium with a built-in microphone stood ready for the upcoming event. The wall opposite the door had been decorated with cheerful, giant, white glittery snowflakes that hung high above a long row of bulletin boards where children's artwork was displayed. Basically, the cafeteria was a rectangular box with two exits, the main double doors where Renner stood and the exit in the kitchen that led to the hallway where he and Tara had just been.

Three men in casual wear, black slacks, black polos, and dark glasses hovered near where Kelsey stood leading music. Those guys were new since the last time Renner visited Raymond's Kids. Renner couldn't get a read on them. No friendly smiles. No eye contact. No hint of recognition.

"Okay, children, now don't forget. You're not to wear your new choir shirts until later today. I want you clean and beautiful when you sing the awesome song for Mr. McCormack, okay…?" She drew that last word out as if she expected an answer.

"Yes, Miss Kelsey," most of them replied in unison. A couple boys weren't paying attention, instead shouldering each other.

"Hey, Miss Kelsey," Renner mimicked the children as they wandered off. "How's the boss?"

She hurried to them, her eyes as wide as saucers. "You poor things! My gosh, you look—"

"Like we've just been beaten up. We get that a lot. What else's going on?" Tara asked. "Where's Lexie."

"Alex is home resting, and Lexie is playing with Squeaks today."

Squeaks was Adam and Shannon Torrey's little boy, so named by Adam after the little guy's unexpected, premature birth on the desert island they'd crash landed on during a TEAM operation. Adam and Shannon weren't married at the time, but Adam delivered the tiny guy who eventually became his son. Fell in love with the tiny infant. Named him Squeaks and the name stuck.

"Alex is home?" That was odd. Renner couldn't recall a day Alex hadn't charged into work needing coffee and needing it right damned now.

"He has the flu," Kelsey replied, but that was still odd. Alex sick? *Did not compute.*

"What's with them?" Renner stuck his chin at the silent men on her six. "You hire bodyguards?"

"Right. My husband owns a security business, so I hire bodyguards behind his back." Sarcasm? From Kelsey? That was new too. "Guys, you all know Tara. I'd like you to meet Renner Graves." She waved them in closer. "He works for Alex. Renner, this is Harvey Warner…"

The hefty guy with the widest shoulders took a half-step forward and extended his right hand gloved in black. "Nice to meetcha," he growled, his upper lip twitching.

"Same here." Renner nodded, now understanding precisely who these men were. That was a soft plastic prosthetic under that glove, not a hand. He'd been one of Montego's victims. "You Air Force?"

"You stupid?" Harvey all but snarled as that same rigid gloved hand hit the middle of his chest. "I'm a Marine! Oo-rah! Least I was—"

"Still are," Renner corrected sharply, "and don't forget it. You're alive, aren't you?" He was suddenly back in the Corps, on parade, ready to stand and fight with good men and women. Sometimes those men and woman just had to remember who they still were. They needed to hear the words. They needed to be reminded that they might not have given all, but they gave all they could.

"Yes, sir!"

"And who are you?" Renner asked the next gentleman, looking him up and down. Inspecting his boots, trousers, belt and shirt like a DI. Not smiling. Just letting him remember how it was to have the muscle of the Corps at your back.

"Private First Class Enrique Rojas, sir." Damned if the guy didn't salute.

"At ease," Renner bit out. "You Mexican, Rojas? Spanish? You one of them illegals from South America?" A good drill sergeant knew how to get under a guy's skin.

"No, sir! I'm American, sir!"

"Good answer," Renner said evenly, the snark in his tone replaced with sudden civility. "Why are you here?"

"To serve Miss Kelsey," he answered, his lower lip trembling.

"Then take those piece of shit glasses off."

Rojas complied, but he fumbled, and Renner caught the sunglasses before they hit the floor. He handed them back, staring at the perspiring but handsome young man with one milky eye. No doubt a souvenir from his time with Montego.

"You've got quite a shiner there, Rojas. You still combat ready?"

Rojas nodded. "Sure am, sir."

"You Army?" Folks might not believe it, but a discerning jarhead noticed the subtle tells and difference between service members.

Rojas nodded again, his eyes glistening.

Renner stabbed an accusing finger at Kelsey. "Do you love her?" he bellowed.

"Yes, sir!" Rojas screwed his lips, biting them. He turned to Kelsey, who stood there as surprised as everyone else. "Sorry, ma'am, but it's true. We all do. You... you helped us. M-me. You showed up. I'll always love you, and I can't thank you enough. I'll put my life on the line for you any day of the week. I will."

"You'll do," Renner said as calmly as he could. These guys all passed muster. Kelsey was in good hands, and it was obvious they loved her in the way all warriors loved mom's apple pie and the pretty girl next door. She was their lady and they would die for her.

The last man stepped forward, his hand already extended, his glasses in his pocket, his eyes smiling, and a big grin on his African American face. "Hey, Staff Sergeant Graves. You might not remember me, but you saved my brother when you were in Afghanistan. He was there when that friendly opened fire in Mazar-I-Sharif. Don't guess you forgot that; I sure never forgot you."

Renner knew instantly who this guy was, but he didn't want accolades for doing his job. "You're Terrell's baby brother?"

Again, with the toothy smile. "Yes, sir, I'm Corporal Zale Warner, and I'm American, too. Just like you."

"Yes, you are." Renner slapped Warner's meaty bicep. "How is Terrell?"

"Terry's real good. Came home and right away got married. He's a police officer in Michigan now, going to be a daddy any day."

"Well, good. Are you guys all here to guard Kelsey?"

"That's what we do." Zale seemed to be the acting leader of this well-built, but silent team. "In case you're wondering…" He stuck one boot forward. "She lopped off all my toes. Might've given me a limp, but she didn't take the Marine outta me. I owe that bitch… Sorry, Miss Kelsey, but I do. And I owe America. If anyone's taking Catalina Montego down, it's gonna be me."

"You're fine," Kelsey said, "but I think you'll have to stand in line if you want to end her."

Renner asked, "So you guys watch over Kelsey while she's here—"

"Yes, sir, and there's more of us. *Others,* I mean. We've got a schedule. This morning's me, Harv, and Ricky. We're on duty until two, then Dallas, Rafe, and Jim usually take over until she decides to go home. Today's gonna be different though. We'll all be here until it's over."

Renner had almost forgotten how these men had all identified as a collective 'we' or 'us' while in Montego's clutches. That was how she'd controlled them, by using their innate sense of brotherhood against them. Torturing or murdering one in front of the others made everyone else compliant and weak.

"But who watches over her until she's safe at home?" Tara asked, eyeing the men through slanted eyelids. "How do you know for sure Kelsey makes it all the way home?"

"Don't you worry none, Miss Tara, but…" Zale's shoulders lifted. "We kinda follow her until we know she's safely aboard the boss's chopper at Reagan."

"You follow me?" That caught Kelsey by surprise.

Zale nodded, his soft brown eyes filled with mischief instead of the pain glittering in Ricky's or the anger in Harv's. "Yes, ma'am, we do, and we aren't going to stop even if you say so."

In typical Kelsey-style, she hugged each of them. Damn, she looked like a little girl hugging giants. After each man had stooped and patted her back, she stepped away, wiping her face. "I never knew. Thank you. That's so thoughtful. Does Alex know?"

By then Harv and Ricky had pocketed their dark glasses. Harv's eyes were gray, Ricky's a clear coffee-brown. "Yes, ma'am, he does," Harv replied. "He pays us, but we'd do it anyway. It's our privilege to take extra special care of you."

"That husband of mine," she said, shaking her head. "I guess we all have our secrets, don't we?"

"Don't be too hard on him," Zale said. "He's just doing what good men do."

"Don't worry. Alex has my back and I have his."

"Damned good to meet you," Renner said as he shook hands with Kelsey's three warriors again, this time as a friend. "You guys ever need anything, call. I'll be glad to come back and kick your asses."

"Yes, sir," Ricky answered, a soft smile tweaking his lips. "Pleasure to meet you, Staff Sergeant Graves."

"Renner, just Renner. My staff sergeant days are behind me."

"Yes, sir. Thank you, sir."

When the men stepped back, Renner turned his attention to the lady of the house. "How'd you sleep last night?"

Kelsey waved him off as if sleep meant nothing.

"Kelsey…" He cocked his head, needing a better answer. "You're starting to scare me. It's like I'm watching you transform into Alex."

"Oh, fine. If you're really asking if I stayed home," she replied, returning the stare, "the answer is yes. But I didn't sleep. I have too much on my mind, and there's still so much to be done. How could Jed do this to me?"

"You'll be fine," Tara said as she turned a full circle, scrutinizing the cafeteria. "Place looks okay to me."

"No, it doesn't. The floors haven't been polished since Thanksgiving. The windows, the bathrooms, the chairs… Oh, my gosh, the chairs need to be wiped down. I'm sure there's sticky jelly and peanut butter fingerprints all over them, and—"

Renner held up both palms. "Relax. This is a home for lost kids, not uppity politicians. Raymond's Kids isn't supposed to be perfect. Like the kids you built it for, it's a messy work in progress. They're the ones you want to feel comfortable here. Not the press."

He nodded at Kelsey's stacks of over-sized pillows tucked into and over-flowing the double-wide closet behind one cafeteria door. Different colors, shapes and sizes, each child chose the pillow they wanted for the on-the-floor sit-down meetings Kelsey held at Raymond's place. Most times, those meetings were story-telling time, nothing formal. Despite strict state regulations to operate a home of this nature, Kelsey made it real. The cooks provided homemade cookies and popcorn on request. There was someone on staff twenty-four-seven. She did everything to soften the rough edges of transitioning from homeless to foster care for some, and she provided medical treatment, counseling, or safe shelter for others. Her staff loved her. The kids adored her. Even the governor had his eye on Raymond's Kids. The concept of integrated childcare for children at risk worked.

"Hell, let the governor sit on the floor like the kids do. He's nothing special. Don't start thinking you have to impress him now, Kels. Stay true to who you named this place after."

Damned if she didn't tear up again.

"Way to go, Renner." Tara punched his shoulder. "You sure know how to make friends."

"I do my best," he answered, but then waved a hand under his nose. "But I would invest in a good room freshener if I were you."

"Same old Jeremy," Tara deadpanned.

"I can do that. Room freshener and pillows, it is. Maybe I'll cancel those trays of hors d'oeuvres and order pizza instead." Kelsey's chest heaved as she blew out a long breath. "I'm so glad you guys showed today. Pillows and pizza will be so much easier, and clean-up will be a snap. I've got plenty of paper plates and—Whew. That's actually a great idea."

"You'll do fine," Renner told her. "Don't sweat the small stuff."

"Because Montego's the real problem," Kelsey muttered darkly.

"She is," Renner agreed, the day suddenly more somber than it had been seconds ago. "Would you mind if I talked with Aaron? Is he around?"

Her shoulders lifted. "We've already discussed security for tonight." She glanced toward the hallway on her right. "He might be in the men's room. Check that way. Tell him you work for Alex. He'll know why you're here."

"I can wait. Nothing urgent. I don't want to bother him."

Tara pointed down the same direction. "Scram. He won't mind. Besides, us girls need to talk."

"Yes, young lady," Kelsey fussed. "Why aren't you in the hospital?"

That was Renner's cue to run like the wind. He ambled down the hall to the men's room, then leaned against the wall opposite the door and waited. And waited. Someone was in there. A toilet kept flushing. At last Aaron exited, fastening his belt. He was bald now, but still, like Bruce Willis, what women would call good-looking. Tall and more gaunt than trim, he wore jeans and a long-sleeved, hunter green, USMC t-shirt. Work boots. A half-smile.

"Are you lost?" he asked, a gentle glitter in his eye.

Renner stuck a hand out. "I'd like a couple minutes of your time if you can spare it. Renner Graves."

Aaron met Renner's hand with a solid grip. His lips pinched as he sized Renner up and down. "Obviously you know who I am. Marine?"

"Damned straight. Just like you."

"You're one of Alex's guys."

"Heard you were invited to join the gang, too."

Aaron's gaze rolled back toward the restroom behind him. "Would if I could, but nah. Stomach runs my life now, I'd never last a day in the field. So, what brings you here? Bodyguard for a day?"

"Looks like that position's already filled."

"Ah, you met the guys."

Renner nodded. "It's a good thing you guys are doing here. Let me guess. You're staying in the basement."

"Yes, we are. So, what do you want?" Aaron crossed his arms over his chest, displaying Montego's handiwork on his left hand where one-knuckle stumps remained instead of four fingers.

"I had questions," Renner admitted, "but now I can see I was wrong. None of you are involved with Montego. Still, I need to ask, do you have any idea who's helping her? Seven men are missing as of yesterday, and you know as well as I do, she can't do this by herself."

"She never did…" Aaron breathed. "Before Seth offed her brother, Roland helped set her up in that hellhole of a warehouse where she kept us. Have you seen it?"

"No, but I heard about it. State's still got it under lock and key."

"They need to burn it. Roland was the genius who planted those pressure plates and bought the chipper." Aaron's shoulders flinched talking about the torture he'd survived. "And I promise, all it takes is the right incentive, and a guy'll do whatever he can to save himself."

"Are you guys doing anything to find her?"

"No," Aaron replied. Quickly. Too quickly.

Not that Renner believed him. He offered another handshake. "Good talking to you. I'll be around."

Aaron looked past his extended hand. "She's coming, you know. Today. Here. That bitch is coming here. Do you know why?"

"Because Kelsey's here," Renner replied gently, concerned this man might be worried for his men or his life.

"Guess again." Aaron widened his stance in the way of all alpha males. Those missing digits didn't diminish the Marine in this guy, not one bit. "She thinks she still owns us, Staff Sergeant. Yeah, she might go after Kelsey to torture Alex, but she knows damned well where we are. Why do you think she smooth talked McCormack into doing that goat rope here, inside Raymond's place? With all these kids? He already made his announcement, why does he need a ribbon cutting ceremony on top of yesterday's press release? With the weather as bad as it is? Hell, the workers he sent over yesterday haven't even cleared a spot for the press to watch McCormack make a big deal out of lifting that first shovelful. I'm telling you, Alex took Montego's brother and then he took us away from her. Mark my words, she wants her slave army back. That's why she's coming. I have a really bad feeling this next show of hers will be the frosting on her 'Fuck America' cake. But you also need to know..."

Renner waited while Aaron breathed. His chest heaved. In and out. Steadily. Slowly. As if he'd zenned out to regain the calm he'd lost. He seemed lost in space, his gaze fixed on Renner but looking through him. At last, he rubbed his good hand over his forehead. "Alex didn't find all of us last time, Graves. There were—are—more victims." The cords in his neck tightened. "More men. Nine more. That I know of."

"Jesus Christ, why haven't you said anything?"

"Because I didn't know about her other prison, torture chamber, whatever you want to call it, until today. But I didn't want to say anything because Kelsey's worried enough. These guys got away from Montego last time, somehow. They escaped the same kind of crap-hole we were in. One of them contacted me early this morning, told me everything, including details only *we* would know. Guess McCormack's announcement shook the bushes and these guys fell out. They're pissed and they're hellbent on revenge. They won't come in."

"What do you mean? As in they won't come into Kelsey's?"

"As in they won't go to the police. Montego castrated them, Graves. They're not just victims, they're monsters, tortured in ways you can't imagine. The guy I talked to said they stay apart to stay angry. They don't want help or handouts. Only Montego. And it doesn't matter how they get her."

"Sounds like they just went to the head of the line."

Aaron nodded. "But if they show today, if they go after her at any cost…"

Renner saw where he was going. Holy Jesus. Clusterfuck in progress. "They'll hurt or kill anyone who gets in their way."

"And the bitch will get away again. You need to cancel this show."

"And lose our shot at taking Montego down? No. We don't know anything for sure. All we've got is the word of some guy who claims to be her victim. Have you seen him? Do you know his name? Can we be certain any of this is credible intel?"

"No, I haven't met him," Aaron admitted, "and he wouldn't give me a name. Said he knew me, though."

"How? How could he find you?"

"Easy. Every time Montego's name comes up in the news, Alex's name comes with it, then mine by association. He's the hero. I'm the fucked-up poster boy of all she did to me and my men."

"Then stand with us," Renner urged. "I'll make sure Kelsey's got double-protection in case these guys do show.

We'll move the kids to a secure location. Together we can bring that bitch down. You with me?"

Aaron swallowed hard, his throat muscles working, his jaw tense. It took a moment, but at last he said, "We are with you."

Not *I'm* with you. Not *we're* with you. But *'we'* are with you. The collective *we*, as if he'd just spoken for all the males Montego had ever tortured.

Made Renner wonder all over again who Aaron Pope was and exactly what he had become.

Chapter Twenty-Six

"You're still hurt," Kelsey insisted. "Why didn't you stay in the hospital?"

"You're a great one to talk. Told Alex about that shiner yet?"

Kelsey's hand flew to her bruised cheek and eye. "You can see it?"

"Like a lighthouse." Tara gave her best friend her wickedest scowl. "You need better make-up, girl. The light coverage crap you use won't hide a neon sign like that."

"Darn," Kelsey muttered as she headed out the cafeteria doors. "Help me. I don't want anyone to know I've been hit until I have the chance to tell Alex."

"What'd you use yesterday?"

"The same brand, but the bruise wasn't as bad then. Mostly just yellow. Great, just what I need, something else to worry about."

Tara followed Kelsey across the hall to her office. "Wow, you came prepared," she said when Kelsey opened her backpack and started dumping jars of make-up on the desk.

"Hurry. Which do you think will cover best?"

One looked as good as the next. "Hold your arm out. Let's test."

Dab after dab met the inside of Kelsey's arm until they decided which foundation provided sufficient coverage. It took seconds to cover the bruise. "You still need ice to slow the swelling. Hold on. Let me grab one of those tiny chill packs you use on the kids when they get a boo-boo."

"Grab one for yourself," Kelsey called out. "Make that a couple. Have you even looked at yourself today?"

Come to think of it... "Umm, no. I've been kind of... busy." Busy all over Renner. Man, was it hot in here? Tara leaned into the full-length mirror behind Kelsey's door, avoiding her friend's sharp eyes. "Crap-a-roni, what the hell?" Make-up was not going to cover the mess that her face was. "That jerk! Why didn't Renner say anything? I look like Frankenstein!"

"Oh, you do not, you big baby. Sit down. Here." Kelsey backed Tara into the chair next to her desk and tipped her chin up, assessing the damage Jorge had done, angling her head from side to side. Humming. Making those sweet little sounds only Kelsey made when she knew you were hurting but she didn't want you to know how bad you looked. "Those butterfly bandages over your eye make you look like a bantamweight boxer who just got her ass handed to her, that's all."

"Give it a rest. Both my eyes are black, Kels. I look like a friggin' raccoon."

Kelsey's lips curved with suppressed humor. "And you called me out for my little shiner? It's nothing compared to yours."

That was actually funny. Tara chuckled. "My bad. Damn. He did a number on me."

"What else did he do to you?"

"I don't want to talk about it. Just glad Renner got there when he did. Thanks for calling him instead of—"

"The police or Alex, yes, I know. It's always easier to keep things like this lowkey. So, Renner, huh?"

Tara nodded, her cheeks warming at the thought of that kiss. "He does seem to show up in the darnedest places."

"That he does," Kelsey murmured as she licked her thumb and rubbed something off the middle of Tara's forehead. "Alex thinks a lot of Renner's mom."

"Oh, yeah?"

"He ever tell you about his dad?"

"We've only just met, remember?"

"Sometimes that's all it takes," Kelsey murmured, though it sounded like she meant that more for herself than Tara. "Renner's dad, Metro PD Detective Cody Graves was murdered in the line of duty a few years back. Brenda took it hard. Heck, the whole city took it hard. There was a parade. Flags flew at half-staff. A lot of businesses shut down. Because Alex had worked with Cody before, Brenda asked us to walk with her and her daughter behind the hearse. Renner was in the Corps and deployed then. His CO said he was unreachable, working some covert op in Pakistan. Alex managed to locate him, but Renner chose not to come home. There. You look— passable."

Tara looked up at Kelsey. "He missed his dad's funeral?" *Unbelievable.*

"Yes. I'm not sure why. Alex never said, but for Renner to have chosen his job over his mom and dad, tells me his mission was extremely important."

That's why he drinks, Tara thought. *That's what's eating at him. He regrets his decision.*

"So how do we look?" Kelsey asked as she tugged Tara up to look in the mirror.

The resemblance was uncanny. "Mah-velous. We look simply mah-velous, dah-ling."

"Hey, lady, where's Tara?"

Kelsey looked up from where she knelt polishing the front door, glass-cleaner in one hand, paper towels in the other. "Hi, Renner. She's around here somewhere."

"Didn't we agree you were ordering pizza instead of cleaning?"

She grinned up at him. "Oops. Guess I am a little OCD. It's just that these windows—"

"Can wait. Come on. Up, up, up." Renner gave her his hand, fluttering his fingers to get her to move. "Off the floor. We need to talk. With Montego coming—"

"Bet I know what you're thinking," Kelsey said as she lifted to her feet. "Don't worry. The kids won't be here when Jed arrives. I've already made arrangements with Sister Betsy at the Catholic orphanage. She and her staff are taking everyone on a field trip to National Harbor. They've earned Christmas money. They need to shop. The bus will be here any minute."

This woman had thought of everything. "What about your choir?"

Her shoulders lifted. "I changed my mind, canceled that right after I ordered pizza. No child wants to sit through a presentation just to sing a song anyway. Boring."

"Now you've got it. But listen…" Renner scanned the front entry of the repurposed high school. Crown molding, probably wood. Drop ceilings, most likely a fire-retardant combination of compressed paper, plastic, and fiberglass. Fire alarm. Extinguisher. "Mark and a couple other agents are working with me this afternoon and tonight. They'll be here soon and I've got to run. What time's Jed arriving? Is there a schedule of events you'd like to tell me about?"

"Sure. I don't have printed programs, but basically, he and Governor Tillis both arrive at six, Jed first, the governor second. I'll meet them here and escort them into the cafeteria."

"The press will already be here?"

"They're setting up at five."

Renner didn't like that scenario at all. "Not good. I don't want you anywhere near Montego."

"But Raymond's Kids is my place and—"

"And Mark and I'll handle the meet and greet, while you wait with Tara—"

"While I wait with Tara? Renner," she said with authentic school-marm authority. "In case you haven't noticed, this is *my* place. I'll be the one welcoming Jed and Governor Tillis, not you or Mark. I know you've got my back, but I refuse to be bullied. Besides, I have to accept the actual check tonight. Montego will be with Jed when I do. You can't do that for me. It wouldn't be right. Yesterday was just the press announcement. Tonight's the financial passing of the torch. Trust me, I've done this before."

He had to look twice at the Kelsey he thought he knew and the one standing in front of him now, challenging him, her lips pursed and her head up, staring him in the eye. "But it's only for show. He'll probably just hand you a record of transfer, a fake receipt. What difference will it make?"

"But I represent Raymond and all the kids who've passed through these halls. Me, not you or Mark." Kelsey's head came up with fire in her eye. "She's threatened my family for the last goddamned time. She wants a fight, she's got one."

Renner shook off the sense of Alex emanating from this petite, classy, brown-haired Amazon warrior with a bottle of *Windex* in her hand. Fierce didn't begin to cut it. This was the hand that rocked the cradle. By hell, it really did rule the world.

"Then you and me are going to be intimately acquainted, because tonight, I'll be stuck to your ass until this cluster—, err, goat rope's, over." He wanted to stab himself with a rusty knife for slipping into grunt-speak—with Kelsey of all people.

She blushed. Kelsey Stewart, who'd just declared herself the supreme lady of the keep—*thank you very much*—blushed like an embarrassed teenage girl. Now that was the boss's wife he knew. "Well, if you say so," she murmured. "It would be nice having a right-hand man at my—"

"Hey, guys." Thank God! Tara appeared out of nowhere and interrupted, saving him from further humiliation.

Renner scratched that ache between his eyes, the one caused by the perpetual frown that seemed to be etching a canyon with each passing minute. One more complication and that ache would turn into an actual divot. "Sorry, ma'am, but it's my job to keep you safe and—"

"No, it isn't," Kelsey politely interrupted, her tone as patient as if she were talking to one of her kids. "Your job is to apprehend Montego. Look around. Do I look like I'm in any way unguarded?"

"Well, ah…" Now that she mentioned it, he had passed Harv in the hall. Zale and Ricky were clearly visible on the other side of those sparkling clean windows. Both out in front, one at the top of the steps, the other posted near the flagpole. Both on guard. All three men capable and seemingly her devoted sidekicks.

Okay then. Renner could keep his distance for now. The rounds in his pistol on the other hand, that—he couldn't promise.

"What'd I miss?" Tara asked, looking first at Kelsey, then to Renner, her brows lifted.

"We're discussing personal safety," Renner replied evenly.

"Anything I can help with?" asked the woman who should be home resting, instead of rambling around this halfway house like she was simply back on the job after a night on the town.

"You can let me drive you home," Renner said. "Kelsey's got things handled here."

"Nah, I thought I'd hang around for a while," Tara answered, her fingers light on his shoulder, her eyes bright. "You know, make sure all the kids get on the bus. Put out the welcome mat. Stuff like that."

Renner ran his thumb over her cheek, relishing the feel of her skin, the angle of her jaw as he cupped her face. "Why the make-up?"

Both Tara's shoulders lifted. "Didn't want to scare the kids. No big deal."

"Did you see Brandon and Turley shoving each other while we were singing? Did you get a chance to talk to them yet?" Kelsey asked.

Tara nodded. "Not sure what really happened to them yet, but yeah. We had a little chat."

"They've been picking at each other since yesterday. Once this is over, I need to sit down with them."

Great. Just what Renner didn't need, another complication. "Are we talking kids with knives or gang affiliation?"

"No, just twin seven-year-old brothers who showed up on our doorstep four days ago. Family Services already interviewed them and their parents. They're mine until a foster family takes them."

"Abuse?" he asked.

"That's the thing, one says yes, the other vehemently denies it," Kelsey answered.

"And yet here they are," Tara added dryly. "So, yeah. I need to hang out, see who needs to talk, who needs to cry. You know, the normal stuff lost kids do when their worlds fall apart. But go. I'll be okay."

"Nah, I'm staying." Renner didn't need a tux anymore. Not for pizza.

Chapter Twenty-Seven

Tara stood in the kitchen, watching Renner and Aaron with Mark Houston, Seth McCray, and Beckam Garner, all handsome-as-hell, kickass males who somehow made everything around them seem small and fragile. They were standing at the wide-open cafeteria doors, embroiled in a heated debate. All dressed the same as Renner. Black polos, jeans, and boots, all wearing identical black TEAM jackets, which she now knew concealed holsters and pistols, maybe a knife or two. Except for Renner. He was in his leather cut, looking more like he'd just ridden in with a motorcycle club.

They'd arrived an hour ago, and together with Kelsey's guys—aka the ones Montego had previously tortured, but who now lived on-site as guards slash men-who-had-nowhere-else-to-go—they'd cleared the entire building of perceived threats. As expected, the worst they'd found was Jessica's stash of *Pepperidge Farm Goldfish* hidden under some t-shirts in the bottom drawer of her dresser. That girl. Did she think she could get away with not sharing her special treats with her favorite arch nemesis and verbal sparring partner? *We'll just see about that.*

Since she'd arrived in the same grungy clothes Jorge had beaten her in, Tara had showered in Kelsey's private bathroom, then changed into one of the many spare outfits Kelsey kept on hand. She and Kelsey could've been twin sisters the way this soft hunter-green sweater top and these dark brown jeans fit. Rider brand. Interesting.

Tara should have known Kelsey would loan her something practical and sturdy. She never ascribed to the latest fads or high fashion. She was one of those steadfast, practical bargain shoppers who purchased reliability instead of glitz. And Tara knew why. She'd seen the scars Kelsey covered with make-up, long sleeves, and high collars. And Kelsey had seen Tara's scars. They'd both suffered at the hands of heartless bastards, and they both knew the high cost of their past mistakes of trusting the wrong kind of guys. How could Tara not love Kelsey? They were sisters of the same heart who'd somehow found each other.

But tall, dark, and handsome Mark Houston was definitely chewing Renner's ass. He made a thundercloud look cheery, standing there with his thick arms crossed over a wide muscular chest, glaring at Renner, who was no slouch. And Renner was certainly up in Mark's grill. His gorgeous face hadn't stopped scowling since his senior agent had arrived.

Renner's boots were spread, his shoulders back, and his chin jerking toward the exits, then the kitchen. Man, he was fierce when on duty. Tara wished she knew if that heated debate was about her not staying at the hospital like a good girl. Not that she'd intended to run home or stay in bed and lick her wounds in the first place. Not today with Kelsey about to face the most evil woman in the world. Friends showed up, damn it.

Mr. McCormack's advance team had arrived to set up some kind of a scale model just inside the lunchroom doors. Tara couldn't see what it was from where she stood, but it didn't take them long before they were gone.

Jeremy had left when his shift ended; the kitchen staff, too. The bus had come and gone, and Tara had made extra sure all twenty-seven Raymond's Kids were on it. She'd counted heads, then to avoid a *"Home Alone" Kevin's-in-the-attic!* incident, she'd personally talked with each of her little angels and reminded them that Santa was definitely coming to Raymond's Kids in a couple days—if they were good. She'd even had them singing Christmas songs by the time she'd stepped off the bus and waved goodbye. Almost made her tear up. Not quite, but almost.

Besides Renner's four-man team, Kelsey and Tara, the only ones left in these hallowed halls were Kelsey's guys. All of them. Some were in the kitchen, helping out, filling plastic pitchers with fruit punch or ice-water, or whatever Tara asked them to do. A couple others stood ill at ease watching over the buffet table where paper plates, napkins, an ice bucket, and plastic utensils had been organized to ensure an even flow. Yet others patrolled the halls and perimeter.

But all were armed beneath their bright red Raymond's Kids hoodies, and all were wary, edgy as cats in a lightning storm. Tara imagined as much as they dreaded the return of their evil mistress, they yearned for it. They needed to see Montego's ugly face again, if only to prove they'd survived her utter cruelty. That they'd lived despite her and they were still men. You could feel the tension radiating off Aaron's guys. It was in the air. In the distance between each of them. You could almost taste it.

That Montego would soon accompany Jed McCormack into this safe place where the remaining sixteen dangerous, angry, adult males she'd tortured now lived, spoke to either her insanity or that she really did own a pair of brass cojones.

Which she'd probably cut off some poor guy. Because she was that cruel.

Bile thickened at the back of Tara's throat at the thought. It wasn't even a bad joke, because Montego had done precisely that to the mystery nine, the guys who Tara now knew had contacted Aaron only a day ago. It'd be good to know if those men were real, and if they planned to crash Jed's party. The sun had just gone down. The night was young. What a scary day this could turn out to be.

Stacks of pillows stood ready to encourage or discourage the press or politicians who showed. Kelsey had personally arranged them, five to a stack along the outside of the cavernous room. Man, it seemed so much bigger without the lunch tables and chairs. Kelsey had also asked the kind folks at Dan the Man who'd delivered the pizzas, to cut them in narrow slivers instead of their usual robust wedges.

"I didn't even put out plastic utensils. Less is more," she'd said with a mischievous twinkle in her eyes. Translated—the less food, the quicker everyone would leave.

There was not, and never would be, any alcohol served, not here at Raymond's Kids. This was a kid-safe zone. That made it safe for recovering alcoholics, too. Yet there stood Renner, standing up to his boss, his finger in Mark's face, and doing it with a full flask of Jack or Hennessy or, hell, Tara couldn't remember which Renner preferred—one poison was as bad as another—hidden in his jacket pocket.

The two men were evenly matched, but damn. Tara couldn't keep her eyes off Renner. He made his senior agent look meek and ordinary. Tame. Maybe it was just the leather jacket. Maybe it was knowing he dared carry a forbidden flask while on duty. But maybe it was just—him. All hard angles.

But sweet. Considerate. Not a mama's boy, but a man who respected and adored his mother. A man who treated women right, but wasn't afraid to fight.

Tara shook her romantic feelings off. She had her own mission tonight. She needed to be ready, which was why she'd taken up residence in the kitchen where it'd be easier to slip away when the time was right.

Thankfully, the florist had come and gone already, the handsome, if not ostentatious, display of red roses now sitting on the floor in front of the wooden podium where Kelsey would soon stand and deliver her welcome. But they were blood red roses, the flower reserved for lovers. Tara had always found that pairing odd. Pink would've been better, it was sweeter. Maybe yellow, it was sunnier. Blue would work too, if you dyed the flowers to match the color of a summer sky. Any other color would've been better than fresh blood.

But hey, what did she know? Only that love hurt like a bitch, and she'd tasted enough blood from mashed lips or a bitten tongue during her short, painfully sad excuse of a marriage. But love had had nothing to do with those worthless vows, had it? She'd never loved Jorge, not for a second. If anything, she'd lied to herself when she'd told herself to be daring and brave that night. That it was love at first sight. That he was everything he'd said he was. Then she covered her stupid mistake of a marriage with enough alcohol to pickle her brain. If it hadn't been for Kelsey...

Tara drew in a deep, cleansing breath remembering the night she'd arrived at Raymond's Kids. Remembering her BFF's genuine kindness and unconditional love for the filthy, smelly wreck of a woman she'd been. That kindness was why Tara stayed now. She loved Kelsey like a sister, and she intended to stand by her as Kelsey had lovingly stood by her. To be here for her friend no matter what happened tonight. Because one thing was certain. That bitch Montego would meet her match tonight. One way or the other.

"Two national news vans just pulled up, ladies and gentlemen," Zale's big voice boomed over everyone's earpieces. "Another's turning in now. Are we ready?"

"I am," Tara said as she took a deep breath and smoothed a hand over her hair, which was natural and red at the moment. She dusted a stray piece of lint off her sweater and shouted across the expansive room, "Hey, Renner! Hey, Mark!"

Both men turned and waved, but were much too involved in their discussion to answer. Which was just as well.

She waved back, that one little chore accomplished. It was important they both see her. Now. While she was dressed inconspicuously in Rider jeans and a sweater. While she was still Tara, and before she transformed again. Which she had to make happen in a minute or two.

It was almost showtime.

Renner stepped back from Mark, pissed at the quandary Jed McCormack had once again put them in. *Shit!* Was dementia behind that arrogant son of a bitch's decision to put Kelsey at risk? Had to be. The ass had just phoned Kelsey to tell her he'd turned the official presentation of his new wing over to LuAnn, as in aka Catalina-fuckin'-Montego. Like she was his wife or something. Like she deserved to breathe the same air as Kelsey.

What was wrong with McCormack? He'd dropped Kelsey straight into that serial killer's bloody hands. It was all Renner could do, to not march out and shoot the billionaire in the head the second the dumbass arrived. Jesus Christ! What else could go wrong?

As if in answer to his question, the press arrived, those hellhounds all but running to the podium to set up their mics, and knocking Kelsey's carefully arranged pillows out of their way. Trampling everything in their haste to be first with the story—whatever the hell that was—elbowing, complaining, and just plain being assholes. The two national reporters who'd arrived seemed more levelheaded. Their staffs were by far more professional and courteous. But those local stations and the gossip rags? Renner wasn't sure there was any such thing as free press anymore. They looked more like a pack of wolves and hyenas circling a kill.

Renner had just been telling Mark all he knew about Aaron's intel on the other nine men who had escaped Montego. Mark took that news well considering most of The TEAM was OCONUS, as in outside the United States. Several were absolutely unreachable and none were able to show up in time to assist. Not that Kelsey didn't already have one helluva bodyguard presence between The TEAM and Aaron's men. Still... Renner wished he had an army.

Interestingly, Aaron's guys weren't tripping over each other's feet like he'd expected. If anything, they worked in sync like a group of USMC cadets on parade, almost as if they'd practiced this scenario before. Which spoke to the leader Aaron was. For a man who'd endured what he'd suffered at Montego's hands, Aaron Pope had made a startling comeback. Renner suspected Alex was behind that, too. The Boss had his fingers in everyone's business.

Fortunately, Renner had also informed Mark earlier that, instead of finger foods and wine, there would now be pizza, punch, and paper plates. Hence no tuxes, which made guarding Kelsey easier. No chance for broken wine goblets, and no dress shoes with slippery soles, either. A small plus in the middle of this ridiculous nightmare that could turn to shit in a heartbeat.

Because of the press, the pillows were being stored, and Aaron's men were tasked with setting up rows of chairs. At the moment Tara was out of sight in the kitchen. Kelsey stood at the cafeteria door with him and Mark, wringing her hands, ready to welcome McCormack and Tillis while Harv and Ricky hovered over her like guardian angels.

Once that private welcome ended, Kelsey and her bodyguards would then usher the statesmen and Montego to their reserved seating in front of the podium. The rest of the hundred-plus fold-up chairs would be open to the press and whoever, politician or civilian, were interested enough to show up on a wintery night like this one. After everyone was seated Kelsey would welcome her audience and introduce Jed McCormack. After he said a few words, he was supposed to turn the mic over to LuAnn, aka Catalina Montego.

Which would put her at the front of the room.

She'd be exposed.

No one else would get hurt if, say, someone should just happen to shoot her while she was out in the open.

It'd be perfect. A double tap and down she'd go. Done. Eliminated.

She couldn't kidnap, torture, or murder any more military men. The nightmare would end.

For one split second, Renner wondered at the gift old man McCormack had unknowingly dropped into his lap when he'd offered Montego the center stage. How easy it would be. Addled or not, it was the perfect opportunity to take her out.

Made a man reconsider how much he valued truth, justice, and all Mark had said. But in the end, no. Hell, no. Renner shook that option out of his head. As much as he wanted Montego dead, he would not tarnish all The TEAM stood for. He would not betray Alex, Kelsey, or the family he loved. His dad, for Christ's sake. He could never be as good a man, but he sure as hell would not betray Cody or Brenda Graves. Hell, no.

Renner refocused, took a deep breath, and swallowed hard.

Since the podium stood opposite from the kitchen, the length of the cafeteria between them, Montego, the press, and the audience could be easily observed. The kitchen was where Seth and Beckam would take up their final positions once the ceremony began. The kitchen window's aluminum screen would come down, well, mostly down. The lights would go off, and, unbeknownst to everyone but Mark and Renner, two of the TEAM's deadliest snipers' scope would target Montego through the narrow slit where the screen and the counter met. Once she stood up to make her presentation, her head and upper body would be visible well over above the audience. She'd make one helluva target if she tried anything.

Renner, Mark, Seth, and Beckam were wired, their earpieces keeping them in constant touch. Kelsey, Tara, and Aaron were, too.

For now, Renner stood alert with Mark at the cafeteria entrance, where they could see all venues: both hallways, front entrance, rear exit, Kelsey's office, restrooms, and the kitchen exit into the hall. But Renner's burgeoning need to eliminate Montego had now combined with the sense of impending doom stalking him. It pushed his internal anxiety into the red zone. This media circus had better be over within the hour. He needed a drink.

"Everyone ready?" Mark asked, his eyes somehow darker, deadlier tonight.

Renner nodded as *'Copy that'* came back from all major players. There'd been no sunset this afternoon, not even a break in the weather, just a bone-chilling drizzle in the dense, heavy fog. Outside, spotlights bathed the parking lots with a surreal mist that looked as if someone was shooting a horror flick.

And shit. Renner realized his first mistake. The north and west sides of this building were not lighted as well as the south and east side were. Visibility outside was rapidly reducing to zero. Which shouldn't matter since the only exits were south and east. But he should've considered any and all limitations Montego could now turn into advantages.

"Tango One just arrived," Seth advised. Another shit. Tango One, aka McCormack was the reason for this event. Only his entourage had pulled into the lot behind Raymond's Kids. They were coming in through the rear exit instead of the front entrance Kelsey had meticulously polished to impress.

Would've been nice to have known that in advance. Renner should have asked. Details, details. No operator could ever have enough details. Those were the things that plugged the holes that tore through every strategic plan ever created. More intel. More ammo. More time.

"Copy that," Renner replied evenly. "Mark's on his way to you, Seth. Beckam?"

"Tillis has a chauffeur. Did you guys know that?"

"Focus, Beck," Mark said as he marched to intercept McCormack and Montego at the rear exit. "Is Tillis here?"

"Yes, sir. Front parking lot. He's getting out of the car now."

"Heads on swivels, people," Mark murmured. "You got eyes on Montego yet, Seth?"

"Oh, yeah. She's out of the car, no winter coat, but she's wearing a helluva lot of sparkly nothing. That skirt's so high and her top's so low, she might as well have worn Band-Aids with straps. Of course, the reporters are swarming her. Lots of strobes flashing. Wait. McCormack... Shit, umm, sorry, Boss, but McCormack's just standing there. She looks like a frickin' Kardashian, but he looks like he forgot where he is."

"That's it. I'm going—"

"No, Kelsey. Follow the plan," Renner bit out as he reached for her hand and missed. "Mark's already on his way to intercept."

But the lady in question had already zeroed on her friend and was headed out of the cafeteria. "That poor man. I will not let him stand alone," she bit out as her heels pounded the linoleum. "Not after losing Lois like he did, and not while I've got all these resour—"

"No need, ma'am," Seth interrupted smoothly. "I'm here and I'll make sure he gets to Mark. You stay in the kitchen where you belong, and Mark'll bring him straight to you like we planned."

"The kitchen?" Kelsey snapped even as she stopped and turned back to the cafeteria. "Where I belong?"

"He meant with Tara," Renner soothed. "Gosh, Kelsey, stand down. It's not like he meant you should be barefoot and pregnant in the kitchen. Everyone's here to help. Give us a chance."

"I know, I'm just..." Kelsey growled, her eyes glistening as she rejoined him. "I just need this damned night over, Renner."

"Copy that," he replied smoothly while he turned her toward Tara who stood at the open kitchen window waiting. "But now's not the time to lose your cool, Kels. Let's do this right, okay? Keep calm a little bit longer for Alex and Lexie. Let's end Montego once and for all."

"And for my guys," Aaron added quietly over the wire, his tone more controlled than Renner felt at that moment.

"Yes, s-sorry," she stuttered. "I'm sorry, Aaron. Of course. This isn't about me. It's about you and everything she did to your guys. I really do know that."

The poor thing was unraveling. But Jesus, the last thing Renner needed was for Kelsey to confront Montego. She might kill the bitch on sight. That could be good, and that could be bad. Especially with the press ready to twist and fabricate the truth to feed their propaganda machines.

"Good evening, Jed," Mark's suave voice came over their earpieces. "Good to see you again, sir. May I take you to Kelsey? She's been waiting all day for you."

"Why, why sure." Jed's halting confusion came over the earpieces loud and clear. "So good to see you again, too, but... where... where's Lois? I took a wrong turn somewhere, and... I think we were going out for dinner. It's dark and I'm hungry enough, but I'm afraid I lost her in this crowd. Do you know where she is? You're taller than me. Can you see her?"

"I'm sure she's around here somewhere, now let's get you in out of this cold," Mark soothed.

Renner bit his lip as he watched Mark usher the kindly statesman up the back steps, through the double-wide glass doors, and into Kelsey's domain. Jed had just provided irrefutable proof for what Renner had suspected all along. McCormack was senile. Thank God, Mark had him now. But if he'd gone and married Montego since that press release yesterday… If he'd been stupid enough to forgo a lengthy, legal prenup…

God bless America. Renner refused to dwell on all that would mean for McCormack Industries, the nation, every man and woman in the service.

Mark had his arm around the old guy's shoulders now, leading him very much like a lost child. "There she is," Mark said when they spotted Kelsey.

"Oh, I know her," Jed exclaimed. "That's… that's… umm…"

"Kelsey, look who wandered in from the cold," Mark called out graciously.

"Jed," she cried as she ran to him and took his hands. "I am so glad you're here. What a stormy night! Is the fog still rolling in? We'll sure be in trouble if it gets cold enough to freeze, won't we?"

"Ah… well… umm…" He looked up at Mark who still had a tight hold on his elbow. "I'm afraid you made a mistake. That's not my Lois, young man."

Young man? My Lois? Renner forced his eyes off the too-tender scene. He couldn't bear to witness the great man crumble, not when Montego had just stalked into Raymond's Kids like a long-legged movie star with paparazzi stuck to her ass, calling out, "LuAnn! LuAnn! Look this way. Smile!"

Bright red Angelina lips twisted with what had lately become her famous fake smile. Even a dumb grunt like him could see through that conniving mask, but not the self-aggrandizing press. Beckam was glued to her six, but still she stopped the procession to pose for a selfie with some idiot male reporter who'd stuck his cell phone in her face. Laughing like they were besties. Strutting up the hall like she and the media were BFFs. Signing another moron's brand-name purse with bright red marker: LuAnn.

Renner growled at his team. "Heads on swivels, people. Let's end this fuckin' show once and for all."

Chapter Twenty-Eight

Alex woke slowly. Still dragged out. Still sick enough to stay in bed all day and night and...

Hell, no. He launched to his elbows, wiped his eyes with the heels of both palms, and blinked the drugging influence of that damned flu out of his head once and for all. It took a couple minutes to wake up enough to get his bearings. Kelsey's side of the bed was empty again. The house was too quiet, the hallway leading from their bedroom, too dark. She wasn't home. Neither was Lexie.

He recognized the thoughtfulness of his sweet wife in the single red rose she'd left in a crystal bud vase on his nightstand. Kelsey was always conscious of little stuff like that. She'd tuck 'I love yous' in his shirt or suit pockets, other love notes to be found when and where he'd least expect them. Folded inside a sock when he was a long way from home. Stuck to a dollar bill in his wallet on long days at the office. Or simply taped to the visor in his car where he'd find it on his drive to the helo-pad. She always found a way to be there with him.

But the neatly scribbled artwork beside it was Lexie's doing. She'd drawn a stick dad with a grumpy face inside a big red Crayola heart, then covered the rest of the sheet with a mess of Xs and Os. Yeah, that was him all right, always too grumpy and short on time. Always leaving…

Made him smile and remember. Abby used to leave masterpieces like this. Little girls… He'd never understand what on earth he'd done to deserve two perfect daughters.

"Kelsey," he called out in case he was wrong. "You home?"

No *'Be right there, honey!'* came back to him.

Well, damn. She must be swamped at work again. Alex pushed to his feet. *That's okay. It's time I surprise her for a change.*

Renner couldn't stop looking at Montego, his sharp eye tracking every gesture and sideways glance, every barely noticeable nuance of the treacherous woman. The way she stuck her manicured nails in her thick black hair and pushed it off her face. The way it always fell back over her shoulder to cover her face and hide those lying eyes. The way her facial features changed from big-smile schmoozing to cold-blooded focus in the blink of a heavily-lined eye. The way her gaze shifted with slick, practiced ease to the kitchen every time she turned to speak with someone sitting behind her. It was as if she knew she were being watched, as if she enjoyed the cat-and-mouse game.

From the moment she'd waltzed through Raymond's doors to the second she sat her ass in her assigned seat and crossed her long legs at her knees—not at her ankles like a lady would have—she'd acted giddy at the media attention. But Renner knew better. Thanks to Seth, who had thoroughly documented Montego while he'd all but lived undercover in Cuba, Renner had studied her for months. The entire TEAM had. She wasn't a star like the press believed. She was a poisonous snake, again poised to strike at the heart of America.

The cafeteria had filled with the District's finest, from politicians Jed worked with to his wealthy business friends and associates. All were decked out in their finery. And all were soon either going to love pizza and punch, or they were going to leave Raymond's disappointed and hungry.

The kitchen screen was nearly all the way down and Seth and Beckam were lying behind that screen, watching Montego through their scopes. Poor Kelsey seemed flustered, as if it took all her nerve to be courteous to the barely dressed and downright bawdy woman as she seated her in the front row. Pillows would have been so much more fun, watching Montego plant her barely covered ass on the floor.

But when she grabbed Kelsey's hand and pulled her close after she'd sat down…

When she said whatever she told Kelsey, so low it didn't come over Kelsey's hidden mic, every nerve in Renner's body jumped in alarm. "Mark! Don't let her get—"

But Mark hadn't needed to be told. He was already on his feet, angling his body between the women while he tugged Kelsey away from Montego.

"What'd she tell you?" Renner asked once Kelsey was safely seated at the end of the row beside Mark and away from Montego.

"That I have no idea how happy she is to finally meet the beautiful lady behind the great Alex Stewart." Kelsey tossed her head as she mimicked Montego's smoky voice. "The liar. I met her the morning she nearly killed Beau. I was there when he died in my kitchen! On my floor. I cleaned his blood off that floor. God, I hate her."

"You and me both, Kels. Take a deep breath." *Because I sure am.* By then Renner's heart was hammering up his throat at what could've easily been a close call. "Let's remember this night may not be what we think it is. It could really be just another stupid publicity stunt. And the press is watching. We don't want to do anything too crazy." *Like kill her.* "Just don't go near her again, okay? And don't forget to call her LuAnn." *Instead of you raving bitch.*

"But that's not all, Renner." Kelsey sounded like she was grinding her teeth. "She asked where Alex is tonight. She actually thought I'd tell her."

"Don't worry, I've got you," Mark whispered, his arm around her shoulders but his face turned to the podium as if everything were normal and she wasn't having a quiet meltdown. "This will be over soon."

Renner had no doubt Mark would fall in the line of duty before he let anything happen to Kelsey. But things still happened, and this was no ordinary serial killer they were dealing with. Renner was glad to have Mark at Kelsey's six.

Because Montego didn't think like other people. As hard as it was to admit, there was a certain evil genius behind people like her. Serial killers were extremely adept at seizing opportunities most people didn't see and would never think of. They used the simplest opportunities to hurt, maim, or kill. Like Ted Bundy, they operated outside the law, but they also thought outside the boundaries of ordinary comprehension and perspective. They saw the world differently. Everything was a tool to be used and discarded. Even people.

Renner knew damned well this trumped-up media circus had nothing to do with McCormack and everything to do with Montego. "Is she wearing gloves?"

Mark shook his head, signaling he'd heard.

"Damn, that's too bad." But she wouldn't be wearing gloves. She was barely wearing anything. Which should've eased the out-of-control sense of dread slithering up Renner's spine. But damn, it didn't. Something was very off about this foolish, risky spectacle he was witnessing.

All was not as it appeared, but what was he missing? What other mistakes had he made, and what was he not seeing? Montego was damned near naked. She had no place to hide a gun or a knife. Poison, yes, which was why he'd panicked when she'd grabbed onto Kelsey. But Kelsey was fine, and everything seemed perfectly normal. Which meant something was very wrong.

"Kelsey, it's time," Renner prompted, his throat tight and dry. "Go be a shining star."

"Oh, that's real funny, me a star," Kelsey muttered in his earpiece as she lifted to her feet from the seat beside Mark and walked to the podium. "All I need now is to trip and fall on my face in front of everyone. I can see the headlines…"

Her audience couldn't see her talking, not with her thick, brown hair cascading over her shoulders, her head up and her shoulders back. She'd stuck with casual tonight, wearing brown pants and a light-yellow blouse. The black casual suit jacket made her look professional and sharp, yet still laid back. When she turned and faced everyone, she looked tired and nervous. Shy. But the moment she leaned into the podium's built-in microphone, her countenance changed. She smiled. Her face brightened. And there she was again, Alex's girl.

"Governor Tillis. My good friend, Jed McCormack. And the lovely media giants who showed up, I don't know why..." Kelsey said with dramatic affectation. She paused then to let the round of applause and laughter die down. Everyone knew why the press was there. Ratings.

Renner didn't miss that she hadn't acknowledged LuAnn, aka Catalina, hadn't even glanced at the murderess, or called her bitch. Which would surely have made front page news. Kelsey was definitely better than him. He couldn't help thinking, *'You go, girl!'*

"It's my unique pleasure tonight to welcome each of you into my home away from home, to Raymond's Kids, an innovative concept of integrated care that the most vulnerable segment of our society needs. I'd take you on a tour, but as you know, one of the District's free clinics resides at the front of our building, and I never disturb them unless it's urgent. They're the frontline heroes in our fight against homelessness. The work those men and women do there is what brings most of our kids to us here."

Another round of applause. Kelsey went on to explain the gentle giant behind the naming of Raymond's Kids. She talked about how she and Raymond had met during the precarious kidnapping she'd endured a couple years back. How she—of all the least dangerous people in the world—frightened him— a monster of a man/child afflicted with a rare pituitary disorder that had ended his short life.

Man, she was a natural at this. The audience grew silent when she described how she'd grown to love Raymond during those few trying days, and how he'd been sorely used by the truly wicked woman who'd kidnapped Kelsey. She told her audience how that woman had used hamburgers to bribe poor, sweet Raymond, how she'd beat him when he was scared and bullied him when he'd cried. How he'd died helping Kelsey, and how losing him that night broke her heart.

"That was when I decided to do something for all the Raymonds in the world. All my lost boys and girls. But I couldn't save everyone, could I? I'm just one person, right?" she asked, drawing her listeners in.

By then the cafeteria had stilled. Necks craned forward. Everyone waited.

Kelsey's gaze moved slowly across the rows and rows of Jed's and Tillis' admirers, smiling at some, winking at Jed, but not for one second making eye contact with Montego.

At last Kelsey shrugged and murmured into the mic, "But I am *one* person, and I could save *one* lost child." She cleared her throat and licked her bottom lip. "And if I could help one homeless child, why not two? Or three? Or another and another until…?"

She performed a flawless Vanna White maneuver, her hands lifted and her eyes bright as she gestured toward the artwork covered wall to her right. "I give you Raymond's Kids and the person who made all this possible, my dearest friend, the man who should be president, Mr. Jed McCormack!"

The audience erupted, every last one of them up on their feet, cheering as Jed stood. For a second there, he almost looked presidential. Renner blinked at the transformation in the man. The reporters went wild, they were everywhere. Snapping pictures while Mark escorted Jed forward. Capturing Kelsey's beaming smile as she stood front and center and clapped for Jed.

But damn, Montego was good, on her feet and clapping along like she cared about Jed—when it was doubtful she cared about anyone. Smiling as if her sharp black eyes weren't peeling Kelsey's skin from her body, slice by bloody slice. And that get-up she'd worn tonight—holy shit. Hard to miss those voluminous, mocha colored breasts spilling over her too-tight glittery spandex tube-top, or the tanned thighs her mini-mini-skirt barely covered. Montego made Madonna look like a chaste virgin. If there were a way she could've looked coarser, or more like a two-bit hooker, Renner didn't know it.

He scanned to the barely lifted rolling divider from where Seth and Beckam watched over Kelsey. They would soon vacate their station after McCormack finished whatever he was going to babble about. Which seemed another one of Renner's glaring errors tonight. Jed was in no condition to speak coherently, much less handle the media glare or any reporter's leading questions. He had no idea where he was. So why the hell was he here?

"We should've called this off, Mark," Renner whispered, knowing full well he'd just broadcast that second-guess to everyone with an earpiece.

"I thought he'd snap out of it," Mark murmured even as he escorted Jed to the podium. "He has before. He might still."

"Trust me," Kelsey whispered. "I'd rather accept the fake check from Jed, or whatever he needs to give me, than that woman. I'll help him get through this. You'll see. I won't leave him. We'll be fine."

"No," Renner said, his gut churning out a definite storm warning. "Get him and Kelsey out of there, Mark. This is all wrong. We can't go through with it."

Renner saw his final error then. Saw her. A slender woman with long, sleek, chocolate brown hair had just stepped out from the third row, walking with purpose. Dressed exactly like

Kelsey. Same color pants. Same suit jacket over the same light-yellow blouse. Her head down. She walked quickly. Too quickly. Straight for the podium.

"Everyone down! Montego's got help, Mark!" Renner yelled as his pistol snapped into his palm.

In that same instant, someone on the front row popped yellow smoke, and the stampede commenced. Women screamed. Men bellowed. But they all turned tail and ran for the exit where Renner was standing, knocking over chairs and stepping on each other in their haste to save themselves. Coughing. Choking. Shoving him out of the way as they fled into the hall.

By then, dense yellow smoke completely concealed Kelsey and the first ten or so front rows.

"Mark!" Renner bellowed. "Everyone! Save Kelsey and Jed! Can anyone see her?"

"Copy that," Aaron growled. "I've got her."

"Where's Jed?"

"Safe," Mark hissed. "He never left my side."

Thank God! "Then where's the bitch?" Renner growled as he fought against the panicked crowd, leading with his shoulder, butting men and women, reporters and senators and senators' wives out of his way. "Where's Montego? Seth! Beckam! You seeing her?"

"Negative," both men replied in unison.

"Can't see anything in this shit, Renner," Seth replied. "Coming your way as soon as we pack up."

"She has to be here! Move it," Renner ordered the last teary-eyed reporter as he cleared the front row. "Shit, someone open the front doors. Aaron, you got any fans?"

"In the supply room, but I'm not leaving this lady."

"Kelsey?" Renner cried out.

"I'm okay, Renner. I'm good. She did it again, didn't she?"

"Hell, I don't know what she did other than create panic…" Renner spun on his heel, his brain working to understand what had just happened. "Shit. Where'd she go?"

By then visibility was partly cloudy to clearing.

"Did anyone see her? Did she leave the building?"

"Negative," Zale reported. "None of us saw anyone leave, and we've been watching, sir."

Which meant she was still inside somewhere. She had to be.

"Guys, get Kelsey and Jed out of here," Renner ordered.

"Let's go to my office," Kelsey said.

"Copy that," Mark replied. "On our way."

Adrenaline poured into Renner at the seemingly perfect puzzle Montego had created. He watched dutifully while Mark ushered Jed across the hall. Aaron and Kelsey followed.

But if Montego was the only one missing, if she truly had fled the building for some unknown reason, even if she was still inside, who cared? Renner could track her now that the main players were safe. She'd missed her prime objective tonight. That was something to be proud of until—he knew who he wasn't seeing.

"Tara!" he bellowed, his heart racing as his boots carried him back to the kitchen. "Have you seen Tara?" he asked Seth and Beckam. "Was she here?"

Both men looked up from where they were packing their rifle cases. "She was until we set up shop, then she split," Beckam replied.

"Where'd she go?"

Seth's shoulders lifted. "Said you were cute, that she was going to stand by you, that she didn't want to miss the show."

"Then where is she now?"

"I left Jed and Kelsey together. She's armed now," Mark said calmly from behind him. "Don't worry. Tara can take care of herself. We'll find her."

But Renner knew better. Tara was that dark-haired woman who'd come out of nowhere at the last moment. She'd purposely dressed like Kelsey tonight. She'd meant what she'd said, that she'd do anything to help her friend.

And he'd been a fool. Too focused on Kelsey and Montego, he'd missed the obvious. Somehow, Tara had walked right past him, and then kept her back toward Seth and Beckam until Montego popped the smoke. That had to be what happened. Tara had also believed Montego was here tonight for a different reason than schmoozing the press. She hadn't known what it was, but she'd been prepared to protect Kelsey the only way she knew how. By becoming Kelsey. Montego had no idea that her little smoke bomb would create enough confusion to fool even her.

Renner's worst nightmare had come true. "Montego's got Tara," he whispered.

"How?" Aaron asked through his earpiece. "My guys are all over this place, inside and out. They would've seen and apprehended her."

"I don't know..." Renner could barely speak. He truly didn't understand how Montego and Tara could've disappeared into thin air. He'd been at the exit, Seth and Beckam at the kitchen exit. She hadn't gotten past them. But then he knew. Montego had escaped and she'd kidnapped the wrong woman.

"She thinks she's got Kelsey, but she kidnapped Tara instead." He ran across the hall and pounded on the locked door. "It's me, Kels. Open up!"

The door swung open. Kelsey stood there, her arm around Jed, her pistol pointed down.

"Where's your security camera footage. I need to see it right damned now," Renner ordered. "There's still time. We can apprehend her."

"What happened?"

"Montego kidnapped Tara." Man, his heart felt like an Abrams tank had parked on his chest.

"Jed, you stay here," Kelsey said as she scrambled into the hall with Aaron on her six.

Of course, Jed-the-Meek took the nearest seat, sitting there like the lost man he was. It didn't get any sadder than this. The man who'd bankrolled both Alex's TEAM and Raymond's Kids, now just as lost as the children she rescued.

"Mark, we need to get those people out of here," Renner ordered.

An ashen-faced reporter stuck her mic in his face and asked, "What's your name? You look important. Who are you and just what happened here tonight? Was this simply another hoax? Another publicity stunt to get more funding for this pathetic excuse of a charity? And where is LuAnn? What'd you do to her? Talk to America. We have a right to know." By then she was screaming at him, her voice in entitled, demanding, panic mode.

Renner squared his shoulders and looked straight into her cameraman's lens. "You want the truth?" he asked, his heart on his sleeve. "You think you can handle the truth?" And now he was channeling Jack Nicholson.

"That's what I asked, isn't it?"

And enough! Renner snapped the mic out of that ballsy woman's grip and gritted his teeth, staring at America but aiming for Montego. "My name is USMC Staff Sergeant Renner Graves. You hear me, Catalina Montego? You understand what I'm telling you? Look at this face and remember it, because I'm the last thing you're going to see. I don't give a damn what you call yourself now. LuAnn. Catalina. Or asswipe. I'm coming for you. So run, you goddamned bitch." Renner clicked the mic off, then handed it back to the reporter. "There. Now you've got a story."

"Wait!" she squealed, chasing after him. "You think LuAnn's really that serial killer, Catalina Montego?"

"No further comment," he shot over his shoulder.

"Way to go, big mouth," Mark murmured, keeping his reprimand low as he fell into step alongside Renner. "You just made yourself a target, not what we need."

"I don't give a shit. She wanted a war, now she's got one."

"Come with me. You need to see what Aaron found."

"Where is—" He spotted Kelsey with Aaron outside the kitchen door. *Oh, thank God.* She was still safe and protected. "What?"

She waved him forward. The crowd of Aaron's men gathered around her parted like the Red Sea had for Moses hundreds of years ago. And Renner lost it.

"Shit, shit, shit!" he snarled, now looking at something else he hadn't known existed. A hidden door! About three-by-three, it dropped into a chute that led to the basement—or outside.

"You," he said pointed to the nearest man. "Go downstairs and—"

"There's nothing there," Aaron said. "We live downstairs. This chute has to go outside."

Renner suppressed an urge to kick something. This was how Montego had gotten Tara out of the building. Once that smoke filled the other end of the room, she'd forced Tara down this chute and into someone else's waiting arms. What a clusterfuck. He should've studied this building's blueprints closer, better, quicker! Hell, Jed should've given him more time to do his job right!

"I didn't know this was here," Kelsey whispered. "It must've been how they sent their full lunchroom trash down to the main garbage bin when this was a functioning high school."

You think? Renner bit his tongue at the panic hammering his heart into oblivion. The chute led to the west side of the building where there weren't enough lights. Where it was extra dark. Where someone had obviously been waiting with a vehicle large enough for Montego and her prey. Tara. Where Renner had made his first error.

"Tell me you at least have security cameras there?" Renner asked, trying not to sound like an ass, but pissed as hell.

"Yes, I do. I can get everything up and running in my office," Kelsey replied. "I'm sor—"

Renner's right hand came up, demanding silence, not excuses. He had no more patience to give, not even for Kelsey. "Just take me there. Mark, Seth, and Beckam, do not let Jed McCormack out of your sight, and will someone please get rid of these people? The party's over," he called out.

Notice he didn't say *'fucking people'*? That ought to count for something.

Mark shot him a warning glare but complied. And yeah, Renner knew he needed to stop treating his senior agent like a junior agent. But shit. *Tara!*

He all but shoved Kelsey into her office. Aaron sat at her desk now, watching the big screen Renner also hadn't realized she owned. But hey, look. Another secret panel. Only this one was actually an armoire that matched her solid oak desk. So it didn't count. "Find anything?"

Aaron nodded, pointing as he rewound the footage. "The garbage chute leads directly from the kitchen to this point right here. It's hidden in this alcove, but watch…"

Renner shut the overhead light off to see past the reflection on the monitor. The tape showed a black van parked at the westside curb, its lights off. A wintery night and fog made it hard to see the plates. Then two black shadows materialized from the alcove, one with a bag over her head, the other pushing the first forward. Montego shoved Tara and she slumped into the open van door. Still no headlights. Not even taillights flickered when the van pulled away.

With his blood thrumming in his ears, Renner said, "Okay, now we know how."

"But how could Montego have known we had a chute?" Kelsey asked. "I work here and I didn't know."

"Tara must've known. She must have told her," Aaron said.

"Which might be how Tyson's getting out of the building," Kelsey said thoughtfully.

Another thing Renner hadn't known. Not like he'd had enough warning to perform a thorough search of this old building. Not that McCormack had given him or Kelsey sufficient time to prepare for the snake he'd brought into this safe place. Jesus Christ! What else could go wrong?

"But why Tara?" Kelsey asked, wiping tears Renner didn't want to see. Couldn't see. Not now. Not with his heart and his reason for living in Montego's cold-blooded hands. God damn it, everything came back to Kelsey.

"She did it for you," he told her, fighting to see through the shimmer in his eyes. "Tara dressed like you tonight. Ten to one she didn't know Montego was going after you or Jed, but she'd prepared, just in case. She made certain she was on her feet. It was just dumb luck she was right and that Montego smuggled in a smoke bomb, probably in her heel. Montego thinks she's got you, Kels."

Her slender fingers cupped her mouth. "No—" she croaked.

"I'm sorry, but yeah." Renner swallowed hard. "Tara told me how you saved her life the day you welcomed her to Raymond's Kids. She loves you, Kels, and because she does, she made herself a target. She planned this all along."

Kelsey dissolved into tears, and Renner turned away, fighting his terror. He'd seen what Montego did the night she'd kidnapped Beau. That time she'd taken just his little finger. While Renner knew the pain Beau suffered, he couldn't help worrying what Montego would do to a woman who'd had the audacity to deceive her, especially when she'd fully believed she finally stabbed Alex where it would hurt him the worst. At his heart.

Instead, she'd stabbed Renner's heart. And it was killing him.

Chapter Twenty-Nine

Once again. Maybe one last time. Tara shook off the effects of the knock-out drug Montego had plunged into her neck when they'd gone down that chute to her getaway van. The concrete floor beneath her was damp, kind of slimy. It smelled bad, though Tara wasn't positive that she wasn't smelling her own blood. But the sickening sweet stink of urine? Couldn't be her. Just could not. That would mean she'd been so scared she'd lost control and wet herself. But Tara wasn't scared, and she wasn't that kind of wet. Not yet.

Her sluggish mind wandered. She was concerned, maybe. Thoughtful. But not for one second did she doubt her decision to save Kelsey Stewart's life. This was precisely what Renner would've done, if he'd had the girlish figure. But he just plain didn't have what it took. There really were some things only a woman could do, and standing in for her best friend was one of them.

That smoke bomb was quite a surprise. Tara took that as a sign that she'd been meant to save Kelsey. Coincidences didn't just happen.

"Please, get… can you get off my foot?" some guy whined.

Tara jerked awake. Instinctively, she rolled to her butt and away from that voice. Where had Montego taken her? And what was that putrid smell?

"Who are you?" she asked as she lifted her arm to cover her nose as the stench worsened.

"R-Roger," he answered, sounding more like a ten-year-old kid than a man. "Jesus, you're a… a woman?"

"Last time I checked, yeah," she answered, trying to keep her cool.

"I'm Gilbert," another voice said.

"Pete."

"Samson, here."

"Antonio, but you can call me Tony." That one came with a definite flirty Bronx accent and a tight twinge of pain.

"Shy," the last voice rasped. He sounded sickly. Weak.

"Gary."

But it was too dark to make out faces. "There's seven of you?" she asked. "Where am I?"

"In hell," Shy murmured hoarsely. "With us."

"And we got us an angel," Tony piped up. "You gonna save us?"

"Shhhhh, you gotta rest, Shy," one of the guys said, maybe Roger. "Stop talking or you ain't gonna last. But please, ma'am, you gotta get off my foot. It's… God, I don't want to scare you, but it's still bleeding."

"Bleeding? Oh, my gosh!" Tara eased her calf off the hard lump she'd thought was a rock. "I'm so sorry!"

"'S okay," he groaned as he pulled his foot from under her.

That's what the smell was. These men. That foot. *Shit!* as Renner would say if he'd been here. Montego hadn't planned to just kidnap and kill Kelsey. She'd meant to torture her like she'd tortured these men.

Tara decided right then and there, she was not going to die at Montego's hands. She'd survived one asshole. She could survive another. But first…

"Shy?" she asked. "I'm no angel, but you sound like you're badly hurt, am I right?"

"We're all badly hurt, ma'am, but yeah. Shy got it the worst."

Tara couldn't be sure which man said that. They all sounded so ragged, so much the same.

"Cuz I wouldn't cry," he whispered. "She likes it when guys cry."

Oh, damn, this was so, so bad. Tara swallowed hard, then said, "So maybe, somehow, I can help." That seemed the best solution. She helped kids, and these guys were all just big kids. As far as she could tell, they weren't restrained any more than she was.

"D-don't t-t-touch me," Shy whimpered. "Just them. Just help them."

Which meant he needed critical care, and he needed it first. Tara pulled that damned wig off, the same one she'd worn the night she'd first showed up at Raymond's Kids. She'd been traveling incognito back then. But once again, it served its purpose. It had kept her safe. It would keep Kelsey safe now.

This place was cramped, crowded, and stifling hot, which made no sense at this time of year. Tara didn't have a clue what those conditions meant. She hadn't come across any places warmer than the heat vents over Metro stations that crisscrossed the District when she'd lived on the streets.

"Talk to me, Shy," she said calmly. "I'm coming to you. I can help. I know I can. Just reach out and take hold of my hand—"

"No. Please, no. You can't help. Not me. Please…" He broke into shuddering sobs. "D-d-don't. J-just don't."

Tara stopped, kneeling and facing darkness with no way to know where any of these men were. "I just want to help."

"You can't help us, ma'am," Roger said, his tone as hopeless as Shy's. "It's too late. There isn't anything to do for Shy now but pray for him to die. Pray for us, too. You wouldn't happen to have a gun on you?"

She shook her head in the dark, even though she knew none of these guys could see her.

"I figure that's a no," he muttered sadly. "Too bad. I'd pray for a bullet myself."

"We can't give up hope," she told him in her best imitation of Kelsey.

"Yeah…" Shy whispered. "Yeah, we can, Ma'am. It's easy… easier… than…" It sounded as if his last breath had just wheezed out of him.

"Shy?" Tara panicked. "Shy? Talk to me. I can help. I know—"

"Shhhhh," Roger hissed. "He's gone."

"He's dead?"

"Yes, ma'am. It was only a matter of time. We tried to help him for days. There was nothing you could've done."

"But…" She couldn't think. Couldn't breathe. Poor Shy had just died less than five feet from her. She could've helped! She could have… "What… what'd Montego do to him?" she asked as tears started to flow.

"You don't want to know. What are you wearing? Any extra clothes? A jacket maybe? You got any water on you?"

"No water, but I've got a jacket. You want my clothes? You can have them."

"Only what you can spare, ma'am. Just need to make a couple tourniquets, that's all."

"Oh, sure." Tourniquets, just tourniquets to stop yourselves from bleeding to death before Montego comes back to kill you. By now Tara was shivering, but not from the cold. "I-I can rip my sleeves and pant legs off, too. Here you go," she said as…

R-r-i-p-p-p-p-p! Who needed sleeves when men were dying?

"Thank you, kindly," Roger said gruffly. "You have no idea what this means to us."

"Spare a couple pieces for me?" Antonio's voice for sure.

"She hurt all of you," Tara whispered, understanding now. Montego had taken fingers, toes, and limbs from these men. Maybe more. Off came her shirt. "Here, let me do that," she told Roger as she tugged it back and proceeded to turn that shirt into bandages and tourniquets and anything else these guys needed.

"Ah, thanks," Roger whispered, his voice ragged and broken as she wrapped part of her jacket around his foot, then tied it with a narrow strip of her shirt. "You're very kind. Sure sorry you're here, though."

"I'm not," she declared bravely. That quiver in her voice didn't mean anything.

Roger didn't reply, and Tara was certain he was crying. For her.

So was she.

Chapter Thirty

Renner was still in Kelsey's office. Still pissed at himself and everyone else on this son of a bitchin' failed op. Renner couldn't believe that no one—no one!—knew where Montego had gone or where she could be. Not any of Aaron's men. Not Aaron. The security footage didn't extend far enough into the street to know if that van had turned left or right. Ember was hard at work searching traffic cams in the area, but that took time. Time Tara didn't have.

Christ on a cracker! She could be dying right now. Or already dead.

"Shit!" he hissed for the umpteenth time.

"We'll find her," Aaron said quietly. He'd been saying that since this *'event'* had turned to crap, and it was working Renner's last nerve.

"She's smart," Kelsey added. "She escaped Jorge when they lived in Colorado and—"

"Sir, you need to step back!" Beckam bellowed from the rear exit where he was supposed to be keeping watch for… Oh, whatever. Who cared? There was no sense watching the henhouse now that the fox had come and gone.

"I will shoot you, now back off!"

Renner scrubbed a hand over his face, pissed at yet one more interruption, one more thing he'd failed to consider. He'd barely cleared the door, when he was confronted with

Beckam's broad back, his boots planted, his butt taut, and both arms extended forward, his pistol in some guy's face.

"What's up, Beck?" Renner asked tiredly.

"Sir, yes, sir, this jerk-off refuses to stand down."

Said jerk-off peered around Beckam with one lethal gray eye. "Are you in charge of this fucked up mess?" he asked, his voice an exact duplicate of Christian Bale's Batman. Deep. Distorted. Dangerous.

The guy's eyepatch made him look like a pirate. Heavy burns mottled his lower left cheek and jaw. Both eyebrows were missing. Renner doubted any hair existed beneath the knitted skull cap pulled tight over his head. He had to be the leader of Montego's other nine.

"You're another of Montego's victims?" Renner asked as more men filed into the hall.

"None of your business. I asked you a question. Are you in charge or not?"

"Yes, I'm in charge," Renner declared, since Mark had run Jed home to his penthouse. "And I asked you a question. Are you another of Montego's victims?"

Aaron was at his side by then, stretching his good hand to the stranger. "They're not victims, Agent Graves. This man is a survivor like me. Hello, I'm Aaron Pope. We talked earlier today."

The stranger's nostrils flared as he sneered at Aaron, who still held his hand out in friendship. "Did you kill her?"

"I've got more tangos entering the rear exit," Beckam advised. "Seth, where are you? Come in, Seth."

"Right up behind these guys," Seth answered, nice and easy. "There's eight altogether, Beck. Another one stayed with the vehicle they ditched three blocks south. That makes nine. We got a name yet, Boss?"

"Working on it," Renner replied as he eased back on his frustration. "I know you and your men don't belong to Montego," he told the stranger. "I'm sorry I misspoke. But right now, she's got one of my people and—"

"Fuckin' asshole!" the pirate hissed. "You should've killed her on sight! What'd you do, invite her in for tea and crumpets, you sons of bitches?"

Beckam stepped a foot back, aligning himself with Renner who was now in the center of the hall. By stepping out of Renner's way, Beck revealed the rest of the stranger's body. The metal knee-brace on his left leg. His black gloves, the left one with rigid curled fingers, the right gripping a nasty, blued, six-and-a-half-inch 44. Magnum, right out of *"Dirty Harry."*

Renner's self-righteous attitude deflated at the atrocity Montego had committed against this man. At the degradation he'd suffered. "You're right, sir, I should've killed Montego the second I saw her, because I sure as hell knew we were all going to be outplayed. Only there are laws about gunning down unarmed women just because you've got a feeling. And…"

"She ain't no woman."

"…now Montego's taken one of our women who—"

"You let her get someone? How long ago? When, damn you? When?"

"I didn't let her take anyone—"

"An hour ago," Kelsey interrupted, her head held high as she stepped around Renner and Beckam. "I'm Kelsey Stewart, and I run this—"

"I know who you are, ma'am. You're Alex's wife."

"I am," she said proudly. "May I know your name, sir?"

He scowled. He growled. But at last the pirate brushed past Aaron's hand and took hold of Kelsey's. "Tom," he said with a curt nod. "That's all you need to know. I'm Tom, and these guys are my… my men. Our car ran out of gas or we would've been here sooner and… Hell, it don't matter." He turned on Renner. "You dumb fucks let her get away. We wasted the trip."

"Watch your mouth," Renner snapped, ready to smack this guy for his atrocious language.

Tom's nostrils twitched. He cast a look at Kelsey, then muttered the most insincere apology Renner had ever heard. "She's heard worse if she was dumb enough to marry a Marine."

"You're right," Kelsey snapped back. "I have heard worse, but this is my house, Tom. My rules. And the sewer doesn't run through here, so there'll be no more crass language, understood?"

"Yes, ma'am," he grumbled, his nose still bent out of shape.

Before he had time to toss another comment, Renner asked, "Do you know where Montego might have gone?"

And off Tom went on another rampage. "Now how would I know? Haven't seen that twisted bitch in months. You think we helped her? Is that what you're accusing—"

Despite his vulgarity, Kelsey had yet to let go of Tom's hand. "We're not accusing you of anything, but my friend risked her life to save me tonight, and I'm very worried…" Her voice cracked. "Tom, I'm scared Montego's hurting Tara while we stand here and argue about whose is bigger. You know how cruel she is. Please. Won't you help me?"

Renner took a step back, giving Kelsey room to what she did best. When Tom growled and shook his head, she dropped his hand and covered her mouth. The muscles in her neck tightened, and Renner knew she was on the verge of tears again. Hell, he was, too. This was his fault, every last fuckin' mistake of this entire fuckin' night was his fault. But Tara was the one who would pay for it.

He couldn't stand to see the rancid acceptance in this guy's eye. Tom had clearly come here to kill Montego, not to rescue or help anybody. He was past the point of civility. Which happened. Some survivors had been through so much they became as cold as the person who'd tortured them. They'd had to. That was how they'd survived, by learning to live through the pain and wretchedness of being turned into a monster. Of having lost the person they once were.

Tom wouldn't help. He didn't know how.

Renner blinked. His throat closed. His heart broke. Jesus, he had to wipe his face when the first tears breached the dam and—

"She might've taken her—there," Tom told one of his men, the one standing behind him at his left. "You thinking what I'm thinking?"

The gray-haired man's head bobbed. "Maybe. If it's still deserted."

"Where?" snapped out of Renner like a flash of lightning. "What's deserted?"

"I don't want your help," Tom spat, his eye on Renner again. "Understand? I don't need it. We—us—we don't need nothing from the likes of you. It's too late. You didn't come looking for us, not once. We don't owe you nuthin'. Do we, men?"

A growly smattering of agreement sounded from the group. Most of his men hadn't come forward, but hung back like shadows who didn't want to be seen, trapped between Seth at their rear, the people standing with Renner forward. Aaron. Kelsey. Beck. Some of Aaron's men, Kelsey's guys.

"But we need you, sir," Renner said as evenly as he could before he fell apart and outright begged. "Can you help us, just tonight? Where do you think Montego might be?"

"Where she, umm, err, where she kept us," Tom replied quietly. "There's an old meat-packing plant off Interstate 495."

"The one by Joint Base Andrews?" Aaron asked.

Renner didn't like the tremor to Aaron's tone.

"That'd be the one," Tom replied somberly. "Only you'd better run while there's still something left of your girl to rescue. It takes sixty minutes to heat the boiler, and Montego likes to play with fire. She's never had a woman at her place before."

"Seven men have gone missing since she returned from Cuba," Aaron interjected. "You think they could be there?"

Tom shrugged, but his eye tracked Renner like a hawk. "She only had two places I knew. The one Alex found last year and the one she kept us in."

Renner shoved past Tom's group of wounded men and all but exploded past Seth and out the rear door. "I'm out of here."

"Wait!" Kelsey cried behind him. "I'm coming!"

"No," he called over his shoulder. "Not this time. Stay here where you'll be safe!"

"But I have a chopper."

That she did. Renner hit the skids, his hand already on his car's door handle, his heart a throbbing beast of anguish at every passing second. "How long until it can be here?" he asked, the tears in his eyes turning Kelsey into a blinding cloud of glistening stars.

She held up five fingers, her cell already at her ear. "Ben. I need you at Raymond's Kids right now. Yes, it's an emergency. Okay, I understand, but hurry, and please fly safe."

"Well?" Renner asked, trying to hold it together as Seth, Beckam, Aaron, Tom and his men formed a half-circle around him and Kelsey in the damp fog. Like it or not, Seth's heavy hand came to rest on his shoulder. Renner shrugged Seth off. It was either that or break down.

"Ben's my pilot, err, Alex's pilot. He said he'd be here in four. He had already refueled the chopper and filed a flight plan to take me home, so he just has to post an update and he's good to go."

"How long's that going to take?" Renner asked, icy fear creeping up his spine, counting down the seconds to each one of those long four minutes.

"He's on his way now, Renner," Kelsey said pointedly. "Can someone please go inside and get my coat? Bring one for Tara, too. And some blankets. She might be cold."

"On it," Seth and Beckam said simultaneously. Off they went. By the time they returned, Ben had touched down in the parking lot, the rotors kicking up a crystalized fog that stung like a thousand BBs.

"How many can that chopper take?" Tom asked, scrubbing his scruffy jaw with his rigid fingers.

"Twenty," Kelsey answered brightly as she opened the door.

Which meant Tom and his men planned to ride along with Renner. He didn't care who came until Kelsey put her foot on the two-step ladder to climb aboard.

"No, stay!" he told her. "Please?"

"But this was my idea," she argued. "Tara needs me. It's my fault she's in trouble."

Renner shook his head no even as he shut the door in her face and told Ben, "Go, go, go!"

"But she's my boss," Ben stalled.

"And there's a good chance she'll die tonight if she comes with us, now go!"

One woman in peril was enough.

Chapter Thirty-One

Tara wiped the sweat from her brow, tired and frightened. After tying multiple tourniquets, she was fully aware of what she was now up against. Torture, depraved and gruesome. Bloody. Utterly, thoroughly frightening.

Pete had no fingers on his right hand, just four lacerated, bleeding knuckles and a thumb, the same as Aaron's hand. She couldn't tie a tourniquet, so she'd fashioned a padded bandage.

Because Montego had taken his toes, Antonio's right foot was hot and swollen, his calf soft with infection. Tara had tied a tourniquet at his ankle even though she knew she'd hurt him when she did. But he'd kept telling her, "tighter, please, I can take it, tighter" until tears streamed down her face. What she'd suffered at Jorge's hands was nothing compared to what these men were suffering tonight.

Poor Gary Desmarais hadn't been physically tortured yet, but he was definitely in shock and way too quiet. Probably drugged.

The bandaging, tying off of so many tourniquets, and knowing where to put her hands and feet so she didn't inadvertently hurt someone while she'd worked, made nursing difficult in the dark. Yet even those small victories spelled doom if she'd infected these poor men's injuries more than they already were.

From what Tara could tell, they were imprisoned inside a square concrete room without doors or windows. Instead of cold like a basement, this room was uncomfortably muggy. One wall was warm enough to make her believe there was a furnace behind it. Combine that with the wide range of body odors, the stink of excrement, and sweat pouring off five extremely sick men, and yeah. Taking a breath without throwing up was a challenge.

Of the five, Antonio, aka Tony, the flirt from New York City—not the Bronx he'd informed her—was in the worst condition. Racked with a high fever, he fluctuated between shivering and sweating. Because she'd used her shirt and jacket for the tourniquets everyone needed, there was nothing left to fashion into a pillow for him. Just a worthless, lumpy pillow. That was all he needed to be a tiny bit more comfortable, and she couldn't even offer that. Instead he'd thanked her for *'torturing him'* with a tourniquet—her words, not his—then laid down and pressed his cheek to the filthy concrete floor in this hellhole. He said it was cool, that it helped him feel better. Tara doubted that.

Roger leaned his back against the wall at her right, Samson beside him. Both men were breathing heavily. Pete, Gilbert, and Gary leaned against the opposite wall, while Tara sat cross-legged in the middle of the men, alongside Tony. Shy's body now lay parallel to the wall between Gilbert and Samson. Roger had carefully shoved him there when he'd made room for Tara.

Her lips were parched from the relentless heat and her throat was sore. A bottle of water would've been nice, but she refused to complain. Asking for anything seemed cruel, considering how long these men had been without water and food.

"You okay, kid?" Roger asked wearily.

"As good as I can be, but please call me—"

"Stop. Don't say it," he ordered. "We don't need to know your name. Kid will do."

"But I know who you all are."

"You only know first names. You can't be sure we didn't lie to you."

"I didn't lie," Tony murmured, his voice tight. "I'm Antonio D'Angelo, and my father's Giuseppe. My mother's Lenna Genova of the Milan Genovas, you know, in Milan, Italy? She and Papa own a vineyard north of West Point. Please don't tell them how I died, ma'am. Make something up. Tell them I got shot or I drank myself to death. Anything but this."

Tara reached through the dark and found the back of his arm. "You're not going to die," she whispered, lying through her teeth.

"Yeah, I am. All of us are."

Tara would've argued if she hadn't still had these men's blood on her hands and arms, probably on her face, too. The longer she'd worked to stop their bleeding, the more she knew she could never withstand the depraved tortures they'd suffered. What kind of animal cut off another person's fingers and toes? A foot? An ear! There'd been nothing to be done for Gilbert, no way to apply a tourniquet. Montego had taken his left ear. Even now, he moaned while he rocked and bled into a piece of Tara's shirt, trying to soothe himself. It wasn't working.

"Stop it," Roger said. "Just stop. Don't make things worse."

Gilbert moaned. "Not like things can get worse."

"It can if we know her name. It can when—if she gets hurt," Roger snapped. "So stop already. Just shut the fuck up."

"Yeah, you're right," Gilbert sighed. "That would be worse."

"Umm," Tara said, her mind spinning at the awful implication of—worse. "Pain's pretty much the same for every—"

"No, it's not," Roger ground out. "It's... it's different when females c-c-cry. T-trust me. It's bad enough being tied down and made to watch a guy getting cut or sawed on, but a w-w-woman…" A thump sounded from his general area. Might have been his head hitting the wall behind him. "God, just get this shit over."

"How'd you get so unlucky?" Samson asked quietly. He sounded younger than the others but trying to be tough. "I mean, to end up here with us?"

Tara huffed through her nostrils. "I had a different plan than this tonight, trust me. I work at a halfway house for runaway kids. Do you guys know who Jed McCormack is?"

A couple grunts came back to her. Roger said, "Yeah. Went to Iraq with Brady, his son."

"Well, tonight he paid us a visit. He made a big donation, and he wanted to do it in public, but he brought his girlfriend with him and—"

"He's got a girlfriend?" Roger asked. "Since when?"

"Yes. Ever since his wife died, he—"

"Lois is dead? No. How'd that happen? When? Jesus Christ!"

Tara stilled, not sure how much to tell this man. He'd been in Montego's clutches a long time if he didn't know Mrs.

McCormack had died. "How long have you been here?" she asked instead of answering.

"Forever," he replied, his voice tired and dry as if his soul were already dead and simply waiting around for his body to get the message.

"As in months?"

"Yeah. Months."

"I hate to tell you, Roger, but Lois McCormack died six months ago."

He made an odd, sad sound, a choking, growling, grinding sound that broke Tara's heart.

"How'd she get to you?" Roger sounded like a big guy.

"We just got back from the Philippines. Went out for drinks and dancing. Guess I got a little crazy with the wrong bitch. Woke up strapped to a... her... table. That's when she took my first toe."

Tara could hear him trying to swallow. It sounded like Roger couldn't make his throat work.

"You never finished telling us how you ended up here, ma'am," Samson reminded her quietly.

Tara wiped a hand over her head, wishing she had an elastic to keep her hair out of her sweaty face. She drew in a belly full of air and told them about Jorge and her marriage, about his terrorist link, running away and divorcing him. She told them about her prescription drug habit, about wandering into that halfway house in DC one particularly dark night. About being saved. She told them how she'd never had a sister, but she'd found one that night. By the time she was through, poor Tony was snoring, but the rest of the guys knew Montego not only had her hooks in Jed, but that Tara had intentionally walked into Montego's trap in order to save Kelsey.

"You're shittin' me," Gilbert hissed. "You decided it'd be better to let that bitch torture you instead of someone else? What are you, stupid?"

And that was okay. Gilbert was in pain, and that gaping, oozing hole on the side of his poor head where his ear used to be was badly infected. He didn't mean what he said.

"Guess I'm as stupid as men who go off to war or combat then," she murmured, rubbing the back of Tony's arm, wishing he were awake. Wishing he were Renner. "I'd rather Montego hurt me than my sister, wouldn't you?"

"Yeah. Yeah, I would," Gilbert answered somberly. "Sorry, ma'am. I've got two sisters. One's older, one's younger. You're right. I'm sure as hell glad they're not here."

"Me too," Tara whispered as she wiped a new batch of tears. "Just wish we weren't here either, guys. I mean, I don't even know what you look like, but I—"

CRASH!

"What was that?"

"God, no," Roger growled. "The boiler. She's... shit. She's back."

Chapter Thirty-Two

The abandoned meat packing plant occupied an acre on the far east side of a long rectangular stretch of land alongside the interstate. Asphalt covered the area surrounding the plant. An eight-foot-high chain-link fence surrounded the parking lot. No trespassing signs marked twenty feet intervals on that fence. A chained double-gate barred the main entrance. A reasonable person could never gain entry. Good thing Renner wasn't reasonable.

The helo had already coasted over the property for a quick look-see. No lights shone from the front office windows. The only sign that someone was indeed home—the POS utility van parked alongside the loading dock behind the building.

Renner's plan was simple. Montego had a driver. Montego had Tara. Montego and her buddy driver were going to die.

But getting into the building without being seen was the problem. The lair that The TEAM had discovered in Alexandria had been one helluva diabolical nightmare that had nearly ended Maverick Carson, another TEAM agent's, life. Seemingly a derelict warehouse from the outside, the interior opened into one wide space. All walls and a high ceiling with metal struts, at first blush it appeared to be what it looked like from the outside—empty.

But unbeknownst to Alex, Beau, Maverick, and Gabe when they'd B&E'd, the entire floor—which had appeared solid—had actually concealed an array of individual concrete cells, each capped with a benign steel plate designed to hold a man's weight. But only for so long. Like the treacherous black widow spider Montego was, each of those steel plates had also concealed a spring actuator. They were pressure plates, that, within seconds of someone stepping on them, dropped the trespasser into either one of her victim's cells or onto a bed of steel spikes.

Maverick fell onto steel spikes that afternoon. He would've died had Alex, Beau, and Gabe not been there to commence immediate life-saving measures. By the end of the day, he'd been in critical care and in surgery, and The TEAM had rescued nineteen tortured, starved, feral men. Alex's USMC buddy, Aaron Pope, had been among them. Renner hoped to make Tom's nine and those still missing seven, Montego's final victims. Her swan song if he had his way.

It was well known she had access to unlimited resources. One didn't come up through the ranks of an international crime family like hers without inheriting the blood money they'd left behind when they'd died—all violently. Which made Renner certain nothing about this derelict building was what it appeared to be.

"Is the parking lot solid?" he asked Tom through their headsets.

Tom's head bobbed. He'd grown more somber and less nasty now that they were hovering over the place where he'd been tortured.

"What can you tell us about the place?" Renner needed specifics. "Are we going to run into any booby-traps? Early warning systems? Poison darts?" He didn't really think there were poison darts, he just said that to get Tom's waning attention back on track. The man seemed to be lost in his thoughts.

By now Ben had landed the chopper near the trees on the parking lot at the far west end of the property. Montego's second lair lay due east at the opposite end of the property. While freeway lights cast a dim light on the front of the building, the entire rear was pretty much shadow. A full stretch of cracked asphalt parking lot lay between Renner and Tara.

Tom gestured with his prosthetic hand at the ominously silent building. "I hate to admit this, but I, umm… I helped her carry some, umm, stuff, through that rear bay door right there. Second closest to us. I, umm, yeah… stuff…"

By *'I umm, yeah, stuff'* Tom really meant he'd dragged the men he'd helped Montego dope and kidnap into this godforsaken place. He'd probably helped her torture some of them, too. Some of the very men who stood with him now. Young, stupid, heterosexual male military members who had, for one night, used their dicks instead of their brains. Like Jed, they'd fallen for Montego's poisonous charms and woke up in Hell.

Renner knew she'd used ungodly means of controlling her male victims—forcing them to watch as she tortured other men—or worse. She'd used mind-altering drugs to obtain them, but she'd also fed body parts and still living, screaming men into the maw of the industrial woodchipper Alex had found at her first lair.

But why hadn't these guys ganged up on the bitch—just one time? That's all it would've taken. They were men. Bigger. Stronger. They could've fed her to her own damned chipper and ended this unholy nightmare months ago.

As if he'd read his mind, Aaron placed his fingerless left hand on Renner's forearm. No pressure. No gentle clasp of fingertips. Just the four-knuckled dead weight of what was left of a proud man's hand that had once palmed an NBA basketball. "A guy will do anything to save his buddies, Agent Graves. That's her power. Her genius. She probably understands us better than we understand ourselves."

That was all he had to say. Renner swallowed his opinion and asked Tom again, "What else? If we can get in there without her knowledge, what else will we find? Pressure plates?"

Tom shook his head, his one eye glistening. "She loved that place up north more than this one. That place belonged to her brother, you know. That's why the fancy setup and all the traps. He's the one who did that for her. She adored Roland. Talked about him all the time. If you ask me, them two weren't just brother and sister, if you catch my drift. But this place here was just... just..."

"Just what?"

Tom sucked in a quick breath, steeled his spine, and said, "Where she fucked us." The muscles in his neck constricted. "Then she... she… you know."

Renner knew. Castration without anesthesia would've been damned hard to endure or watch.

"I'm sorry for what you and your men went through," Aaron said, "but we've got a second chance here tonight, Tom. You and me, we can save Tara and those missing men, if Montego's got them. You need to tell us everything you know. Let's go in strong and prepared this time. Let's be men again."

The pirate in Tom turned that single, sharp eye on Aaron, then on Renner. His lip curled. He nodded one curt nod. "I know where she kept us. I can get us that far. And it's all concrete. Ain't no way she could've installed pressure plates in those floors. Want to bet she's conceited enough to think me and my guys ran like scared little dogs with our tails between our legs? Want to bet she thinks we weren't never coming back? That she's safe?"

"I'm not a betting man," Renner bit out. "But tonight, all I've got is riding on you, buddy."

The pirate in Tom blinked. Twice. That one eye glistened, and Renner knew he hadn't been called buddy in a while.

"Thank you, sir," Tom murmured hoarsely.

Renner gave him an answering nod. Trusting Tom. Trusting Aaron. "Then let's end this once and for all. Take us in, Tom. You lead, we'll follow."

Chapter Thirty-Three

Tara sat in the dark, her knees pulled tight into her chest, her arms around her legs. Her heart hammered after that loud noise and what Roger had said. The men had all moved away from the sole exit, over to the wall farthest from the door, preferring to cower with Shy's dead body. But Tara couldn't leave Tony. He hadn't stirred, and he was so sick. She refused to show Montego one speck of fear. It hadn't worked with Jorge.

By now, the tension and heat in this concrete dungeon were unbearable. Rivers of sweat poured between her breasts and down her back. Her hair was all but plastered to her head and neck. As frightened as she was, she climbed to her feet, determined to meet Montego like a woman, not a coward. If Montego thought she'd go down easy, she had another thing coming. *The bitch!*

Until the door creaked open and a blinding light hit her in the face. Tara lifted one hand to block the glare, trying to see the psychotic woman who'd terrorized the East Coast for too damned long.

Instead, a male voice snarled at her. "You."

"No," she shot back at him. She could barely see beyond the beam of bright light aimed in her face.

"She wants you," he said.

"I heard you, and I said no," Tara replied. "If she wants me, then tell her to get her fat ass in here and get me herself."

The guy grunted. "It don't work that way."

Tara planted her feet. "It works that way now."

He grunted.

She grunted back at him, surprised at her sudden bravado. But she was tired, damn it. Tired of bullies and bitches. "The fuckin' buck stops here," she growled at her warden, if that's what this guy was. "Now. Tonight. Go get Catalina Montego. I want to talk to her. Go!"

"Do what he says," Roger whined, back to sounding like a little boy instead of a man. "Please. Don't make this guy mad."

Montego's henchman stood waiting.

"Why should I?" Tara asked. "If she's going to kill me anyway, then she needs to man up and do it. Why wait?"

"B-b-because she won't hurt you when she comes," Gilbert said. "She'll h-h-hurt us. Then you'll do whatever she wants. You'll give her anything, even p-p-parts..."

Tara tried to swallow, but she had nothing to work with. No saliva. No breath. *Parts.* Montego had already dismantled these men, bit by bit and part by part. But would she do that to a woman? Or was it just men she hated?

Speak of the she-devil. Catalina Montego peered around the corner, her haughty nose in the air. "What's taking so long?" she asked her male slave.

He pointed a finger at Tara. "She said no."

Montego's lips curled into a salacious smile.

"Oh," she said. Just "Oh" as she slid into the room like a viper, her eyes black and soulless, her lips still bearing that hint of an evil smile. She'd changed out of her hooker ensemble and into a long, dark velvet dress. The slit up her right thigh revealed most of her leg; the corresponding slit down the center of her outfit, most of her breasts. Not a good look for someone as big as she was. The outfit made her look fat and sloppy. She needed a bra and a corset—one of those old-fashioned kinds made with whalebones. That ought to work.

"Aren't you the clever one?" she asked Tara. "Did Mrs. Stewart put you up to this little deception? Is she paying people to die for her now?"

"Kelsey has no idea I'm here," Tara asserted, still acting the part of a tough girl instead of a cowering wimp—which she knew she'd soon be reduced to once Montego got down to her disgusting, dirty business. But hey. Why not go out with a bang?

Montego took three steps toward Tara, her sharp gaze flashing from the men cowering behind Tara, to poor Tony, then back to the men again. "Where's the wig you used to trick me?"

"How would I know? I've been busy," Tara bit out. "Why don't you come in and look for it?"

Man, it'd sure be nice if just one of the guys got on his feet and at least stood beside her. Or behind her. Maybe they could work together to bring this lunatic down. Two against two made the odds even. Kind of. Five against two would've been better. Wasn't that what soldiers were supposed to do? Fight back? Even when they were injured?

A genuine grin curled Montego's lips. "Yes, I see you've been very busy, and perhaps a thank you is in order."

"No," Roger growled. "Don't do it."

"You dare speak?" she hissed, her eyes wide now, her brows raised.

Instead of answering, Roger made a funny sound.

"Him," Montego ordered her slave. "The one on the floor. He's useless. Bring him."

Tara couldn't help thinking, *'My God, what have I done?'* as she stepped over Tony's legs, protecting him. He was still unconscious, but he would've done the same for her, wouldn't he? "Stop!" she yelled as the henchman set his light on a hook near the door and headed her way. "You're not taking him anywhere."

Which meant nothing to the guy. His fist shot out and hit Tara square in her chest, knocking her backward onto her butt. She'd barely missed landing on Tony. By the time she could draw a breath and climb back to her feet, he'd grabbed Tony's ankle and was dragging him out the door.

Poor Tony never made a sound, but Tara did. "Stop!" she yelled. "You can't take him!"

Montego cocked her head, her long ebony locks now cascading over her shoulder and her eyes as flat and lifeless as a ghoul's. She wrinkled her nose at Tara. "You're smart. Brave. Want to join me? You might learn something."

Adrenaline flooded Tara with two very loud demands. Run! Fight! She was shaking and she knew Montego could smell her fear. But she would not go willingly. Never!

"Don't hurt him," she snarled. "He's sick. He needs medical—"

"He's not sick, he's dying," Montego said as calmly as if she'd just mentioned a change in the weather. "You may not be who I first thought you were, but we can still be friends." She held a slender hand to Tara, canted her head, and coaxed, "Come on. Together we can watch how easy it is to make grown men cry."

Somebody, maybe Roger, groaned behind Tara, and she swallowed hard. Still facing Montego, she told Roger, "I'm sorry." Then, to make it look authentic, she turned her body partly toward him and his guys.

Montego stepped closer, her grasping fingers reaching for Tara's arm.

Guess again, bitch. Tara had already cocked her hand—the one in the shadow, the one Montego could no longer see—into a powerhouse knuckle sandwich. Just as Montego's ice-cold fingers contacted Tara's skin, Tara followed through and punched her in the face.

"Roger! Help!" she screamed, facing the zombie-like men who were supposed to be at her six. "Gilbert! Pete! Now's our chance! Come on, get up. Help me. We can win! Just—!"

Down Tara went as another needle struck her neck. She stumbled to her knees, blinking, trying to stay focused. Too late she realized Montego hadn't intended to grab her. Just to subdue her. With drugs. It was too, too late.

Not that Roger, Samson, Gilbert, Pete, Gary, or poor, poor Tony cared.

Tom was good for his word. He led his men, Renner, Seth, Beckam, and Aaron directly through the door on the dock and into a dark corridor that was wide enough to accommodate forklifts.

Into the bowels of Montego's lair they went, each now armed with a government-issued LED tactical light Velcroed to their shoulders, just like in the old days. This operation felt like others Renner had been on in the Corps. Nothing but shoulder pats and hand signals as Tom took them through a maze of hallways and deeper into ground zero.

Heavy equipment grumbled somewhere up ahead and the air in these concrete corridors had grown oppressively hotter. More humid. But Renner had heard no screaming. Which meant Montego wasn't torturing anyone yet. Renner didn't want to think what she might do to Tara.

Tom fisted his right hand, signaling a full stop, and their hurried advance ceased. Until now, Seth and Beckam had been quiet, just following orders.

"Sir, I think we'd accomplish more if we broke into separate groups. Is that doable?" Beckam directed that question to Tom.

"Agreed. This hall splits into a T up ahead. Some of us…" Tom gestured at his men and Renner. "Will go left. The rest of you…" He pointed at Seth, Beckam, and Aaron. "Go right. That way'll lead you to the boiler room behind Montego's workshop, if that's what you want to call it. Shut that fucker down and haul ass back here. We should be inside her, umm, dungeon by the time you get back. Understood?"

"Copy that," Beckam and Seth replied simultaneously. Like the good troops they were, they turned right at the T with Aaron, while Renner went left with Tom and his men. Another sound, this one mechanical, higher pitched, sounded behind the double doors ahead. But not as high as Tara's scream, "No!"

The muscles in Renner's thighs bunched with the need to run, but Tom's hard plastic prosthetic hand hit him in the chest. "Don't you goddamned dare go in there to save your girlfriend and spoil everything," he snarled. "This ain't about one person, this is about taking Montego down once and for all. This is a revenge killing, damn you. We get to finish her. Us! We! Not you!"

Tara screamed again, one long, drawn out, "Noooooooooo!"

Renner couldn't think, couldn't focus. Until Tom hit him again. "You've got to be the man that young lady needs you to be, Agent Graves. Engage. Focus. Know the rules!"

Just that fast Renner's inner sniper shoved his softer, more thoughtful, human side out of its way. His spine turned to steel. His heart stopped beating, and he was a highly-trained USMC machine, hardened in battle, ready to do whatever it took to get Tara out of there. "I know the rules."

"Are you ready then?" Tom asked from the doors where he'd molded C4 over the lock.

"Ready," Renner growled, primed now. Ready to kick ass. Dying to kill.

The blast went off just as Tara screamed, "No!" again.

Renner put his shoulder to the door and promised, "Hang on, baby. I'm coming."

Chapter Thirty-Four

"No! Stop! You can't do that!" Tara screamed at the wicked woman lashing Tony to a wooden plank that would soon be fed into the gaping maw of a woodchipper as big as a full-sized truck. Its wide intake feeder led to filthy metal augers that led to—God!

She couldn't bear to think what that chipper did to a man's body. For now, the wicked machine sat humming. The augers weren't spinning, just frightfully threatening. One only had to see it to know what Montego used it for. A foot-deep aluminum trough sat below the chute leading out of the chipper. Dark stains on the concrete floor beneath the machine and trough testified to the chipper's previous, horrifying use.

"Oh, but I have to," Montego replied as she wound another bungee cord around Tony's ankles and secured the hooked ends tightly together. She was a study in morbidity. Gone was the velvet. Now she wore black coveralls, the sleeves puckered at her wrists, and long black gloves tucked into her sleeves. She'd pulled her hair back from her face, every last strand secured beneath a black rubber cap. Black rubber boots that came up to her knees completed her extremely efficient, frightening ensemble.

"Isn't this why you dressed to look like Alex's little wife tonight? Weren't you dying…" She paused to look at Tara, her face contorted with sick, sadistic amusement. "…to see where

I do my best work? Isn't that why you deceived me into thinking I finally had the woman I wanted?"

"You wanted Kelsey? Is that why you targeted Mr. McCormack, to get at Kelsey? Why? What'd she ever do to you?"

"I don't really want her. She's just a means to a perfect end. And Jed…" Montego blew out a bored sigh. "…has outlived his usefulness. I'll take care of him when I return to that mausoleum he calls a home tonight."

"You want Alex then? This is about him? What'd he do?"

Like Tony, she'd found herself lashed to a wooden board when she'd come to in this… this dungeon that stunk of blood and death and fear. Only her board came with hinged sections like arms that now had her spread-eagled, her wrists and ankles restrained in metal cuffs that allowed no room to move. Still wearing her bra and pants, she fought against the wood, searching for the one weak spot that would get her out of there. She hadn't found it yet.

The room where Montego did her 'best work' was large, rectangular, and concrete with cold bare walls, dusty ductwork high overhead, and a concrete floor that sloped toward a large, rusted floor drain. Green rubber hoses dangled from ceiling hooks. Heavy-duty shop brooms stood against the wall far to Tara's left. Huge steaming vats waited beside her now, boiling oil at her left, boiling water at her right. Three portable spotlights on tripods aimed their bright beams, one at the chipper, the others at the wooden cross that held Tara and a metal table with chains, and… *Oh, my God, stirrups!*

Montego's shoulders lifted. "Of course, I want Alex Stewart. He thinks he's better than me, above the law. That he can come into my country, into my home and hurt me. His mistake was thinking he could get away with that, that I wouldn't hurt him back. I intend to show him how wrong he is." She said that as if there were no reason to lie or hold anything back, as if she feared no reprisal.

Which meant she intended to kill Tara. "But he's a good man. He loves his country."

"But does he love you enough to sacrifice himself to save you?" Montego asked, one brow spiked.

"Why should he? He barely knows me. He's married. He loves his wife, not me."

Montego made a dark, sinister sound. "Ah, but that's where you're wrong. I've watched him these last few months, and I've seen how he suffers the loss of every serviceman. He doesn't even have to know them, he still takes responsibility for each death or injury, for every coffin. In a way, I've come to respect him, maybe even love him."

She stretched the bungee cord then let it go with a mean snap. "Which is why I want his bitch, that Kelsey. Trust me. I've loved a few men in my life, but him more than any others. It's only fitting I give him the best gift a woman can give a man... A piece of his wife over there..." She fluttered her fingers at the wall to her left. Then to the right... "A piece over there... And the great Alex Stewart wouldn't be able to do a thing to save her. Not a thing. Just watch. And scream. And know for certain the woman he truly loves is—me. Not that insipid creature he calls wife."

Montego loved Alex? God. This woman was insane. "Wait. You've been killing and torturing men all these months because you love Alex Stewart?"

She tipped her head back and laughed. "You'll never understand the complexity of hate and love, how close they are, or how the slippery feel of their blood is…" Montego's chest heaved as she filled her lungs, then let loose a growling, breathy, "…orgasmic."

A full body shiver shuddered over Tara. "You're right. I'll never understand."

"But you will…" Montego said in a sing-songy voice as she lifted her face to the thing suspended from the ceiling that Tara hadn't noticed until now. A movie camera, the red light under its lens blinking. *Oh, shit.*

Gone went the last of her courage, every foolish, wishful, pretentious bit of it. Montego was filming this—her. She meant for Alex to see everything that Montego would do to her. Every cut. Every scream. Every base defilement.

For that one split second, Tara hated Kelsey. It didn't make sense, because with all her heart she truly loved the woman who'd saved her life. They were survivors born of similar tragedies. They were soul sisters who'd lived and endured. And despite her temporary panic, Tara wouldn't change her mind. She wouldn't trade places with Kelsey even if she could. She took back her fleeting feeling of hate. She wouldn't wish this nightmare on her worst enemy. But love did hurt. Every damned time. And it was really going to hurt tonight.

At least Tony was still unconscious, but—

"No!" Tara cried again. She could see his face now. He was dark-haired, olive-skinned, and so, so young. He didn't look like a soldier. He had a beautiful babyface. He was Giuseppe and Lenna D'Angelo's little boy. But Montego had turned the augers on. She really was going to feed him into that chipper like a piece of meat.

"Please, I'll do anything you want, just don't hurt him. Can't you see you've already done enough?"

Montego's head jerked up. "Anything?" She snapped her fingers at the tall, angular man helping her.

He shuffled to her side, his head down like a whipped puppy. Oh, God, he was another victim. His ear was missing.

Tara's heart sank. "Hey you. W-what's your name," she asked, directing every beat of her heart at yet another poor tortured man who just might be her only hope. Tony's last hope. She needed to make contact with this guy's soul if he still had one.

Which made Montego smile, if that's what you wanted to call what her twisted lips and her soulless eyes did. "Please stop bothering him," she said, her voice gone soft and ultra-feminine. "He can't help you; he wouldn't even if he could. I own him, you silly thing."

"You can't own another human being," Tara told the nameless male, wishing she could get him to look at her. Maybe seeing a defenseless woman would jog something lose in his demented, zombie head. Maybe there was a shred of humanity in him.

"Yes, you can," Montego insisted. "It's easy. Want to watch how it's done?"

"No. I don't." Tara leaned back into her wooden crucifix, for that's what this wooden framework was. Her body was no longer hers, not restrained like it was on a contraption that Montego could easily raise or lower, lifting Tara's feet over her head or spreading her arms and legs wider if she wanted.

Montego stretched one hand out to her henchman and—

He slapped wickedly sharp cutting-shears into her open palm, then grabbed hold of Tara's left foot.

No! Just no! "Please don't do this," she begged him.

He still refused to look at her, the coward.

"But I have to do this. You don't believe me," Montego purred. She was not a good-looking woman up close. There was an evil spirit to her, an inky black shadow deep inside her. In her eyes and in her countenance. It was part of her. Like poison. Like death.

"I can see it on your face. You're scared, but you still don't think I can own a man's soul. But I do, and I can own yours, too. I'll show you how it's done." The jaws of the shears opened and closed with a click like alligator jaws. "It's simply a matter of what you're willing to give up to let your boyfriend live."

Tara swallowed hard, her mind spinning at the brutality of what was about to happen.

By then the henchman had released her foot and walked back to the woodchipper. He looked at Tara, then placed one hand deliberately on one of the machine's many handles, the other on Tony's securely bound legs. He'd go into that hopper feet first. If he came to then… If he woke up shrieking and screaming and... He could watch his body being churned to death.

"Anything," Tara cried, knowing how much this would hurt, but steeling herself to keep Montego from harming Mama D'Angelo's baby boy again. He could still survive. He should!

Yet she prayed with all her heart, *'God, oh, God, please don't let this happen. Not to Tony. Not to me! Save us, Renner.'* Why his name burst into her mind at the end of her prayer, she didn't know, but yes. *'Send Renner,'* she pleaded with her Heavenly Father. *'Please. Send Renner! He'll save us all.'*

The sleek, smooth blade of the shear's pincers came down around her littlest toe, pinching it, cutting a half circle of skin. Just the skin. Tara still had her toe and most of the flesh around it. But she shook at the degradation of the cruel act Montego had done, the humiliation of once more not being in control of her life, her freedom, or her body. Shadows of Jorge swelled around her. His evil spirit was here.

She swallowed hard. Afraid to breathe again. Afraid to think. Afraid to take her eyes off the gleaming scissors now lifted above her foot to her big toe.

Montego widened its shiny pincers. "You have to be more specific," she said, her voice low and sultry as if this despicable act of depravity was turning her on. "*'Anything'* is *'nothing'* if you don't understand the cost of losing it. What's that stupid American saying, *'You don't know what you've got until it's gone'*? So, choose wisely. Know what gifts you've got now. Decide what you value most, and what you can live without. Only after you've freely given, will I let your boyfriend live."

By then Tara's lips were bone-dry, and it was hard to talk. Her head all but bounced from fright against what would soon be her wooden deathbed. But she had to try. "For how l-l-long? Will you let him leave? Will you let everyone leave if I s-stay with you?"

Montego shook her head, her black eyes piercing. "No one leaves me."

"Then what… God! What do you want?" Tara cried, her voice nothing more than a wisp of despair. She knew it now. No one could save her. No one was coming. Renner didn't know where she was. How could he? She'd done this to herself, and even if she screamed her hardest, no one could hear her through these concrete walls. Roger was right. They were all going to die in this prison. Only Tony would not die tonight. Somehow, she would make sure of that.

"My, my, my, you still don't understand, do you?" Montego asked as she stepped alongside Tara's arm, jerked a lever and stretched her arm wide. "It's not what I want, it's what you want to give me. What you are willing to sacrifice of your own free will to save your boyfriend? A finger?" she asked as she traced her fingernail up the inside of Tara's arm. "A hand? An arm?"

"A t-toe?" Tara asked timidly, ashamed she had whined like Roger. That it was her ego that had brought her here, that had reduced her to bartering her body away. She could almost see Jorge grinning behind Montego's shoulder, laughing at this ungodly comeuppance.

Montego's visage changed as if by magic. A glitter replaced the flat black stare. Her lips twisted into a sick, joyful smile. "See how easy it is?" she breathed into Tara's face, those awful eyes now fastened on Tara's lips.

Bile crept up her throat at the thought of Montego kissing her. Another wicked debasement, somehow worse than having her toe severed. Tara would never be able to lick her lips again and think of Renner's first kiss. His taste. His soft touch. His genuine concern for her. Was it love? God, she hoped so. It would be nice to have been loved at least once in her life by an honest, decent man.

"Which toe?" Montego whispered, stroking Tara's cheek like she would a sick child's. But purring, the sadistic bitch. How had Jed McCormack ever tolerated sleeping with this woman? She reeked of too much perfume and sweat.

Turning her head away from her tormentor, Tara squeezed her eyes tight. There was no need to watch now. There was no escape. The 'gift' had to be given. She had to commit. Only then would Tony live to see another day. "Little toe," she whispered, her heart pumping up high in her throat. "J-j-just my little toe."

"Not good enough," Montego sing-songed again. "You have to say it like you mean it. Beg."

"P-Please… Just my little toe, please…"

"See? That wasn't so hard now, was it?"

The auger churned to life. "Wait!" Tara growled. "You said you'd let him live."

Montego's eyes narrowed. "And you, you stupid little pig, believed me. Now watch!"

Oh, God, no! Tara couldn't watch. Not poor Tony and not the cold blade nestled into the still bleeding cut around her toe. She felt the first sharp pain that would only get worse. A tear of regret trickled down the side of her head and—

"Get your son of a bitchin' hands off that woman!" some guy roared.

Montego jolted upright and—pffft, the seductress was gone. In her place, the dominatrix bitch hissed, "How dare you bring your little group of merry men back here?" She strutted toward the man who'd spoken, the shears—thankfully—in her hand, waving them forward. "Come in, boys. Join the party if you've got the balls. Oh wait. I've got them, don't I?"

"Shut the fuck up," the stranger bellowed.

Tara's belly expanded with a full breath. "Thank you, God," she whispered.

But who was the scarred, one-eyed man aiming a gun at Montego? And who were all those scary looking guys behind him? Renner! Mixed in with all those guys. It was Renner!

Chapter Thirty-Five

Christ on a cracker, what a gruesome sight. Renner cleared the doorway behind Tom, the men whose names he still didn't know, on his six.

Tara lay across the room to his left, stretched over an X-shaped frame. A crucifix, damnit. Some unconscious guy was tied to a board on the other side of the room, that board in the hands of a skeletal man the size of Lurch off *"The Munsters,"* or some other eighties, black-and-white sitcom rerun. Looked like Lurch meant to send that kid feet first into the industrial-sized, two-wheeled woodchipper, a monster of a diesel. Had to cost tens of thousands, the thing was heavy machinery, as big as a tractor. A heavy chain kept its tow bar anchored to the floor, but God damn. This had to stop.

"You drop him, I drop you!" Renner yelled, walking straight at the idiot who had to be another of Montego's twisted sidekicks.

The guy's eyes popped, his gaze on Renner's pistol. Yeah, he damned well knew Renner could and would kill him. Scarred, his fingers and face hideously deformed—make that mutilated—he stood nearly seven feet tall. Renner pegged him to be Air Force. Maybe a Coastie. He didn't have a thick enough neck to be a jarhead.

Lurch settled the board to the floor, then dragged it away from the chipper. Like a good boy, he slapped the handle that shut the machine down. The auger stopped spinning.

"No!" some bitch screamed. And there she was, Catalina Montego, back at Tara's side with pruning shears in her black-gloved fingers. So that was why no one had ever found DNA. She'd dressed like some maniac surgeon from a horror movie when she murdered and tortured. All in black and on her way to Hell.

"Back off," she commanded.

Really? Me? Back off? "Why should I?" Renner cocked his head. "I'm not the one who backs off, not tonight. Can't you see I've come with the men you tortured? Can't you see they're ready to kill you?" He almost laughed. It felt good finally coming face to face with her, knowing she was done terrorizing American military. Knowing that with just one shot he could kill her.

Her nostrils flared even as she stared him down. "I think you have it all wrong, Mister..." She made a fluttering gesture with her fingers, willing him to answer.

"Agent Renner Graves, at your service," he replied, his pistol now aimed at the middle of her chest, between those breasts she'd rubbed all over McCormack, over that sucking black hole where a heart should have been. No head shot today. Only full body. This woman was going down like the rabid dog she was.

"Agent Graves," she purred. "Of course. Let me guess. Alex Stewart sent you. You're another one of his."

"Nope. He doesn't even know I'm here."

"But he will," she said as she took an imperious step toward him. "Trust me, he will."

"How the hell do you figure that?" Renner met her step with two of his own. This woman had her nerve.

Montego cast her gaze upward to a—

Shit. A camera. She was filming what she was doing to Tara.

"Renner!" Tara cried out. "Behind you!"

Renner whirled to find that Tom, the son of a bitchin' liar, now had his weapon trained on him. "Sorry," he croaked, shrugging like he was embarrassed.

"You're with her? This was all a setup?" Renner cursed, his gaze taking in all seven of Tom's men, their weapons now zeroed on him, too. WTF? Was this why Tom split the team? Why he'd sent Seth, Beckam, and Aaron off in the opposite direction? Were they in trouble, too? Had he sent them straight into another group of alleged escapees? Was this her plan all along, to lure more of Alex's men into this shithole?

Tom held out his prosthetic hand. "Give me your piece, Agent Graves."

"Why don't you just try and take it," Renner spat as he shifted the reticle at the end of his weapon's barrel to Tom's ugly face. No way he could miss this head shot. "You were working with her all along. You fuckin' bastard!"

"Not really," Montego said, her voice a chilling mix of triumph and threat. "But Tommy and I have worked together before. He owes me and he knows it."

"You don't owe her anything!" Tara called out from her cross. "None of you men owe her anything. You're better than she is. You're honorable. You're righteous. For God's sake, you're Americans! You're free!"

Something about Tara's frantic rant registered deep in Tom's eye. He blinked, then blinked again. His head canted, then shook as if he had something in his ear. But then his lips twitched.

"Don't make me kill you in front of your woman," he told Renner. "Look around. We have the upper hand, not you. Us. Now, be a smart guy. Hand it over."

"Like hell," Renner promised even as he scanned the men at Tom's back and all those barrels now aimed at him. "I didn't come all this way to go home empty-handed. Back the fuck off or die first. Your call."

Tom leaned forward. "Then do it. Shoot me. You can't kill us."

"Us?" Renner asked, finally understanding what was happening. These men had all been brainwashed in the most heinous ways. Plus, they were back tonight where it had all started. Where their worst defilement had happened. "What happened to Tom? Just you? Just Tom, the pissed-off man who wanted to kill Catalina Montego with his bare hands?"

Tom's men all chortled behind him, but it sounded more like they were choking instead of laughing.

Something was wrong with this crazy picture. Okay, a helluva lot was wrong here. They were in a dungeon after all, but Renner had one of his gut feelings. He forced a swallow, then tipped the muzzle of his pistol back onto Montego.

"You first," he told her. "Let Tara go or you die first. Trust me, these men at my back are all good guys. They don't listen to you anymore."

"No!" Tom bellowed. "We can't—"

"You see that's where you are wrong," Renner said as calmly as he could, his eye still on his target. "Maybe we can't, but you can. There is no us or we anymore, Tom. There is only you and each of your individual men. There is only me and my woman and that poor guy over there who Montego planned to turn into pulp. There's only that big bastard of hers who's too chickenshit to fight like a man. And then there's the bitch who cut off your balls and probably fed them to you, who probably laughed while she did it, am I right? There is just Montego. She's nothing special, look at her. God, she's an ugly bitch up close, isn't she? But she's just her, Tom. And you're still you. What. Do. You. Do?"

"Simple. I k-k-kill you before you h-h-hurt her."

"Are you sure about that?"

Tom didn't sound so sure.

"Why?" Renner asked, still keeping it civil. Still keeping his cool. Still watching wide-eyed Tom, who had suddenly turned into Montego's mindless drone, out of the corner of his eye.

"Shoot him," she ordered, her command short and sharp. "Kill him now! Then I'll let you play! All of you!"

Whatever that meant.

Tom took a step toward Renner, his weapon on target, the index finger of his only working hand on the trigger.

"You're going to let her do it to you again, aren't you?" Renner goaded, more certain than ever that these tortured men had somehow fallen into Montego's power just by being back here. Where she'd forced them to watch each other's bloody humiliation. "Are you going to let her have your balls again, Tom? Oh, wait. She's already got them. What are you going to let her have next? The rest of your arm? Your other leg? She's already got your manhood. Jesus, why don't you just bend over and let her give it to you again? She's more man than you guys ever were."

Tom growled, but he didn't fire. The guys behind him seemed spellbound. Frozen.

"You, Tom. Just you. Just each one of your men, the guys I know damned well you would die for," Renner said even as he swallowed what might be his final breath. "This is about you and what you decide to do next. There is no 'us'. There is no 'we'. There never was, buddy. Montego used you before, man. She used your brotherhood and your manhood against you."

He licked his lips, hoping something he said was getting through to Tom and his guys. "But tonight, you can each start fresh. You can be men again. She can't make any of you do what you don't want to do. Not anymore. Not ever again. Understood? Catalina Montego's hold on you is over. Finished. You came here with me tonight to save my woman, didn't you? Didn't all your men trust you to save Tara? Isn't that why you guys are here? Isn't that what each of you want? What you need? To do what's right and be men again?"

Lurch growled from somewhere behind Renner, but Renner relied on Tara's perfect, sweet face and the love shining in her true blue eyes to keep him alive. She'd warn him if he had anything to worry about at his six. Renner knew it then. He trusted her with his life.

And just that fast, his heart settled into a steady beat. He knew what he had to do. For Tara and for each of the tortured men pointing their weapons at him. For Aaron. For Kelsey's guys. And for Alex, the primary target of Montego's cruelty. He had to end Montego. It was the only way to break her spell.

"You can't have my buddy Tom," he told her with steel in his voice. "Alex Stewart sent one of his best into Cuba to end your asswipe brother, but he only sent me to end you. Sorry, but you're gonna have to settle for second best, because you're not worth shit."

His index finger settled against the grooves notched in his pistol's trigger. He drew a bead on the evil woman staring back at him and—

Her chin came up. "You're wrong. I own every last one of these bastards' worthless souls. I made these pigs who they are, and they are loyal! Do you hear me? Loyal!" Her chin lifted higher even as she glared down at the men she'd tortured into servitude. "Look at them. They're nothing but a sniveling, whining pack of cowards ready to do my will. My will, not yours!"

"See that's where you went wrong," Renner replied smoothly. Calmly. "They didn't come here tonight to do my will. I never forced them, all I had to do was ask. They're free men, Montego. They always were. Tom and his army came because they wanted to help. They came because they don't believe in you anymore. They're free and they're proud. They're American soldiers."

"Ah—" Tom started to speak.

"Shut up!" Montego spat, her eyes gone an interesting shade of pitch black, the pupils now expanded, filling her stare with pure evil. Her upper lip twitched, an interesting touch of total insanity. "Know your place, you freak! Kill this worthless excuse of a man before I do. Or would you rather another hot bath?"

"No," Tom said, so quietly that Renner thought he hadn't heard correctly.

"Do it!" she shrieked, dark, ugly veins popping across her forehead. "I said kill him!"

And Tom said, "No," again. Louder. Clearer. He lowered his pistol to his side.

Renner allowed a small breath of relief, his weapon still on Montego—

Until Tara yelled, "Renner! Watch out! No, don't!"

He expected a bullet in the back of his head, but ended up with a bear hug around his arms and chest as Lurch lifted him off his feet and set him aside like he was a kid.

At the same time, Tom roared, "Kill the bitch, boys!"

Tom and his men ran Montego down. Lurch joined in the mob, running with them.

The shock on her arrogant face before she turned tail and ran was priceless. But holy shit! These guys were pissed. Renner ducked as Tom's ragged army raced past him to the woman who'd tortured the life out of them.

"Stop!" she commanded when they cornered her at Tara's left, right near the steaming vat she had no doubt planned to use on Tara. "You will do as I say or—"

Smack! Tom's prosthetic hand dealt a hard slap that knocked her head to the side. He ripped her rubber skull cap off. Then his eye patch.

"Or what? You'll slice out my eye again?" he taunted as his men closed in around her. Circled her like the pack of wolves she'd turned them into. Each willing to bite off his own appendage or limb to save his brothers. But never to save himself. She'd done that. She'd used their brotherhood to destroy their souls, only now... they'd finally remembered who and what they were.

"You'll die for that," she hissed. "All of you. I'll cut you so—"

Smack! Tom hit her again. This time he ripped her coverall down the middle, the snaps torn and scattered to the floor and her cleavage on display.

She still came up with fire in her eyes, wiping the back of her hand over her bleeding lip. The same hand that had, only months ago, cold-bloodedly snipped Beau's little finger off, put it in a bag, and sent it to Alex. The same hand that had sent men screaming to their deaths in her chipper.

And it was time to move. Renner ran to Tara and had her off the cross in no time. She clung to him as he lifted her into his arms and removed them from the center of that shitstorm to the opposite side of the room near the door. Only then did he put her on her feet.

"Are you okay?" he asked, eyeing her bloody toes. "She didn't hurt you too much, did she? Can you walk?"

She nodded, her gaze still fastened to the scene across the room.

"Hey, don't look. See me. Just me," Renner said as he lifted Tara's fingers to his lips, counting each of them, needing to make sure she was whole, and that the blood pooled under that treacherous cross wasn't hers. Not a drop of it. *Thank God.* He'd never been so happy for ten fingers and ten toes as he was right now. He pulled a couple bandages up from his jeans pocket and knelt, wrapping her tiny, bloody toe. Tears flooded his eyes again. Damn Montego for hurting her.

"I'm fine, Renner," Tara breathed, her fingertips trembling on his shoulders. "Now that you're here, but…"

Lifting to his feet, he peered down into tearful eyes, loving this brave woman with every beat of his warrior's heart. "What, baby? What do you need? What can I do for you?"

"Please save Tony," she cried, pointing at the poor kid still trussed up across the room. "He needs a medic. He's dying."

"Oh, shit, yeah," Renner exclaimed as he dodged Tom's men, pulled the knife out of his boot, and freed Tony's emaciated body from the plank. Speaking into the mic pinned to his jacket collar, he sent Mark a terse mayday. "Need EMTs at this location. STAT." He provided the location as well as GPS coordinates, then buzzed Ben, Kelsey's pilot, with an update, and told him to ready the chopper. They had a hero to save.

"Let's go," he told Tara as together, they carried Tony out of Montego's killing room. They'd barely cleared the door, when Seth, Beckam, and Aaron appeared in the hall, all three men bloodied.

"Ran into those other missing men," Seth said, his face ashen as he took Tony out of Renner's grip and pulled him into his chest. "One guy's dead—"

"Shy," Tara whispered. "I was with him when he died."

"Are you guys hurt?" Renner asked, needing first things first.

"Yeah, well…" Beckam cleared his throat. "No. The blood's not ours. It was, umm, Shy's. He was in bad shape. You should see these guys, Renner. That bitch hacked them up pretty bad. Already called for back-up. Ben's on his way in to assist until they get here. Guess he used to be a PJ."

PJs were Air Force pararescue specialists known for their expert battlefield care of trauma victims as well as combat search and rescue. They were the medical heroes behind every firefight and every battle, behind every serviceman and woman who made it home alive.

"Looks like this kid needs Ben, too," Seth said as he looked down at the guy Tara knew as Tony in his arms. "Where is she? Did you end her?"

A blood-curdling scream echoed up the hall from those double doors.

Tara stopped cold, her eyes wide. "They'll kill her," she said quietly.

More screaming. More bellowing.

"I sure as hell hope so," Beckam declared without an ounce of sympathy.

Renner met her question with a frank stare. "What do you want me to do?" he asked, ready and willing to listen and obey—this woman and this woman only. For the rest of his life. All Tara had to do was ask.

Another scream, this one more terrified. More frantic. More human...

Seth grunted, a male sound of satisfaction, not concern.

Beckam stood silent, not shifting his boots, but not a hint of doubt on his face that Montego was finally getting all she deserved. And Renner knew what he had to do.

"Wait here," he told his guys as he handed Tara over to Beckam for safe keeping. "I'll be right back."

And back into chaos he went.

My God, what a horrific scene. Renner closed the doors behind him. Tara didn't need to hear or see what was happening to the witch who'd planned on torturing her and filming it like the sick fuck Montego was.

Tom's men were no longer men. They were wild animals, growling and cursing each other, hissing over who got to keep which trophy, which lip, which finger. The body parts of the evil woman once known as Catalina Montego now lay strewn in a circle of feral beasts, all of them covered in her blood. Even Lurch, her one-time slave, held what was left of a hand.

Fighting the bile creeping up his throat, Renner recognized the stink lifting up from the carnage. The mix of body parts, blood, and bowels. But he also recognized Karma when he saw her at work. Catalina Montego had murdered innocent men in the most heinous manners, and she'd done it for months. She'd tortured them for her sadistic pleasure. She'd earned this, her just reward. But it had to end.

Lifting his pistol to the closest ceiling vent where a round couldn't ricochet, he fired one shot and bellowed over the report, "Enough!"

Like a scene out of a bad sci-fi flick, the men stopped in their tracks. All on their hands or knees, they glared at him as if he were the freak in the room. As if he had his nerve disturbing them. Until slowly, finally, intelligent awareness flickered back to life in the blank pits of their wild eyes. Tom lifted his head from where he knelt over what was left of Montego's torso. His lip snarled, but there was recognition in his eyes. No hostility. No challenge. Shit, he was holding her head.

"It's over," Renner told Tom and his men. "You guys need to think about what you've done here. The police will be waiting outside for you. You can either leave here with pride and give yourselves up, or you can go out like the pigs Montego trained you to be. You can end up dead like she is, or you can start over. But each of you has to let the past go. Now. Here. You've completed your mission. You saved lives tonight. I've got my woman back and my guys found the other missing men. It's finished."

Tom gave him a chin nod. "Aye," he replied, wiping the blood off his chin. "That it is."

"Meet you outside," Renner said before he left them to whatever they thought they needed to do next. When he closed the door behind him, he found Tara waiting. God, she was a sight for sore eyes.

"I heard a shot. Are you okay?"

He pulled her into his arms and buried his face in her hair, thankful she hadn't seen what he had. Breathing her into the shadowy memories stuck in his mind. Needing her light and her love. Her heart. "I am now."

She looked up at him, sad and tired, yet glowing. And then, like she had once before, she curled her shivering body into him and said, "Take me home. Please. Take me home."

And Renner knew. He would march into Hell for this woman. Only for these true blues. Only for Tara.

Chapter Thirty-Six

Kelsey stood watching the wintery sky in the cold parking lot of Raymond's Kids with Mark at her side, diligently searching for running lights that would signal Renner's and Tara's arrival. It had been hours since Renner had called with a sitrep. She knew Montego was dead, literally torn apart by the very men she'd tortured. Which seemed a just and fitting end for the wicked woman. She'd hurt so many innocent military members in her short time in America. Their families too. She deserved more than one death, but one would have to do.

Seth and Beckam had also located the recently missing military members, who were now on their way to the nearest hospital. They'd refused to be separated, had actually fought off the Virginia State Police officers who'd simply tried to remove their dead companion's body from where Seth had laid him on a police gurney. Renner'd had to speak to them, then Tara, too. At last the men relented, and the battered man Kelsey knew only as Shy was finally on his way home. And that was good.

At last his worried family would know where he was. Their nightmare may not have ended like they'd wanted and hoped and prayed all these months, but nightmares seldom ended well. At least, it was over. Sometimes that was the only good that came out of, what Kelsey knew from her own sad experience, had to have been a heartbreaking storm.

Renner had told her, with a definite hint of pride in his voice, that Tom and his men had gone willingly into FBI custody. Covered in Montego's blood, they'd been singing and jubilant when at last they'd marched out of that meat-packing plant and into the bright glare of a hundred state police spotlights and rifles. And the ever-present media.

It seemed something only a man could understand—the barbaric pride of a kill. But Kelsey understood the psychology behind that pride. It wasn't too long ago she'd been forced to defend herself and her sweet man/child, Raymond, against another wicked woman, that one the despicable mother of the murderer who'd killed Kelsey's precious baby boys.

Which only proved once again that life did go on. That tears eventually dried. That, like it or not, the sun would continue to rise, and snows and rains would fall. That your broken heart would keep beating until you found a way to live around the hole in it.

A thick blanket settled over her shoulders. Drawing it tighter under her chin, she said, "Thank you, Mark. This is thoughtful, but you should go home. They shouldn't be long now."

Two strong arms engulfed her. A warm male body pressed against her backside. It wasn't Mark. Kelsey bowed her head. Alex was here.

"I love you, sweetheart," he breathed into the crook of her neck.

The dam she'd been holding back broke loose, tears spilling down her cheeks like two rivers she could never seem to control.

"Hey, what's all this about?" Alex murmured as he turned her into his chest and tucked her head under his chin, his hands big and strong and warm on her back. His chest broad and solid.

And she was home again, encircled in all that was right and true in her world. God, she needed this man. Alex always had, and would always be, her bedrock and her life force. He'd made her the woman she was today, and she loved him for it.

"I had to do it," she whispered contritely.

"I know," he replied, ever her most faithful companion. Ever her one true love.

"Renner has the DNA evidence I stole, only now we don't need it, and…" She choked, all of her sins laid bare to the one man in the world she adored. "I'm sorry I borrowed Ben and your helicopter. I should've asked. I shouldn't have just taken it."

"It's yours, too," he said evenly. "Always. Use it whenever you need it. Ben doesn't mind."

"And I bought a lock for our medicine cabinet. Lexie will never get into the melatonin again. It's a good thing she only gave you three."

He never hesitated, his hands never stopped rubbing the life back into her shoulders and up into her neck. Finally, able to relax after the past few hectic days, she pressed her ear into the strong beat of her man, listening to him breathe. Knowing they were going to be okay.

"I knew you'd come," she whispered, warmer now.

"Always," he told her, his rumbling baritone the answer to all her prayers. "I ache when you ache. I smile when you smile. That's how it works. You're my better half. You should know that by now."

"Which is why I had to do it," she said honestly. "I couldn't stand to see what she was doing to you again. I couldn't let her keep hurting you. It had to stop."

"Copy that," he murmured, nuzzling his cold nose between her shoulder and neck, breathing her into his soul the same way she breathed him into hers.

"Lying to you was the worst thing I've ever done. I'm so, so sorry."

His arms tightened.

"She deserved what she got, only I wish she'd died before she'd hurt Beau or Tom, before she killed Shy or... or anyone."

"Don't feel sorry for her."

"I don't. She was a monster, only now…"

Alex rocked her, swaying there in an empty parking lot with fog swirling around them. Loving her. Forgiving her. Never once doubting her.

"Now you show up and make everything better."

"That's my job, and I'm damned good at it."

A tiny chuckle bubbled up Kelsey's throat. "Yes, you are. You do an excellent job."

"I do."

"And you're humble."

"Humility's overrated when you're in love." Alex eased back from her then and took her head in his hands, his thumbs on her cheeks, wiping her tears away as he ducked down to peer into her eyes. "I think that's my best trait, Kelsey. I love you and Lexie more than I can ever tell you. Nothing is as important as my girls."

"I don't deserve you," she murmured, her heart filled to bursting and her eyes still doing their thing.

Alex tipped her head a scant bit to his right, his eyes clear and dark with love. Slowly, gently, he closed the distance and kissed her, his mouth wet and warm. Softly demanding. Never rough, never harsh. Asking.

He pulled back then and snuggled her back where she belonged. Under his arm. Into his heart. It wouldn't be much longer now. Renner and Tara would be back soon. Then Kelsey would take Alex home and love him the rest of the night.

Kelsey was exhausted, Alex could easily read that in the dark circles under her eyes. He felt it in the way she'd sighed when she melted into his arms. But DNA evidence? That she stole? That Renner had? What was that about, and why hadn't Renner reported it?

Unless he'd told Mark, in which case Mark might not have thought to mention it when Alex showed unexpectedly at Raymond's Kids in the middle of the night. That made sense. Alex had been out of communication for twenty-four hours. He did feel better, but come morning he'd still demand a full sitrep from Renner. He'd ask about that DNA evidence, too, but not tonight. It could wait. There was no urgency now that Montego was finally—thankfully—dead.

But what Alex wouldn't give to have been there in Renner's shoes, to have seen her die. Albeit dismemberment was a gruesome way to go, Alex had as much sympathy for her as he'd had for her perverted, pedophile brother. Zero.

Decent people deserved sympathy and empathy, not the Montego siblings. Those two had earned their hard deaths. It was nature at her most primal. Dog against dog. Strong against weak. Right against wrong.

But this op had hit too close to home for Alex's comfort. Kelsey had gotten involved. Which made Catalina's death even more satisfying. That Renner had had a hand in it, albeit indirectly, reflected on Alex and The TEAM. They stood for something, damn it. Alex was proud of every last one of his men and women.

What he didn't care about was Kelsey's use of the chopper. That's what it was there for. When they'd moved out of Alexandria and settled near the Shenandoah, he'd purchased the helicopter to get them both back and forth whenever needed. He'd meant what he'd said. It was hers as much as his. Everything he owned was hers.

But Lexie gave him three *what?* Melatonin? What the hell was that? And there was now a lock on the medicine cabinet? *Okaaaay.* That was new, but Kelsey would explain in time, and if she didn't? Well, that was where trust came in. It was kind of like the sun. A guy didn't always need to see it to know it was there.

Right now, right here, Alex had his life back. This was all he'd wanted through the turmoil of this past year. If Kelsey wanted to stand in her parking lot all night, he'd stand here with her. This was her show, and she'd proven herself to be one damned capable woman. How could a man not love that?

Only when she called this vigil off would they go home together, and then he'd make love to her until she fell asleep. He'd hold her and kiss her long after she nodded off. He finally got it now. The rest of the world could damned well wait. It wasn't what was truly important in his life anyway. Only Kelsey and Lexie.

Her cell rang. Still pressed tight against him, she tugged it out of her pocket, checked the caller ID and answered, "Yes, Ben." Pause. Big sigh. "Oh, okay. Yes, I agree. It's too dangerous and you've done enough. Please tell them I love them both." Another pause. "I don't know how to thank you. Please don't take chances because of me. Yes, that will be fine. Goodnight." The phone went back into her pants pocket.

Clouds heavy with the long-awaited snowstorm hovered over the city. The fog filled quickly with flakes. It was time to go home. Yet Alex kept quiet. He'd stood in stormy weather on other cold nights like this while tracking other notorious terrorists. Those nights hadn't been nearly so lovely. He'd been alone then and in hostile territory, not standing with his arms around the only woman in the world with the power to make his heart beat. Not breathing in her unique perfume while feeling the exquisite peace that always came with the first snowfall of the season.

As a kid growing up on his grandparent's farm in West Virginia, there'd been times he'd played in the snow all day, when he'd gaped like a turkey at the burgeoning sky with his mouth open, catching lazy, white snowflakes on his tongue. There was a yearning silence hidden within those storms of solitude. A reverence, if you will. Like the heavenly silence of that first silent night, Alex breathed in the sweet warmth and delightful scent of his wife, now mixed with the scents of snow and ice. There were those who couldn't wait to die to go to heaven. Not him. He already had his arms around it.

"The weather's too bad," she murmured. "Ben's landing at Reagan. Renner and the guys will go home from there."

"Makes sense," Alex replied. Still waiting on his woman. He was comfortable now. He'd planted his feet, he could stay here for hours.

"Let's go home, Alex."

Ah, words he lived for. "Your wish is my command," he murmured before he tipped her face up and bussed a quick kiss to her lips.

"Damn, you're good," she said as she eased away.

He grabbed onto her hand and steered her toward the street where he'd parked his truck. "I know, but I'll be really, really good once I get you home."

That made her smile. She swung their joined hands between them, and suddenly, they were newlyweds again. Just married. Not a care in the world but how to undress each other fast enough to get back into bed.

"Where's Lexie camping tonight?"

"At Squeak's house. He's turned into a chatterbox. You should hear him sing *'Ghostbusters'* with Adam. Lexie loves that movie."

Alex rolled his eyes at the song that would soon be coming to his house. "Have you ever made love when the snow's falling?" he asked his wife at her door.

She glanced up at him, tiny white crystals on her eyelashes, bigger snowflakes suspended in her hair like so many stars. "Sure. Lots of times. When we leave the curtains open, remember? It's romantic watching snow fall while we're snuggled warm in bed."

His breath caught in his heart. God, she was lovely. So beautiful. He lifted a hand to cup her cheek, threading his fingertips around her ear and into those warm chocolate tresses. She closed her eyes and leaned into his hand, her lashes like velvet butterfly wings on her cheeks, her love for him the purest he'd ever known in any woman. "No. I meant in the snow. Outside. In the middle of a snowbank with snow falling around us."

He heard her swallow. He was pretty sure her answer to that crazy notion was a solid 'No!' Still, he waited.

"Wouldn't it be cold?" she asked, her brown eyes sparkling, her brows arched.

"At first."

"Have you ever done anything that crazy before?"

"Haven't wanted to until now."

"You want to? You're serious? Would there be blankets? A fire? Something to keep us—"

"Trust me?" he asked, wanting her with all his heart. Alex didn't know how this crazy suggestion would work or if it'd turn out like he envisioned. He just knew that making love tonight, with his wife cocooned in the crystal silence of winter's first snow, seemed somehow holy and right.

Her face blossomed with that inner glow she seemed to carry inside wherever she went. "Always, Alex."

And there it was, the truth their lives revolved around. Trust.

Alex swept Kelsey off her feet and into his arms. With one step onto the running board, he tucked his fairy queen into her magic GMC sleigh. They might be an old married couple, but tonight… their adventure was just beginning.

Chapter Thirty-Seven

Tara watched the snow outside the helicopter swirl against its bubble windshield. She'd heard the air traffic controller at Reagan issue a winter weather warning over her headset. Guess she wouldn't be sleeping at Raymond's Kids tonight, which was a little upsetting. She'd been looking forward to hugging Kelsey to make sure she was okay. The whole 'seeing is believing' thing. Not that she hadn't believed Renner, but in a way, Kelsey had been there with her in Montego's lair tonight. Tara just wanted to know.

She'd also heard everything Ben and Renner told Kelsey, who'd been waiting at Raymond's Kids for their return. That was Kelsey, for you. As vigilant and as patient as the day was long.

Renner hadn't said much since he'd spoken with her, which was just as well since their ear protection headsets made every conversation public. Tara couldn't believe the nightmare with Montego was finally over, or that Renner—a man she'd just met a couple days ago—had saved her life twice in the short time they'd known each other.

But what amazed Tara more was the diverse lives that had unknowingly intersected to end Montego. Aaron and his group of wounded warriors. Tom and his misfits. Renner, Seth, Beckam, and Alex. Kelsey. Even Montego herself had caused her own demise in a self-destructive, convoluted way. She was the one who'd mangled, minimized, degraded, and violated her male victims. What had she thought? That treating others like that would make them her friends? For a while, it might have made them her puppets, yet, in the end, she'd totally miscalculated those soldiers' resilience and the depth of their hatred for her, a hatred she'd instilled with painful accuracy. That they hadn't boiled her alive in one of those steaming hot vats in that awful room was small comfort considering what they did do to her. Those last seconds of her life had to have been horrifically frightening. Only Tara couldn't quite believe that Catalina Montego had ever been afraid of anything. She hadn't seemed to have even the tiniest shred of humanity. So yeah. What goes around had certainly come around tonight.

Tara leaned against Renner's chest, needing to hear his heartbeat, to know that good men did exist. Now that she was safe, she was supposed to feel better. Instead, her heart pounded like a bat had gotten caught in her ribcage. She wanted to run away, into the storm. She wanted to hide and forget what Jorge and Montego did to her, what Tom and his men had done to Montego. She wanted the screams in her mind to stop, hers and Catalina's. She wanted to feel good again. Clean. Normal.

Instead she curled into a ball on Renner's lap, her knees under her chin and her arms around her knees, frightened and still alone. He said nothing, just wrapped his arms around her and pressed his chin onto the top of her head as if he understood. God, this feeling of dread was suffocating. She'd come so far. Why couldn't she shake it off and laugh that everything was over?

Jorge was in FBI custody. Didn't they ship creeps like him off to Guantanamo Bay or somewhere just as distant? Montego really was dead. Tara didn't need to see what was left of her corpse to believe Renner. He wouldn't lie. He was everything trustworthy in her life. He and Kelsey and Alex and his team. Aaron and his men. They would all stand with her. Then why was she unraveling now when she had her life back?

Because Jorge's wicked spirit had been there tonight too, and because his evil promise lingered: *You cannot escape me. I have eyes everywhere. I will find a way to drag you to Mecca, and there you will die like the whore you are.*

'But I'm not a whore,' she thought. *'I only did what I had to do to stay alive.'*

She could almost see his cold, black eyes fill with scorn as she recalled what he'd said so many times before: *You are and always will be what I made you. A dog. An American dog.*

Which was pretty much what Montego had said to Tom and his men. *"I made them. Look at them. They're nothing but a sniveling, whining pack of cowards ready to do my will. My will, not yours!"*

That had to be all this ugly feeling was. Montego's words reminded Tara of Jorge. Only Renner was right. Montego wasn't worth shit. Neither was Jorge. They were just two crazy people who hadn't been unique or special at all. Just cruel.

At last Ben finessed the chopper onto its private pad in the secure and private area east of the main Reagan terminal. Finally, she and Renner were safe on the backseat of one of the few brave cab drivers out in the storm.

Only then did Renner say the words she needed to hear. "You're staying with me, Tara. At my place. All night. Tomorrow too. You okay with that?"

Until then, she hadn't been sure where he was taking her, her place or his. Her stress wheezed out of her like the air out of a leaky tire. "Oh, thank God. Yessss."

Renner took Tara to his humble home. It wasn't much. Tucked in the pines along an unnamed river that was more often than not just a stream, he gave the cabbie a big tip, told him to be careful driving in this wintery weather that would close the District come morning, then escorted Tara into his single-home bungalow. The rustic little house was the first thing he'd purchased when he'd returned from his whirlwind tour of America. It made his mom happy that he'd decided to stay near her, but to Renner, it was just a place where he kept important stuff. His big screen. His bike. His mail.

Once inside, he turned the thermostat to higher than fifty and the gas fireplace to cheerful. The place would warm quicker that way. Making a quick pass through his living room, he scooped up clothes and jackets, kicked boots and shoes out of Tara's way with a hurried, "Don't just stand there. Have a seat."

"Knock it off," she teased as she peeled out of his cut, revealing her white, practical Playtex bra. "You're a guy. I wasn't expecting clean and tidy."

"It's clean," Renner corrected as he dumped the armful he'd gathered into the hall closet to be dealt with later. He grabbed a clean t-shirt off the hanger for Tara. "Mostly."

Yawning, she dropped cross-legged in front of the fire and tipped forward to warm her hands. "Man, what a night."

"Yeah," he agreed. "Here. Figured you might want something to cover up with."

The whole flight back she'd been giving him mixed signals, snuggling in close like she had at the hospital, then turning remote and stiff, curling into a ball. Despite her state of undress, he still wasn't sure where he stood with Tara, so Renner kept his distance while she slid into his shirt. Instead of curling around her on the floor like he wanted to, he took the chair nearest the fire and let her set the rules.

"You want coffee?" he asked, surprised at his lack of needing a stiff drink. His flask had been in his jacket all night, but his jacket had been on Tara during the ride home. He hadn't thought of it until he'd offered her coffee instead of beer. That in itself was new. Normally he would've drained that flask dry after what he'd seen and done today.

The universe had definitely tilted, and everything was different now. Even Tara seemed more relaxed. Renner was feeling oddly resilient. Successful. He'd fulfilled one helluva tough mission. After months of worry that had all but eaten Alex alive, Kelsey was safe. She wouldn't be flying off another hi-rise anytime soon. Montego was dead; her threat to servicemen everywhere eliminated. No doubt there. Even rat bastard Jorge was in FBI custody and destined not to see the light of day for a very long time.

Renner still didn't feel as good about that last item as he did the others. There was more satisfaction in a final double tap that ended evil once and for all than in knowing that taxpayers everywhere would now 'get' to support, feed, clothe, and otherwise pamper that murdering ISIL terrorist for the rest of his life. *If* the court system got it right this time and sentenced Jorge to life without parole. Which, on a good day, was doubtful.

Right or wrong, a definite high came with a mission that ended in an elimination instead of a jail sentence. The culmination of years of training and experience had paid off. Not that the press would ever focus on details like that. Those jackals were after fresh meat, which meant they'd gleefully spotlight the atrocity Tom and his men had done to end Montego, instead of reporting Tara's bravery in saving Kelsey's life, or Seth's and Beckam's gentle care of Shy's body and the tortured men they'd rescued. God knew the press had enough weird, crazy footage of Tom and his men marching into police custody while belting out one military song after another, from the *'Army Goes Rolling Along'* to the Corps' proud *'The Halls of Montezuma'*.

Renner'd had one of those full-body cringes when he'd heard Tom and his demented followers singing the USMC song. Because conquering heroes, Tom and his men were not. Yes, they'd done what needed to be done, and they'd ended a vicious killer. But they'd sunk to Montego's level to do it, and that was the difference between them and Tara, Seth, Beckham, and Aaron.

Which, at a fundamental level, also explained why Jorge was still alive, and why tax-paying Americans would now pay for his living expenses. Because Renner was as bad—or as good—as anyone on The TEAM. Simply because ninety-nine percent of American servicemen and women the world over operated according to strict ROEs, rules of engagement, based on justice and honor. They had a code, and they upheld that code even in the worst of times.

But Montego *was* dead. That much was certain, and Renner felt like basking in the night's success, another odd sensation for the loner he'd become. Usually, he would be in bed by now, belly up and snoring. Drunk and passed out. But because Tara'd unknowingly had possession of his flask until now, and he hadn't thought to ask her for it, his mind was rather clear. He could see.

His fingertips still itched to trace the smooth skin on her back, to slide up under the sleek red hair spilling over her shoulders like a cape, and massage her shoulders. Or something else. Damn it, he wanted to lay her down and eat his way up her delectable body. Instead he waited and watched the gas log put on a show that almost looked natural. He watched how that fire cast golden light into the room and over Tara, adding golden hints of flame to her fiery tresses.

"No, I'm good. Coffee would just keep me awake," she answered, her voice weary and—pensive.

Okay, no foreplay. No eating. She was tired. He could live with that. Women were never as horny as men anyway; they weren't made that way.

"Shower's down the hall," he murmured, keeping his tone passive and low. "Clean towels are in the linen closet just outside the bathroom."

He wasn't going to assume their previous close encounters meant anything to her, although, they'd both meant the world to him. Kissing Tara had breathed life into the hollowed-out pit of a soul he'd come back with from the wars. She'd filled him with something he wasn't ready to let go. He wasn't nearly as depleted as he'd been when this whole mess started, and it wasn't just the prospect of sex. He had no doubt sex with Tara would be off the charts, but it was quiet times like this that meant something more, something different.

That was the thing about the excess adrenaline still roaming his body. It amped a guy up, made him want to screw the daylights out of the first woman that came along. Not that Renner had ever indulged in the debauchery of post-combat sex, but the battle was real. Mankind might build rockets to take him to the moon, but deep down, he was still a primitive SOB with a hard-on from hell in his pants. He was the conquering hero, and Tara was sweet and close and...

No. Just, no. Renner scrunched his face, blinking to get his mind out of the gutter. He took a slow breath of reality. Tara was one hell of a survivor, and yeah, she was here with him in his house, but he would not put his best moves on her. She deserved better. A helluva lot better. They needed to be able to relax with each other. Talk, just for the sake of talk.

"I've got an extra room. Stay here and get warm, I'll go make the bed," Renner said because he had to, now that he'd made the offer. The spare bed was basically just an extra mattress he'd bought. Still in its original plastic wrap, he'd laid it on the new box springs he'd bought the same day. A new headboard leaned against the opposite wall in his spare room. He could have that bed put together in under thirty minutes, have it made by then, too.

"No, don't," she said as she turned her shoulders to him. "Please. Let's not make this any bigger than it has to be."

"Well, okay." Renner sat cross-legged beside her, his hands on his knees, wondering what she'd meant by that.

Tara smiled that same sad smile she'd given him up in her attic that first night. That *not now and maybe not later either* smile. "I don't know how you do it," she murmured.

Renner had no idea how he did it, either. But hey. He'd been going without sex for a couple years now. He could do it again. Not like he had much choice given how he didn't go looking for it like he once had. The perks of drinking. Either you partied with another alcoholic who was female, or you withdrew into yourself and became a loner because there was nothing nice about that female drunk the day after. Drawing in a deep breath, he stared at the fire, not ready to open his mouth and stick his foot in.

"How did you carry on after losing your dad?"

"What?" he asked at the sudden shift in conversation. Okay, maybe just in the conversation he thought they were having.

Her shoulders lifted. "Your dad. Do you ever wish you'd made different choices? That if you had, maybe he'd still be alive?"

"You been talking to my mom?" Not likely. There hadn't been time.

She shook her head. "No, but my mom said my dad's been sick, and I think it's because of me."

"And somehow you found out my dad's gone." Renner noticed how the flame burned blue in the heart of the fake log instead of bright red or orange.

"I'm sorry. Kelsey told me. Was it supposed to be a secret?"

He shook his head even as he said, "No. Not a secret at all, and I do miss him, but no. Nothing I did contributed to his death. He was on duty during the last presidential inauguration. You know how crowded DC gets during official events. Some asshat just happened to bring a gun. When he pointed it at the

First Lady and screamed, the Secret Service closed in to protect her, and my dad closed in on the guy with the gun."

"And he shot your dad. I remember now. I'm so sorry."

Renner's chest expanded with yet another deep breath that never came close to easing the pain or the loss that still sat like a brick on his chest after all these years. But he'd been raised by an Irish woman with the love of God in her heart, and he knew better than to wallow in self-pity. Yes, they'd all cried plenty back then, but not a day went by Renner hadn't thanked that same God for the kind of man and father Cody Graves had been.

"The thing is…" he said slowly. Thoughtfully. "Mom and I always knew Dad might go down in the line of duty. He and Mom talked about it with Mo and me when we were old enough to understand. And yeah, I miss him. I do. But don't mistake missing him for fear or depression or any of that crap."

"Is that why you drink?"

Renner shook his head. "Folks might think that. It probably makes sense on the outside, but no. I started drinking when I was a kid, long before I joined the Corps or lost Dad. You know, everyone else is doing it, I dare you, so blah, blah, blah…"

"If everyone else jumped off a cliff, would you do that too?" she asked softly, teasing.

He grinned at her. "You sound just like Mom, but yeah. I was a pretty dumb kid. I probably would have jumped off that cliff back then, just to prove I could do it and they couldn't."

Renner rubbed the center of his breastbone over that hole in his heart. "You have to understand, Dad was a father to be proud of, and I still am. He served his country and his president, and he loved Mom and us kids. Just because he died before his time doesn't make me one of those crybabies who needs rehab and drugs or alcohol because Daddy died. I don't, and that's not why I drink. Honest. When he died, I knew it was up to me to honor him by living the way he did. By stepping up. He was the reason I joined the Corps in the first place, and yeah. He also knew I might go down in the line of duty. I mean, we're all going to die, right? The best thing Dad ever taught me was to live so well that, when it's your time to go, you leave this life knowing you've done your best every single day."

"Was he always bigger than life?"

Renner nodded, remembering. Aching. "Absolutely. I swear he was ten feet tall."

That summed up Metro PD Detective Cody Graves perfectly. Dark-red hair. Always smiling. Always bigger than life. A man's man who knew how to fix plumbing and cars, bikes and squeaky doors. Who knew how to pitch a perfect fast ball. Always there for his kids and wife until the day he wasn't.

"Sounds like my dad," Tara said wistfully.

"I guess that's how all good dads must look to their kids. He coached my city league baseball team. We took regional that year," Renner said on a sigh. "What's up with your dad?"

"Mom said he's sick," she whispered. "While I've been off living my life like an inconsiderate selfish brat, thinking everything's about me, he's been worried about me and…" She leaned her chin to her fist, her elbow already cocked at her knee. "I'm the reason he's sick. I know it."

"Parents are like that. They worry themselves sick even when they shouldn't. So call him. Talk to him. He'll feel better and so will you. I know Mom worried every time I deployed. I thought of not telling her when I was leaving, that it'd be easier if she didn't know. But I'm pretty sure she would've kicked my ass if I had."

"What makes some kids so stupid?" Tara asked quietly, still mesmerized by the flames dancing across the gas log.

"They're not stupid. They're like you and me, just trying to figure things out." But then he stuck his foot in his mouth and asked, "Where was your coach when you were out being stupid?"

She didn't seem to notice his inadvertent blunder at calling her stupid. "Trying to get through to me. Threatening to pull me off the team if I didn't shape up. Badgering me to practice harder and longer and... I just wanted to ski, Renner. But joining the Olympic team killed the joy of winter for me. It turned the sport I loved into drudgery and blisters and shin splints, every damned day. Some days my ass hurt from falling on it so many times. I just wanted to live my life my way for a change, you know? Go back in time to laughing all the way downhill, then skiffing in sideways at the last minute, braking just in time to hit the lift lines and start all over again. That's why I drank and acted out, and that's what led me into Hell. Like a stuck-up Hollywood diva, I wanted it all. I rebelled."

He let her vent, wishing she'd actually look at him. But maybe it was better this way. Confession was good for the soul. Didn't mean you had to make eye contact to do it.

"My name is Renner Graves," he said carefully. Deliberately. "And I am an alcoholic."

That got her attention.

"You're right, Tara," he said evenly, her bright eyes on him now. "I'm an alcoholic. I didn't really realize it until tonight, at least I didn't want to admit it, but yeah. I wanted that flask, only it was in my jacket, and you were wearing it, and—"

"And you didn't want to ask me for it because you didn't want me to think you were—"

"Wrong," he finished for her, staring into soft blue eyes that had gone misty around the edges. "I'm wrong and you're right and... Jesus, this is hard." He interlocked his fingers, his elbows on his knees, and took a deep breath, sick at what he'd just admitted but never more certain it was right. "Yeah, it's true. I have a drinking problem. I am an alcoholic."

He swallowed hard, thinking on everything he was giving up with those few words. The fire in that first satisfying shot. The gradual buzz and the hum of the second and third. The fourth. The comradery of alcoholics the world over. The taste of dogshit in his mouth and hair on his teeth the morning after...

"I can help," she offered meekly.

He gave her the flat palm of his hand and a stern headshake. "Nope. I have to do this alone. Thanks, but… you know that."

She nodded, her mouth skewed to the side like she was biting the inside of her cheek. "It'll be hard."

Another big sigh. "Yeah, well, so was the Crucible. If I can do that—"

"Wait, what?"

"The Crucible. It's a kick-ass test recruits go through before they earn the right to be called Marines. There is something you can do now though, you know, to help."

She climbed off the floor and right onto his thighs where he wanted her. "Yes?"

Chapter Thirty-Eight

He placed his palms on her hips, his thumbs skimming over the crease between her belly and her thighs. These pants had to go, that practical bra, too.

As if she'd read his mind, Tara leaned into his face and whispered into his mouth, "Help me out of these clothes?"

He undressed her in seconds. She did the same with him. And they were on the carpet in front of the fire, bare-assed naked and sparks dancing in her eyes. Like at Crazy Eights and in the hospital, she took control, straddling his hips, her body so perfect she was making him cry.

For reasons he didn't want to examine, she needed to be in control, and Renner went willingly where she led. Sex was never about domination. It was play, pure and simple. Exploration and that elusive sense of communion. Not work. Besides, she really should've gone back to the hospital. That bump on the back of her head was no small thing. He didn't want her on her back… at least, not yet.

But when she tipped forward, her breasts fell soft and heavy in his happy hands, her nipples peaked and hard and—

Christ, resistance truly was futile. He took gentle possession, rolling one perfect nipple between his finger and thumb while he swallowed the other. While he held her as tightly as he dared, ever conscious of her cracked ribs.

The heavenly scent of her skin filled his nose. Part feminine sweat, part some nameless flowery bouquet, he suckled until she pulled back. But then he sucked harder, loving the sound coming from the back of her throat as he consumed first one, then the other tip, stretching her breast. Daring her to come. But if those noises meant what he thought they meant…

"Yesssss," she hissed, her hair flung over her shoulders. An actual glow suffused every inch of her body, announcing her coming. Then, "Oh, Renner, yes!"

He let her breast go with a satisfied pop, grinning at the luscious sight of his woman in the throes of one quick as hell lightning strike. Her nipples were dark and swollen, and he was one damned happy man.

Still throwing aftershocks, she began to move, rubbing against him and driving him nuts. Sliding one hand between their bellies, he found what he'd wanted. She was steaming hot and ready. That alone, just touching her, told him he wouldn't last long enough for her round two if he didn't hurry.

Renner eased Tara up just high enough to plant himself where he wanted to go. He meant to take this next part as slow as he could. She'd been with a monster, and she was still recovering from her recent encounter with the bastard. Renner didn't want what they did to each other now to remind her of anything that asshat did. But day-um. Tara wasn't holding anything back. With the sweetest feminine grunt he'd ever heard, she impaled her slick body onto him and he was in heaven. So tight. So sweet. He closed his eyes at the sensations lapping up his spine and tightening every muscle in his body. One thrust was all it would take and this first time would be over.

He tried to hold on but she started to move. Up and down. In and out. Making those same little needy sounds. Those adorable ohs and ahs and groans and whimpers and—

She screamed, and he exploded along with her, right through the roof and into the wintry sky like a blazing pair of rockets bound for heaven. Renner held onto her for the ride of his life, his fingers dug into the cheeks of her ass as deeply as her fingertips stabbed his shoulders.

God. Damn. Yessss.

An annoying bell sounded in the far back of his mind, warning him of—something. But logic had taken a backseat during the consummate pleasure of here and now. Tara's pretty face was all he could see, her hair, her eyes. Pleasing her was his only ambition; her satisfaction, a goal he would excel at. The sense of foreboding faded. How could he think with this goddess riding him, her silky soft tangles pouring over his face and chest like the softest scarlet rain from heaven?

His nostrils flared at the musky sweet scent of sex, and Renner was ready to go again. He didn't understand how, but he was, and she was right there with him. Rocking onto him. Her palms splayed over his chest, and her eyes closed. His hands filled with her backside, and his mouth suckling at her generous breast. But that gentle, satisfied smile on her lips was what spurred him on. Urged him. Made him thrust harder and deeper. Faster. Intending this one only for her, his queen. His goddess.

She made that whining, coming sound again, and—*yes, yes, yes!* She came all over him, melting like honey. Damn, damn, damn. Life didn't get any better than pleasuring the woman who'd brought sunshine back into his life. Renner held her hips as she came undone, her femininity squeezing him, milking him, urging him upward with her soft feminine growls and groans and…

It began again. A lick of lightning started up from his tailbone, rocketing skyward. Into her, his only universe. Only her...

Jesus, he flew and he was very sure she flew with him this time, too. How could she do that? What a rush!

At last, Renner fell back to earth with his arms and soul, his heart, finally full again—filled with Tara. He lay there with his eyes closed, breathing hard but so much at peace, content to absorb the sublime sensation of her body weight on his. Her warm breath in the hollow of his neck. Her hair spread like a luxurious cape over him. What a ride. But what a landing, too.

"Umm, hey there," she murmured, her heart still pounding. "Do you have any tissues or… Oh, wait. There's my underwear."

"You had underwear? When?" he teased. He couldn't remember anything once she'd unsnapped her bra and those soft, sweet breasts fell in his face.

"I don't want to make a mess," she said as she eased her panties between them. "You say when."

He shook his head. "Never gonna happen. I'm happy right here." And then it hit him. Shit. "Please tell me you're on some kind of birth control, because, baby—" Yeah. Right. B.A.B.Y.

She winked. This delightful woman winked. "Are you kidding? Do you honestly think I'd take a chance of that bastard knocking me up? Ever?" She shivered. "Of course, I'm on birth control. He never knew but then he never asked. He just assumed he owned me."

Ugh! Renner squeezed his whole face shut. He should have asked, too. He'd never had unprotected sex before now, and he didn't know what made this time different, other than the goddess in his hands. His mama didn't raise no fools. Until now. "I'm sorry. I should've asked earlier. Hell, I should've—"

"Oh, stop," Tara purred, those magnificent breasts still delightfully warm against his chest, her nipples turning into diamond-hard tips again. Made Renner forget what he was saying and thinking and worrying about and... *Oh, hell. Whatever.*

"It's my body. Sex and birth control are my responsibilities, too," Tara told him, a glint of rowdy mischief in her eyes. "It's the twenty-first century. What do you think I am, some poor little housewife who lets her big, strong man make all her decisions for her?" She wriggled her backside when she said that.

He couldn't help that his palm landed a gentle spank on said ass. "I could see you in an apron. Naked. When I get home from work at the end of a long hard day."

Those sparkling blue eyes widened. "I could see you with a ball gag," she said with attitude and a toss of her head.

"A what? Are you into...?" *Oh, God, no.* As much as he'd love seeing her in leather, Renner's manhood cringed at the thought. "Whips? Chains? BDSM?"

She made the cutest frowny face and shook that red silk cape of hers into his face. "No way! I just had to top that apron insult of yours. But no. Eww, no. I don't get the thrill in letting a man beat you. Been there. Done that. The hard way. Trust me, rape it isn't sexy and it wasn't fun."

Something inside Renner broke then. He tugged this audacious, competitive woman down to his level, cupping her stubborn winner-take-all jaw carefully between his palms, thumbing the warm blush on her cheeks and blinking to keep his tears at bay.

"I will never hurt you, Tara," he told her as he tipped her lips to his and kissed her gently. Completely. "Ever," he breathed in her mouth. "If you don't know anything else about me, please know that."

But Renner could definitely understand how she'd gotten herself into trouble. Tara led with her chin. She tended to come off tougher than she really was. He and she were quite the pair, him with his never-back-down-from-a-dare chip on his shoulder, her with her tough-girl want-some-of-me? routine. They'd both made stupid decisions that they were living and dealing with now. Guess that was called life.

She moaned then as he rolled her over and planted his knees between her legs, making sure he didn't bump her head. A word crawled up his throat from his over-flowing heart, not choking him, just sitting there, letting him know he could call on it if it needed to be spoken. Looking down on her, watching the glow in her eyes and the way she licked her lips while eyeing his mouth, Renner knew he loved this woman. Yes, she'd made her share of mistakes, but didn't everyone? Tara fought for her friends with her whole heart. She should've been a Marine.

But things had happened so quickly between them these last couple days, and she'd already told him she didn't love him, that she might want to spend time with him. Might. Not marry. Not move in. Just get to know each other better.

Yet his heart ached to tell her. To ask her.

"So umm…?" He thrust his hips forward suggestively.

A smile blossomed over her face. "Umm, yes," she said as she matched his forward thrust with one of her own. Her nose wrinkled. "I could do this all night."

And yup. Renner was head over heels in love with this fierce, sexy woman. He could do her… All. Night. Long.

Tara lay wrapped in Renner's arms, watching the fire. He was asleep, or at least his eyes were closed and his breathing was even. He'd relaxed. That alone was a nice change from his normally tense demeanor. They'd made their mad dash into the restroom, but only to clean up enough to return to the blanket-bed he'd made in his living room. He'd grabbed a couple pillows and two comforters from his extra bedroom, one for a mattress, the other for a cover. Which Tara didn't need. She'd never felt safer than lying with Renner with all her sins laid bare.

The only thing she hadn't bared yet was her heart.

But her long journey from bondage was finally over. Did she dare dream that this interlude with this particular man could be more? And therein lay Tara's problem. She'd been stupid before. Make that she'd been an outright raving idiot when she'd tossed her life and her freedom to the wind and married What's-His-Name. Not that Renner had yet asked her to marry him. He hadn't. Not that she'd expected he would or even wanted to. But if he did…?

That was what scared her. She licked her lips, her heart thumping at how badly she'd suffered through her last mistake. Decisions that had once seemed obvious were now complicated and frightening. There was no such thing as happily ever after. True love was a joke. There were no princes on white stallions, either. There was only experience, and it was a cruel, hard teacher.

The back of her head still hurt from where she'd cracked it on the concrete floor back in that butcher shop. Her thick hair covered the bump, and people were prone to forget it was there. But her ribs were still plenty tender. While the cuts Jorge had decorated her arm with seemed to be healing, the back of her hand where *Grumpy Cat* had once glared back at the world was damncd sorc. It couldn't be stitched, and it hurt every time she flexed her fingers.

And… okay, yes, she was scared of commitment. Scared shitless. As much as she wanted Renner to protect her, she knew that wasn't the way life worked. You either stood up for yourself or you chickened out. How well she'd learned that lesson, not only at Jorge's hard hand, but while staring down Chicken Springs, Mount Ogden Bowl, or shredding the halfpipe off Snow King, her favorite runs at Snow Basin, Utah. That was where she'd tested her mettle as an Olympic hopeful. That was where she'd crashed and burned. But by hell, she'd kicked back into her bindings, and she'd skied those dangerous runs again. Over and over until fear was just a jokester along for the rides of her life. Man, those were the days. She'd been on top of the world. Headed for fame and fortune. Her name on a box of cereal.

So why was she afraid now? Why couldn't she nestle back under the covers alongside this to-die-for naked, handsome man she knew she loved now that she was safe?

"Hey," he grumbled, his voice hoarse with sleep. "You're taking the covers."

"Oops, sorry," she said as she turned to pull the blanket over him.

Instead, he rolled her into his arms and onto her back, the flames from that log flickering like magic in his darkened eyes, one hand cupping her skull. "Can't sleep?" he asked as he smoothed her tangled tresses off her face while he nestled his hips between her legs.

"Just thinking," she said, opening wide for him, loving the way his body fit into hers. Wanting him back again, tucked deep inside. The way Renner fit so easily into her pelvic cradle was so much more intimate than what Jorge had done to her body. This night with Renner had been about making love and discovery. He'd been careful and gentle. Playful and sweet. Never impatient. As strong as she knew he was, Renner didn't have it in him to be cruel.

"Don't think so hard, Tara. Trust me, it's not healthy, especially at night. That's when I do all my worst imaginings," he whispered as he planted a warm wet kiss on her mouth and gave her what she wanted. His length and his heat. "Things always look worse at night."

Wasn't that the truth? Tara ran a hand over his head, loving the lush cool feel of his hair sifting through her fingers. Loving him, but afraid to tell him even as she pushed forward to seat him deeper. "You really are my hero. I know you guys don't like to hear that, but I owe you my life, Renner. Think about it. We've only known each other three days, and when I needed you most—"

He covered her mouth with his, swallowing her fear and her doubts, rocking into her. Filling her. Making her believe. Tara closed her eyes and let the storm that was Renner Graves roll over her. If this truly was love, it was perfect. It was divine.

This was his gift. He knew how much she needed soft and sweet and slow.

Chapter Thirty-Nine

Brinnnngggg! Damn. Renner peeled one bleary eye open, his arm still snug around Tara. Her head was on his chest and her one palm was splayed delightfully low on his belly. But his cell was in his pants and his pants were… Hell, he didn't know where they were. *Brinnnngggg* went his cell again, and he wondered why he'd selected that annoying old-style telephone ring instead of a nice quiet buzz he could ignore. Maybe because that call was his Mom?

Tara yawned. "Your phone's calling you."

That earned her a playful smack on her bare ass. "You think?"

"Wait here, I can get it for you," she mumbled sleepily even as she lifted to her hands and knees and—

Holy Jesus, Mary, and Joseph. That woman had his glowing pink handprint on one cheek of her very fine ass. But when she turned that ass around and tossed his pants in his face, Renner's whole body sprang to attention.

"Stop staring," she teased, wiggling her sexy derriere, which jiggled her breasts, which short-circuited his brain, and—

"Come here," he growled even as his phone rang again.

"Phone first. Sex later."

"Awww…" All he heard was phone sex. "…but I've been good—"

Brinnnngggg!

"Damn it, Mom," he complained as he fumbled his phone out his jeans pocket and answered, "Do you have any idea what time it is?"

"What kept you?" she asked, as sweet and as nosy as ever, not bothering with his question.

"Just waking up. What do you want?" *And make it quick, I've got someone to do.*

Tara was laying on her stomach by then, her blanket shoved aside and every inch of her body delectably bare and ready for breakfast. He licked his lips, eating her up with his eyes while his ears tried to listen to something about Christmas dinner and eggnog and Midnight Mass at Saint Patrick's.

Renner blew Tara a kiss, crooking his finger for her to come closer if she dared.

Uh, uh, her head shake answered, but he was pretty sure there was yes, yes in her eyes.

"Renner! Did you hear anything I just said?"

"Umm…" *No.* "Yeah, Mom, you want me to bring eggnog to dinner and, umm…" *Shit.* "No. Sorry. I've got a lot on my mind. Say again."

She laughed. "I said I guess we won't be seeing you come Christmas morning, not with you being recognized by the honorable Governor Tillis and Mr. Jed McCormack for heroism in the line of duty. My guess is you'll be too busy hobnobbing with the president by then to remember you're making eggnog."

"Excuse me, but what are you talking about?" Renner honestly thought she'd been drinking a little early this morning. "Me hobnobbing with who?"

"Never mind, but do me a favor, boyo of mine. Read the paper or at least turn on the news. You and that pretty woman you brought into my place a couple nights ago are front page news. Then call me and we'll talk. Get a move on."

"Umm, yeah. Bye, Mom." Renner traded his cell for the big screen remote in time to catch breaking news. "Come here," he told Tara, motioning for her to sit beside him. She did, still naked, still delectable. He guided that cute ass onto his lap as some national news reporter talked over a camera shot of him carrying Tara out of Montego's ghoulish meat-packing plant last night.

"Wow," Tara breathed as the camera zoomed in for a close, personal picture of Renner's grim face, his hand firm at the back of her head and her head on his chest. She'd had her eyes closed as if she'd been saved, which she had. But he looked pissed and fierce and mad as hell, as if he dared anyone to step one foot in his way.

"Alex isn't going to like this," Renner deadpanned even as the reporter said, "There he is now! That's our homegrown hero with just one of the many people he rescued! Renner Graves, of—"

"Don't do it," he growled, but the reporter beamed like giving the entire world his address was a good and right thing to do. "Jesus Christ," he hissed, angry all over again and his personal security violated.

"I can't believe she said that," Tara murmured. "I wouldn't like everyone knowing where I live."

"Me either," he replied, trying to keep his cool.

As if on cue, his cell buzzed like an angry hornet from the floor where he'd dropped it. "Speak of the devil," Renner muttered before he answered, "Yes, Boss?"

"You and I need to talk," Alex bit out. "My place. One hour."

"Copy that," Renner answered, but then had to ask, "As in at your home or the office?"

"My home, but make that two hours. Kelsey's telling me you might not be up yet since you were late getting in last night."

"I'll be the—"

"And bring your girlfriend," Alex ordered before the connection went dead.

Renner stared at his phone, surprised it wasn't smoking in his hand, just as surprised that Alex knew Tara was with him. Not like that was a big secret, but he couldn't help wondering who else knew.

"What's he mad about now?"

"Not sure, but if he already knows that reporter blew my cover, that'd be enough."

"Still, why would he be mad at you over that and not her?"

"Not sure, but let's get moving. We can grab breakfast on the way."

Showering together wasn't as pleasurable or as long as Renner had planned, but driving west to Alex's home with Tara at his side was great. He caught a quick glance at the woman by his side. Dainty, yet brave. A traumatized risk-taker. Beautiful despite her bruises and bumps, yet kind despite them. She sat there quiet and peaceful, watching the road and traffic.

After the steady go-go-go of the last few days, Renner realized just how much he'd needed this quiet time with Tara. They seemed to fit together, like a pistol fits a hand. Okay, so that wasn't the most romantic metaphor, but it felt right. It felt good. Pistols didn't fit a guy's hand until after hours and hours of practice and muscle training, until that weapon became an extension of that hand, like a finger or thumb. Until it became a part of him.

There was no lightning bolt, no brilliant epiphany to convert him. Just his hand in hers and the quiet everyday silence that stretched between them. He could feel it happening deep inside. The warmth. The flood. This was what he wanted, this thing—whatever it was—right here. This sense of finally getting it right. Of belonging...

But damn. She'd wrapped her wet hair into a tight bun after their first couple's shower, and that bun had unraveled with every mile. By the time he pulled his TEAM vehicle up to Alex's gate, she'd gone from prim and proper to downright sexy, X-rated hot, hot, hot. Especially in his USMC t-shirt that came nearly to her knees.

What Renner wouldn't give to back this ride out of Dodge and grab a room at the nearest hotel. But yeah, not happening. Not with Alex on the war path.

Several other vehicles lined both sides of the street. Harley's red Jeep, Maverick's new Chevy pickup, Taylor's ratty old truck, which Renner knew had once belonged to Maverick's brother who'd died in Afghanistan. A brand-new Mercedes he didn't recognize. A Porsche—had to be Zack's. Mark and Libby's much larger family van.

Interestingly, the driveway gate was open, something that hadn't happened in over a year. Renner opted to park on the street in case Alex needed to leave in a hurry. No sense poking the bear.

"Let's do this," he said as he ushered Tara along the brick walk to the Stewarts' front door.

Cute little Lexie swung it open before he had a chance to knock. "Hi, Unca Renner!" she squealed as she barreled into him and hugged his leg.

"Women just can't keep their hands off you, can they?" Tara teased.

"It's a gift," he said as he scooped Lexie over his head and set her on his shoulders. "Brrrrr, aren't you cold?"

She snagged his ears, bouncing like they were handles and he was her horse. "It's almost Chwistmiss!"

"Yeah, well that doesn't make me a reindeer. Settle dow—" Renner's mouth dropped.

"Surprise! Surprise!" Lexie squealed, bouncing harder and faster.

Surprise nothing. It was—Lois McCormack. Standing there. Breathing.

"Ma'am," Renner managed to spit out. "Um, ah—you're not dead."

She stood there very much alive, her palm resting on a very proud Jed McCormack's forearm, with that genuine motherly smile she was so well known for beaming on her pretty face. "No, I'm not, Agent Graves, and thanks to you, I finally have my life back."

That almost made him sound like a miracle worker. Both silver-haired and kindly featured, Mr. and Mrs. McCormack looked healthy and happy, and, well, Jed looked smarter than he had in months.

"What's going on?" Renner asked his boss as Tara closed the door behind them. "Did you know?" *You son of a bitch!*

Alex didn't look any happier than Renner felt. He shook his head from where he sat with his arm around Kelsey, across the room on the stone ledge in front of his fireplace. Both dressed casually in jeans and matching gray sweaters, they looked steadily at the McCormacks.

Quite a few TEAM agents were also there, all with their wives at their sides, all dressed casually with a cup of steaming something in their hands. All somber as hell. Zack and Mei Lennox. Mark and Libby Houston. Harley and Judy Mortimer. Gabe and Shelby Cartwright. Taylor and Gracie Armstrong. Adam and Shannon Torrey. Beau and McKenna Villanueva. Maverick and China Carson. Others.

The TEAM members who'd been on overseas operations had been recalled, just like Alex did the last time Montego came to town. Seth and Beck were noticeably missing, as were Connor and Hunter. Rory, Lee, Eric, and Jake, too.

"What's going on…" Jed stepped forward and grabbed Renner's hand, "…is you, young man."

"But I thought…" Renner didn't know what to say. "I thought you were losing your mind or that you'd already lost it. Sir." He meant to say, *'Sir, you crazy son of a bitch.'*

Alex huffed like he might be as pissed at Jed and Lois as Renner was. Harley outright laughed, but it came out stilted and off-key. But Jed grinned and exclaimed, "Good! That means I fooled you, too. It was easy fooling the press, but you guys were something else. I really had to polish my acting skills to pull this one off. But remember when we all thought Alex had been killed? Well, we thought if the president could pull something like that off, then, well, so could we."

Silence answered his less than enthusiastic explanation, but Kelsey topped it off when she said quietly, in her no-nonsense voice, "Lexie, climb off Uncle Renner and go play upstairs with your cousins. Hurry, sweetheart. Daddy and I want to talk with your uncles and aunts."

Lexie's cousins were the agents' children. Her aunts and uncles were the somber faced agents and wives. Once Renner set Lexie to the floor, she scurried off, still squealing, "Surprise! Surprise!" blissfully unaware of the storm clouds gathering behind her sweet little derriere.

"Good?" Renner asked McCormack once Lexie was gone, his temper rising. "Excuse my French, sir, but what part of this… this cover-up, is good? I carried your damned coffin that day," he told Lois pointedly, "and I felt like shit doing it." He didn't mean for his voice to shift from curious to pissed off to accusing as quickly as it did, but… *Fuck! Who fakes their death, then expects everyone who loved them to just forgive and forget?* "You must have no idea what you meant—mean—to us. Losing you was like losing my dad all over again."

Renner could still remember the day they'd buried Lois, because it reminded him of what he'd missed by not being at his mom's side when she'd needed him most, of not being one of those chosen to carry his dad's coffin. Of trying to act tough and manly in front of his USMC brothers while his heart broke. But making the tough decision to stay on task on that special operations mission in Pakistan, was something he knew Cody Graves would have surely done. So he'd missed his dad's funeral. He hadn't missed a day of that incredible man's life, and that was what counted. All those living years…

Lois came to him quickly and cupped his jaw, her eyes misty as she peered up at him. "I'm so sorry for hurting you, Renner, and for hurting everyone else, too. But we had to lure that beastly woman back into America. She had to be stopped once and for all time. It was the only way we could think to get her here. Can you ever forgive me?"

Damn, he wanted to cry. "Forgive you for what? For being alive?" God, this was so fucked up! He swiped a quick finger under his nose. "There's nothing to forgive, ma'am, but— fuck!" And now he was cursing a woman. "All. This. Time…" He set his jaw, not going to fall apart with his teammates watching.

Jed stepped up into him then, blocking everyone but Alex's and Kelsey's views. "We had to get that conniving woman back into America, Renner," he told him with deliberate firmness. "She was killing us, too. Please understand. Lois and I knew she was greedy. We had to make her believe she could actually weasel her way into McCormack Industries, that she could get her hands on my name and fortune. And to do that, we had to make her believe Lois was dead."

"But I saw you…" Renner said accusingly. Plaintively. God, he wanted to hit something! Jed would do. "You looked like you enjoyed her company, sir. And she wore your wife's jewelry. Those diamonds. You gave them to her." Renner glanced at Lois, wondering if she knew what else Jed had given Montego.

"That was my idea," Lois explained evenly, her chin up and so very much like Tara that Renner had to wipe his eyes to see clearly. "I told Jed to give that bitch anything she wanted, well, except for him. She couldn't have him. Not really. He just had to make her think she could."

Jed had the grace to blush as he dipped into his jacket pocket and pulled out a plastic bag of Tattle Tales. "Trust me," he said as he handed them to Renner. "What you think you saw, Agent Graves, was precisely what Lois and I needed you to see."

"But she was… all over you." *You lying rat bastard.*

Jed nodded. "Yes, but that, unfortunately, had to be part of the plan. I needed her to believe I was growing more and more senile, that I was losing my mind. Wasn't really that, excuse the double entendre, *hard,* if you know what I mean. Us old guys don't exactly have what it takes to party all night anymore."

"That was my idea, too," Lois interjected as if her saying that made everything better. "I saw what that woman did the last time she was here, and every time, all I could see was her hurting my Brady. No mother should have to live through what Montego..." Lois made a distasteful face, her lips pinched and her nose twisted as if she couldn't bear to say the woman's name, "...did to those poor boys."

"No, they shouldn't," Kelsey murmured, "but you could've taken us into your confidence, Lois. I mean, we are family. You should've trusted us."

"We do trust you," Jed said, "but if you recall, Alex went through this very same ordeal during President Tom Adams' first term. Tom needed everyone to think Alex was dead and—"

"You think I've forgotten that?" Kelsey snapped, her fingernails digging into Alex's knee. "God, I still have nightmares!"

Alex visibly cringed at the true anguish echoing in his wife's voice at the betrayal that had struck everyone. But Jed and Lois had betrayed the whole nation. The press would have a field day with this stunt, just like they did years ago when President Adams had tasked the FBI to make it look like Alex had been murdered. In the process of working that involuntary yet crucial presidential covert operation, Alex had outed the true betrayer, Vice President Winston. He'd been the money-man behind the home-grown terrorist organization, *Chaos*

Now. They'd planned to unleash a dirty bomb in the District while, at the same time, they'd planned to assassinate President Thomas Beauregard Adams.

But the emotional cost had been especially hard on Kelsey. Renner knew the stories. Not only had she completely believed that her husband had been murdered—the FBI had actually done an exceptional job faking his death—she'd been targeted and nearly killed. Unbeknownst to everyone, including Alex, she'd also been pregnant with Lexie, which made forgiving the FBI impossible for Alex. Even now, he moved his arm protectively around her shoulders, tipping her into his side, his eyes gone icy and cold as he stared Jed—his friend—down.

Lois turned to face Kelsey, a tear glistening in the corner of her eye. "Oh, honey, believe me, we wanted to tell at least you kids. But we saw how this evil woman worked and how hard you took every death, Alex. Jed's been worried for months about his good friends. In the end, right before I 'died,' we decided we couldn't take the chance that she'd lash out at you more than she already had. She'd already struck at Alex through Beau. All it would've taken was for one word of our deceit to get out, and, well, you know how wildfires start in the District."

Alex didn't say a word.

Jed drew in a deep breath. "Which is why I needed to meet with each of you here today. I betrayed your trust, and I'm truly sorry. There's no way to compensate you for what Lois and I did, and I would never insult you by throwing money at you. Tomorrow morning, I'll pay for my sins on national television. I plan to re-introduce Lois at the award ceremony, and explain why we did what we did. But I need you good men and women to forgive me first, because you are my family, my sons and daughters."

Tears leaked out of the corners of his eyes, but Jed brushed them briskly away. "To be honest, you kids are why we do what we do at McCormack Industries. I'd give my right hand to have Brady back, but…" Jed clutched Renner's bicep then, as if holding on for dear life. "…but I've got you, son. You and your brothers and sisters in arms. Please, please forgive me."

"Forgive me, too," Lois said, her eyes bright with uncertainty, both hands on Renner's wrist.

He couldn't have gotten away from them if he'd tried. Which he didn't. She seemed to need this motherly contact, and for a second there, he thought he saw Brady in her gentle features. Renner hadn't personally known the guy, but every jarhead knew the story behind Brady McCormack's unlikely rescue and the man sitting calmly across the room with his arm around Kelsey. Alex was the one who'd saved Brady's life. Just like he'd saved President Adams' life…

Well, shit. Renner didn't know whether to laugh or cry at these two old people. He still felt stupid and used. Angry. But it made sense now, how Jed had come unglued when he'd first thought Lois's headstone was vandalized, then how quickly he'd calmed once Montego started her slut routine. Renner chewed the inside of his cheek. Jed had kept his distance from Montego, appearing with her in public, but not going home until late. Not spending every minute of his days with her, which most infatuated males would have if they'd truly been in lust or love.

How he'd seemed to fluctuate between savvy, intelligent businessman and doddering old fool. And diamonds were just rocks, as far as Renner was concerned. Jed could well afford to toss all those expensive gifts he'd given Lois over the years out the window and buy her bigger and better.

"You screaming about her headstone was just an act?" Man, that had looked so real.

McCormack nodded. "I almost gave myself away that night. Wasn't sure I fooled her or not."

"You fooled me," Renner admitted. But still… "I don't want your award. Keep it." *Shove it.*

"It's not my award, Agent Graves," Jed replied, a stern note in his voice. "It's a Congressional Special Award, a one-time thing created especially for you. The whole nation has been watching this mess with Montego, aka LuAnn. Like you, most of them believed I'd lost my mind until they saw that final news report. Honest to God, she had the press eating out of her hand, didn't she?"

He ran his fingers over his thinning silver hair, fingers that Renner realized were bent with arthritis and age. "But Americans are not as stupid as the press thinks, and neither were you, Renner. You saw through Montego from the start, and you're the one who tracked her down. You've dogged her since that day in Arlington. You're the one who led your team into her den, and you're the one who—"

Renner's palms came up. "Stop. No, sir, it wasn't me. It was Tom and his men. He knew where she was, and he's the one who—"

"Tom told us everything you did for him and his men," Jed said quietly. "He's not as crazy as you think. He knows he and his men are probably on their way to an institution for the criminally insane. They need serious help. He admits that, but he said if not for you, they would've gone down fighting that night. Suicide by police, that was how they'd planned it, to go out in a hail of gunfire, blood, and grit. But whatever you told them there at the end, well, you made them think, and you made them believe. Tom said you turned them into men again."

"I'm no hero," Renner ground out, fighting his tears. *Goddamnit!*

"Yes, you are," Lois said sweetly as she slipped past his defenses and wrapped her arms around his chest, pulling him against her in a smothering motherly hug. "You're just like my Brady, Renner. You are your father's son. Believe me. Cody's looking down from heaven right now, and he's so proud of you."

Well, damn. That didn't help, bringing up his dad like that. Nestling under his chin like his own mother would if she'd been here. Her holding onto him while The TEAM watched, blinked, and sniffled. Renner was fighting a losing battle. He swallowed his pain down where it belonged, in his heart.

Lois stepped back, one hand still on his arm, while tiny sparkles filled the corners of his eyes thinking about the horrific battles each of Montego's victims had ahead of them. At the godawful cost of war in general, both abroad and at home. At the downright wickedness of evil people like Montego and the bastard who'd killed his dad just because he was pissed at the president. None of it made sense, but evil never did. It just was.

Renner felt Tara's fingers then, twining into his. Holding onto him. Holding him up. He tugged her into his side, needing the warmth of her body. Her courage. Her incredible heart. She settled against his hip like she belonged there, and by hell, she did. With her, he could do anything. Even forgive...

"Think of it this way," Alex said from across the room. "You're not accepting this award because you're the hero of the day, Renner. You're accepting it on behalf of men like Tom and his men who will never be recognized for all they endured. For the survivors Montego left in her wake and all the bodies we still haven't found. For the names of victims that we may never know. Because they were and are heroes. You'd march into hell for your brothers, wouldn't you?"

Stupid question. Renner had already done that. He nodded, not sure he could answer without his voice cracking.

"Then be that guy," Alex said, his voice steel. "Man up and stand tall and give them something to be proud of again. Don't let anyone forget them."

Well, shit, shit, shit.

"Here, here," Harley interjected somberly from where he sat with his arm around Judy. His hazel eyes were bright with tears, and he was doing all the sniffling. Poor tender-hearted Harley. "Proud to know you, Renner Graves. But then, I already was damned proud to call you my friend."

"Me, too," Judy said sweetly, her green eyes glistening as bright as her tender-hearted husband's. She'd leaned her head against Harley's shoulder. God, what a pair.

"I second the motion," Mark added, then murmured, "Junior agent," very clearly, letting Renner know he might've stepped out of line once or twice the past couple days. He and his blonde wife Libby were every bit the powerhouse couple Harley and Judy were. Like Alex and Kelsey. Hell, like every couple in this over-sized living room. They all had what Renner wanted.

The fight shuddered out of him. He squeezed Tara tight, afraid to look down at her, afraid what he'd see in her pretty eyes. But so thankful she was at his side.

"This has been one helluva tough mission, people," Alex added, "but it's over. Take the next two weeks off. I don't want to see any of you until January."

"Yeah, tough," was all Renner could make his mouth say as he acknowledged his boss.

Alex and Kelsey looked good together. They looked happy, him with his arm around her, her with her hand on his knee. Like they loved each other. Like Renner's dad and mom used to look before—

Damn, he needed a drink.

"You're telling me," dark-haired Beau Villanueva growled from the loveseat where he sat with McKenna, their baby girl, Essie, asleep on his lap. "I'd give my right arm if none of this ever happened. But hey…" He raised his left hand, then wiggled his brows and all five working fingers. A big shitty grin consumed his ugly face. "I damned near did."

That broke the tension. A couple people chuckled, but Renner wanted to cry. He didn't have what Alex and Kelsey, Beau and McKenna, or most of these agents had. At the end of this day, it was quite possible that he'd still go home alone. That Tara meant what she'd said. And he understood, he did. She needed time to heal.

"Trust me, this week will be hard for me and Jed, too," Lois told him, her eyes bright and sad at the same time. "I still have to tell my daughter-in-law I'm alive, only now Melissa's married that awful Tucker Chase fellow, and he's FBI, and he'll probably have us thrown in jail for the rest of our lives."

"You're already dead," Harley deadpanned, his eyes bright with Mortimer mischief. "He can't put you in FBI jail, ma'am."

That brought a hearty round of chuckles, until Alex intoned, "Tucker's not so bad." Uncommon praise for a former SEAL who still believed everyone else wanted to be him.

"So, you're not losing your faculties?" Renner asked Jed, needing to look into the man's bright eyes to be sure. "You're not senile or tetched or…?" He tapped his forehead.

"No, son, no, I most certainly am not tetched." Jed claimed Lois's hand, grinning like the man he'd been before anyone had ever heard of the twisted Montego dynasty. "In fact, I'm on my way to Congress Monday morning. I'm going to propose they let me pay back what they spent when Lois's funeral shut down Washington, DC. Do you think they're smart enough to do that?"

"No, sir," Renner said tightly. Damn, even Jed had Lois to go home to now.

Jed cocked his head, his eyes suddenly teary and tender. "But can you ever forgive me, son? This lie has been especially hard on you. I know that, and I'm sorry I avoided you these past few weeks. But having to go home to my penthouse, knowing she'd be there, pawing at me and, umm, other things…" He shivered. "I'll never be able to repay you for what you did for me and my wife. For America."

Jed stretched out his hand and this time, Renner accepted it. Lois sniffed. Some former Marine in the room gave a grunt of approval. Might've been Alex. Or Mark, Zack, Taylor, Gabe, Maverick or—hell, it could've been Kelsey. She'd been sounding more and more like a Devil Dog lately.

"Hey, everyone, I've got French toast, eggnog, and homemade applesauce," she chimed in. "It's in the kitchen if you're hungry."

"And bacon," Alex added. "Peppered and regular. Grab your kids. Let's eat."

Renner found himself caught in a friendly tide of guy hugs, wifely hugs, and one very tight strangling hug from Kelsey. "Thanks for keeping my secrets," she whispered in his ear, "but I told Alex everything last night."

"Yes, and thanks for having her six," Alex murmured behind her, his hand in Renner's face. "I still can't believe she jumped off that high-rise in Hillcrest Heights. She's just as bad as you. You're quite a guy."

Renner accepted the praise humbly. "It was my pleasure," he said even as Tara piped up with, "Well, of course he is. That's why you hire men like him, isn't it?"

Alex's brow lifted like he had more to say, but he offered nothing, just brushed by Renner and Tara on his way to the kitchen with Kelsey.

"Let's eat," Tara said.

"Ah huh," Renner replied, his boots rooted where he stood, his gaze caught on the fine Irish bar next to where Alex and Kelsey had been sitting. Had to be solid wood, maybe something Alex had crafted. Beautifully carved Celtic crosses and ivy marked the polished front panel. A white bar towel sat neat and folded beside a dozen seductive amber bottles of temptation. The friends of a lifetime... Jameson. Bacardi. Jose Cuervo. Patrón. Others.

Alex wouldn't mind. All Renner needed was one stiff drink. A quick shot would go down smooth and easy. Just one. That was what real men did, they tossed one back, and it gave them the burn and the energy to move on. To keep fighting. Fighting men had been doing it for centuries. No one had to know. The guys might even expect it from him. Couldn't let them down, could he? They had his back and he had theirs and—

Tara's fingertips graced his chin, tugging his gaze from the bar back to her trusting blues. "You do what you have to do," she told him earnestly. "I'll be in the kitchen. Don't be long."

But he knew what she meant, and damn it, Renner didn't need her permission, nor anyone else's, but—

Tara was a recovering alcoholic. So was Harley. They'd both stayed clear of that bar and those bottles. They hadn't even seemed tempted. Yet Renner knew they were just like him. Tempted plenty. Alcohol didn't let anyone get away without a fight. A fight he was now embroiled in. So, how'd they do it?

He stared that bottle of Irish whiskey down. Stay or go? Man up or man down? Live to die another day or pickle his liver like a weakling with Satan riding his back, spurring him. on. Not covering his six. Never loyal. Just spurring him endlessly on for one more shot, one more sip, half-pint or bottle or handle. One more, and then another until it killed him. Until Tara left him for good—

Damned if something Detective Cody Graves had said a long time ago didn't bubble up to the surface of Renner's mind. Something about how sometimes the better part of valor was walking away from a fight. Knowing when to fight. Knowing who you were really fighting. That guy with the big mouth or—you.

In the end, all came back to Tara. She'd told Renner precisely what he'd needed to hear, to do what he had to do. Well, first Renner was going to *do* breakfast with a strong cup of coffee and a hearty slice of peppered bacon. Then he was going to *do* a quick retreat back to his or her place, where they could be alone and naked the rest of the day, maybe tomorrow, too. And then, he was going to *do* Tara.

Jack Daniels and his friends couldn't beat that.

Chapter Forty

Tara rubbed her nose into Renner's chest like a cat in heat, craving his touch and his scent. Every last one of his kisses. Loving the way he clutched her backside when she came. The way he always handled her poor banged-up head gently as if he knew where that bump was. How he knew where every last one of her injured ribs were and avoided them with precision. Which hadn't been easy the way they'd feasted on and off each other's bodies yesterday. Yet this morning she felt better. Relaxed. Finally, ready and able to face the world. Maybe spit in its eye.

Better yet, they had two weeks off together—two weeks!—to play and relax. In the shower. In his bed. On his sturdy kitchen table. Or on the counter while the pancakes she'd tried to make fluffy burned instead to a smoky crisp. Surely the neighbors heard the smoke detectors screaming.

Or they could play at her, ahem, loft. Mr. Marchant had to have noticed she hadn't been back. Or maybe he'd seen the news. He might be worried. It was time to go home.

"I'll race you to the shower," she said as she licked her way up Renner's neck, then covered his mouth with hers. The man had a rugged five o'clock shadow that graced the hard line of his cheeks, jaw, other assets she adored. Who knew whisker burns could hurt so good? Yet they did. On her lips and chin. Her breasts, that had even now perked for his attention. The inside of her thighs. He'd marked her body in the most delicious places and—

The shower could wait.

Urgently, she nipped his lower lip, sucking it like he'd suckled her breasts. Hinting. Then hinting a little harder until he opened those beautiful deep blue eyes and rolled her over.

"Good morning," he growled down at her before he poured kisses over her face.

It didn't take long until they were both sweating and flying again. This man knew her body too well, and that made her happy in ways she'd never imagined. This was making love. Kiss by kiss, he'd banished all thoughts of her nightmares. When she woke now, her first thoughts weren't to run and check her locks. Her past was finally behind her. She really could fly.

"Come with me," he murmured, his voice a sexy rumbling command her body couldn't seem to ignore. So, she did, her heart opened wide as her body exploded.

At last, Renner sagged into her, his breath hard in her ear, but his body just as relaxed and satisfied. Satiated. For now. She too knew a few things he couldn't resist. Mostly she just had to undress, but he liked her mouth on him—everywhere. And she lived to make him throw his head back and roar. She loved his fingers in her hair while she worshipped his body. If this gentle dance of persuasion they seemed to be locked in step with wasn't love, she didn't know what love was. He already owned her body and soul. Her heart. He just didn't know it yet. She hadn't told him.

And just like that… "I love you, Renner," spilled easily off her tongue.

His head came up, sweat glistening on his brow, but that adorable bright light in his eyes. Gah. She knew it then. He didn't have to say it. He loved her, too.

Her heart overflowed down her cheeks.

"Please tell me I didn't hurt you," he begged hoarsely, that sad smile back on his mouth.

She couldn't speak, could only shake her head.

"Good," he purred, "because I know you love me, baby. You've been showing me nothing but love since we met."

She nearly choked. "Even when I pushed you off that high-rise?"

He nodded, bowing the top of his head to her chin as his mouth latched onto her nipple. "Even then," he mumbled. The man had no trouble talking with his mouth full. "And you need to know I love you, too. All of you."

She nestled her nose into his hair and against his scalp, breathing in the spicy, sweaty scent of him. Loving every last epithelial, every molecule. Holding onto him and all that he'd brought into her life. Courage. Ferocity. Love, soft and sweet and kind.

His head came up again as he let go of her nipple with a satisfied pop. He grinned like the happy male he was. This man was a pleasure to love. He was a gift and she was never letting him go.

"How about we take a nice long bath instead?" he asked, his mouth still shiny wet.

"I'd like that. But then I should probably go back to my place. I'll have bills to pay and I want to let Mr. Marchant know where I've been."

"I want you here with me. All the time. Would you ever consider moving in—"

"Yes. Yes!" she all but squealed. "I'd like that very much."

"Today?"

Tara nodded, grinning like a fool. "Yes, please. I'm myself, I'm strong again. More, I don't know, stubborn, I guess you could say."

That raised his brows. "How could you possibly be more stubborn?"

Yeah, he had her there. "It's a good trait." She laughed. "It keeps you focused on your goals long after others quit on theirs."

"It also gets you into trouble."

Well, yeah. There was that. "But only winners have the perfect blend of tenacity and willpower." Her back stiffened automatically at that. "And only winners believe they can do anything. It's never more than a matter of *'where there's a will, there's a way'*. Right?"

His hands slipped under her hips and ended up cupping her backside. Renner took a deep breath. "Right, but how willful are you? A good marriage takes hard work."

Tara stopped breathing. Was he asking...?

"I know you said you wanted to take time getting to know each other, but..." He looked down to where their bodies were still warmly connected. "I don't want to wait. Move in with me. Stay with me. Marry me. Win with me."

"Yes," she whispered, afraid if she spoke too loudly, she'd wake up from this once-in-a-lifetime dream.

When Renner smiled, the sun poured out of his heart, and he was smiling now. "I love you, Tara," he whispered.

Aww... She cupped his beautiful, manly face. There wasn't a twinge of sadness in his eyes. Only the purest love. His cheeks cracked wide open. Even with whiskers, he looked like the happiest kid on earth. And so was she.

Talk about goal-oriented. All Renner needed was a mission, a directive, or an order, and he was ready to go. He and Tara had already gone to her place and met with her buddy, Mr. Marchant, the gray-haired older gent who didn't mind taking her rent, but never came through with simple, basic things like fire escapes or enough extinguishers.

How he'd ever acquired a certificate of occupancy or a housing business license amazed Renner. Which made him look differently at the other four apartments on the first level of this older Victorian. The house itself was not in bad shape. It was the owner who was out of touch with state and city regulations, out of compliance. Renner didn't want to think about how much insurance old man Marchant had—or didn't have. Probably not much, certainly not enough.

Renner had learned the hard way about licensing and insurance requirements after his dad died. His mother woke up one day and sprang into action, intent on getting back on her feet and on with her life. She'd brushed her hair and threw her shoulders back, and she'd used some of the payout from Cody's life insurance to buy a has-been tavern, now registered at city hall as the profitable enterprise, Crazy Eights.

Like the energetic, and okay, stubborn woman she had been and still was today—Renner cringed at the fact that he seemed attracted to that particularly bristly female trait— Brenda Graves opened a pub where Cody's fellow detectives and MPD officers could linger after hours, where they could be among friends. Where they could laugh or cry while they threw one or a dozen back. Where she could look out for them and make sure they didn't drive once they'd gone over her two-beer limit. Not that she stopped them from drinking any more than she'd stopped him after two beers. She'd just mothered them. Maybe smothered them. Made sure they got home to their loved ones at night. Called their wives to tell them where their men were and why. It seemed Brenda had found a new mission in life—making sure that none of Cody's friends died on her watch.

She should've been a Marine, too.

Which was why Renner was on his fifth trip to the garbage receptacle in Marchant's rear parking lot. The fewer combustibles Tara left behind when she moved, the safer this entire building would be. At least until Renner had some free time to help this guy with his rent issues and insurance. That was all Marchant needed, a helping hand to get the place back on track. He might have to ante up and pay a few late fees or fines, but that was doable. Consider it a lesson learned.

"Only one more," Tara called down the stairs after Renner.

"Okay, lock up after me. I'll be right back."

"You bet."

He waited until he heard her feet pounding down to the first floor. Then click, and he jerked the back door open. Mr. Marchant stood on the small concrete porch, dressed in a red winter jacket and boots, sweeping the latest snowflakes off the steps.

"Here, I can do that," Renner said as he dropped the tidy white kitchen garbage bag off the edge of the porch. "You take a breather."

"Thanks," Marchant said with a puff. "Seems the older I get, the less oxygen there is in the air."

"You okay?" Renner asked, his sharp eyes taking in his new friend's condition.

"Pshaw, yes. Just get winded faster these days. That'll teach me for smoking when I was young and dumb."

Renner had to smile at that. He was still young enough to be that kind of dumb. "Well, we all have our favorite bad habits, don't we?"

Marchant took up residence on the concrete side of the porch. "Sure wish I knew who's leaving those damned cigarette butts for me to clean up."

"What butts? Where?"

"Over there." Marchant gestured to the garbage receptacle.

"Today?"

"Every damned day. If I ever catch him or her..."

Renner dropped the broom and ran to the receptacle. Oh, hell, no. Clove cigarette butts. Lots of them, one still smoking through the freshly fallen snow. Beside the receptacle where Renner was fairly certain Jorge had stood while he'd watched Tara.

Renner ran past Marchant and back into the house, his heart in his throat. "Tara!"

Chapter Forty-One

Tara had just stripped the bedding off her bed when someone stepped out of her tiny walk-in closet. She hadn't known anyone was there until a hand came out of nowhere and slapped over her mouth and nose. Then she felt an arm tighten around her neck, gloved fingers against her lips, and something sharp in her ribs. A knife. She couldn't scream, couldn't call out. Didn't dare. That would put Renner and Mr. Marchant in danger. She wouldn't do that.

"There now," an American voice soothed like this guy wasn't trying to kill her. The sharp thing in her already sore ribs cut deeper, lancing her shirt and her skin. "You do as you're told, I might let you live. Call your boyfriend. Tell him you're too tired. He needs to go home. Make him."

She might comply if this creep would take his hand off her mouth. Tara smelled body odor and tooth decay. Clove cigarettes. Whoever this guy was, he wasn't Jorge. But he knew Jorge. Which meant he was Indonesian or Syrian, or— just another terrorist.

Unable to speak or reason with this guy, she went along while he shoved the back of her legs, edging toward her bedroom door. When she grunted, needing him to let go of her mouth long enough to do as he'd ordered, the blade in her side cut deeper.

Tara was damned if she obeyed, damned if she didn't. She couldn't win. This guy had no intention of letting her talk, probably because he knew she'd scream. And she would. She had no intention of letting him kill Renner or Mr. Marchant.

By then they were standing in her front room. She could see out her window. The wintry storm had finally quit. The sky was clearer and no flakes were falling. Clouds still hovered low and gray over the District. And there Tara stopped dead in her tracks. She wouldn't go willingly, not to what she knew waited for her. This guy might as well kill her right here and now. That was what terrorists did.

Until she heard boots pounding up her stairway. Renner.

"No!" she tried to warn him, but her scream came out muffled.

Her assassin hissed, "Silence!" cutting her again.

The door burst open and Renner was there, his eyes black, his face devoid of emotion. The two pistols he relentlessly carried were out of their holsters and fastened on her and the man hiding behind her like a coward.

"Andy White," Renner barked. "Let her go."

"Ahmed Al-Yousif!!" her abductor bellowed. "I am Ahmed Al-Yousif. There is no more Andy White."

Tara cringed. Dear God, the man slowly knifing her to death was Jorge's blood-thirsty buddy. But he had two names. He must be a traitor.

Renner never blinked, never took his eyes off White/Yousif/Whatever. Just looked at her and told her as steadily as if he were reading the news, "I'm here now. You're going to be okay."

But Tara knew better. The blade in her side was no toy, and she was already bleeding. And Renner couldn't hide the sweat beading on his brow or the hard glint in his eye. God, please let that glint be that stubborn determination they'd talked about. She could use some.

Tara shook her head at Renner, trying to tell him to just leave. Save himself.

"Don't. Move," he ordered, his voice steel, wrapping around her like an unbreakable promise.

But breathing was already a struggle. Blood ran warm and thin down her leg. It would only take one stab, one stumble, and she'd be dead. There was no way she'd make it out of this standoff alive. Tara closed her eyes, prepared to die if it meant saving Renner.

"Let her go, White," Renner ordered again. "Or die."

Tara was pale and bleeding, standing in a pool of her blood. Andy Asshat had to comply or Renner would soon have no choice but to shoot through her to kill him. Not an option he ever thought he'd be faced with. Yet here they were, AW hiding behind yet another human shield, prepared to die a chicken shit martyr. Renner wanted to grant that wish. But shooting Tara was not how he wanted this to end.

God, help me.

"She's a pig," Andy spat. "Just another American whore. She deserves to die."

Yeah, well so do you, jerk-off. "Why?" *Keep him talking.*

"She led my brother astray."

"And who would that be—?"

"Jorge! Jorge Poerbatjaraka! My brother!"

"As in biological brother or philosophical brother or asshole brother…?"

"Shut your mouth! All Americans are pigs! Fucking pigs!"

That's it. Get mad. Get stupid.

Renner took another sideways step toward his target and zeroed down on Tara's right shoulder. It had to be a through and through. Clean shot. Slow and steady. He couldn't afford to hit bones or organs. But God. This was Tara's sweet delicate body he was aiming to shoot. Breathing had become impossible.

Yet he taunted, "You talk to your mom with that mouth?"

"I have no mother! No father but Allah!"

"Then tell your buddy Allah hello for—"

Tara bowed as if she knew what was coming, and damn it! She'd put her head directly in his line of sight. Renner couldn't take the shot. He'd lost his one perfect chance. He bit his lip, shifted both reticles and—

Pew! Andy White's head snapped to the side. Then… *Pew! Pew! Pew!* The knife in his hand dropped and red mist splashed the wall behind Tara. Behind Tara. Not through Tara.

Renner had her down on the floor and in his arms before Ahmed the Asshole fell. But WTF? He hadn't fired the kill shot. It came through her one and only window. Someone across the street fired it. That shot could've been for Tara or him.

"Ow," she cried, doubled over and holding her side.

"Stay with me, baby," he murmured, thumb-dialing 911 even while he carried her into her windowless kitchen and set her ass on the table.

Boots pounded up her stairs, and he had no choice but to drop the phone and aim for the door as he shielded Tara with his body. Whatever ISIL asshole dared come to White's rescue would die.

Instead, it was Hunter Christian peering cautiously around Tara's doorjamb. "He the only one?"

"That was you?" Renner hissed at his fellow TEAM agent. "Yes! God, yes, only Anderson White. He's alone."

"You sure?" Hunter asked as Connor Maher squeezed past him into the room.

Renner shook his head. "Thought I was sure before, but he must've been hiding in—" God, where? This place was so damned small.

"No worries," Hunter said as his rifle led him into Tara's living room, then into her bedroom where he checked her tiny closet. "Right. Place is clear. I spotted, but Connor took the shot."

Both men carried McMillan TAC-338s, complete with Leopold Mark 4 3.5-10x40 LR/T scopes, in their gloved hands. The precision weapon was one of the best sniper rifles in the business.

"We've been tracking White for days," Hunter called out from wherever he was now. "Bastard got away from the FBI and us this morning. Blew up the dive-hotel he was staying at downtown. Killed two of Metro PD's finest."

Connor headed straight to Tara, his blow-out kit in his hand. "Medics are on their way. Metro police, too," he reported as he handed his weapon over to Hunter, then laid Tara back onto her table. "Get her shirt off, Renner."

"Renner," she cried, her face sweaty and her eyes brimming.

"It's okay, baby, you're safe now," he said, his hands already ripping past her buttons, tearing the shirt off her left shoulder to get at the stab wound in her side.

Connor handed over a thick pad of cotton packing, which Renner pressed over the narrow slice, needing to slow the bleeding. "Did he hurt you anywhere else? Did that bastard—?"

"No," trembled off her lips, and Renner wanted to kill White again for hurting her at all.

"QuikClot?" Renner asked Connor, even as sirens sounded nearby.

"Coming right up." While Connor ripped the foil wrapper, Renner lifted the saturated packing. Connor poured a healthy dose of the hemostatic dressing over the wound and pressed another thick pad of clean packing over that.

"It stings," Tara murmured, tears streaming down the sides of her face.

"Hey," Renner crooned, leaning over her and stroking her forehead. "This is nothing, Tara. Trust me, us guys have treated worse. White only wanted you to bleed. You're going to be okay. A few x-rays, some stitches, and you'll be on your feet in no time. You'll see."

"Is there anything you can't do?" she asked, blinking up at him.

He still had one hand pressed hard into her side. "Yeah," he admitted, his voice gone hoarse. "Apparently, I can't shoot you."

"Me?"

"That was my plan. Shoot one round through your shoulder to kill White. Bastard was using you as a human shield. I couldn't just stand there and let him cut you."

"White?"

Renner explained who Anderson White, aka Ahmed Al-Yousif, was. By the time he finished, the medics and police had arrived. A Metro PD officer yelled up the stairway, "Hands up! Everyone! You're surrounded."

"Come on up!" Hunter drawled back, then hissed, "Shit. They're going to take my rifle again."

Standard protocol. Police interrogation. Confiscation of all evidence. Hours and hours of redundant questioning.

"Let them," Connor replied easily. "It's not like we don't have more."

"Yeah, but—" Hunter never finished his thought. MPD had arrived along with two medics and a gurney that only fit sideways through the door.

Tara clung to Renner's hand as the medics took over. Two MPD officers patted Hunter and Connor down. Took their rifles. Made them empty their pockets and divest themselves of all other weapons. Their knives. Their ammo. As usual.

"You guys do good work," the one medic commented after he'd lifted the soaked packing to diagnose Tara's wound and found her bleeding had slowed. "Glad you were here. Only we can't transport you to ground level, ma'am. The stairwell's too narrow for our gurney."

Of course, Tara lifted to her elbows and boldly declared, "I can walk."

Which made Renner smile. "Like hell," he growled as he scooped her carefully off the table and into his arms. "You hold on tight to me."

She melted into him with a whimper. "Always."

Chapter Forty-Two

It was the Sunday before Christmas. Tara wouldn't be allowed to leave the hospital for another day. Because of her previous concussion, she'd had to undergo more tests on her head, stress tests on her heart, and she'd answered hundreds of MPD questions. The officers were extremely thorough, as were the kindly FBI agents who'd visited her last night and were back again this morning. It seemed Special Agents Ky and Eden Winchester had been working with Renner's friends, Hunter Christian and Connor Maher, tracking the ISIL terrorist known by the media as Ahmed Al-Yousif, but whom Renner called Andy Asshat.

Interestingly, Ky and Eden were married. Tara couldn't help but wonder if all married people developed the level of communication they had. They seemed to know precisely what the other was going to say before they said it.

Before he'd left to attend the award ceremony, Renner'd told Tara to watch out for the Winchesters. She hadn't the time to ask what he'd meant then, but she liked them. A lot. Ky had a laidback way about him, and he loved talking about his son. Give him an opening, and he dove right in. She could easily read it in his eyes. He clearly adored his wife and son. Eden was the same as her husband, professional, yet warm and friendly.

"Would you mind?" she asked as she angled the overhead television screen where everyone could see it.

Tara didn't have a set at home, had never been a TV addict, but she didn't want to miss Renner's public debut on national television. The event was being broadcast by all major networks, as well as local news channels. Vice President Owens was presenting the award. The stage was lined with huge red poinsettias, a garland of red, white, and blue twined between the plants.

And there he was, looking especially handsome in his black suit, black tie, and a bright red poppy she'd personally pinned to his lapel. On stage between Mr. and Mrs. McCormack. They looked more nervous than he did. Tara fell in love with Renner all over again. The way the laugh lines at the corners of his eyes crinkled at VP Owens' lame joke. The way Renner stared into the camera, that cocky dimple in his chin. Yeah. That guy.

Tara loved him a thousand times over. And then some…

Renner stared unblinking at the crowd. Everyone expected a humble thank-you for this prestigious once-in-a-lifetime congressional award. But that wasn't what they were going to get. Not from him. Not today.

This event was supposed to take place in the Oval Office, but ended up at the John F. Kennedy Center for the Performing Arts. Which was just as well. There were nearly as many reporters here this morning as spectators.

But this was just another dog and pony show, one of many he'd been at and given during his military career. Renner hoped Tara was watching, because he planned to never, ever, do this again.

Alex and Kelsey sat in the front row with his mom, his sister Maureen and her daughter, Frankie. The TEAM and their families filled the rows behind them. Then Aaron's men, decked out in suits and ties, spit-and-polished shoes, lined the following rows. They were nervous and it showed. Even outgoing Zale Warner. He hadn't stopped licking his lips since he'd sat down. And it was easy to read hypervigilance every time he rolled his eyes. The hardest part of surviving was still—surviving. Going out in public. Dark noisy places. Always too many people. Yet there they were, tall and proud and holding it together.

Jed McCormack had finished gracefully explaining to the country how he and his wife had deceived them in order to snare Catalina Montego. He talked about all those phony interviews he'd included her in, even explained what went on behind closed doors, which ended up being embarrassing for him. Then Lois took her turn at the podium, her tone that of a mother out to save every last one of *'her'* boys and girls in the service.

"What would you have done if you'd been in my shoes?" she asked bluntly, her chin set in defiance. "Our servicemen and servicewomen put their lives on the line every single day for us, while most of us sit in our cushy homes, in our civilized towns and cities, and we dare to armchair quarterback their every move. They suffer in silence while we second-guess, judge, and criticize everything they do. Denounce me and my husband if you want. Pretend this was nothing more than a publicity stunt, if you will. I. Don't. Care."

She got a standing ovation for that in-your-face defiance.

"And I'd do it again," Lois declared, every bit the patriot that her husband was. "I'm willing to bet that every single proud military mom and dad, every mother and father, grandmother and grandfather, sister and brother of our courageous sons and daughters would've done the same thing. It worked, didn't it? Jed and I lured that witch back to our country—ours, not hers—and Alex Stewart's TEAM took it from there. Think with your hearts, people. Who do you love more?"

Gentle, sweet Lois McCormack faced those glaring spotlights and opinionated reporters head-on, and she told Americans everywhere, "Don't think for one second that I wouldn't do it again. I can afford to lose fair-weather friends. What I can't afford to lose is our young military. To that sadistic woman, I said, no more. No more soldiers..." She paused long enough to scan the audience. "No more sailors." Another pause. Another meaningful scan. "No more Marines like my Brady." Damn, Renner wiped a tear at that. She was killing it. "No more Coasties and no more airmen. Do you hear me, America? I said... No. More."

The audience exploded to their feet. A roar went up.

But the damned woman wasn't done. After the applause, hoorahs, and whistling died down, she leaned into the mic and stated, loud and clear, "Catalina Montego or LuAnn or whoever she wanted us to believe her name was, is dead. Now let's get on with our lives and remember what we stand for. I'm holding a barbeque picnic at Joint Base Andrews today at four o'clock. It's free for every veteran, their family and friends.

I'm celebrating. I hope you'll join Jed and me there. God bless America."

Another resounding cheer. Another standing ovation. And Lois McCormack could've run for the United States presidency right then and there and won by a landslide.

Vice President Owens took the podium back then. He applauded all Jed and Lois McCormack stood for, and forgave them for tricking him and the rest of America. He said a few other things too, but when he called out, "And now…."

Renner's stomach fell to his feet. How could he top anything Lois or Jed had said? Dry-mouthed and on wooden legs, he joined the VP center stage.

Owens said a lot of nice things. He made a few jokes, but he'd never served in the armed forces. He didn't really understand the cost of war like Jed, Lois, and Renner did. Some of what he said was true, but some of it was trite and self-serving. Throughout the initial chitchat and then the official handing over of another piece of shiny metal, Renner focused on Alex, wishing he were in charge of the presentation. Alex knew, damn it. This award would mean more then.

At last VP Owens stepped back and the podium belonged to Renner.

He stuck his chin at Americans everywhere. He thought of Tom and all that he and his men had gone through—just because they were military. He thought of Aaron, who watched him now from behind Agent Lee Hart's broad shoulder. Renner brought his gaze back to Brenda Graves, the first woman he'd ever loved and would love until his last breath. She winked at him like this was no big deal. And suddenly—it wasn't. He smiled at her, so damned proud to be Cody's and Brenda Graves' son. So damned proud to be an American.

He cleared his throat and said, "Good afternoon, America."

The audience gave him an appreciative smattering of applause, which was all he deserved.

"As you all know, my name is Staff Sergeant Renner Graves. Former active duty Marine. Always a Marine. But that's not important, and if you're like me, you'll forget me the second I step off this stage. I know I would. But what you need to remember are the American men and women fighting somewhere, right now, for you and me. What you need to remember is that it only takes one…" He lifted his index finger for all to see. "One. Just one. One man. One woman. To change the world. Montego sure as hell did that, didn't she? But thanks to a group of warriors hardened in the worst kind of hell imaginable, she's terrorized us for the last time.

"Do I deserve this expensive looking medal and all these accolades?" He shook his head. "No. I don't. I'm not the one who ended Montego, and I didn't go after her so I could stand here today. Yet here I am…" He spread his arms.

Once again, the audience recognized him with another smattering of get-on-with-it-so-we-can-go-home. And that was okay. Renner wanted out of there, too. But Tom and his men, all those military members Montego had mutilated or murdered, and all their families deserved so much more.

"So, indulge me a minute or two while I tell you who *we* are," he said, his gaze riveted on Aaron as he purposely used that collective word. "*We* are not heroes. *We* don't like the word and *we* don't believe it. Don't you believe it, either. Because *we* are no different than you. No better. No smarter. But *we*…" He stuck his chin at Aaron. "…are America's sons and daughters. *We* are college students and backyard mechanics, moms and dads if we are lucky. *We* are peanut-butter-and-jelly and a cold glass of milk on a long, hot day when *we* are too tired or too lazy to fix a real dinner. *We* are cold Bud-Lite on Super Bowl Sunday, and Coney Island hotdogs in the middle of Times Square.

"*We* are Fenway Park, the Boston Red Sox, the New York Yankees, and every baseball team in between. *We* are Irish and Vietnamese, African American and Native American. *We* are Catholic. *We* are non-believers. *We* are *"see-the-USA-in-your-Chevrolet"* and fireworks on the Fourth of July. We are Ajax: *"Stronger than dirt.* Burger King; *"Have it your way"*. And *we* promise you…" He cleared his throat then. "I mean I promise you…"

His eyes zeroed back to his mom who was crying, then to Kelsey, also crying, finally to stone-faced Alex, who wouldn't be caught dead crying. Man, he loved all three of them. They were family. Those men and women several rows behind them as well.

Renner ended at Aaron, who was now sitting forward in his seat, his fingers steepled beneath his chin and his eyes glimmering. That man exemplified endurance, solitude, and sheer grit. He'd endured Montego's cruelty, and he'd turned his hatred of her into something better. He helped lost children. Now *there* was a hero.

"I…" Renner raised his hand high above his head, his index finger extended, pointing to heaven. "That's me, Renner Graves. Just me. Just I. And I promise you…" He nodded at Aaron, "that I will bear all my country asks of me, brother. And I will bear it gladly if it saves one…" Renner swallowed hard, his heart breaking for all who'd died serving America. "Just one of my brothers or my sisters. And that, ladies and gentlemen, is what ended Montego's death grip on the East Coast. Men like me who walked into Hell to save just one."

Alex was the first out of his seat as the audience thundered to its feet. He nodded at Renner, clapping his approval, his mouth pressed into a tight line like he needed to hit something. Renner knew the feeling.

But Aaron stood there behind Lee Hart with tears running down his face, saluting, openly falling apart. His men too, and that, right there, proved that Montego hadn't destroyed them. The men Montego had hurt the worst were still in the fight. Better yet, they had the rest of their lives ahead of them to prove her sorry ass wrong.

Renner nodded at Aaron, offered Alex the same recognition, then walked off stage. He'd done what he'd come here to do. He needed to get back to Tara.

Chapter Forty-Three

Tara was packed and ready to go. She'd convinced her doctors she'd be okay, then convinced Ky and Eden Winchester to leave. *"Really, just leave, I'll be fine."* She'd dressed in the new clothes Kelsey had dropped off, a simple white blouse with acid-washed jeans. New underwear and socks. A pair of white Converse running shoes. By the time Renner pushed her door oprn, she was dying of anticipation. She had a man to love, and love him, she did. With all her heart.

And there he was. Breathtakingly handsome in his tailored suit, complete with suit jacket, pressed slacks, white shirt and tie. Until now, she'd only seen him in casual black jeans, shirt, and his leather cut. Now he looked like a professional businessman. A gentleman. His hair was parted and combed, and he'd shaved.

Her heart did a triple backflip in her chest. She'd always loved a man in uniform, but this guy was something else. He made that suit look good.

But a sad smile was back on his face. Once again, the warrior in him had come home depleted and weary. She ran to him, needing her hands on his neck and her mouth on his lips. Needing to help him forget.

"I watched you," she cried, kissing his cheeks and chin, his mouth and lips. Trying to distract him. "I heard what you said, and you were magnificent. Everyone loved you."

He growled out of his jacket, one hand at the small of her back as he tossed it aside. "Don't care what everyone thinks."

"Then let's go home."

"To where? Your place is a crime scene, and I've been outed. I can't go back there."

"Where'd you stay last night?"

"Hotel," he mumbled into her open mouth, still kissing and licking his way into her heart.

"Then we're going to your hotel room."

"Hold that thought," he murmured as he walked her backward to the bed and hoisted her up onto it. Resting one knee between her legs, he climbed on top of her, one hand in her hair, the other cupping her hip. "You," he breathed in her face, "should stay here until they actually medically discharge you for a change."

"They did release me."

"You bullied them into releasing you."

She shrugged both shoulders. "So? You bullied them last time; I bullied them this time. I don't want to be here without you." Tara's heart ached for this man. His eyes were so sad, the whites tinged with red, his eyelids swollen. This day had been hard on him. "I saw your mom on TV, Alex, Kelsey, and some of your other friends, too."

His chest expanded with a drawn-out sigh, his eyes focused on his fingers in her hair. "Yeah, everyone showed up. That was nice. Did you see Aaron?"

She shook her head, loving the feel of Renner's body pressing her into the mattress. Neither were fully on the bed. Their legs extended off the side; her knees were bent, but his were stiff and stovepiped. He had to be uncomfortable. "What about Aaron?"

Renner looked into her eyes then. "He's alone, Tara. All those guys are alone, and that bothers me a lot. I'm thinking of taking them out on my boat."

"You own a boat?" There was so much she didn't know about this guy.

"Yeah, it's no big deal, just a fishing boat. Nothing fancy. A pontoon. I figured me, you, and our dog—"

"Wait. What dog?"

He smiled down on her then, a real smile, the kind that spilled sunshine over her and warmed her from the inside out. "The dog we're going to get as soon as we're married. He can be our first baby, while we, you know…" Renner thrust his hips forward, "practice."

Tara's eyes filled at the sight of him finally thawing. "Yes, practice. Let's go to that hotel room and practice. Take me home, Renner. Make love to me. I need you inside me. Because you're already in my heart."

She didn't mean for that to hurt him, but his eyes brimmed. He nodded, suddenly overcome and unable to speak. "Yeah," was all he ground out.

Tara lifted her chin and tucked his head to her breasts. She couldn't fix the world, but she could soften its rough edges like only a woman could do for her man. She could be here for him whenever he needed her. Hell, she might even learn how to cook and bake for this guy.

"I've always wanted a dog," she murmured into his combed hair, kissing his head. "But we didn't wait to have sex. Why wait to get a dog? A puppy would be fun." And he seemed to need the companionship only dogs offered. Hope he also needed all those other little things that came with owning a dog.

His fingers adeptly unbuttoned her blouse, and Renner nestled his nose between her breasts, breathing hotly into her bra. His chest expanded. She could feel his cheeks wrinkle with a smile against her skin.

"Where do you want to live? Colorado?" he asked, licking the side of her breast. "Your parents are there."

"But my life is here." She let her fingers dip low on his back, loving the feel of his full weight on her. "I have a good job and Kelsey needs me. Raymond's Kids need me. Where do you want to live?"

"With you," he said simply, his tongue a sizzling hot brand on her sensitive skin.

Tara pressed her cheek to the top of his head. "I'll go anywhere you want to go," she told him sincerely. "But right now, let's get out of here. I have a man to love, and I don't want to be disturbed while I do it."

Like a true gentleman, Renner pushed to his feet, then held out a hand for her. Tara settled her much smaller hand into his, then lifted to her feet, aware for the first time of all she felt for Renner Graves. Here she stood with her shirt unbuttoned and her man coming undone. But Renner was so much more than just a man. He was her heart and her soul, her reason for living and dying. He was everything.

He pulled her against his chest, still looking down at her, his eyes a deeper blue. "What would you say to a New Year's Eve wedding? I know a place—"

"Yes," Tara told him, her arms around his neck and their bodies warm against each other's. "Let's do it."

"But I want your parents to be here. Your dad said—"

"Wait. You talked to my dad?" That was just plain sweet.

"Of course. I had to ask him for your hand in marriage, didn't I?"

Oh, damn. This man was breaking her heart. "You did? When?"

Renner's face split into a handsome grin. He was simply, beautifully, breathtakingly handsome when he smiled. "Last night while you were sleeping. I talked to him right here in this room. Talked with your mom, too. He's already bought tickets. They'll be here the day after Christmas. Noon flight out of Denver."

Tara didn't know what to say.

Renner shrugged like it was no big deal. "If I'm rushing things, tell me. I can slow down. We can wait."

She shook her head. "I'm done with waiting and I'm done with running."

"Does that mean you're also done playing Robin Hood?"

She had to smile at that. He'd remembered. "Yes, I'm done stealing from the rich, especially since Jed and Lois are stepping up to completely finance Raymond's Kids."

Renner stopped and scooped her into his arms. "Then let's get out of here. Let's go home."

Tara nestled under his chin. She was already home. Wherever Renner went, there she would be. At his side. Forever. It didn't—couldn't—get any better than this.

Chapter Forty-Four

Christmas had come. Christmas had gone. It was early April, cherry blossom time in the District. Renner sat in the captain's chair of his well-used, but seaworthy, double-decker pontoon boat. He'd dressed accordingly today, in swim trunks and a button-up shirt with tails that flapped in the breeze. Ray-Ban polarized aviators protected his eyes. They were heading east on the Potomac, dodging river taxis and smaller watercraft, bound for a day of fishing. The wind was east by northeast, coming in off the Atlantic. Brisk enough to water your eyes, but nothing to worry about. No storm warnings. Only smooth waters ahead.

Tara lounged beside him on the cushioned seating that rimmed the inside of the hull, while Aaron and several of his men helped themselves to the ice chests full of soda and beer, cold cuts and sandwich fixings. A couple guys, Renner wasn't sure who, had staked out the top deck that served as both roof over half the lower deck, and a damned good place to lounge while they fished.

This was the second time Aaron and several of his men had accepted the invite, but this was the first time Aaron brought a lady. Her name was Tiffany. Sly Harvey brought a girlfriend, too. Another Tiffany. Thanks to the underhanded matchmaking efforts of the clever women of The TEAM. The wives. God bless them.

Their diligence in introducing Aaron and his guys to any available women they knew, stemmed from that single little comment Renner had made to Tara. He'd simply said that it bothered him to see Aaron alone. Leave it to the women to take that to heart and start dropping innocent little hints that so-and-so needed someone to fix a leaky faucet under her kitchen sink—or walk her dog, or fix her car, or any number of little invitations to get to know a few more women other than just Kelsey and Tara. To take a small risk. To step outside their comfort zones.

Of all things, Maverick Carson had then stepped up and hired the hardest cases, the five of Aaron's guys who'd withdrawn into themselves to go work for him. Jim Sellers, Cory Ralston, Bruce McCoy, Tiny Alvarado, and Merle Perkins were now ranch hands, living like cowboys in a bunkhouse and working with some of the biggest horses Renner had ever seen. Percherons. Maverick and China owned a couple dozen head of what China called her kids. Big damned kids.

Among other things, the Carsons ran *Everyone's a Cowboy,* a local therapeutic riding program designed to give special needs children hands-on experience riding horses. Affiliated with the Professional Association of Therapeutic Horsemanship, internationally known as PATH, *Everyone's a Cowboy's* reputation for reaching out to all children, no matter their disability, exceeded all others in the region. And now the men Montego had all but destroyed, were healing as they too worked with those children, some who had worse disabilities than they did. It was a win/win that still made Renner's eyes water. God, he loved America.

"Hey there, tough guy," Tara murmured as she slid onto his lap and ran her fingers over his head.

He swiped a quick hand across his eyes, but yeah, she'd seen. She knew he was having one of those days when everything made him miss his dad. Being out here on the river used to be his go-to place to meditate, curse, cry, or just plain brood and get sloppy drunk. But he was sober now, one hundred three days and counting. With Aaron as happy as a clam and his guys along for the ride, Renner couldn't help remembering the man he missed most. Ghosts and all that...

"I know a secret," Tara whispered in his ear, licking him, tickling, breathing life back into him.

"Oh, yeah," he asked, drawing her under his arm and into his side, pretending he wasn't dwelling on the past, that it hadn't sneaked up and ambushed him again. "Who are you matchmaking now? Roger or Gilbert?"

"Not Gilbert. He's marrying that cute nurse he met in the hospital next Friday. You know, the one that turned him onto that doctor who builds prosthetic ears."

No, he hadn't known, but how cool? Roger and Gilbert were two of the men that Montego had lured into her web. "Really? Damn, that's great. Make sure he invites us to the wedding, okay?"

"We already are, but that isn't what I needed to tell you."

"So, spill, Mrs. Graves. You know your secrets are safe with me."

Tara eased far enough back in his arm that he looked down at her. Into her. She smelled of sunblock and wind and that flowery perfume she liked. Dressed in navy blue shorts, his white USMC t-shirt, and boat shoes without socks, she did look different today. Happier. Or something. Her bruises were long gone and her red tresses fluttered behind her. She looked carefree, so he pushed the stick forward and their boat went faster. Her hair streamed behind her like she was flying. God, she was beautiful, and he loved her so damned hard.

They'd bought a home out west past the Bull Run Regional Park, near the city of Haymarket, way west of the District. It seemed the right thing to do. It put them between the too-busy city where he could still be close to his mom, but far enough from the Shenandoahs that he wasn't too close to his boss. They were just off Interstate 66 in another bungalow, this one with room to expand.

"Did you buy a dog?" he asked. She'd wanted one since he'd brought it up, but she wanted a Yorkie. He leaned more toward something bigger. Maybe a Rottweiler or a Great Dane. A lab. They liked the water as much as he did.

"Nope," she said, bringing one hand around, those fingers tiptoeing up his chest to his chin.

"You know you own me, Mrs. Graves. Whatever you did, whatever you bought, I'll love it. Just say it."

She bit her lip, which meant whatever she had to tell him, it was going to be good.

He grinned down at her, falling in love all over again. They'd already proven they could overcome any obstacle, climb any mountain. All they needed was to be together, and they were unstoppable. He knocked his forehead to hers. "Just say it, baby. Go on. Surprise me. Make my day."

"Well, umm... You know how we're fostering Jessica?"

His brows arched at what he hoped Tara would say next. "Yes?"

"Well, umm—"

"Family Services won't approve us? They won't let us have her? Why not?" Her parents had already signed over their rights. What was the hold-up?

Tara shook her head, her lips pinched. "It's not that. It's, umm…"

"You're killing me," he growled, pissed that DFS could ever deny sweet little Jessica being with the woman who'd loved her on sight. "Just say it, baby. Tell me."

She drew in a deep breath and blurted, "Jessica's going to be a big sister."

"We're… Wait. What?" He couldn't believe it. Renner wanted to dance. Shout! So, he did. "We're pregnant?" he asked for all the world to hear.

Tara nodded.

Tears flooded his eyes. He bellowed again, "We're pregnant!"

"You're what?" Aaron asked from somewhere behind him.

But Tara was crying, and he didn't know why. "Don't you want to be?" *Oh, please be happy for us. This is such great news. Jessica needs a family. God, so do you and me and… Please be happy.*

She nodded, her eyes squeezed tight and tears trickling down her cheeks. "Yes," she whispered, her voice trembling. "Yes. I just wasn't sure you wanted to be. It's so soon and—"

He crushed his mouth to hers, swallowing those doubts. Inhaling her fear. Laughing at his silly woman while he cried with her. God, they were a couple of pansies.

"It's never too soon," he told her once he stopped mugging her. "Remember what you told me?" he asked, blinking hard and trying his damnedest not to look as sappy as he felt. But this was a dream come true, a dream he hadn't realized he'd wanted until he'd literally fallen into Tara's life. "*'We fly together. All the way. Are you with me?'*"

Tara smiled as her precise words came back to her. "I love you so much, it hurts sometimes, Renner," she breathed into his face, her arms around his neck and those lovely breasts mashed against his chest. Her lovely red hair whipped around them like an Irish blessing, chasing every last one of his blues away.

This amazing woman loved him, and she was pregnant with his child. *His* baby. *His* little boy or his little girl! Was there anything better?

Hell, no.

The End

Thank you for reading Renner's story

You are the key to this book's success!

Please tell other readers why you liked RENNER by leaving an honest review at the retail site where you purchased it.

Recommend it to your friends. Lend it. Most of all, enjoy it!

Other Irish Winters' best-selling books/series

In the Company of Snipers

Alex
Mark
Zack
Harley
Connor
Rory
Taylor
Gabe
Maverick
Cassidy
Adam
Lee
Ky
Hunter
Eric
Jake
Seth
Beau

Coming soon:
Beckam

Deuces Wild
King of Hearts
Joker Joker
One-Eyed Jack
Ace

Hearts and Ashes
Smoke
Ash

SOBs Novels
Angel
Assassin

Coming soon:
Julio's story

The best way to keep up with my new releases, giveaways, and actionable intel is to sign up for my spam-free newsletter at IrishWinters.com.

Preview of ADAM

In the Company of Snipers, #11

There comes a time when a man has to do what a man has to do. For Junior Agent Adam Torrey, that moment had come.

"Sir, we are currently at thirty-five thousand feet and holding."

Adam nodded one curt acknowledgment to the Air Force crew out of Ellsworth Air Force Base, stepped to the vibrating loading ramp of the powerful C-130, and, with a backward step and a cocky wave, he pitched his body forward into the midnight sky. The flight chief's acknowledgement, "Jumper away," faded in his earpiece.

Frigid air whipped Adam, making him instantly thankful for the polypropylene thermal undergarments beneath his TEAM flight suit. He leveled his six-foot, three-inch frame into a belly dive, his arms and legs extended like a giant bug descending to the planet below.

Man, I love my job.

HALOs, high-altitude low opening parachute jumps, were not uncommon in his line of work, at least for him. Known by everyone on The TEAM as the flying squirrel, the ex-Navy SEAL thrived in the weightless realm between earth and sky. All agents working for Alex Stewart had to be capable, physically fit, and qualified to jump. The day a man couldn't perform he was put to pasture, or worse, turned into something dead called a *senior agent*. Adam was an ex-Navy SEAL, a man of action and a lethal sniper. He never intended to graze clover. He loved the sensation of flight too much, the freedom of falling, the heady rush of air over, around, and seemingly through his body.

Specialized equipment allowed this miracle, and he relied on it. Every last piece of it. From the Special Forces HALO helmet with its oxygen mask strapped snuggly over his nose and mouth, to the goggles that allowed peripheral vision and much-needed facial protection, to the backlit altimeter on his wrist, that registered nothing at the moment, its altitude range less than his. The lightweight auxiliary pack strapped to his belly provided a measure of assurance if his main parachute failed. His gloves kept his ten digits warm enough.

God, what a ride.

The experimental GPS wrapped around his wrist matched its digital partner's lack of information. No matter. They'd both flash on soon enough—within seconds if the new technology behind them functioned as expected. The GPS was part of the reason for this extreme jump. This was its maiden flight, its beta-test, and he was just the man for the job.

Until it kicked in, supposedly at a higher altitude than others now on the market, he gloried in the adrenaline rush, free-falling to what very well could be his death. Therein lay the rub and the magic of a precision drop—all the risk of dying only to pull up at the last possible second and spit in the stone-cold eye of the Grim Reaper.

Nothing like it in the world.

The fact that another brave soul had recently made a twenty-four-mile high jump from the stratosphere only proved

Adam's point. Some men were made to fly, and he was one of them. This ordinary jump of nearly seven miles straight down was enough for the adrenaline junkie he'd become. For now. Maybe someday he'd match that other guy's record. Maybe not. Adam truly didn't care about records. Just the fall. Just the flight.

He liked that initial *'What the hell have I done?'* sensation in his gut, even more so because he understood the physics behind a HALO, the very real concept of terminal velocity when the downward force of gravity equaled the restraining force of drag. Law of gravity. Risk of splat. Gotta love it.

Every HALO jump involved unique dangers—the frigid cold, decompression sickness, and hypoxia. Death never lingered more than a heartbeat away. But the thrill. The view.

He could've pulled his body into a compact, cylindrical projectile, secured his arms to his sides and his legs together instead of splayed like they were, in order to increase his speed. Skydivers called it free flying, when a man's body became more bullet than flesh and blood. But as much as Adam loved the thrill of downward acceleration, he loved the journey more. Only HALO jumps brought him this close to Heaven. He truly loved the sea, but God, he loved the sky more. In the sky he was free, not so much bird as shooting star. On land he became a bulky beast of burden bound to the earth's core. A turtle. Why hurry a three-minute ride?

Suspended between earth and space, it seemed time stopped on a night like this one. No moon tonight, just the constellations and Ursa Major glittering in the sub-polar altitude, crisp and clear. Adam's buddy, Polaris, shone exactly where the pointer stars in the bowl of the Big Dipper indicated it should be. The North Star beckoned like the true friend it was, as constant and a thousand times squared more reliable than any woman he'd ever known. Always beckoning him home.

His failed relationship with his ex-girlfriend and ex-nightmare flashed to mind. The one he'd been damned glad he left behind. But none of that mattered now. He forced his very disciplined mind to the work at hand. Shirley was old news, the poison of her manipulative grasp at last diluted with enough good times mingled with plenty of scotch.

The experimental GPS digital readout flashed to life right on schedule, reminding him he had better things to do than dredge up the past, like finding that wayward drone.

Impact in less than two.

South Dakota lay below, now the site of a lost prototype, the multi-million dollar HH UAV, the Hummingbird Hawk Unmanned Aerial Vehicle. Named for its compact but predatory stealth design, it had gone down during its initial test flight out of Ellsworth Air Force Base, just a few miles away. Its advanced technology made it immeasurably valuable in the world of military intelligence. All of DoD held its breath when they'd heard it went missing. The CIA, too. This was their baby, their future, and now their worst nightmare. Too many foreign powers wanted the technology behind this particular drone. Russia. China. Terrorists. Allies.

Ellsworth had been alerted. They knew he was dropping in tonight, but were advised not to engage in the search, only to assist with the drop. For now, this operation was just him, a missing baby bird, and maybe a few barking rodents.

The peculiar nature of his mission still nagged, though. The very capable folks at Ellsworth would've been happy to retrieve the UAV. They could've, and they should've. The request for a HALO was one hundred percent unnecessary, but the CIA said, *'Hell, no,'* to the Air Force offer to assist. Hands off. Like the control freaks they were, the spooks demanded a non-defense-related contractor perform the retrieval.

Enter the man responsible for developing the prototype, Mr. Paul Reagan, inventor and billionaire CEO of the prestigious Reagan Industries out of northern Virginia. He'd made the CIA's paranoia look tame when he'd circumvented them and went straight to Alex Stewart, the owner of the covert surveillance company, The TEAM. Before the Air Force or CIA could shoot off their well-prepared rebuttal, the deal between Reagan and Alex was struck.

One agent and one only would handle retrieval. Given his aptitude for HALO drops, it was a no-brainer from the get go. Adam Torrey, ex-Navy SEAL, was the best flying squirrel on The TEAM, and in transit before his boss's signature had dried on the dotted line.

But why one agent only? Why a HALO? Why not Ellsworth's assist? Very odd indeed.

Checking altimeter and GPS coordinates again, Adam allowed a small smile of success. No meteorological events interfered with his flight tonight. Smooth descent. Right on target.

Earth approached fast.

Fifteen thousand.

His favorite country western song popped into his head, its heavy bass a heartbeat that matched his philosophy. What *was* life for if you didn't live it? And man, this was living at its most extreme.

Eight thousand.

His GPS flashed once. Then twice. His target might as well be already acquired and the mission over. Smoothest drop ever.

Six thousand.

Thicker atmosphere at the earth's surface brought warmer temperatures. Almost time. He stalled the inevitable, wishing he didn't have to land.

Four thousand.

Two.

Begrudgingly, Adam jerked the ripcord. *Whoosh.* The flat-black nylon, eight-celled, ram-air canopy released, stopping death in its tracks, and offering a few breathless seconds to view the LZ before his boots hit the dirt. Drifting toward touchdown, the sight below was all he expected. Prairie. Flat. Damned dark.

He activated another specialized tracking device, set to pick up the HH locator signal only. Just in time. South Dakota rushed up to meet him. To be safe, he removed the night-vision goggles from the zippered pouch on his belt and strapped them around his neck. It never hurt to be prepared. Freedom lived in the heavens. Not on earth.

He braced for impact, his knees bent and his senses sharp, primed for any and all possibilities.

Oomph. Touchdown.

Adam rolled as he landed, expelling nothing more than a soft grunt that none heard, unless the few curious prairie dogs scampering out of his path mattered. Gathering big handfuls of the black nylon, he stuffed it into the empty nylon bag he'd brought with him, using those same few minutes to survey the wide-open space around him. The pure sounds of the dark Dakota night met his ears...

Smoothest landing ever.

Once he'd stowed his gear, he let the rucksack drop from his back. It carried what-if supplies like water, MREs, medical supplies, and his all-important EPIRB, his emergency position-indicating radio beacon.

The feeling that this was some bizarre game persisted, mostly because a HALO drop into harmless South Dakota made no sense in the wary world of a black operator. HALOs were last-option only, the safest way into deadly terrain. Not prairie. Why, oh why old man Reagan, the billionaire eccentric behind this op, had demanded such a high-security measure in the middle of grassland seemed irrational and foolish.

But there was a job to be done, and until an adversary presented himself, Adam had no reason for alarm. The soft green glow from the screen displayed a map of his immediate area, a red dot pinging a heartbeat less than three clicks to the northeast and the exact position of the missing drone. Good enough.

Setting a steady pace, he jogged toward it, watching where he stepped. Landing in a prairie dog hole could snap a man's leg. He had no intention of being airlifted for such a stupid mistake, not after the exhilaration of this perfect drop.

The sweet Dakota air smelled good at 0245 hours. Cool. Pleasant. And a good run relaxed a man. It allowed the adrenaline overload from the falling out of the sky to burn away. He checked the tracker again. Less than a thousand meters straight ahead. Instantly, his very analytical brain provided mathematical equivalents. Three thousand, two hundred, and eighty-one feet. One thousand, ninety-four yards.

Man, I love my job.

A prairie dog barked off to his left. Then another. Adam grinned at the exhilaration of a night so rare. He wasn't even breaking a sweat. What's more, this very expensive, very top-secret UAV would be home in its cradle before the world knew it had gone missing.

The tracking device that indicated he was nearly on target sounded steady beeps. Slowing his gait, Adam glanced to his right and then left. Only grass and more grass. All good. How hard could it be to find a two-foot long baby bird, attach it to a miniature aerostat, punch the can of helium to inflate the balloon, and let it fly away home? Not hard at all. Once the prototype was airborne, a larger UAV would snag the line between baby bird and the aerostat with a specially designed pincer attached to its nose. By the time Adam's boss inhaled his first cup of coffee in far-off Virginia, the baby bird would be back in its hanger at Reagan Research, and all would be well.

As big a fiasco as this loss might have been, the mechanics of baby bird's rescue would once again prove the undeniable need for drones in defense and industrial missions. A drone rescuing another drone. Technology upon technology. The world was an amazing place, and Adam reveled in it. It helped him fly.

Brushing his palms over the knee-high grass, Adam let it tickle his splayed fingers. Everything about the prairie was just plain magic. Buffalo used to roam here. The Lakota, too.

The GPS pinged louder, leading him straight to his prize. A dark shadow carved into the tall grass revealed the landing skid, and ultimately, the smooth body of the tiny predator. He knelt, one knee to the ground in awe, pulling the little guy gently out of the shallow depression of its crash-landing. The weight of the tiny drone surprised him. He'd expected more, but it felt less than twenty pounds. Coated in flat-black, radar-absorbent material, the overall smooth design contributed to its invisibility. It was the perfect predator. Small. Invisible. *Deadly.*

He cradled it tenderly, proud of his skill and aptitude. *Best day ever.*

"Come on, little guy. Let's get you home."

He pushed to his feet with a sigh of relief. In the moonlight, the drone didn't appear damaged, other than a few scrapes along one side of its sleek metallic skin—nothing a good buffing wouldn't solve. He committed the serial number from the metal plate at the edge of its polycarbonate nose to memory: UVZ172661. And hot damn. Operation Baby Bird was nearly over. *Way to go, Torrey!*

A soft whirring overhead, the telltale ruffling of silky nylon ballooned tight with air, interrupted his self-congratulations. Adam jerked his gaze heavenward. It couldn't be. Another jumper? Here?

Nothing revealed itself, but his ears hadn't lied. He crouched to one knee and hunkered low in the tall grass. With the infant UAV tucked tightly to his chest, he let nature provide the camouflage while he went into full alert.

Sliding his night vision goggles up over his face, the world turned lime green. His sixth sense screamed, *"You're not alone,"* but no other sound rent the silence. No boots on the ground. No motorized engine. No un-oiled squeak of a control lever to bring a parachute or a one-man glider to pinpoint landing. Nothing.

He held his breath, trusting his gut more than his ears or sight. But who was out there, and why? Better question—how could anyone have known he was there? Or was he just that paranoid?

A rippling breeze parted the tall grass ahead of him for mere seconds. He'd switched to NV too late. From up high, somebody dropkicked the side of his head, hard, but not hard enough to make him release the baby in his arms.

Adam crouched to adjust his goggles, searching after his assailant. And there the bastard was. A lime-green tinted man sat beneath a triangular-shaped paraglide floating overhead, as silent as the night itself. An engine noise would've confirmed the visual, but there was none. Whoever this guy was, he'd banked and was coming around again, no doubt thinking he'd rendered his target unconscious.

Guess again. Adam growled low in his throat. The predator in him sprang to life. Two could play that game.

Rolling to his back with the baby still in his arms, he waited until his assailant was nearly on top of him again. But this time, automatic rounds strafed the ground alongside Adam. Enough was enough! He flipped to his stomach, set the drone down, and charged the would-be assassin.

Surprised, the guy banked sharply. Too sharp. With a running leap, Adam grabbed his ankle and jerked. Either the idiot hadn't buckled up or the harness broke. *Umph.* Down he came, hitting the dirt hard. Adam followed through with a kick to the guy's midsection. His boot connected with body armor. The guy had anticipated trouble.

Good to know. Me too.

Reaching to his ankle holster, Adam pulled his knife up, and—

"Got it!" a woman shrieked behind him. He whirled as another black silhouette materialized against the midnight sky. Whoever she was, she now had the HH.

He cocked his arm back and hurtled his knife at the thief. *Bull's-eye!* She grunted, sagged, and collapsed limp in her harness. The paraglide continued into the night with the tiny drone tucked into the silvery netting beneath the woman's seat.

No way! Adam ran with long-legged strides, his lungs bursting and every muscle on fire to get that damned HH. The nearly silent engine offered the barest hum as he closed the distance, his heart pounding with adrenaline and rage. No one—and I mean *no one*—messed with Adam Torrey.

Six more yards. Maybe less. Almost there. *Almost got it.* He forced his last reserve of strength into a final lunge, stretching with all he had to secure that baby bird again when—

BLAM! A wicked blast of fire and pain caught his shoulder. It spun him around and turned him into a ragdoll, tumbling end over end through the grass. Forward momentum finally ceased when he came to a breathless stop, face up, blood streaming out of the hole in his chest. A universe of stars swirled overhead. He had no way to reach his gear bag. Thunder rumbled too close. Not thunder. Maybe boots on the ground. Running fast. Coming straight toward him.

A black shadow descended, cruel and cold.

The butt of a rifle.

The last thing he saw.

About the Author

Irish Winters

…is a best-selling author of military romance who, when she isn't writing, dabbles in poetry, grandchildren, and rarely—as in extremely rarely—the kitchen. More prone to be outdoors than in, she grew up the quintessential tomboy on a dairy farm in rural Wisconsin, spent her teenage years in the Pacific Northwest, but calls the Wasatch Mountains of Northern Utah, home. For now. She believes in making every day count for something, and follows the wise admonition of her mother to, "Look out the window and see something!"

Connect with Irish online:
On Facebook: https:/www.facebook.com/author.irishwinters
On Twitter: https://twitter.com/irishwinters1
Or at www. IrishWinters.com